THE BATTLE OF COURTRAI

Lion of Flanders Vol. I

HENDRIK CONSCIENCE

The Lion of Flanders

Two Volumes in One

TRANSLATED FROM THE FLEMISH

INTRODUCTORY ESSAY ON
FLEMISH AND DUTCH FICTION
BY A. SCHADE VAN WESTRUM

A FRONTISPIECE AND A
BIOGRAPHICAL SKETCH

**Fredonia Books
Amsterdam, The Netherlands**

The Lion of Flanders
(Two Volumes in One)

by
Hendrik Conscience

ISBN: 1-4101-0392-7

Copyright © 2003 by Fredonia Books

Fredonia Books
Amsterdam, The Netherlands
http://www.fredoniabooks.com

All rights reserved, including the right to reproduce this book, or portions thereof, in any form.

In order to make original editions of historical works available to scholars at an economical price, this facsimile of the original edition is reproduced from the best available copy and has been digitally enhanced to improve legibility, but the text remains unaltered to retain historical authenticity.

THE LION OF FLANDERS

VOLUME ONE

CONTENTS

	PAGE
INTRODUCTION	5
LIFE OF CONSCIENCE	17

BOOK FIRST

CHAPTER I	19
CHAPTER II	35
CHAPTER III	57
CHAPTER IV	79
CHAPTER V	94
CHAPTER VI	113
CHAPTER VII	146
CHAPTER VIII	164

BOOK SECOND

CHAPTER I	189
CHAPTER II	209
CHAPTER III	233
CHAPTER IV	249
CHAPTER V	278
CHAPTER VI	294
CHAPTER VII	331
CHAPTER VIII	356
CHAPTER IX	384

INTRODUCTION

AN introduction to the two novels selected for this series of "Foreign Classical Romances" to represent Flemish and Dutch literature would be utterly inadequate to its purpose if it were restricted in scope to the work and life of their authors, without reference to their relation to the two great currents now converging in a common Dutch-Flemish literature. Of the older of these two movements, the Fleming, Hendrik Conscience was the father and the most brilliant and successful leader. His name ranked with that of Scott in the international world of letters of the first half of the nineteenth century; he was translated in that day into every language of Europe, and even into some of its dialects; but, admirable as were his gifts as a teller of historic tales and a delineator of the daily life of his people—for he was a modern realist before modern realism was practised, as well as a romancer in the heyday of romance—his real service lay in that he revived a dying tongue, fought for its life through poverty and early lack of support, until, aided by others, he won a victory that has been felt in Belgian affairs of state as well as in Belgian letters. At the beginning of the nineteenth century Flemish was a dialect debased by the hordes of conquerors who had swarmed over the "cockpit of Europe" through the ages, an uncouth idiom spoken only by the Flemish peasant. despised by French-

Introduction

man and Walloon, derided by the Hollander, repudiated by the French-speaking Fleming of standing and culture —a speech without pliability, strength, or beauty, whose resources did not reach beyond the simple requirements of ordinary, everyday life. Conscience left it a language worthy of literary usage, capable of rising to all demands that authorship could make upon it, flexible, sensitive, modulated: a tongue that could sing in tender verse and speak in noble prose.

It is for this service to a nationality that Belgium, Walloon as well as Flemish, honors the memory of Hendrik Conscience to-day, for this that it honored him during his lifetime as few leaders of art and culture have been honored before their death. The movement begun by him was carried into other spheres. It was his genius and the spirit of his colaborers that revived the artistic consciousness of a sturdy race which, through centuries of turmoil and oppression, had resisted almost irresistible forces of amalgamation and annihilation from without. He came at the right moment, when peace and liberty settled upon these Low Countries of the south; he saw the opportunity and forced it to results with unflagging energy. He nursed back to strength a racial pride that had long been moribund; he revived a national consciousness all but extinct.

The Congress of Vienna, which noted the end of Napoleon's sway, made of the northern and southern Low Countries a kingdom that was divided against itself from the first. In 1830 the irresistible conflict broke out, and the Kingdom of Belguim arose, a free country at last. Of the two nationalities within this little new realm, it

Introduction

was the Walloon, whose relation to the French may be compared with the relation of the Flemings to the Dutch —it was the Walloon, strangely enough, who set about the creation of its commerce and industries; it was the far more backward Fleming who, in the face of derision and official as well as social opposition, set about reviving the love and practise of the arts.

The little Belgian kingdom quietly proceeded with its industrious task of winning its right to a place among the nations of Europe, which had almost forgotten its recent creation when the novels of Hendrik Conscience were brought to its attention in translations that included Russian and Czech and the Scandinavian tongues, as well as German, French, and Italian. With his third novel, "the Lion of Flanders," presented in these volumes, Conscience won his place in the literature of the world, which he held to the end of his busy career; the titles of his books mount up to a hundred. But while he was hailed as a great author by all Europe, the deeper and more enduring value of his work, which is the rehabilitation of a language and the founding of a literature, was understood only in Belgium itself and in Holland. Modern Flemish-Belgian literature began before Walloon-Belgian literature, which was for many years loosely classed with the French, a disadvantage under which it labors even to-day. It is, indeed, likely that Walloon-Belgian literature, like the literature of the French-Swiss cantons, will ultimately be merged with French letters, and it has been the parallel aim, in recent years, of the Flemish authors to secure uniformity of the written language with the Dutch.

Introduction

Conscience could not go so far as this, of course, for a very good reason: Had he written in Dutch, he would simply have become a Dutch author, without the least influence over the corrupted dialect he wished to raise to a place of honor. Therefore he wrote in Flemish, but with the awakening touch of a true genius. The language grew under his master pen; he drew from it humor and pathos, descriptive range and flight of eloquence, yet he never forced it to service beyond its power. Instead, he discovered, by patient search and study, the needed word, the desired turn of phrase, the happy idiom, long forgotten, or long condemned to the most menial of prosaic uses. His style is clear and flexible, intimate without being familiar, and of an admirable simplicity. His search for the buried treasures of word and phrase in the archives of old Flanders served a second purpose: it yielded him the material for his historical novels. It is beyond doubt that in this field Conscience took his cue from Scott, like the rest of the romancers of that day. It was a period of which historical fiction was one of the logical products. The downfall of Napoleon had been followed by a revival of patriotism, still more by a desire to forget recent national humiliations in the glory of earlier national triumphs. Conscience drew with that gifted pen of his the glories of medieval Belgium; so that, while his Flemings were reveling in their ancestors' noble deeds as told by him, they discovered at the same time with wondering delight the dignity of their olden speech and its resources.

But in his efforts to foster a language and the feeling of nationality it gives, Conscience had still another

Introduction

string to his bow, in his charming tales of contemporary Flemish life. They are worthy of a seventeenth century Dutch painter, these homely pieces, so full of tenderness and understanding, so near to the heart and the daily existence of his own people. Conscience was a modern realist long before the days when modern realism began to be preached as a literary tenet. He was a tender-hearted artist, who saw and loved what is beautiful and ennobling in simple lives, as well as the sorrow and the sin. To one who knows Flanders and its people, their language, customs, and habits of thought, these stories have a charm more potent and enduring than even that of the historical tales. But the world at large, not possessing the key of personal knowledge to their value as pictures of men, women, children, homes, and fields, while recognizing their workmanship, will probably pronounce hereafter, as in the past, for the romances, with their brave pageantry and deeds of derring-do. Among these "The Lion of Flanders" undoubtedly stands first.

Difficult as was his undertaking, Conscience's battle for the Flemish tongue and a Flemish literature was won within a decade after the publication of his greatest novel. His French father had turned him out for daring to write a Flemish book—for debasing himself and throwing doubt upon the social status of his family by betraying his thorough knowledge of this peasants' lingo. His seventieth birthday was made a national holiday by Walloons as well as Flemings, for nothing but this very wickedness!

Conscience was not the only founder of the Flemish movement, but he was undoubtedly the most influential

Introduction

of them all. He saw the importance of going to the people and working upward with them and through them, instead of beginning the propaganda at the top, among the literati, and graciously bending down toward the masses. Him even the simplest Fleming could understand; in him even the lowliest recognized a brother. He did not write their songs, but he wrote their tales, which they took into their homes, and with them his national spirit that thenceforth they made their own. After Conscience's death the Flemish movement expanded its scope. Success in the field of literature naturally resulted in a determination to secure official recognition for the language. It took years of agitation to force this recognition of Flemish upon the Belgian Government, to force the passage of laws prescribing its use side by side with French in the law courts and in official documents. To-day Flemish is the only language used at the University of Ghent; King Leopold, whose father was one of Conscience's earliest friends, and his patron through life, has made public addresses in the once despised tongue. There is a national Flemish theatre now in Belgium; to crown it all, a Royal Flemish Academy has existed these many years

Coming now to the consideration of Dutch literature, it may be stated, first of all, that Dutch itself has several dialects. Of the two dialects of the tongue beyond the boundaries of Holland, Flemish, as we have seen, has been reclaimed and has made common cause with literary Dutch; the other dialect, the "Taal" of the Boers, is hopelessly corrupt and crippled, having lost most of its grammatical forms and all its flexibility in the course of

Introduction

its long silence on the lonely Veldt, and through disuse of any but the most elementary terms during two centuries of constant struggle for bare life and mere existence. Here, too, a return to the language of Holland in print and writing, if not in speech, was in progress when the recent South African War broke out. The movement will undoubtedly be resumed with great application when the Boer finally recovers from the ravages of the three years' struggle.

Dutch, one of the dialects of the Teutonic littoral, did not begin to differentiate itself from German until the beginning of the twelfth century. There is ample documentary evidence of this, whereas philologists are much hampered in their researches into the origins of Flemish by the total lack of manuscripts in the dialect older than the middle of the same century. It is not likely, however, that its origins differed greatly from those of Dutch, beyond the more than probable addition of Frankish and even Romance influences. Neither tongue produced through the Middle Ages any original literature worth mentioning—the record is one of dreary historical chronicles, translations of the Arthurian romances and of the songs of the *trouvères*, a borrowing from English, French, and German sources. The Flemish versions of "Reynard the Fox" may be mentioned here, but that great animal epic was originally written in Latin, and is of unknown authorship. In the Low Countries, as elsewhere, Latin was a powerful obstacle to the development of a national literary language during the Middle Ages. Thomas à Kempis wrote in it, and Erasmus. During the time that elapsed from the beginning of the

Introduction

twelfth to the end of the sixteenth century the two tongues diverged considerably.

In the Netherlands, as in Germany, the Reformation, not the Renaissance, was the cause and the inspiration of a national literary language and a national literature. Upon the Dutch the Italian Renaissance made, indeed, but a slight impression. Its sensuousness could find no echo in the hearts or minds of freemen who had been robbed of their rights and forced to bow to absolutism and its denial of freedom of conscience. It took a sterner aim in life than that of the Renaissance to attract them; priestcraft and the "divine right" supporting it drove them to embrace the Reformation, political as well as religious. To be sure, the lighter touch, the Italianate influence, is not missing in the Dutch literature of the seventeenth century; nor, on the other hand, does it lack the coarseness that is characteristic of the period of the Synod of Dort. But at the core this literature is morally sound and serious. Soaring with the outward power and inward prosperity of the Dutch Republic, this literature declined with them, until, at the end of the eighteenth century, Dutch letters, like the country's naval power and its standing in Europe, sank to a level of utter insignificance. Waterloo brought a revival of national feeling and pride. A new literary "school" rose, flourished, and was dethroned by still younger men. And these, having gradually wandered into an uninspired, uninspiring rut of mediocrity, were in their turn driven from the places of honor by the leaders of the great so-called "Sensitivist" movement in Dutch letters, which began in the year 1880.

Introduction

It was a Donnybrook fair sort of an insurrection at first. These young enthusiasts of the eighties, inspired by a deep, genuine love of letters, did not always stop to consider how hard they struck, or how fair. Of course, there was the usual desire to *épater les bourgeois* —to startle the Philistines—in this case quite understandable, however, because the greatest Philistines in the Holland of that period were undeniably its literary Mandarins. The young band fought hard, receiving blows more unfair than any it gave. The defense was, indeed, mostly confined to offensive personalities. This literary revolt was against matter as well as against form; it was a rising against a literary aristocracy; it had its social as well as its purely artistic side. Indeed, it was more or less socialistic in some of its manifestations from the very first. And no wonder, for the many foreign influences that contributed to the outbreak (Dutch literature has always been very susceptible to foreign influences) ranged from Shelley to Tolstoy, and from him to Baudelaire, Gautier, Poe, Huysmans—a Fleming writing French—and, above all others, to Zola. No wonder that conservative middle-aged Holland shuddered and protested.

The band of insurgents set about remodeling the literary uses of the language in a manner of their own, somewhat after that of Meredith and James; they made progress, won the day, and have been justified of their doings by the results, these fifteen years or so. Now that their leaders have reached middle age, the impetuousness of youth has died out. In their turn they incline toward conservatism; they contemplate what they have

Introduction

achieved, and retain their faith in it. But instead of further development along the lines hewed out by them, another general revolt may be impending—although of this there is as yet no positive sign. The only token thus far of a waning of the influence of the "Sensitivist" school of 1880 is the appearance of independents, of authors who repudiate all idea of allegiance to, or derivation from, all schools and movements in general, and this one in particular. From the foreign standpoint, Maarten Maartens would be considered the most prominent of these independents; but he, writing in English, is not accounted a Dutch novelist by the Dutch. There remains, then, as the first independent of real and growing importance in contemporary Dutch letters, the author of "Eline Vere," "Majesty," and "Fate."

Louis Couperus is beyond doubt the leading novelist of Holland to-day, the only one of its living authors, moreover, who has earned and received the distinction of translation into English, French, and German. His place is beyond the ranks of national authors; he stands among the writers who have international fame—with Matilde Serao, Hermann Sudermann, Pierre Loti, Marion Crawford. His versatility is great, for he ranges from the novel of contemporary manners to a decidedly obscure mysticism. He claims not only literary independence but absolute originality, a somewhat sweeping claim that can not be allowed without many qualifications. It is true, none the less, that his literary descent is exceedingly hard to trace. He is strikingly Dutch in "Eline Vere," which, notwithstanding his disclaimer, belongs to the "Sensitivist" school in atmosphere and treatment, though

Introduction

most decidedly not in manner. It is a study of the moods of a young woman who lacks the firmness of purpose that character gives, while at the same time it is a delightfully vivid and truthful picture of the social life of The Hague, the "village capital" of Europe. "Majesty," a thinly disguised tale of royalty hemmed in by anarchy, is cosmopolitan; it might as well have come, certain allowances being made, from a German, or a French, or even an English or American pen, as from his.

The critics of Europe are puzzled by Couperus's case. A Frenchman has declared that he is decidedly not a student of contemporary French fiction, that he does not "derive" from the French psychological novelists; a German has sought to account for a certain seriousness in his work through a distant Scottish ancestor (the family name is said to be a Latinization of Cowper)—as if Dutch ancestry itself did not suffice to explain this trait; while, finally, a Dutchman has offered the suggestion that the secret of Couperus's elusive individuality as a writer should be sought in the impressions received by him as a boy during his five years' stay in Java, where his father had been appointed to a judgeship, this Indian influence being brought forward, of course, in interpretation of the author's mysticism. The explanation of these conflicting views is, however, rather simple. Each book of Couperus published thus far has presented some new phase of his mind, and the international trio of critics did not base their verdicts upon the same book. It would be wiser, probably, to defer all attempts at definitive appreciation or criticism of this able Hollander

Introduction

until he has at least reached the youth of old age. So far as he has gone, he has certainly demonstrated a marked degree of originality; but for all that, he is, at least in some measure, indebted to the "Sensitivist" school which he denies, and in lesser measure to the modern Frenchmen. Withal he remains typically Dutch in essence.

"Fate" is the most characteristic of Couperus's novels translated into English, the book in which he apparently has given most of his own inner self, of his intimate personal attitude toward life. Its conception of Fate harks back to that of the classic Greek dramatists, its modern setting making the ancient note all the more striking. The story, then, here offered, is certainly worthy of representing in a foreign tongue the only Dutch novelist who is of the company of the world's masters of fiction to-day.

A. SCHADE VAN WESTRUM.

LIFE OF CONSCIENCE

ONE day, twenty-five years ago, the Belgian people united in doing honor to a man of national celebrity. Only two years later another incident occurred evoking general tributes of respect and admiration toward the same popular individual. The festival of 1881 was held to solemnize a literary event, the publication of his one hundredth volume by Hendrik Conscience; and in 1883 thousands and thousands of Belgians, belonging to all classes, followed his bier, forming an obsequial procession that at once betokened grief for his loss and triumph for his memory.

This novelist, who wrote his stories in Flemish, was born at Antwerp in the course of the year 1812. After attending local schools, young Hendrik at the age of twenty enlisted in a Belgian cavalry regiment, where he advanced to the rank of sergeant. But in 1836 he left the army to become private tutor in the royal family. His august pupils having grown up, he was given an official position of some importance at Courtrai, whence he ultimately removed to Brussels, as director of

Life of Conscience

the public picture galleries, continuing in this post until very near the end of his days.

During his brief military career Conscience wrote some popular songs, and the year after his retirement brought out the first of a long series of historical novels, "The Year of Miracles" (1837). "The Lion of Flanders," which was published in 1838, and "Arteveldt" (1849) might be mentioned as two of his early successes. "The Fisherman's Daughter" (1893) and "Ludovic and Gertrude" (1895) were two of the best known among the historical novels he produced in old age. Never wearying of the Flemish people as a subject for his muse, he not only wrote many volumes describing their past and keeping alive their traditions, but composed a large number of tales concerning their manners and customs, their character, their ways of thinking, their home life in town and country. Especially famous among these domestic canvases—genre pictures, a painter would call them—is "What a Mother Can Suffer," which appeared in 1843. Other titles to be noted in this category are "The Conscript," "The Miser,' "The Poor Gentleman," and "The Curse of the Village."

THE LION OF FLANDERS

BOOK FIRST

CHAPTER I

THE east was reddening with the first doubtful rays of the morning sun, still enveloped with the clouds of night as with a garment, but at the same time making a perfect rainbow in each drop of dew; the blue mist hung like an impalpable veil on the tops of the trees, and the flower-cups opened lovingly to the first beams of the new daylight. The nightingale had more than once repeated his sweet descant in the glimmering dawn; but now the confused chirping of the inferior songsters overpowered his entrancing melody.

Silently trotted a little band of knights along the plains of West Flanders, near the small town of Rousselare. The clank of their arms and the heavy tread of their horses broke the rest of the peaceful denizens of the woods; for ever and anon sprang a frightened stag from out the thicket, and fled from the coming danger as on the very wings of the wind.

The dress and arms of these knights were alike

The Lion of Flanders

costly, as beseemed nobles of the very first rank, and even greater still than they. Each wore a silken surcoat, which fell in heavy folds over the body; while a silvered helmet, beplumed with purple and bright-blue feathers, decked his head. The steel scalework of their gauntlets, and their gold inlaid kneepieces, flashed brightly in the beams of the rising sun. The impatient foam-besprinkled steeds champed their shining bits, and the silver studs and silken tassels which ornamented their trappings glanced and danced right merrily as they went.

Though the knights were not armed at all points in full battle-harness, yet it was easy to see that they were by no means unprovided against a possible attack; for the sleeves of their shirts of mail were not hidden by the sleeveless surcoat. Moreover, their long swords hung down at their saddlebows, and each one was attended by his squire, bearing his ample shield. Every knight bore his cognizance embroidered upon his breast, so that at a glance the name and descent of each might easily be known. At that early hour of morning the travelers were little inclined for conversation. The heavy night air still weighed upon their eyelids, and it was with the utmost difficulty that they struggled against sleep. All rode onward in silence, wrapped in a kind of dreamy half slumber.

A young man strode along before them in the

The Lion of Flanders

road. His long waving hair flowed over his broad shoulders; eyes of heaven's own blue glowed and flashed under their brows, and a young curly beard fringed his chin. He wore a woolen jerkin, drawn into his waist with a girdle, in which he bore the broad-bladed, cross-handled knife in its leathern sheath, at once the appropriate weapon and distinguishing ensign of a free Flemish burgher. It might easily be seen, from the expression of his countenance, that the company to which he was acting as guide was not to his taste. Doubtless his heart was full of some secret design; for from time to time he cast upon the knights a look of peculiar meaning. Lofty of stature, and of unusual strength of build, he stepped along so quickly that the horses could hardly keep pace with him at a trot.

They journeyed on thus for a while, till at last one of the horses stumbled over the stump of a tree, so that it came upon its knees, and had wellnigh fallen over altogether. The knight fell forward, with his chest upon his steed's neck, and was as near as possible measuring his length on the ground.

"How now!" exclaimed he in French; "my horse is gone to sleep under me!"

"Yes, Messire de Chatillon," answered his neighbor, with a smile, "that one of you was asleep is plain enough."

"Rejoice over my mishap, evil jester that you

are," retorted De Chatillon; "asleep I was not. For these two hours past I have had my eyes fixed on those towers yonder, which are certainly bewitched; for the farther on we ride, the farther off they seem to be. But so it is; the gallows will be one's portion ere one hears a good word out of your mouth."

While the two knights thus twitted one another, the others laughed right merrily at the accident, and the whole cavalcade woke up out of its somnolency.

De Chatillon had meanwhile brought his horse upon its legs again; and, irritated with the quips and laughter which resounded from every side at his expense, drove his sharp spur (after the manner of the time, he wore but one) fiercely into the animal's side, which thereupon first reared in fury, and then rushed headlong among the trees, where, within the first hundred yards of its wild career, it dashed itself against the stem of a gigantic oak, and sank almost lifeless to the ground.

Well was it for De Chatillon that, as the shock came, he fell or threw himself sidewise from the saddle; notwithstanding this, however, he seemed to have had a severe fall, and it was some moments before he moved either hand or foot.

His comrades came round him, dismounted, and carefully raised him from the ground. The one among them who had been the readiest to make merry over his former mishap seemed now of all the most tenderly concerned for him, and bore on his countenance an unmistakable expression of real sorrow.

"My dear Chatillon," he sighed out, "I am heartily grieved at this. Forgive me my idle words; believe me, there was no harm meant."

"Leave me in peace," cried the fallen knight, now somewhat recovering himself, and breaking loose from the arms of his companions; "I am not dead this time, my good friends all. Think you, then, that I have escaped the Saracens to die like a dog in a Flemish wood? No; God be praised, I am still alive! See, St. Pol, I swear to you that you should pay on the spot for your ill-timed gibes were we not too near in blood for such reckoning between us."

"Come, be reasonable, my dear brother, I pray you," replied St. Pol. "But I perceive you are hurt; you are bleeding through your coat of mail."

De Chatillon drew back the sleeve from his right arm, and then noticed that a branch had torn the skin.

"Ah! look!" said he, quickly reassured, "this is nothing, a mere scratch. But I do believe that Flemish rascal has brought us into these accursed roads on purpose; I will inquire into that matter; and if it be so, may I forfeit my name but he shall hang on this very oak of mischief."

The Lion of Flanders

The Fleming, who was all the while standing by, looked as if he understood no French, and eyed De Chatillon firmly and proudly in the face.

"Gentlemen," said the knight; "only look at the peasant, how he stares at me! Come here, rascal! nearer, come nearer!"

The young man approached slowly—his eyes fixedly bent on the knight. A peculiar expression hovered over his features—an expression in which wrath and cunning were strangely united; something so threatening, and at the same time so mysterious, that De Chatillon could not repress a slight shudder.

One of the knights present, meanwhile, turned away, and walked off some paces through the trees, with an evident appearance of dissatisfaction at the whole affair.

"Tell me now," said De Chatillon to the guide, "why have you brought us by such a road? and why did you not warn me, when you saw the stump in the way?"

"Sir," answered the Fleming, in bad French, "I know of no other way to Castle Wynandael; and I was not aware that your honor was pleased to be asleep."

And with these words a scornful smile played about his mouth, and it might easily be seen that he was turning the knight into ridicule.

"Insolent!" cried De Chatillon; "you laugh—

you make jest of me? Here, my men! take this rascal peasant and hang him up! let him be food for the ravens!"

The youth laughed yet more contemptuously, the corners of his mouth twitched yet more violently, and his countenance became alternately pale and red.

"Hang a Fleming!" he muttered; "wait a little!"

Upon this he retreated a few steps, set his back against a tree, stripped up the sleeves of his jerkin to his shoulders, and drew his bright cross-handled knife from its sheath; the mighty muscles of his arms swelled up, and his features became like those of an angry lion.

"Woe to him that touches me!" thundered from his lips: "Flemish ravens will never eat me; French flesh suits their stomachs better!"

"Lay hold of him, you cowards!" cried De Chatillon to his men; "seize him, and up with him! Look at the poltroons! are ye afraid of a knife? Must I defile my hands with a peasant! But no, that must not be, I am noble; and like must to like, so it is your affair! Come, seize him by the collar!"

Some of the knights endeavored to pacify De Chatillon; but most of them took his part, and would willingly have seen the Fleming swing. And assuredly the men-at-arms, urged on by their master, would have fallen upon the youth, and in the end overpowered him, had not at this moment

The Lion of Flanders

the same knight drawn near who had just before gone a few steps aside, and till now had walked up and down absorbed in thought. His dress and armor far surpassed those of all the rest in magnificence; the lilies in a blue field embroidered upon his breast showed that he was of royal blood.

"Hold, there!" cried he, with a stern look to the men-at-arms; while he added, turning to De Chatillon: "You seem to have forgotten that it is to me that my brother and our King Philip has given the land of Flanders in fief. The Fleming is my vassal; it is I that am his lord and judge, and you have no right over his life."

"Am I then to submit to be insulted by a common peasant?" asked De Chatillon, angrily. "By my troth, count, I know not why it is that you always take the common man's part against the noble. Is this Fleming then to escape with the boast of having put to scorn a French knight unpunished? And you, gentlemen, say, has he not richly deserved to die?"

"Messire de Valois," said St. Pol, "I pray you let my brother have the satisfaction of seeing this Flemish fellow swing. What difference can it make to you whether the pig-headed rascal lives or dies?"

"Now listen, gentlemen," cried Charles de Valois, thoroughly roused, "this inconsiderate talk is extremely displeasing to me. I would have you

The Lion of Flanders

to know that the life of one of my subjects is no small thing in my eyes; and it is my will that this young man go his way unmolested and unhurt. To horse, gentlemen; we waste too much time here."

"Come along, Chatillon," muttered St. Pol, turning to his brother, "take the horse of one of your people, and let us start: after all, De Valois is no true man; he holds with the people."

Meanwhile the men-at-arms had replaced their swords in their scabbards, and were now busied in helping their master to remount.

"Are you ready, gentlemen?" asked De Valois. "If so, let us make haste and get on, else we shall be too late for the hunt. And do you, vassal, walk on one side, and tell us when we have to turn. How much farther have we to Wynandael?"

The youth took off his cap, bowed respectfully to his preserver, and answered: "A short hour's ride, my lord."

"By my soul, I don't trust the fellow," said St. Pol; "I believe he is but a wolf in sheep's clothing."

"That I have long suspected," interposed the chancellor, Peter Flotte; "for he eyes us like a wolf, and listens like a hare."

"Hah! now I know who he is!" cried De Chatillon. "Have you never heard of one Peter Deconinck, a weaver of Bruges?"

"You are certainly wrong there," observed

The Lion of Flanders

Raoul de Nesle; "I have myself spoken with the noted weaver of Bruges, when I was there; he is a far deeper one than this fellow, though he has but one eye, while our friend here has two, and those none of the smallest. Without doubt the lad is attached to the old family, and is not overwell pleased at our victorious arrival to thrust them out and take possession—that's all. Surely we may well forgive him his fidelity to his country's princes in their evil days."

"Enough of this," interrupted De Chatillon; "let us speak of something else. Do any of you know what it is that our gracious King Philip really means to do with this Flanders? If he kept his treasury as close as his brother De Valois's lips, by mine honor it would be but a poor life at court."

"There you're right," answered Peter Flotte; "but he is not so close with every one. Keep your horses back a little, and I will tell you things of which assuredly you wot not."

Curious to hear what it was he had to tell, the knights drew together about him, and let the Count de Valois get somewhat in advance. As soon as he was far enough not to hear what was said, the chancellor proceeded:

"Listen! Our gracious lord King Philip is at the bottom of his treasure-bags. Enguerrand de Marigny has persuaded him that Flanders is a very mine of gold; and in that he is not so far wrong, for here there is more of gold and silver than in all our France put together."

The knights laughed, while one and the other nodded assent.

"Hear further," proceeded Peter Flotte: "our Queen Joanna is deeply embittered against the Flemings; she hates this high and haughty people more than words can express. I myself have heard her say that she would like to see the last Fleming die on the gallows."

"That is what I call speaking like a queen," cried De Chatillon; "and if ever I have the rule here, as my gracious niece has promised me I shall, I will take care to fill her coffers, and send Master Peter Deconinck, with all his trumpery of guilds and city companies, to the right-about. But what business has that rascal listening?"

Their Flemish guide had, in fact, drawn near unobserved, and was drinking in every word that passed with attentive ears. As soon as he saw that he was noticed, he darted off, with a strange burst of laughter, among the trees, then halted at some little distance, and unsheathed his knife.

"Messire de Chatillon!" he cried, in a threatening tone, "look well at this knife, that you may know it again when you feel it under the fifth rib!"

"Is there none of my servants, then, that will avenge me?" cried De Chatillon in fury.

The Lion of Flanders

Before the words were well out of his mouth, a burly man-at-arms had dismounted, and was making at the youth sword in hand; but the latter, so far from defending himself with his weapon, put it up again into its sheath, and awaited his adversary with no other arms than those two sinewy ones with which nature had provided him.

"Die thou shalt, accursed Fleming!" cried the man-at-arms, with uplifted sword.

The youth answered not, but fixed his large piercing eyes on the soldier, who suddenly stood still with amazed look, as though all courage had at once forsaken him.

"On! stab him! kill him!" cried De Chatillon.

But the Fleming did not wait for his foe to come on. With a dexterous side-spring he threw himself within the sword's point, caught the man-at-arms with his powerful grasp about the waist, and dashed him so mercilessly head foremost against a tree that he fell to the ground without a sign of life. A last shriek of despair resounded through the wood, and the Frenchman closed his eyes forever, while a final spasm convulsed his limbs. With a frightful laugh the Fleming placed his mouth on the dead man's ear, and said in a tone of bitter scorn:

"Now go and tell thy lord and master that Jan Breydel's flesh is no food for ravens;—a French carcass is fitter meat for them."

The Lion of Flanders

And with this he sprang into the thicket, and disappeared in the depths of the forest.

The knights, who had meanwhile halted, and become anxious spectators of the scene, had not had time to exchange so much as a word with one another; but, as soon as they were recovered a little from their first astonishment, St. Pol exclaimed:

"In very truth, my brother, I believe that you have to do with a magician; for, as God is my helper, this is not according to nature."

"The place is indeed enchanted," replied De Chatillon, with a disconsolate air; "first my poor horse breaks his neck, and now I fear here is a faithful follower's life gone;—a most unlucky day! My men, take up your comrade, and carry him as well as you can to the nearest village, that there he may be cared for or buried, as his need may be. I pray you, gentlemen all, let the Count de Valois hear naught of this matter."

"Of course not!" was Peter Flotte's ready answer. "But let us now spur on a little; for I perceive Messire de Valois just at this moment disappearing among the trees."

Thereupon they gave their horses the reins, and soon overtook the count, who had meanwhile trotted steadily on, and did not now notice their approach. His head, with its silvered helmet, drooped in thought upon his breast; his gauntlet, keeping mechanically its hold of the reins, rested

The Lion of Flanders

carelessly on his horse's mane; his other hand clasped the hilt of the long sword that hung down beside the saddle.

As he thus rode on, immersed in thought, and the other knights by signs to one another jested at his displeased air, Castle Wynandael, with its massive ramparts and lofty towers, was slowly rising before them.

"Hurrah!" cried Raoul de Nesle, joyfully; "there is our journey's end. Spite of the devil and all his works, here we are at Wynandael at last!"

"Would that I could see it on fire!" muttered De Chatillon; "the journey has cost me a good horse and a faithful servant."

And now the knight with the lilies on his breast turned to the others and spoke:

"This castle, gentlemen, is the abode of the unhappy Count Guy of Flanders—of a father whose child has been taken from him, a prince who has lost his land by the fortune of war, which has favored us. I pray you let him not feel that we come as conquerors, and be careful not to embitter his sufferings by any words of affront."

"Think you, Count de Valois," snappishly interposed De Chatillon, "that we know not the rules of knightly good breeding? Think you that I am ignorant that a French knight should be generous in victory?"

The Lion of Flanders

"You *know* it, as I hear," replied De Valois, with strong emphasis; "I pray you, therefore, let me see you *practise* it. It is not in empty words that honor lies, Messire de Chatillon. What avails it that the precepts of knightly bearing come trippingly from the tongue, if they are not at the same time graven in the heart? He that is not generous in his dealings with those beneath him can never be really so with his equals. You understand me, Messire de Chatillon."

This rebuke excited the object of it to the most furious rage, which would certainly have broken out into words of violence but for the interposition of his brother, St. Pol, who held him back, and at the same time whispered in his ear:

"Hush, Chatillon, hush; the count is right. It is but due to our honor that we add no sufferings to the old Count of Flanders: he has troubles enough!"

"What! The faithless vassal has made war upon our king, and so offended our niece, Joanna of Navarre, that she has wellnigh been irritated into sickness; and now he is to be spared, forsooth!"

"Gentlemen," repeated De Valois, "you have heard my request; I do not believe that you will be wanting in generosity. And now, forward! I already hear the dogs; our approach too has been observed, for the bridge falls, and the portcullis is raised."

The Lion of Flanders

The Castle of Wynandael (its ruins may still be seen near Thourout, in West Flanders, hard by the village of the same name), built by the noble Count Guy of Flanders, was one of the fairest and strongest existing at that day. From the broad moat which compassed it rose high and massive walls, above which again, on every side, a multitude of watch-towers were conspicuous. Through the numerous loopholes might be seen glancing the keen eyes of the bowmen and the sharp steel of their arrows. Surrounded by the ramparts rose the pointed roofs of the lord's dwelling, with their guilded weather-cocks glittering in the sun. At the angles of the walls and in the fore-court stood six round towers, which served for hurling missiles of all kinds upon the foe, to keep him aloof from the body of the building. A single drawbridge crossed the moat, and made a way from the island fortress to the surrounding woods and vales.

As the knights drew near, the sentinel gave the sign to the guard within, and immediately the heavy gates creaked upon their hinges. The tread of the horses was already sounding upon the bridge, and the French knights passed on into the castle, between two rows of Flemish infantry drawn up in arms to receive them. The gates closed, the portcullis fell, and the drawbridge slowly rose behind them.

The Lion of Flanders

CHAPTER II

THE heaven was colored with so pure a blue that the eye failed when it sought to measure the skyey depths; the sun rose radiant above the horizon; the loving turtle-dove was sipping the last dewdrops from the verdant foliage.

Castle Wynandael resounded with one continual cry of hounds; while the neighing of the horses mingled with the cheery tones of the horns. But the drawbridge was still raised, and the passing countryman could only conjecture what was going on within. Numerous sentinels with cross-bow and shield paced the outmost ramparts, and through the loopholes might be discerned a mighty running hither and thither of a multitude of armed retainers.

At last some of the guardians of the walls made their appearance on the upper platform of the gateway, and let the drawbridge down; and at the same moment the gates opened wide, to give egress to the hunting-party which now rode slowly over the bridge.

A magnificent cavalcade it was, and of right high and mighty lords and ladies. First rode the

The Lion of Flanders

old Count Guy of Flanders on a brown steed. His features bore the expression of quiet resignation and unuttered grief. Bowed down by his eighty years and his hard lot, his head hung heavily forward upon his bosom; his cheeks were furrowed over with deep wrinkles. A purple surcoat flowed from his shoulders upon the saddle; his snowy hair, wound about with a kerchief of yellow silk, was like a silver vase hooped with gold. Upon his breast, on a heart-shaped shield, might be seen the black lion of Flanders, rampant in his golden field.

This unfortunate prince found himself now, at the end of his days, when rest and peace would have been the fitting meed for his long toils and struggles, thrust from his high estate and robbed of all. His children, too, deprived of their inheritance by the fate of war, had only a life of poverty and obscurity in prospect—they who should have been the wealthiest among Europe's princes. But though beset with enemies flushed with recent victory, and sorely tried by fortune, the brave old count yielded not to despair one inch of ground in his heart.

Beside him, and deep in discourse with him, rode Charles de Valois, brother to the King of France, who seemed desirous of impressing on the old count some views of his own into which the latter did not very readily enter. The battle-sword at

The Lion of Flanders

the French chief's side had meanwhile given place to another of less formidable proportions, and the knee-pieces, too, were no longer to be seen.

Behind Charles trotted a knight of haughty air and gloomy aspect. His eyes rolled and flamed within their sockets; and if perchance they fell upon one of the French knights, he compressed his lips, and ground his teeth so violently, that an attentive ear might have caught the sound. Hard upon fifty years old, but still in the fullest vigor of life, with broad chest and powerful limbs, he might well pass for one of the stoutest knights of his day. The horse, too, on which he rode was much taller than any of the rest, so that he showed a full head above any of his companions. A glittering helmet, with blue and yellow plume, a heavy coat of mail, and a curved sword, were all his arms, defensive and offensive: his surcoat, which covered his horse's croup with its long skirt, was distinguished by the Flemish lion. There were few knights of that day who would not at once have recognized this proud champion among a thousand others as Robert de Bethune, the old Count Guy's eldest son.

For some years past his aged father had committed to his charge the internal administration of the land. In every campaign it was he that had led the Flemish armies, and he had earned himself a glorious name, far and near. In the Sicilian

The Lion of Flanders

war, in which he, with his soldiers, had formed a part of the French host, he had performed such wondrous feats of arms, that ever since he was hardly spoken of otherwise than as the Lion of Flanders. The people, which ever cherishes with love and admiration the name of a hero, sang many a lay of the Lion's deeds of valor, and was proud of him who was one day to wear the Flemish coronet. As Guy, from his great age, rarely left his home at Wynandael, and was, moreover, not very popular with the Flemings, the title of Count was equally given by them to his son Robert, who was regarded throughout the land as their lord and master, and met with joyful obedience from all.

On his right rode William, his youngest brother, whose pale cheeks and troubled air contrasted like the face of a delicate girl with the bronzed features of Robert. His equipment in no way differed from that of his brother, except by the crooked sword, which Robert alone wore.

Then followed many other lords and gentlemen, both Flemings and foreigners. Among the former were especially noticeable Walter Lord of Maldegem, Charles Lord of Knesselare, Sir Roger of Akxpoele, Sir Jan of Gavern, Rase Mulaert, Diederik die Vos (*the fox*), and Gerard die Moor.

The French knights, Jacques de Chatillon, Gui de St. Pol, Raoul de Nesle, and their comrades, rode among the Flemish nobles, and each engaged in courteous conversation with such of them as happened to come in his way.

Last of all came Adolf of Nieuwland, a young knight of one of the noblest houses of the wealthy city of Bruges. His face was not one of those that attract by their effeminate beauty; he was none of the carpet heroes, with rosy cheeks, and smiling lips, who want nothing but a bodice to transform them into young ladies. Nature had made no such mistake with him. His cheeks, slightly sunburnt, gave him a look of seriousness beyond his years; his forehead was already marked with the two significant furrows which early thought rarely fails to imprint. His features were striking and manly; his eyes, half-hidden under their brows, indicated a soul at once ardent and reserved. Although in rank and position inferior to none of the knights in whose company he now was, he held back behind the rest. More than once had others made room to allow him to come forward; but their civility had hitherto been quite thrown away upon him—in fact, he seemed altogether lost in thought.

At the first glance, the young knight might have been taken for a son of Robert de Bethune; for—the very considerable difference of age apart—there was no little likeness between them; there was the same figure, the same bearing, the same cast of features. But their dress was not alike; the cognizance embroidered upon Adolf's breast showed three golden-haired maidens in a red shield. Over his arms stood his chosen motto: *Pulchrum pro patriâ mori.*

From his earliest youth Adolf had been brought up in Count Robert's house, whose bosom confidant he now was, and always treated by him like a dear son. He on his part honored his benefactor at once as his father and his prince, and entertained for him and his an affection which knew no bounds.

Immediately behind came the ladies, all so gorgeously attired that the eye could hardly bear the flash of the gold and silver with which they glittered. Each one rode her ambling palfrey; her feet were concealed under a long dress which reached nearly to the ground; the bosom was encased in a bodice of cloth-of-gold; and a lofty head-dress, adorned with pearls, was further decorated with long streamers which fluttered down behind. Most of them, too, bore falcons on their wrists.

Among them was one who quite eclipsed the rest both in magnificence and beauty. This was Count Robert's youngest daughter, by name Matilda. She was still very young (she might count some fifteen summers); but the tall well-developed figure which she had inherited from the vigorous stock from which she sprang, the serene beauty of her features, and the seriousness of her whole de-

The Lion of Flanders

portment, gave a royalty to her air and bearing that made it impossible to look on her without respect and even something of awe. All the knights about her showed her every possible attention, but each carefully guarded his heart against all venturous thoughts. They well knew that none but a prince could without folly lift his eyes to Matilda of Flanders. Lovely as some delightful dream hovered, so to say, the graceful maiden over her saddle, with head proudly uplifted, while her left hand lightly held the rein, and on her right sat a falcon with crimson hood and golden bells.

Immediately after this glittering bevy came a multitude of pages and other attendants, all in silken attire of various colors. Such of them as belonged to Count Guy's court were easily distinguished by the right side of their dresses being black, the left golden yellow. The rest were in purple and green, or red and blue, according to the colors of their respective masters.

Lastly followed the huntsmen and falconers. Before the former ran some fifty dogs in leash: sleuth-hounds, gaze-hounds, and dogs of chase of every variety.

The impatience of these spirited animals was so great, and they pulled so hard at the leashes, that every now and then the huntsmen had to bend forward down to the very manes of their horses.

The falconers bore each his bird on portable

perches. Hawks of all kinds were there, gerfalcons and tercels gentle, hobbies and sparrowhawks; every one with a red hood set with bells on its head and light leathern cases on its legs. Besides these, the falconers had their decoys, false birds with movable wings, by means of which the hawk was lured back from her flight.

The cavalcade once clear of the castle, the way soon grew wider, and the knights mingled promiscuously, without distinction of rank. Each sought out his own friend or comrade, and the time passed merrily in jests and joyous talk; even several of the ladies had found places among the knights.

Count Guy and Charles de Valois were still in front; no one had ventured to take the lead of those two. Robert de Bethune, however, and his brother William were now riding on the one side of their father; and, in like manner, Raoul de Nesle and De Chatillon had taken place alongside of their prince, who, at this moment, with eyes fixed in deep commiseration on the white hairs of the old Count and the depressed air of his son William, was thus speaking:

"I pray you, noble Count, to believe that your hard lot is a subject of real grief and pity to me. I feel indeed your sorrows as though they were my own. Nevertheless, be still of good heart; all hope is not lost, and my royal brother will, I doubt not, upon my intercession, forgive and forget the past."

"Messire de Valois," answered Guy, "you deceive yourself greatly. Your king has been heard to say, that to see the last day of Flanders is his dearest wish. Is it not he that has stirred up my subjects against me? Is it not he, moreover, that has cruelly torn my daughter Philippa from my arms to shut her up in a dungeon? And think you that he will again build up the edifice which he has, at the cost of so much blood, cast down? Of a truth you deceive yourself. Philip the Fair, your king and brother, will never give me back the land he has taken from me. Your generosity, noble sir, will remain recorded in my heart to the last hour of my life; but I am too old to flatter myself now with deceitful hopes. My reign is over—so God has willed it!"

"You know not my royal brother Philip," resumed De Valois; "true it is, that his deeds seem to witness against him; but I assure you his heart is as feeling and noble as that of a true knight ever should be."

But here Robert de Bethune impatiently broke in—"What say you? Noble? Noble as that of a true knight should be? Does a true knight break his pledged word and plighted faith? When we, fearing no evil, came with our poor sister Philippa to Corvay, did not your king violate every law of hospitality, and make prisoners of us all? Was this the deed of a true knight or of a traitor? Say yourself!"

"Messire de Bethune!" replied De Valois, stung by the reproach, "I do not believe you intend to affront or annoy me."

"Oh, no!" rejoined Robert, in a tone which bespoke sincerity; "by my faith and honor, that I did not. Your generosity has made you dear to me; but for all that, you can not with good conscience uphold that your king is a true knight."

"Listen to me," answered De Valois. "I tell you, nay, I swear it to you, that there is not a better heart in the world than that of Philip the Fair; but he is surrounded by a troop of miserable flatterers, and unhappily lends his ear to them. Enguerrand de Marigny is a devil incarnate, who instigates him to all evil; and, then, there is another person who often leads the king astray, whose name respect forbids my uttering, but who is, in very truth, answerable for all you have had to suffer."

"Who may that be?" asked De Chatillon, not without design.

"You ask what every one knows, Messire de Chatillon," cried Robert de Bethune; "listen to me, and I will tell you. It is your niece, Joanna of Navarre, that holds my unhappy sister in captivity; it is your niece, Joanna of Navarre, that debases the coin in France; it is your niece too, Joanna of Navarre, that has sworn the destruction of the Flemish freedom."

De Chatillon's rage at this retort knew no bounds. Furiously wheeling round his horse in front of Robert, he cried out in his face:

"You lie! false traitor that you are!"

Touched in his honor's tenderest point, Robert backed his horse a few steps, and drew his crooked sword from its scabbard; but in the very moment of making his onset upon De Chatillon, he remarked that his foe was unarmed. With manifest disappointment, he put his sword back into the sheath, and, approaching De Chatillon, said in a smothered voice:

"I do not suppose I need throw you down my gauntlet; you know that your words have cast a blot upon me that can only be washed out with blood; before this sun goes down I will demand an account from you of this insult."

"It is well," replied De Chatillon; "I am ready to maintain my royal niece's honor against all opposers."

The two knights resumed their former places in silence. During this short episode, the bystanders had been variously affected by Robert de Bethune's bold outbreak. Many of the French knights had felt inclined to take his words amiss; but the laws of honor did not allow their interfering in the

The Lion of Flanders

quarrel. Charles de Valois shook his head with an air of annoyance; and it was easy to see from his manner how much the whole affair vexed him. But a smile of pleasure hovered upon the lips of the old Count Guy, and turning to De Valois, he whispered:

"My son Robert is a brave knight, as your king Philip experienced at the siege of Lille, when many a valiant Frenchman fell before Robert's sword. The men of Bruges, who love him better than they do me, have given him the surname of the Lion of Flanders, a title which he well deserved also in the battle of Benevento against Manfred."

"I have long known Messire Robert de Bethune," answered De Valois; "and every child, I ween, knows the story, how with his own hand he won the Damask blade he now wears from the tyrant Manfred. His deeds of arms are far and wide renowned among the chivalry of France. The Lion of Flanders passes with us for invincible, and has well earned his fame."

A smile of contentment gilded the old man's face; but suddenly his visage darkened, and his head sank upon his breast, while he sorrowfully replied:

"Ah! Messire de Valois! is it not a misery that I have no heritage to leave to such a son? To him who was so well fitted to bring the house of Flan-

The Lion of Flanders

ders to fame and honor? It is the thought of that, and of the imprisonment of my poor child Philippa, which is fast hastening me to the grave."

Charles de Valois made no answer to the old Count's lament. He was sunk in deep thought, so that even the rein had fallen from his hand, and was hanging from the pommel of the saddle. Count Guy long watched him as he thus sat, and could not enough admire the generous feeling of the brave knight, who was evidently, from his very heart, concerned for the woes of the house of Flanders.

But suddenly the French prince sat up in his saddle, his countenance beaming with joy; and laying his hand, with a sort of confidential familiarity, upon that of the old Count, he exclaimed:

"It is a suggestion of heaven!"

Guy looked at him with curiosity.

"Yes!" continued De Valois, "I will bring it about that my brother, Philip of France, shall restore you to the princely seat of your fathers."

"And what spell of power, think you, have you found to work this miracle, after he has conferred upon yourself the fief that he has taken from me?"

"Give me your ear, noble Count. Your daughter sits disconsolate in the dungeons of the Louvre; your fiefs are gone from you, and their heritage from your children; but I know a way by which your daughter shall be released, and yourself reinstated."

"What say you?" cried Guy, incredulously. "That I can not believe, Messire de Valois; unless, indeed, your queen, Joanna of Navarre, should have ceased to live."

"No: without that. Our king, Philip the Fair, is at this moment holding court at Compiègne; my sister-in-law Joanna and Enguerrand de Marigny are both at Paris. Come with me to Compiègne, take with you the chief nobles of the land, and, falling at my brother's feet, pray him that he will receive you once more to allegiance, as a repentant and faithful vassal."

"And then?" asked Guy, amazed.

"Then he will receive you into his favor, and you will recover both your land and your daughter. Be of good courage, and trust to these my words; for, the queen absent from his side, my brother is all generosity and magnanimity."

"Oh! blessings on your good angel for this saving inspiration! and on you, Messire de Valois, for your nobleness of soul!" cried Count Guy, joyfully. "O God! if only I may be able to dry the tears of my poor child! But alas! who knows whether instead of that, I may not myself find a dungeon and fetters in that fatal land of France!"

"Fear not, Count! fear not!" answered **De Va-**

The Lion of Flanders

lois, "I will myself be your advocate and your protector; and a safe conduct under my seal and princely honor shall secure your free return, even should my efforts be in vain."

Guy let fall his rein, seized the French prince's hand, and, pressing it with fervent gratitude, exclaimed:

"You are a noble enemy!"

Meanwhile, as they thus discoursed, they had reached a wide plain, apparently of endless extent, watered by the gurgling stream of the Krekel. All now made ready for the sport.

The Flemish knights took each his falcon on his wrist; the strings which held the birds were made ready for casting off, and the hounds were properly distributed.

Knights and ladies were promiscuously mingled together; by chance Charles de Valois found himself by the side of the fair Matilda.

"I can not but think, fair lady," said he, "that you will bear away the prize of the day; for a finer bird than yours I have never beheld. What perfect plumage! what powerful wings! and then the yellow scales upon her claws! Is she heavy on the hand?"

"Yes, indeed, Messire," answered Matilda; "and although she has only been broken to a low flight, yet she would be quite a match for any crane or heron."

The Lion of Flanders

"It seems to me," remarked De Valois, "that she is somewhat full in flesh. Would it not be better, lady, to give her food softer?"

"Oh, no! excuse me; no! Messire de Valois," cried the young lady; piqued for her reputation for good falconry, "I am sure you are wrong there; my bird is just as she should be. Something of these matters I think I know; I have myself trained this noble bird, have watched her by night, and prepared her food myself. But quick, Messire de Valois, out of the way; for just over the brook there flies a snipe."

While the prince fixed his eye upon the point indicated, Matilda quickly unhooded her falcon, and cast her off.

The bird gave four or five strokes with her wings, and then circled gracefully before her mistress.

"Off, off, dear falcon!" cried Matilda.

And at these words the bird rose skyward like an arrow, till the eye could no longer follow it; then for some moments, poised in the air and motionless, she sought with her piercing eye her quarry; there, afar off, flew the snipe, and more swiftly than a stone from on high, swooped the falcon on the poor victim, which she soon held in her sharp talons.

"There, Messire de Valois!" cried Matilda, exultingly; "now you may see that a Flemish lady

The Lion of Flanders

can break a hawk! only look, how skilfully the faithful bird brings in her quarry!"

And the last words were hardly over her lips, before the falcon was again upon her hand with the snipe in its talons.

"May I have the honor to receive the game from your fair hand?" asked Messire de Valois.

But at this request the young lady's countenance became somewhat troubled; she looked imploringly on the knight, and said:

"I hope, Messire de Valois, that you will not take it amiss; but I had already promised my first quarry to my brother Adolf, who is standing yonder beside my father."

"Your brother William, mean you not, lady?"

"No; our brothe Adolf of Nieuwland. He is so kind, so obliging to me; he helps me in training my hawks, teaches me songs and tales; and plays to me on the harp; we all in truth heartily love him."

While Matilda was thus speaking, Charles de Valois had been regarding her with the closest attention; he soon, however, convinced himself that friendship was the only feeling which the young knight had excited in her bosom.

"If so," said the prince, with a smile, "he indeed well erits this favor. Do not, I pray you, let me detain you a moment longer."

And immediately, without heeding the presence

The Lion of Flanders

of the other knights, she called as loud as she could:

"Adolf! Adolf!" and joyous as a child, she held up the snipe for him to see.

At her call the young knight hastened up to her.

"Here, Adolf," added she, "is your reward for the pretty tale you last taught me."

He bowed respectfully, and received the snipe with pleasure. The others regarded him half with envy, half with curiosity; and more than one sought to decipher a tender secret upon his countenance; but all such speculations were in vain. Suddenly a loud exclamation called every one's attention to the sport.

"Quick! Messire de Bethune!" cried the chief falconer; "loose your hawk's hood and cast her off; yonder runs a hare."

A moment later, and the bird was hovering above the clouds, and then swooped perpendicularly upon the victim as it fled. It was a strange sight to see. The hawk had struck its claws deep in the hare's back as it ran, and so held fast to it, while both together rushed onward like the wind. But this did not last long; for the hawk, loosening one claw, seized hold with it of a tree, and with the other held her prey so fast, that, in spite of its desperate struggling, there was no escape for it. And now several dogs were uncoupled; these hurrying up, received the hare from the hawk, which

The Lion of Flanders

now, as if exulting in its victory, hovered aloft over the dogs and the huntsmen, exhibiting its joy in the most various sweeps and turns.

"Messire de Bethune," cried De Valois, "that is a hawk that knows her business! A finer gerfalcon I never saw!"

"You say no more of her than she deserves, Messire," replied Robert; "in a moment you shall look at her claws."

With these words he lifted up his lure, on catching sight of which the hawk immediately returned to her master's fist.

"Look here," proceeded Robert, showing the bird to De Valois; "see what beautiful fair-colored plumage, what a snow-white breast, and what deep-blue claws."

"Yes, indeed, Messire Robert," answered De Valois, "that is in very truth a bird that might hold comparison with an eagle. But it seems to me that she is bleeding."

Robert hastily inspected his hawk's legs, and cried impatiently:

"Falconer, hither, quick! my bird is hurt; the poor thing has tried its claws too much. Let her be well seen to; you, Stephen, keep her under your own eye; I would not lose her for more than I care to tell."

And he gave the wounded hawk to Stephen, his trainer, who all but wept at the accident; for the

The Lion of Flanders

hawks he had broken and tended were to him as his very children.

After the chief persons present had flown their hawks, the sport became more general. For two hours the party continued the chase after various kinds of birds of high flight, such as ducks, herons, and cranes, without, at the same time, sparing those of low flight, among which were partridges, field fares, and curlews. By this time it was noon; and now, at the cheerful summons of the horns, the whole party came together again from every side, and proceeded on their way back to Wynandael as fast as a moderate pace could carry them.

On the way, Charles de Valois resumed his conversation with the old Count Guy. The latter, much as he mistrusted the result of the proposed expedition into France, was yet, out of love for his children, disposed to undertake it; and finally, on the repeated insistence of the French prince, resolved on casting himself at King Philip's feet, with all the nobles who remained faithful to him, in the hope that so humiliating a homage might move the conqueror to compassion. The absence of Queen Joanna, flattered him with a ray of hope that he should not find her husband inexorable.

Since their morning's quarrel Robert de Bethune and De Chatillon had not met again; they purposely avoided each other, and neither of them said another word on the subject of what had

The Lion of Flanders

passed between them. Adolf of Nieuwland was now riding beside Matilda and her brother William. The young lady was evidently occupied in learning off some lay or tale which Adolf was repeating to her; for every now and then one of her ladies exclaimed in admiration:

"What a master in minstrelsy Sir Adolf of Nieuwland is!"

And so at last they got back to Wynandael. The whole train entered the castle; but this time the bridge was not raised nor did the portcullis fall, and after a delay of a few minutes the French knights issued again from its walls armed as they had come. As they rode over the bridge De Chatillon observed to his brother:

"You know that I have this evening to uphold the honor of our niece; I reckon on you as my second."

"Against this rough-spoken Robert de Bethune?" asked St. Pol. "I know not what may happen, but I fear you may come but badly out of it; for this Lion of Flanders is no cat to be taken hold of without gloves, and that you know as well as I."

"What is that to the purpose?" answered De Chatillon hastily. "A knight trusts to his skill and valor, and not to mere strength."

"You are quite right, my good brother; a knight must hold his ground against every one, be he who he may; but for all that it is better not to expose one's self unnecessarily. In your place I should have let Robert talk his spite out. What signifies what he says now that his lands are gone, and he is as good as our prisoner?"

"Be silent, St. Pol. Is that a seemly way to talk? Are you a coward?"

As he spoke these words they disappeared among the trees. And now the portcullis fell; the bridge was raised; and the interior of the castle was again concealed from view.

The Lion of Flanders

CHAPTER III

The knight or minstrel, who was admitted within the walls of Wynandael by the hospitality or compassion of its inhabitants, found himself on passing its gates in an open square; on his right he saw the stables, amply sufficient for a hundred horses, before which innumerable pigeons and ducks were picking up the stray grain; on his left were the lodgings for the soldiers and military retainers of all kinds, together with the magazines for the siege artillery of that day; as, for instance, battering-rams, with their carriages and supports, ballistas, which at one cast threw a shower of arrows into the besieged place, and catapults, which hurled crushing masses of stone against the hostile walls; besides scaling-ladders, fire-barrels, and other like implements of war.

Right in front of the entrance lay the residence of the Count and his family, rising majestically with its turrets above the lower buildings about it. A flight of stone steps, at the foot of which two black lions reposed, gave entrance to the ground floor, consisting of a long range of quadrangular rooms, many of them provided with beds for the

The Lion of Flanders

accommodation of chance guests, others decorated with the arms of bygone Counts of Flanders, and with banners and pennons won on many a hard-fought field.

On the right-hand side, in one corner of this vast building, was a smaller apartment, altogether different from the rest. On the tapestry with which its walls were adorned might be read the whole story of the sixth crusade in figures which almost looked alive. On one side stood Guy, armed from head to foot, and surrounded by his warriors, who were receiving from his hands the Cross; in the background was a long train of men-at-arms already on their way to the scene of action. The second side exhibited the battle of Massara, won by the Christian army in the year 1250. St. Louis, King of France, and Count Guy, were distinguishable from the other figures by their banners. The third side presented a hideous scene. A multitude of Christian knights lay dying of the plague upon a desert plain. Among the corpses of their comrades, and the carcasses of horses, black ravens flew over the fatal camp, watching for each one's death to gorge themselves with his flesh. The fourth side showed the happy return of the Count of Flanders. His first wife, Fogaets of Bethune, lay weeping on his breast, while her little sons Robert and Baldwin lovingly pressed his hand in theirs.

By the marble chimney-piece, within which a

The Lion of Flanders

small wood fire was burning, sat the old Count Guy in a massive armchair. Full of deep thought, he was supporting his head on his right hand, his eye resting unconsciously on his son William, who was busily reading prayers from a book with silver clasps. Matilda, Robert de Bethune's youthful daughter, stood with her hawk on the other side of the chamber. She was caressing the bird, without heeding her grandfather or uncle; while Guy, with a dark misgiving of the future, was brooding over the past, and William was praying to Heaven for some alleviation of their sorrows, she was playing with her favorite, without a thought that her father's inheritance was confiscated, and possessed by his enemies. Not that she was wanting in feeling; but, half-child as she was, her sorrow did not last beyond the immediate impression which excited it. When she was told that all the towns of Flanders were occupied by the foe, she burst into abundant and bitter tears; but by the evening of that selfsame day her tears were dried and forgotten, and she was ready to caress her hawk as before.

After Guy's eyes had for some time rested unmeaningly upon his son, he suddenly let fall the hand which supported his head, and asked:

"William, my son, what is it you are asking so fervently of God?"

"I am praying for my poor sister Philippa,"

The Lion of Flanders

was the youth's answer; "God knows, my father, whether the Queen Joanna has not already sent her to her grave; but in that case my prayers are for her soul."

And as he spoke he bowed forward his head, as if to conceal the tears which fell from his eyes.

The old father sighed heavily and painfully. He felt that his son's evil foreboding might but too easily turn out true, for Joanna of Navarre was wicked enough to make it so: nevertheless he would not give utterance to such a feeling, and so he only replied:

"It is not right, William, to sadden yourself with forebodings of evil. Hope is given to us mortals for our consolation here on earth; and why, then, should you not hope? Since your sister has been in prison, you mourn and pine so that not a smile ever passes over your countenance. It is well to feel for your sister; but, in God's name, do not give yourself up to this dark despair."

"Smile, said you, father? smile while our poor Philippa is buried in a dungeon? No, that I can not! Her tears drop upon the cold ground in the silence of her dungeon; she cries to Heaven because of her sorrows; she calls on you, my father—she calls on us all for relief; and who answers her? The hollow echo of the deep vaults of the Louvre! See you her not, pale as death, wasted and faded like a dying flower, with her hands raised to

The Lion of Flanders

heaven? hear you her not, how she cries, 'My father, my brothers, help me; I am dying in these chains?' All this I see and hear in my heart; I feel it in my soul; how, then, can I smile?"

Matilda, who had half listened to these sorrowful words, set her hawk hastily on the back of a chair, and fell with a violent burst of tears and sobbing at the feet of her grandfather. Laying her head on his knees, she cried out piteously:

"Is my dear aunt dead? O God! what sorrow! shall I not then see her again?"

The old Count raised her tenderly from the ground, and said kindly:

"Be calm, my dear Matilda; weep not; Philippa is not dead."

"Not dead!" exclaimed the girl with astonishment; "why, then, does my uncle William speak so of death?"

"You have not understood him," answered the Count; "we know of no change that has taken place with regard to her."

The young girl then dried her tears, casting the while a reproachful look upon William, and saying to him, in the midst of her sobs:

"You are always saddening me to no purpose, uncle! One would think that you had forgotten all words of comfort; for you ever talk in a way that makes me tremble. My very hawk is frightened at

The Lion of Flanders

your voice, it sounds so hollow! It is not kind of you, uncle, and it vexes me much."

William regarded his niece with eyes that seemed full of sorrow for the suffering he had caused her. No sooner had Matilda perceived this look of grief than, running up to him, and seizing tenderly one of his hands:

"Forgive me, dear uncle William!" she said; "I do love you dearly; but do you too think of me, and not torture me so with that terrible word, death, which is now ever upon your lips and in my ears. Forgive me, I pray you."

And before her uncle could answer her, she had already returned to the other end of the room, and was playing with her hawk again, though with tears still in her eyes.

"My son," said Count Guy, "do not take our little Matilda's words amiss; you know she does not mean unkindly."

"I forgive her, sir, from my heart; for, indeed, I love her from my heart. And the sorrow which she showed at my poor sister's supposed death was comforting to me."

And again William opened his book, and read, this time aloud:

"O Jesus Christ the Saviour, have mercy upon my sister! By thy bitter pangs release her, O Lord!"

And as the name of his Lord sounded in the old Count's ears, he uncovered his head, folded his hands, and joined in William's prayer. Matilda set down her hawk again on the back of the chair, and knelt in a corner of the chamber, on a great cushion, before a crucifix.

William went on:

"Blessed Mary, Mother of God, hear me, I pray! Comfort her in the dark dungeon, O Holy Virgin!

"O Jesus! sweet Jesus! full of pity! have mercy on my poor sister!"

Count Guy waited till the prayer was at an end, and then asked, without giving further heed to Matilda, who had again returned to her hawk:

"Tell me one thing, William; do you not think that we owe great thanks to Messire de Valois?"

"Messire de Valois is the worthiest knight I know," answered the youth; "he has treated us with true generosity; he has honored your gray hairs, and even done his best to give you some comfort. I well know that all our troubles, and my sister's imprisonment, would soon be at an end, if it depended on him. May God grant him eternal bliss for his nobleness of heart!"

"Yes, may God be gracious to him in his last hour!" said the old Count. "Can you understand, my son, how it is that our enemy should be noble enough to endanger himself for our sakes, and bring upon himself the hatred of Joanna of Navarre?"

The Lion of Flanders

"Yes, my father, I do understand it, when it is Charles de Valois that does it. But, after all, what can he do for us and my sister?"

"Listen, William. This morning, as we were riding together to the hawking, he showed me a way whereby, with God's help, we may be reconciled with King Philip."

In a transport of joy the young man struck his hands together, and exclaimed:

"O Heaven! His good angel must have spoken by his mouth! And what is it you have to do, my father?"

"I, with my nobles, must go to the King at Compiègne, and throw ourselves at his feet."

"And Queen Joanna?"

"The implacable Joanna of Navarre is at Paris, and Enguerrand de Marigny with her. Never was there a moment so favorable as this."

"The Lord grant that your hope may not deceive you! And when will you undertake this perilous expedition, my father?"

"The day after to-morrow Messire de Valois comes to Wynandael with his suite, and he will accompany us. I have called together those nobles who remained true to me in my misfortunes, in order to inform them of this matter. But your brother Robert comes not; how is it that he has not yet returned to the castle?"

"Have you already forgotten his quarrel of this

morning, my father? he has had to clear himself of the lie direct; of course he is with De Chatillon."

"You are right, William. I had forgotten that. This quarrel may do us harm; for Messire de Chatillon is powerful at the court of Philip the Fair."

In those times honor and good name were a knight's dearest possessions, and not the shadow of a reproach could he allow to pass upon them without a demand for instant reckoning; combats, therefore, were matters of daily occurrence, and excited but little attention.

Presently Guy rose, and said:

"There, I hear the bridge fall; doubtless my faithful nobles are already there. Come, let us go to the great hall."

And immediately they went out together, leaving the young Matilda alone, and took their way to the hall, where they were speedily joined by the Lords of Maldeghem, of Roode, of Courtrai, of Oudenarde, of Heyle, of Nevele, of Roubuis, Walter of Lovendeghem, with his two brothers, and several more, who came in one after the other, to the number of two-and-fifty in all. Some of them were already temporarily lodged in the castle, others had their possessions and residences in the neighboring plain.

All stood with uncovered head before their lord,

The Lion of Flanders

anxiously awaiting the intelligence or command he might have to communicate. After keeping silence for some little time, Count Guy addressed them thus:

"My friends, it is well known to you that the true obedience with which I have ever followed the commands of my liege lord King Philip has been the cause of all my misfortunes. He it was that laid it upon me to call the city corporations to account for their government, which I therefore as a true subject and vassal desired and attempted to do. Then the city of Bruges refused me obedience, and my subjects rose against me. Afterward, when I went into France to do my homage to the king, he made me prisoner; and not only me, but my poor child, who was with me, and who still groans in the dungeons of the Louvre. All this you know; for you were the companions of your prince. Then, as became me, I sought to make good my right with arms; but fortune was against us, and the false Edward of England disregarded the bond we had entered into, and deserted us in our need. Now my land is confiscated; I am now the least among you, and your prince no more; another is now your lord."

"Not yet!" cried Walter of Lovendeghem; "when that day comes I break my sword forever. I know no other lord than the noble Guy of Dampierre."

The Lion of Flanders

"Sir Walter of Lovendeghem, your faithful attachment is truly gratifying to me; but hear me patiently to the end. Messire de Valois has overrun Flanders with his arms, and has now received it as a fief from his brother King Philip. Were it not for his magnanimity, I should not be with you here at Wynandael; for he it was that assigned me this pleasant abode. But this is not all; he has resolved to build up again the house of Flanders, and to set me once more on my father's seat. That is the matter which I have to speak of with you, my noble friends; for I need your help in it."

The astonishment of all present, who were listening with the deepest attention, reached its highest pitch at this announcement. That Charles de Valois should be willing to give up the land he had won and taken possession of seemed to them utterly incredible. They regarded the Count with looks that expressed all they felt; and after a short pause he resumed:

"My noble friends, I doubt not in the least your affection for me; therefore I speak in the full confidence that you will grant me this last request which I now make you; to-morrow I set out for France, to throw myself at the king's feet, and I desire to be accompanied by you, my faithful nobles."

All present answered, one after the other, that they were ready to accompany and stand by their

The Lion of Flanders

Count, where and when and in what way he would. All answered him except one, Diederik die Vos.

"Sir Diederik," asked the Count, "will you not go with us?"

"Surely, surely," answered he, thus personally appealed to, "the fox will go with you, were it to the mouth of hell. But I tell you, noble Count—forgive me, but I must have my say—I tell you, that one need be no fox to see where the trap lies here. What! after once having been caught in this way, will you run into the very same snare again? God grant that all may turn out well; but one thing I tell you, Philip the Fair shall not catch the fox."

"You judge and speak too lightly, Sir Diederik," answered Guy; "we are to have a written safe conduct from Charles de Valois, and his honor is pledged for our free return to Flanders."

The Flemish nobles, well knowing De Valois as a model of knightly honor and good faith, were satisfied to trust to his promise, and went on to discuss the matter with the old Count. Meanwhile Diederik slipped unobserved out of the hall, and wandered up and down the outer court wrapped in deep thought.

Before he had spent much time in this occupation, the bridge was lowered, and Robert Bethune entered the castle. As soon as he had dismounted, Diederik approached, and thus addressed him:

"I need not ask, noble Count, as to the result of

The Lion of Flanders

your affair of to-day: the Lion's sword has never failed him yet; doubtless by this time Messire de Chatillon is on his journey for the other world."

"No," answered Robert; "my sword came down upon his helmet in such sort that he will hardly speak for some days to come. He is not dead; God be praised for that; but another mishap has befallen us. Adolf of Nieuwland, who was with me as my second, fought with St. Pol, and he had already wounded his opponent in the head, when his breastplate failed him; upon which he received a severe wound, I fear even a mortal one. In a few minutes you will see him, for men are now carrying him hither."

"But say, my lord," proceeded Diederik; "think you not that this journey to France is a venture somewhat of the rashest?"

"What journey? I know not what you mean."

"What! you have not yet heard of it?"

"Not one word."

"Well, we set off to-morrow with your noble father for France."

"What is it you say, Diederik? Are you jesting —to France?"

"Yes, Lord Robert. To throw ourselves at the feet of the French king, and sue for forgiveness. I have never yet seen a cat creep into a sack of her own accord; but before long I shall see it at Compiègne, or I am greatly mistaken."

The Lion of Flanders

"But are you quite sure of what you say, Diederik? You fill me with alarm."

"Sure, do you say? Be pleased to go into the hall; there you may see all your friends assembled with your father. To-morrow we set out for our prison. Believe me, then, and cross yourself when you leave Wynandael."

Robert could hardly contain himself for indignation at this intelligence.

"Diederik, my friend," he said, "I pray you have my poor Adolf taken up to my own chamber when he is brought in, and laid upon the left-hand bed. See that he is duly cared for until I can come myself; and send, too, for Master Roger to dress his wounds."

And with these words, he hurried away to the hall, where the Count was still in conference with his nobles, and pressed forward hastily till he stood before his father, not a little to the astonishment of all present; for he was still in full armor from head to foot.

"Oh, my lord and father!" cried he; "what report is this I hear? are you really about to deliver yourself up to your enemies, that they may make a mock of your gray hairs? that the vile Joanna may cast you into fetters?"

"Yes, my son," answered the Count steadfastly; "I am going to France, and you with me—such is the will of your father."

The Lion of Flanders

"Let it be so, then," replied Robert; "I will go with you; but not to fall at the king's feet! God forbid that we should so humiliate ourselves!"

"It must be so, my son; and it behooves you to accompany me," was the unalterable reply.

"I!" cried Robert in fury; "I fall at Philip's feet! I, Robert de Bethune, prostrate myself before our foe! What! shall the Lion of Flanders bow his head before a Frenchman, a maker of false coin, a perjured prince?"

The Count was silent for a few moments; but as soon as Robert's first burst of indignation had subsided, he resumed:

"And yet, my son, you will do it for my sake?"

"No, never!" cried Robert; "never shall that blot rest upon my shield. Bow before a foreigner—I! You know not your son, my father!"

"Robert," pursued the old Count calmly, "your father's will is a law for you: I command it!"

"No!" cried Robert yet again; "the Lion of Flanders bites, and fawns not. Before God alone, and you, my father, have I ever bowed the head or bent the knee; and no other man on earth shall be able to say of me that I have thus humbled myself before him."

"But, Robert," insisted his father, "have you no compassion for me, for your poor sister Philippa, and for our unhappy country, that you thus reject

The Lion of Flanders

the one only means by which we may yet be delivered?"

Robert wrung his hands violently, in a very agony of grief and anger.

"What will you now, my father?" he exclaimed; "do you indeed desire that a Frenchman should look down upon me as his slave? I am ready to die with shame at the very thought. No, never! Your command, your entreaty even, is of no avail. I will not—I can not do it!"

Two tears glistened upon the old man's hollow cheeks. The singular expression of his countenance threw the lookers-on into doubt whether it was joy or grief that had touched him, for at the same time a smile of comfort seemed to hover on his countenance.

Robert was deeply moved by his father's tears; he felt, as it were, the pains of martyrdom in his heart. At last his emotion burst all bounds, and almost beside himself, he exclaimed:

"My prince and father! your curse upon me, if you will! but this I swear to you—never will I creep or bow before a Frenchman! In this thing I can not obey you."

But even amid all his excitement Robert was terrified at his own words. Pale and trembling in every limb, he clenched his hands convulsively, till the iron scales of his gauntlets might be heard grinding upon one another throughout the hall.

The Lion of Flanders

He felt his resolution shrinking, and awaited the curse he had defied in an anguish like that of death.

All present waited for the reply of the old Count with anxious expectation. At last he threw his aged arms round his son's neck, and cried with tears of love and joy.

"Oh, my noble son! my blood—the blood of the Counts of Flanders—flows undegenerate in your veins! Your disobedience has bestowed on me the happiest day of my life. Now willingly could I die! One more embrace, my son; for words do not suffice to express the joy of my heart."

Admiration and sympathy filled the hearts of all the noble company, who looked on in solemn silence, while the old Count, releasing his son from his embrace, and turning to his barons, exclaimed enthusiastically:

"See, my friends; such was I in my younger days, and such have the Dampierres ever been. Judge by what you have seen and heard whether Robert de Bethune does not deserve to wear his father's coronet. Such are the men of Flanders! Yes, my son, you are right; a Count of Flanders must bow his head before no stranger. But I am old; I am the poor imprisoned Philippa's father, and yours, my brave son. I will myself kneel before Philip; since such is the will of God, I humbly submit. And you, Robert, shall go with me; but not to bow the head or bend the knee before the oppressor. Hold yourself, as ever, erect; that so there may be a Count of Flanders after me free from shame and reproach."

The various preparations for the journey were now discussed at length, and many important points were deliberated upon and settled. Robert de Bethune, now calmer and more collected, left the hall, and proceeding to the smaller apartment, where Matilda still remained, he took the maiden by the hand, and led her to a chair; then drawing one for himself, he sat down beside her.

"My dear Matilda," he began, "you love your father, do you not?"

"You know I do," was the reply, while she caressed the knight's bearded cheek with her soft hand.

"But," he continued, "would you not also love a man that ventured his life in my defense?"

"Yes, surely; and bear him eternal gratitude."

"Well, then, my daughter; a knight has risked his life in your father's quarrel, and is sorely wounded, perhaps even unto death."

"O God! I will pray for his recovery forty days, and more too!"

"Do so, my child, and for me too; but I have to ask yet something more of you."

"Speak, my father; I am your obedient child."

"Understand me well, Matilda; we are going for some days on a journey, your grandfather and I,

The Lion of Flanders

and all the knights that are here with us. Who, then, shall give the poor wounded knight to drink when he is thirsty?"

"Who? I, my father; I will never leave his side till you return. I will take my hawk into his chamber, and be his constant attendant. Fear not that I will leave him to the servants; my own hand shall hold the cup to his lips. His recovery shall be my best hope and my dearest joy."

"That is well, my child; I know your loving heart; but you must, moreover, promise me that in the first days of his illness you will keep his chamber perfectly still; make no noise there yourself, nor let any one else do so."

"Fear not for that, father; I will talk to my hawk so softly that not one word of it shall the wounded knight hear."

Robert took his daughter by the hand, and led her out of the chamber.

"I must show you your patient," he said; "but speak low while you are with him."

Meanwhile Adolf of Nieuwland had been carried by the attendants into a chamber of Robert's lodging, and laid upon a bed; two surgeons had bound up his wounds, and now stood with Diederik die Vos by the bedside. No sign of life was to be perceived; the countenance of the young knight was pale and his eyes closed.

"Well, Master Roger," inquired Robert of one

The Lion of Flanders

of the surgeons, "how goes it with our unfortunate friend?"

"But badly, my lord," answered Roger; "but badly indeed. I can not, at this moment, say what hope there is; and yet I have a sort of presentiment that he will not die."

"Then the wound is not mortal?"

"Well, it is and it is not; nature is the best physician, and often works cures which neither mineral nor simple could effect. I have laid upon his breast, too, a thorn from the Holy Crown; the virtue of that relic will, I trust, assist us."

During this conversation Matilda had gradually approached the bed; and her curiosity having led her to look at the wounded knight's face, she suddenly recognized that of her dear friend and playfellow. With a mournful cry she started back, tears burst from her eyes, and she sobbed aloud.

"What is this, my child?" said Robert, "are you no better mistress of yourself than that? Know you not that one must be calm and quiet by a wounded man's bedside!"

"Calm shall I be! Calm when our poor Adolf lies at the point of death! He that taught me such sweet songs! Who shall be our minstrel at Wynandael now? Who shall help me to break my hawks, and be to me as a brother?" And then approaching the bed again, she wept over him as he

The Lion of Flanders

lay insensible, and at last sobbed out: "Sir Adolf! Sir Adolf! my good brother!"

But no answer came. Covering her face with her hands, she fell back in an agony of grief into a chair.

After some little time thus spent, Robert, seeing that she was unable to command herself, and that her presence would be more injurious than useful, took her by the hand.

"Come, my child," he said, "leave this chamber till you are somewhat more mistress of your sorrow."

But she would not leave the room. "Oh, no!" she replied, "let me stay here, my father! I will not weep any more. Let me care for my brother Adolf. Those fervent prayers which he has himself taught me, will I pour out for him by his bedside."

And thus saying, she took the cushion from a chair, laid it on the floor at the head of the bed, and, kneeling on it, began to pray silently, while suppressed sobs burst from her breast, and her eyes overflowed with tears.

Robert de Bethune remained till far on in the night by Adolf's bedside, hoping to see him come somewhat to himself. His hopes were, however, in vain; the wounded man breathed feebly and slowly; nor was there the slightest movement perceptible either in limbs or body. Master Roger, too, began to fear seriously for his life; for a slight fever had made its appearance, and the sufferer's temples already began to burn.

Those of the nobles who were present at the conference and were not lodged in the castle had already taken their departure, not without a feeling of contentment at what had happened; for, as true knights, they rejoiced at having an opportunity of once more doing their old prince a pleasure and a service. Such of them as were the Count's guests betook themselves to their bedchambers. Two hours later not a sound was to be heard at Wynandael but the call of the sentinels, the baying of the dogs, and the screech of the night-owl.

The Lion of Flanders

CHAPTER IV

The journey which, at the suggestion of Charles de Valois, Count Guy was about to undertake, was a matter of no little risk, both to himself personally and to the whole land of Flanders; for there was only too much reason to believe that the King of France would think all measures good which might secure to him as long as possible the possession of those wealthy provinces.

Philip the Fair and his wife, Joanna of Navarre, had, in order to provide funds for their reckless prodigality, drawn, so to say, all the money of the realm into the treasury; yet for all this, the enormous sums which they extracted from the people did not suffice for their insatiable wants. His unprincipled ministers, above all Enguerrand de Marigny, daily incited the king to levying fresh taxes, raising the already exorbitant salt-duty, and laying the most intolerable burdens on all three estates of the realm, regardless of the murmurs of the people and the frequent symptoms of armed resistance. Again and again he expelled the Jews from France, in order to make them pay enormous sums for permission to return; and at last,

The Lion of Flanders

when every other means was exhausted, he resorted to the plan of debasing the coin of the realm.

This debasement of the coinage was a desperate and ruinous expedient; for the merchants, not choosing to part with their wares for mere worthless counters, left the kingdom; the people fell into poverty, the taxes could not be levied, and the king found himself in a most critical position. Flanders meanwhile flourished by the industry of its inhabitants. All the trading nations of Europe and Asia regarded it as their second country, and carried their goods to its cities, as to the universal market-place of the world. At Bruges alone more money and goods changed hands than in the whole of France; the city was, in truth, a very mine of wealth. This did not escape Philip's observation, and for some years he had been occupied with plans for bringing the land of Flanders into his own possession. First he had laid down impossible conditions to Count Guy, in order to drive him into contumacy; then he had arrested and imprisoned his daughter Philippa; and at last he had overrun and seized upon Flanders by force of arms.

Nothing of all this had escaped the old Count's consideration, nor did he in truth conceal from himself the possible consequences of his journey; but his grief on account of his younger daughter's imprisonment was such as induced him to reject no means, however desperate, which might possibly lead to her release. Doubtless, too, the safe conduct promised by Charles de Valois had tended considerably to reassure him.

And now the old Count set out, with his sons, Robert and William, and fifty Flemish nobles; Charles de Valois, and a great number of French knights, accompanying them on the journey.

Arrived at Compiègne, the Count and his nobles were sumptuously lodged and entertained by the Count de Valois, until such times as he should be able to arrange for their admittance to the king's presence. This magnanimous prince, moreover, so well used his influence with his brother, that the latter was quite inclined to fall into his views with respect to the Count of Flanders, whom he accordingly caused to be summoned before him, at his royal palace.

The Count was introduced into a large and splendid hall, at the other end of which stood a throne, with a canopy of blue velvet wrought with golden lilies, and hangings of the like falling on each side to the ground; a carpet, richly embroidered with gold and silver, covered the steps which led up to this magnificent seat. Philip the Fair was pacing up and down the hall with his son, Louis Hutin, that is, the "quarrelsome"; behind them followed many French nobles, and among them one to whom the king often addressed his conversation. This favorite was Messire de No-

The Lion of Flanders

garet, the same who at Philip's command had ventured to arrest Pope Boniface, with circumstances of special contumely.

As soon as Count Guy was announced, the king retired to the steps of the throne, without, however, mounting them. By his side stood his son Louis, while his nobles ranged themselves on either hand along the walls. Then the old Count of Flanders drawing near with slow steps, knelt on one knee before the king.

"Vassal!" said Philip, "a humble attitude truly beseems you, after all the trouble you have occasioned us. You have deserved death, and are, indeed, condemned to die; nevertheless, out of our royal grace, we will now hear you. Stand up, therefore, and speak."

Upon this the old Count rose from the ground and said:

"My prince, and liege lord! with confidence in your royal justice I have presented myself at your feet, that you may deal with me according to your will."

"Your submission," returned the king, "comes late. You have entered into a confederacy against me with Edward of England; you have risen up as an unfaithful vassal against your liege lord; you have had the audacity to declare war against us; and your land has therefore been justly confiscated for your manifold transgressions."

The Lion of Flanders

"My prince," said Guy, "let me find grace before you. Bethink yourself, mighty king, what it is that a father feels deprived of his child. Did I not supplicate you in the deepest woe? Did I not humbly pray you to give her back to me? If your own son, my future lord, Louis, who now stands so manfully by your side—if he were taken from you, and cast into a dungeon in a strange land, would not your grief carry you any length to avenge or to release your own blood and offspring? Yes! you have a father's heart, and that will understand me. I know that I shall find grace at your feet."

Philip cast a look of tenderness upon his son; at this moment he felt for all that Guy had had to suffer, and his heart melted with compassion for the unfortunate Count.

"Sir," cried Louis, with emotion, "for my sake be gracious to him; I pray you have pity upon him and upon his child."

The king, however, had recovered from his emotion, and now assumed a sterner aspect.

"Be not so easily moved by the words of a disobedient vassal, my son," he said. "However, I will not refuse to listen, if only he can make it appear that what he has done has been for his daughter's sake, and not from contumacy."

"Sire," resumed the Count, "your majesty knows that whatever man could do I did, to have my child back; but none of my endeavors availed; all my prayers and supplications were in vain; and even the intervention of the Holy Father was of no effect. What, then, could I do? I flattered myself with the hope of procuring my daughter's deliverance by force of arms; the fortune of war, however, was against me, and the victory was with your majesty."

"But," interrupted the king, "what can we do for you? You have given an evil example to our vassals, and if we show grace to you, will they not all rise up against us, and you, perhaps, once more join yourself to their number?"

"Oh, my prince!" answered Guy, "let it please your majesty to restore the unhappy Philippa to her father, and I swear to you that I shall bind myself with inviolable fidelity to your crown."

"And will Flanders raise the contribution we have imposed? And will you duly repay all the costs of the war which your insolence and contumacy compelled us to make against you?"

"No sacrifice shall be too great for me to repay your majesty's gracious favor: and all your commands shall be humbly and punctually obeyed. But my child, sire; my child!"

"Your child?" interposed Philip, hesitatingly; and his thoughts reverted to his wife Joanna, who, he knew, would hardly with good will release from captivity the daughter of the Count of Flanders.

The Lion of Flanders

Fearing to provoke the wrath of his imperious queen, he did not venture to follow the better movements of his heart; so, without making any absolute promise to Guy on this point, he replied:

"The intercession of our beloved brother has done much for you; and, moreover, your hard lot moves me to compassion. You have sinned; but your punishment has been bitter. Be of good hope; I will endeavor to sweeten your cup. Nevertheless, we can not, on this very day, finally receive you into favor; so great a matter must first have due deliberation. We require, moreover, that you make a public submission in the presence of our vassals here assembled, that you may be an example to them all. Go now; leave us, that we may once more consider what we can do for an unfaithful and disobedient vassal."

Upon this command the Count of Flanders left the hall; and before he was out of the palace the report was universally current among the French nobles that the king had promised to restore him his land and his daughter. Many wished him joy with all their hearts; others, who had built ambitious hopes on the conquest of Flanders, were inwardly displeased; but as they could not oppose the king's will, they took care that their vexation should not be seen.

Joy and confident hope now filled the hearts of the Flemish supplicants; and many a flattering an-

The Lion of Flanders

ticipation was entertained of the liberation and renewed happiness of their country. It seemed to them as if nothing could now disturb the good success of their undertaking; since, besides the gracious reception the Count had met with from the king, the latter had moreover given a solemn assurance to his brother De Valois that Guy should be dealt with magnanimously.

Ye who have striven against fortune, and in this hard struggle suffered sorely and wept bitterly, how pleasantly comes a ray of joy into your darkling hearts! How easily do you forget your pains, to embrace an uncertain happiness, as if you had already emptied the cup of woe; while the dregs, bitterest of all, still remain for you to drain! You see a smile on every countenance, and press the hand of every one that seems to sympathize in your happiness. But trust not the fickle dame Fortune, nor her ever-rolling wheel; nor yet the words of those who were not your friends when you were in adversity. For envy and treason are hidden under the double countenance, as adders lurk under flowers, and scorpions behind the golden pineapple. In vain do we seek the track of the serpent in the field; we feel her poisoned tooth, but know not whence it has stricken us. So does the envious and spiteful man work in darkness; for he knows his own wickedness, and out of shame conceals his evil deeds. The black soul does not show upon the

The Lion of Flanders

flattering countenance; and so his arrows strike us to the heart, even while we hold him for our friend.

Count Guy lost no time in taking the necessary steps for satisfying all the king's requisitions immediately upon his return to Flanders, and for laying the foundations of a long peace, in which his subjects might forget the calamities of war. Even Robert de Bethune seemed to have no doubt of the promised grace; for, ever since his father's appearance at court, the French nobles had on all occasions behaved with the utmost kindness and civility to the Flemings; and as the latter well knew that the thoughts of princes are best read on the countenances of their courtiers, they saw in this demeanor a certain proof of the favor and good-will of the king.

De Chatillon, among the rest, had repeatedly visited the Count, and overwhelmed him with congratulations; but he concealed a devilish secret in his heart, which he contrived to hide with his smiles. His niece, Joanna of Navarre, having promised him that the fief of Flanders should one day be his, all his ambitious projects had centred upon this one goal; and now he beheld it vanishing into thin air before his eyes, like a dream which is gone and leaves no trace behind.

There is no passion of the human heart which more readily and imperiously leads away those who are subject to it into every kind of iniquity than the lust of power; pitilessly it tramples down whatever impedes its path, and looks not round to count the havoc it has made, so steadfastly and constantly does it keep its eyes fixed on the darling object. Possessed by this fiend, De Chatillon resolved in his heart on a deed of treachery, of which his own selfish interests were indeed the real motive, but which he decorated before his conscience with the fair names of duty and patriotism.

On the very same day that he arrived at Compiègne he chose out one of his most faithful servants, and, mounting him on his best horse, he despatched him in all haste to Paris. A letter which this messenger bore gave a full account of all that had passed to the queen and Enguerrand de Marigny, and urgently pressed their speedy return to court.

His traitorous design met with the fullest success. Joanna of Navarre's fury knew no bounds. The Flemings graciously received! Should they to whom she had sworn an eternal hate thus escape her at the very moment when they seemed at last fully in her power? And Enguerrand de Marigny, who had already squandered, or in prospect laid out, the enormous sums which he reckoned on extorting from the Flemish burghers! Both of these foes of Flanders had too great an interest in the destruction of their prey, to allow it thus easily

The Lion of Flanders

to give them the slip. No sooner had they received the intelligence than both hastened back to Compiègne, and appeared suddenly and unexpectedly in the king's chamber.

"What, sire!" cried Joanna; "am I, then, nothing to you, that you thus receive my enemies into favor without a word said to me? Or have you lost your reason, that you are resolved on nourishing these Flemish serpents to your own destruction?"

"Madame," answered Philip, calmly, "methinks it would beseem you to address your husband and your king with somewhat more respect. If it is my pleasure to show grace to the old Count of Flanders, so shall it be."

"No!" cried Joanna, inflamed with anger, "so shall it not be! Hear me, sire! I will not have it so! What! shall the rebels who beheaded my uncles escape thus? Shall they have it to boast that they have shed with impunity the blood royal of Navarre, and insulted its queen?"

"Your passion leads you astray, madame," replied Philip; "bethink yourself calmly, and tell me, is it not right that Philippa should be restored to her father?"

At this Joanna's fury waxed still higher.

"Release Philippa!" she exclaimed. "Surely, sire, you can not think of it! That she may be married to Edward of England's son, and so your own child may lose a throne? No, no; that shall never happen, believe me. And what is more, Philippa is my prisoner; and you shall find that even your kingly power is not sufficient to rescue her from my grasp!"

"Truly, madame," cried Philip, "you are exceeding all bounds! I would have you know that this unseemly defiance much displeases me; take care, moreover, that I do not make you feel it! I am your sovereign, and as such I will be obeyed!"

"And you intend to restore Flanders to this old rebel, and to put him in a position once more to make war upon you? A grievous repentance will you prepare for yourself by so ill-considered a step! For my part, since I see that I am of so small account with you, that a matter so nearly concerning me is to be settled without my being even consulted, I will return to my own land of Navarre, and Philippa shall go with me."

This last speech of Queen Joanna had a powerful effect upon the king's mind; for the possession of Navarre was in truth a matter of no small importance to the crown of France; and Philip would have parted with a great deal rather than that. Joanna had more than once threatened him with retiring to her own states, and he feared that she might one day carry this design into effect. After some consideration, therefore, he replied:

"You are offended without cause, madame. Who

has told you that I intend to restore Flanders? I have not yet come to any determination on the subject."

"You have said enough to let your intentions be seen," answered Joanna. "But be that as it may, I tell you, that if you disregard me so far as to set my wishes and opinion at naught, I will leave you; I will not stay here to be exposed to the consequences of your want of prudence and foresight. The war against Flanders has exhausted your treasury and your people; and now that you have the means in your hands of retrieving yourself at the expense of the rebels, you are about to receive them into favor, and to give them all back again! Never have our finances been in a worse condition; that Messire de Marigny can tell you."

Thus appealed to, Enguerrand de Marigny addressed the king. "Sire," said he, "it is impossible we can continue to pay the troops you are maintaining, for the people can not or will not any longer pay the taxes. The *Prévot des Marchands* at Paris has refused the additional contribution; so that before long I shall not be able even to meet the daily expenses of your majesty's household. To carry the debasement of the coin, too, any farther is impossible. Our only resource, then, is Flanders, where the commissioners whom I have despatched are at this moment engaged in raising the money to help us out of our difficulties. Consider, sire, that in restoring this land to the Count, you deprive yourself of your last resource, and expose yourself to all the consequences of the existing embarrassments."

"What!" said Philip, in a tone of mistrust, "can it be that the whole of the last contribution levied upon the third estate is already expended?"

"Sire," replied De Marigny, "I have had to repay to Stephen Barbette the moneys which the farmers of the tolls at Paris had advanced. There remains but little or nothing in the treasury."

The queen saw with malicious joy the downcast air with which the king received this news, and she perceived that now was her opportunity for obtaining a final sentence of condemnation upon the old Count. Drawing near, therefore, to her husband with a well-dissembled return of gentleness, she thus spoke:

"You see well, sire, that my counsel is good. How can you lose sight of the interests of your own kingdom merely to favor these rebels? They have openly defied you; they have joined with your enemies, and have set at naught your just commands. Seeing that it is their wealth that thus puffs them up, and makes them insolent, nothing can be better in every way than to take from them this superfluity of riches; and as they have all justly deserved to die, they may well kiss your royal hand, and thank you that you do not also deprive them of their lives."

"But, Messire de Marigny," said the king, turning to his minister, "can you find no means of meeting the necessary expenses for some short time at least? For I hardly think that the moneys from Flanders will come in so quickly. What you tell me of the state of things disquiets me to the last degree."

"I know of no expedient, sire; we have already employed too many."

"Listen to me," interposed Joanna. "If you will follow my counsel, and deal with Guy as I desire, I will procure a loan on the credit of my kingdom of Navarre, so that we shall be set free from all anxiety for some time to come."

Whether from weakness or poverty, the king gave way, and agreed to all that Joanna required. The poor old Count was thus delivered into the hand of the traitress, in order to undergo the ceremony of a public humiliation, and then to be kept a prisoner, far away from his own land and people!

The Lion of Flanders

CHAPTER V

THE evening was already far advanced when Joanna of Navarre arrived at Compiègne; and while with threats and cunning she was extorting from her vacillating husband the sentence of condemnation upon the House of Flanders, its unfortunate chief was sitting with his nobles in a large room of his lodging. The wine passed round again and again in silver goblets; and joyful hopes and pleasant anticipations formed the universal subject of conversation. More than one point had already been warmly discussed, when the door opened, and Diederik die Vos, who as Robert de Bethune's bosom friend, was lodged in the same house with the Count's family, entered the apartment.

For a while he stood without speaking, looking at the old Count and his sons, first at one, then at the other. His countenance bore an expression of deep affliction and intense compassion. Joyous and open as his bearing ever was, his comrades were not a little terrified at his unusual deportment; and they suspected that some evil news must have reached him, thus to overcast his countenance and disturb his spirit.

The Lion of Flanders

Robert de Bethune was the first to give expression to this feeling in words. "Have you lost your tongue, Diederik?" he exclaimed; "speak, and if you have bad news for us, spare your jests, I pray you."

"You need not fear my jesting, Lord Robert," was the reply. "But I know not how to tell you what I have to say; I can not bear to be a messenger of evil."

An expression of fear passed over the countenances of all present; they regarded Diederik with anxious curiosity. The latter meanwhile filled a goblet with wine, drank it off, and then proceeded:

"That will give me courage; and in truth I wanted it. Listen, then, and forgive your faithful servant Die Vos that it is from his mouth you hear such news. You are all in hopes of being graciously received by the king, and not without reason, for he is a generous prince. The day before yesterday he found pleasure in the thought of showing himself magnanimous; but then he was not, as now, possessed by evil spirits."

"What is it you say?" cried his hearers in astonishment; "is the king so afflicted?"

"Sir Diederik," said Robert sharply, "a truce to your flowers of rhetoric; you have something serious to tell us—that I can see, but it does not seem to come readily from your lips."

"You have said the truth, Lord Robert," answered Diederik; "hear, then, my news, which it sadly grieves me to have to bring: Joanna of Navarre and Enguerrand de Marigny are at Compiègne!"

These names had a terrible effect on all the company, who, as if suddenly struck dumb, bowed their heads without speaking a word. At last the young William lifted up his hands, and cried despairingly:

"Heavens! the cruel Joanna and Enguerrand de Marigny! oh, my poor sister! my father, we are lost!"

"Well, then, now you understand," said Diederik; "those are the evil spirits which possess the good prince. You see, most noble Count, that your servant Diederik was not so far wrong, when he warned you at Wynandael against this trap."

"Who told you that the queen is at Compiègne?" asked the Count, as though he still thought the matter doubtful.

"My own eyesight," answered Diederik. "Ever fearing some underhand work (for I put no trust in their double-tongued speeches), I kept on the watch, with eyes and ears both wide open. I have seen Joanna of Navarre, seen her face, and heard her voice. My faith and honor on the truth of what I tell you."

"What Diederik tells us is doubtless the truth," said Walter of Lovendeghem; "Joanna is certainly

The Lion of Flanders

at Compiègne, for he pledges his honor that it is so; and she will as certainly use every effort to destroy our hopes from the king, with whom her influence is, heaven knows, only too great. The best we can do is to consider with all speed how to get out of the trap; when we are prisoners, it will be too late."

The effect of this intelligence upon the old Count was such as to depress him even to despair. His position was so dangerous that he could find no outlet from it; escape seemed impossible, for they were in the very heart of the king's territories, or at least too far from Flanders to have any hope of safety in flight. Robert de Bethune chafed like a lion in the toils, and cursed the journey which had thus delivered him bound hand and foot into the power of his enemies.

Thus for a while they sat in gloomy silence—the Count disconsolate and uncertain what to do, and the eyes of all the rest fixed on him. Suddenly a servant of the court appeared at the door of the chamber, and cried with a loud voice:

"Messire de Nogaret, with a message from the king."

A sudden movement sufficiently evinced the anxiety felt by the Flemings at this startling announcement. Messire de Nogaret was the accustomed and well-known instrument of the king's secret commands; and they all supposed that he was now

The Lion of Flanders

come with an armed force to arrest them. Robert de Bethune drew his sword from the sheath, and laid it before him on the table. The other knights grasped the hilts of their swords, and looked fixedly at the door; in which position they still were when Messire de Nogaret entered, who, courteously bowing to the knights, turned to Count Guy, and thus addressed him:

"Count of Flanders! My gracious king and master requires of you to appear before him tomorrow, an hour before noon, and there publicly to ask pardon of him for your transgression. The arrival of our most gracious queen has hastened this command. She has herself interceded in your behalf with her royal consort, and I have it in command from her to assure you of the satisfaction your submission gives her. To-morrow, then, gentlemen! Forgive me that I leave you hastily; their majesties are waiting for me, and I can not stay. The Lord have you in His keeping!"

And with this greeting he left the room.

"Thanks be to Heaven, gentlemen!" exclaimed Count Guy; "the king is gracious to us: now we may go to rest with hearts at ease. You have heard his majesty's commands; be pleased to hold yourselves in readiness to obey them."

The knights now recovered their spirits once more. They conversed for some time upon the alarm Diederik had given them, and the happy

The Lion of Flanders

result which seemed now to await their expedition; while a goblet of wine was emptied to the health of their aged Count.

As they were separating for the night, Diederik took Robert's hand, and in a suppressed voice said to him:

"Farewell, my friend and master! yes, farewell; for I fear it will be long before my hand shall again press yours. But remember that your servant Diederik will ever stand by you and comfort you, in whatsover land—in whatsoever dungeon your lot may be cast."

Robert saw a tear glisten in Diederik's eye which told him how deeply his faithful friend was moved.

"I understand you, Diederik," he whispered in reply: "what you fear is what I too foresee. But there is no escape left now. Farewell, then, till better days."

"Gentlemen," pursued Diederik, turning to the company and speaking aloud, "if you have any commands to your friends in Flanders, I shall be happy to convey them; but I must beg you to be quick."

"What do you mean?" cried Walter of Lovendeghem; "are you not going to court with us to-morrow, Diederik?"

"Yes, I shall be there with you; but neither you nor the Frenchmen shall know me. I have said it, it will take a better huntsman than King Philip to catch the fox. God have you in His guard, gentlemen!"

He was already out of the door while he addressed to them this last greeting.

The Count withdrew with his attendants, and the rest of the company likewise left the apartment, and betook themselves to their beds.

Already at the appointed hour the Flemish knights, with their old Count, might be seen standing in a spacious hall of the royal palace; but without their arms, which they had had to lay aside in an antechamber. Joy and satisfaction shone upon their countenances, as though they were congratulating themselves beforehand on the promised pardon. Robert de Bethune's alone wore quite a different expression from those of all the rest; on it were to be read bitter annoyance and stifled rage. It was only with much difficulty that the valiant Fleming could brook the insolent glances of the French knights; and it was solely consideration for his father that kept him from demanding an account from more than one of them. The violence he was obliged to put upon himself caused a severe struggle in his breast, and from time to time an observant eye might have remarked a convulsive clutching of his fingers, as though grasping something which they endeavored to crush.

Charles de Valois stood by the old Count in friendly conversation with him, awaiting the mo-

The Lion of Flanders

ment when, at his brother's command, he should present the Flemings at the foot of the throne. There were besides many abbots and bishops present in the hall; as also some of the good burgesses of Compiègne, who had purposely been invited to attend the ceremony.

While all present were busily talking over the affair of the Count of Flanders, an old pilgrim entered the hall. But little indeed was to be discerned of his countenance; for the broad-brimmed hat, deeply pressed down upon his brow, overshadowed his visage, which was moreover humbly bent downward upon his breast, with the eyes fixed upon the ground. His figure was concealed under a wide upper garment of brown stuff, and a long stick, with a drinking-vessel attached, supported his travel-weary limbs. The prelates, as soon as they observed him, came up to him and overwhelmed him with all kinds of questions. The one desired to know how it stood with the Christians in Syria, another the last news of the Italian wars, a third inquired whether he had brought back with him any precious relics of the saints, and many other like questions were put to him, such as his character of pilgrim suggested. He answered as one might who had just returned from those distant parts, and had so many wonders to relate that all listened to him with interest and respect. Although the most of what he told was serious and even moving, yet ever and anon came an expression from his mouth of such comic force that the prelates themselves could not refrain from laughter. He soon had a circle of more than fifty persons about him, of whom some carried their veneration for his character so far that they secretly passed their hands over his ample pilgrim's coat, in the hope of thus obtaining the blessing of Heaven.

And yet the mysterious stranger was, in truth, no pilgrim; the lands which he seemed so well to know he had indeed visited in his youth; but that was long ago, and his memory did not always serve him; then his imagination had to stand him in stead;—and often when he told of the wonders he had seen, he chuckled within himself over the credulity of his hearers. The seeming palmer was, in truth, Diederik die Vos, who possessed in unrivaled perfection the art of disguising himself, and of assuming the most various forms and characters. Putting no trust whatever in the royal word, and not choosing, as he had told the Count, that King Philip should trap the fox, he had thus disguised himself, in order to escape the danger which he foresaw.

And now the king and queen entered the hall, with a numerous train of knights and pages, and took their seats upon the throne. Most of the French knights ranged themselves along the walls;

the rest stood together at the farther end of the hall, and near them the citizens who were present. Two heralds, with the arms of France and of Navarre, were stationed, one on either hand, at the foot of the throne.

The king gave a sign, and Charles de Valois came forward with the Flemish nobles. Velvet cushions were placed on the ground in front of the throne, and on these the Flemings knelt on one knee, in which humble position they awaited in silence the king's declaration. On Count Guy's right hand knelt his son William; and on his left Walter of Maldeghem, a noble of high rank. Robert de Bethune was not in his place; he remained at some distance, standing among the French knights, and for a while entirely escaped King Philip's notice.

Queen Joanna's dress was all brilliant with gold and jewels; on her head was a royal crown, which threw back the sun's rays from its thousand diamonds. Haughty and arrogant, she kept casting round contemptuous looks upon the Flemish nobles as they knelt, and grimly smiled her hate upon the old Count whom she purposely kept waiting in his attitude of humiliation. At last she whispered a few words in Philip's ear, who thereupon, in a loud voice, thus addressed Count Guy:

"Unfaithful vassal! out of our royal mercy we have been graciously pleased to cause inquiry to be made about your transgressions, in the hope of finding some ground upon which it might be allowable for us to show you favor; but, on the contrary thereof, we have found that your daughter's imprisonment, with which you excuse yourself, has been only a pretext for your contumacy, and that it is really out of insolent pride that you have disobeyed our commands."

As the king uttered these words, amazement and consternation filled the hearts of the Flemings, who now saw themselves in the trap against which Diederik die Vos had warned them; but as Count Guy made no motion to rise, they too remained on their knees. The king went on:

"A vassal that traitorously takes arms against his king and liege lord has forfeited his fief; and he that holds with the enemies of France has forfeited his life. You have disobeyed the commands of your sovereign; you have made common cause with Edward of England, our enemy, and with him levied war against us; by all which misdeeds and treasons you have justly forfeited your life. Nevertheless, we will not hastily put in execution such our righteous doom, but will still further take time for consideration thereupon; to which end we have determined that you and those of your nobles who have abetted you in your contumacy, be held in safe keeping till such time as, in our wisdom, we may come to a final resolution concerning you."

The Lion of Flanders

But now Charles de Valois, filled with equal grief and astonishment at what he had just heard, came forward, and thus addressed the king:

"My liege! you know with what zeal and fidelity I have ever served you, even as if I had been the lowest of your subjects, and none can say that treachery or falsehood has ever sullied with one spot the shield of Charles de Valois. And now it is you, my liege, that are, for the first time, putting shame upon my honor—upon your brother's honor! Will you make me a traitor? Shall your brother have to hide his head under the reproach of a false knight? Remember, sire, that Guy of Flanders came to your court under a safe conduct from me, and that you make me a liar if you do not respect it."

The Count de Valois had gradually grown excited as he spoke; and such power was there in his flashing eyes that Philip was on the very point of recalling his sentence. Himself regarding honor and good name as a knight's most precious treasure, he felt in his inmost heart the pain that he was inflicting upon his faithful brother. Meanwhile the Flemings had risen, and were listening anxiously to the pleading of their advocate, while the bystanders awaited the result motionless and terrorstruck.

But Queen Joanna gave her husband no time to answer for himself. Fearing lest her prey should escape her, and jealous of her brother-in-law's interference, she passionately exclaimed: "Messire de Valois! how can you dare to stand up in defense of the enemies of France, and so make yourself a partner in their treasons? This is not the first time, moreover, that you have taken it upon you to oppose the king's good pleasure."

"Madame," retorted Charles sharply, "it ill beseems you to couple such a word as treason with the name of your husband's brother. Shall I stand by in silence and allow you to bring infamy upon my name; and so have it said of me that it was Charles de Valois that beguiled the hapless Guy of Flanders to his destruction? No, by Heaven! so shall it not be. And I ask you, Philip, my prince and brother, will you allow the blood of St. Louis to be dishonored in me? Shall this be the reward of all my faithful services?"

It was easily seen that the king was interceding with Joanna, and pressing her to consent to a mitigation of the sentence; but she, in her implacable hatred against the Flemings, scornfully refused to listen; while, at the words of Charles de Valois, a scarlet glow of fury overspread her countenance. Suddenly she exclaimed:

"Ho, guards! Let the king be obeyed! Take the traitors, one and all!"

At this command the royal guards filled the hall, through all the various doors that led into it. The

The Lion of Flanders

Flemish knights allowed themselves to be made prisoners without resistance, which they well saw could avail them nothing, as they were at once unarmed, outnumbered, and surrounded.

One of the bodyguard approached the old Count, and laid his hand upon his shoulder, saying:

"My lord Count, I arrest you in the king's name."

The Count of Flanders looked him sadly in the face; then turned toward Robert and sighed out, "My poor, poor son!"

Robert meanwhile stood motionless, but with restless eye, amid the French knights, whose looks were now curiously bent upon him. Suddenly, as though an invisible hand had touched him with a magic wand, a convulsive shiver passed over his whole frame; all his muscles strained convulsively, and lightning seemed to flash from his eyes; then, springing forward like a lion upon his prey, he cried, with a voice that made the very rafters shake:

"Villain! do you dare in my presence to lay an ignoble hand upon my father's shoulder? There you shall leave that hand, or I die the death!"

And with these words he wrested the weapon from the hand of a halberdier, and dashed forward. A general cry of alarm was heard, and the French knights drew their swords, for at first they were in fear for the lives of the king and queen. This

The Lion of Flanders

fear, however, was soon over; for Robert's blow was struck. As he had said, he had done; the hand which had ventured to touch his father lay, with the arm belonging to it, upon the ground, and a stream of blood flowed from the mangled stump.

The guards crowded round Robert and endeavored to overpower him, but without success. Maddened with blind fury, he played the halberd in circles round his head, so that not one of them ventured within range of his weapon. Perhaps some still more fatal catastrophe would have ensued, had not the old Count, anxious for his son's life, called to him in a supplicating tone:

"Robert, my brave son! for my sake surrender; do it, I pray you, I command you!"

With these words, which he uttered in a tone of the tenderest emotion, he threw his arms about Robert's neck, and pressed his face against his son's bosom. Robert felt his father's hot tears drop upon his hand, and then for the first time understood the extent of his rashness. Tearing himself from the old Count's arms, he dashed the halberd against the wall over the heads of the guards, and cried:

"Come on, then, ye miserable hirelings, and lay hold of the Lion of Flanders! fear no longer; he surrenders."

Again the guards crowded about him, and now made him their prisoner. While he and his father were being led from the hall, he called aloud to Charles de Valois:

"There is no stain upon your arms; you still are what you have always been, the noblest knight in France; your honor is still unimpeached; bear witness all who hear that the Lion of Flanders says this."

The French knights had put up their swords again into their scabbards, so soon as they perceived that there was no danger for the king or queen. As regarded the arrest of the Lion, they left that to other hands; it was a kind of work in which a noble could not with propriety take part.

Very different, meanwhile, were the feelings of the king and of the queen on this occasion. Philip was much depressed and deeply lamented the step into which he had been drawn. Joanna, on the contrary, was full of joy at Robert's resistance, for the offense of wounding the king's servant in the king's presence was so serious that she felt her schemes of vengeance were greatly advanced thereby.

At last the king could no longer suppress his emotion and resentment, and, notwithstanding the resistance of his imperious consort, determined to leave the hall. As he rose from his throne, he said:

"Gentlemen, this scene of violence has greatly troubled us. Much more pleasing would it have been to us could we have shown mercy; unhappily the interests of our crown and realm would not admit of it. Our royal will and pleasure is, that you all use your best endeavors that the peace of our palace be not further disturbed."

The queen now rose also, and was about to descend the steps of the throne along with her husband, when a new incident, at once unexpected and vexatious, prevented her.

Charles de Valois had for some time been standing immersed in thought at the farther end of the hall. The respect which he owed his king, as well as the love he felt for his brother, long struggled in his heart against the indignation which the late act of treachery excited in him. But at last his wrath waxed uncontrollable, and broke loose: now red, now pale, with every sign of the most violent agitation of mind, he stepped forward in front of the queen:

"Madame," he thundered out, "you shall not dishonor me with impunity! Listen, gentlemen; I speak in the presence of God, the judge of us all. It is you, Joanna of Navarre, that exhaust our country's resources by your prodigality; it is you that have ground down the king's subjects by the debasement of the coin, and by extortions and oppressions of every kind; it is you that bring disgrace upon my noble brother; it is you that are the blot and shame of France. Henceforth I serve you not! Henceforth I renounce you as a false traitress!"

With these words he drew his sword from the scabbard, snapped the blade in two across his knee, and dashed the pieces with such violence against the ground that they rebounded to the very steps of the throne.

Joanna was beside herself with shame and fury; her features were distorted with the expression of the most devilish passions, and seemed no longer to have anything womanly about them. Convulsed with rage, she exclaimed:

"Ho, guards, seize him! seize him!"

The bodyguards, who were still in the hall, prepared to execute the queen's command, and their captain was already drawing near to the Count de Valois; but this was too much for the king, who was sincerely and deeply attached to his brother:

"Whoever lays a finger upon Messire de Valois shall die this very day!" he exclaimed.

This threat checked the advance of the guards; and De Valois left the hall without hindrance, in spite of the queen's command.

Thus ended these scenes of treachery and violence. Count Guy was forthwith imprisoned at Compiègne; his son Robert was conveyed to Bourges in Berri, and William to Rouen in Normandy. The rest of the Flemish nobles were also kept in close custody, each at a different place;

and were thus deprived of the consolation they might have derived from friendly companionship in misfortune.

Of all the company, Diederik die Vos was the only one that got back to Flanders, thanks to his palmer's coat, by means of which he escaped unrecognized.

Charles de Valois, with the aid of his friends, immediately left the kingdom, and retired to Italy; nor did he return thence until after the death of Philip the Fair, when Louis Hutin had succeeded to the throne.

The Lion of Flanders

CHAPTER VI

At the time of which we are writing, there existed in Flanders two political parties violently opposed to each other, and who spared no pains to inflict on each other every possible injury. The great majority of the nobles and those in power had declared in favor of the government as established by France, and thence had obtained with the people the appellation of Lilyards, from the well-known bearings of the royal arms. Why it was that they thus took part with their country's enemies will presently appear.

For some years past, what with extravagant expenditure upon tournaments, what with internal wars and distant crusades, the Flemish nobility had very generally fallen into pecuniary embarrassment, and had thus been compelled to raise money, by granting extensive privileges and immunities to the inhabitants of their lordships, and especially to those of the towns, for which they received very considerable sums. Dearly as the citizens had to pay for their enfranchisement, the sacrifice was soon made good with ample interest.

The Lion of Flanders

The commonalty, which had formerly belonged with life and goods to the nobles, felt that the sweat of their brows no longer flowed in vain; they elected burgomasters and councilors, and constituted municipal governments, with which their former lords had no power of interference whatever. The different guilds cooperated for the common interest, each under the direction of its dean, who was its principal officer.

Freedom and security bore their usual fruits; from all the winds of heaven strangers made their way to Flanders, and commerce flourished with a vitality that would have been impossible under the government of the feudal lords. Industry prospered, the people grew rich, and in the pride of independence and power rose up more than once in arms against their former masters. The nobles, seeing their revenues diminished and their supremacy in danger, strove by all means, fair and foul, to check the rising importance of the commons, but with very indifferent success; for the wealth of the towns enabled them to take the field on at least an equal footing, in order to maintain the liberties they had won, and to hand them down unimpaired. In France things were far otherwise; Philip the Fair, indeed, had once, in his distress for money, summoned the deputies of the third estate, that is to say, of the towns, to the States General; but any gain to the people from

The Lion of Flanders

this step was but temporary, and the feudal lords speedily recovered whatever ground they had lost.

What remained of the Flemish nobility had thus entirely lost their supremacy, and had nothing left but the ordinary rights of proprietorship over their estates. Lamenting their bygone power, they saw no other way of recovering it but by the overthrow of the privileges and prosperity of the commons. As no ray of freedom had yet beamed upon France, where a despotic feudalism still exclusively prevailed, they hoped that Philip the Fair would totally change the state of things in Flanders, and that they should be reinstated in all their former power. To this end they favored the cause of France against Flanders, and thus obtained the name of Lilyards, as a term of reproach. These were especially numerous at Bruges, which then divided with Venice the palm of wealth and commerce, and where even the burgomasters and other magistrates, through corrupt influence brought to bear upon the elections, all belonged to that faction.

The arrest of the old Count, and those nobles who had remained true to him, was joyful news for this party. Flanders was now delivered up into the hands of Philip the Fair; and they hoped that by this means they should succeed in canceling all the rights and privileges of the commons.

But the people at large heard of what had taken place with the deepest dismay; the affection which

The Lion of Flanders

they had always borne to their native princes was now enhanced by compassion, and there was a universal outcry against the treachery that had been committed. But the numerous French garrisons, which occupied the length and breadth of the land, with the want of unanimity among the citizens themselves, paralyzed the Clawards (such was the name given to the patriotic party, from the threatening claws of the Flemish lion); so that, for the present, with all their excitement of feeling, they had no spirit for action, and Philip remained in quiet possession of the inheritance of the Count of Flanders.

On the first receipt of the evil tidings, Adolf of Nieuwland's sister, Maria, had proceeded with a numerous retinue of servants and a litter to Wynandael, and brought back her wounded brother to their paternal house at Bruges. The young Matilda, so painfully severed from all of her own blood, was glad to accept the invitation and escort of this new-found friend, and to escape from Wynandael, now occupied by a French garrison.

The house of the Nieuwlands lay in the Spanish street at Bruges. At either angle of its gable front rose a round tower, crowned with a weathercock, and commanding all the neighboring buildings; the arch of the doorway rested on two pillars of hewn stone of Grecian architecture, and over it stood the shield of the Nieuwlands, with their

The Lion of Flanders

motto: *"Pulchrum pro patriâ mori,"* having for supporters two angels with palm branches in their hands.

In a chamber away from the street, and quite out of reach of the sound of its unceasing bustle, lay the wounded Adolf on a magnificent bed. Ghastly pale, and worn to a skeleton by the pain and fever of his wounds, he was hardly to be recognized. At the head of his bed stood a small table, and on it a flask and drinking-cup of silver; against the wall hung the breastplate that had failed before St. Pol's lance, and so been the cause of his wound; beside it was a harp, with its strings loose. All about him was still as death. The window-curtains were half drawn, so that the light in the room was but a doubtful gloaming, and no sound was heard except the painful breathing of the wounded man, and the occasional rustle of a silk dress.

In one corner of the room sat Matilda silent, and with her eyes fixed upon the ground. Her falcon was perched on the back of her chair, and seemed to participate in its mistress's sorrow; for its head was buried in its feathers, and it showed not the slightest movement.

The young girl, formerly so light-hearted and joyous that no grief could touch her, was now totally changed. The imprisonment at one stroke of all that were dear to her had given a shock to

The Lion of Flanders

her feelings which caused everything to appear dark before her eyes. For her the heavens were no longer blue, the fields no longer green; her dreams were no longer interwoven with threads of gold and silver. Sorrow and brooding despair had found the way into her heart; nothing could console her under the torturing image of her beloved father confined in prison and in a foreign land.

After she had thus sat for some time motionless, she slowly rose from her seat, and took her hawk upon her hand. With eyes full of tears she looked upon the bird, and thus spoke in a low voice, while from time to time she wiped away a tear from her pale cheeks:

"Mourn not so, my faithful bird; our lord my father will soon come back. This wicked queen shall do him no mischief; for I have prayed so fervently for him, and God is ever just: mourn no more, my darling bird."

Warm tears trickled down the maiden's cheeks: for though her words seemed full of hope and comfort, yet her heart was all the while oppressed with the deepest sorrow. In a mournful voice she continued:

"My poor hawk, now we can no longer follow our sport in the valleys about my father's castle; for the stranger has his abode in the fair Wynandael. They have cast my unhappy father into prison, and bound him with heavy chains. Now

The Lion of Flanders

he sits and sighs miserably in the dark cell; and who knows whether the fell Joanna may not even take his life, my darling bird? Then we too will die of grief! The thought, the frightful thought alone deprives me of all strength. There now, sit down; for my trembling hand can no longer bear you."

And then, in an agony of despair, the poor child sank back upon her chair; but her cheek grew no paler than before, for long since had its roses faded; and only her eyelids were red with constant weeping. The charm of her features was gone, and her eyes had lost all their life and fire.

Long time she sat, sunk in sorrow, and passing in review the long array of gloomy images which her despair had conjured up before her. She saw her unhappy father chained in a damp unwholesome prison, she heard the clanking of his chains, and the echoes of his sighs of wretchedness in the gloomy vault. The fear of poison too, then so common, or thought to be so, in the mysteries of French statecraft, ever occupied her imagination, and the most frightful scenes followed one another before her eyes. Thus was the poor maiden incessantly tortured, and filled with the most terrible apprehensions.

And now a faint sigh was heard from the bed. Hastily Matilda dried the tears from her cheeks, and hurried to the bedside with frightened anxiety.

The Lion of Flanders

She poured some of the contents of the flask into the cup, raised Adolf's head a little with her right hand, and brought the cup to his mouth.

The knight's eyes opened wide, and fixed themselves with a peculiar expression upon the maiden. An intense feeling of gratitude spoke in his languid glance, and an indefinable smile passed over his pale countenance.

Since he had received his wound, the knight had not yet spoken intelligibly, nor did he even seem to hear the words that were addressed to him. The latter, however, was not the case. When, in the first days of his illness, Matilda had whispered over him in her gentlest voice, "Get well, my poor Adolf! my dear brother! I will pray for you, for your death would make me still more unhappy here on earth," and other like words, which, unconscious of being heard, she murmured to herself behind his couch, Adolf had heard and understood all, though totally unable to reply.

Meanwhile, during the bygone night there had taken place a marked change for the better in the wounded knight's condition. Nature, after a long struggle, had thrown him into a deep sleep, from which he awoke refreshed and with new life and vigor; the sigh which broke from him at the moment of awakening was louder and longer than any breath which he had yet drawn since he received his wound.

The Lion of Flanders

boring buildings, as though fixing them in his memory for future recognition. At last he said:

"Sir Adolf, I must now bid you farewell; ere the day close I will be here again; probably it may be somewhat late; meanwhile, make all the necessary preparations for your journey."

"Will you not, then, allow me to present you to the lady? Moreover, you are weary; I pray you do me the honor of taking refreshment and repose beneath my roof."

"I thank you, sir; my duty as a priest calls me elsewhere; at ten o'clock I will see you again. God have you in His holy keeping!"

And with this greeting he parted from the astonished knight, and turned into the Wool street, whence he speedily vanished into Deconinck's house.

Transported with joy at his unexpected good fortune, which had come upon him like a golden dream, Adolf knocked with the greatest impatience at his door. His dear master's letter seemed to glow between his fingers; and as soon as the door was opened, he rushed past the servant and along the corridor like one mad.

"Where is the Lady Matilda?" he inquired, in a tone which demanded speedy answer:

"In the front room," replied the servant.

He hurried upstairs, and hastily opened the door of the chamber.

The Lion of Flanders

Then rising, she once more fixed her eyes on the knight, and in a glad voice said to him:

"Keep still, Sir Adolf, and move not; that is what Master Roger strictly enjoins you."

"What have you not done for me, illustrious daughter of my lord!" replied Adolf. "How constantly have your prayers sounded in my ears; how often has your voice of comfort cheered my heart! Yes; in my half-consciousness it seemed to me as though one of God's angels was standing by my bedside, and warding off death from it; an angel that propped my head, that quenched my burning thirst with cooling drinks, that constantly assured me that death should not yet have dominion over me! God grant me health and strength again, that I may one day be able to pour out my blood for you!"

"Sir Adolf," answered the maiden, "you have risked your life for my father; you love him as I love him; does it not, then, become me to care for you as for a brother? The angel you saw was, without doubt, St. Michael, to whom I have constantly prayed in your behalf. Now I will hasten and call your good sister Maria, that we may rejoice together over your better health."

She then left the knight, but in a few moments returned, accompanied by his sister. Joy at this sudden improvement in Adolf's condition was visible, not only upon her countenance, but in her whole air and bearing. Her movements were quicker and lighter, her tears no longer flowed, and now she could find cheerful words for her favorite. Immediately on her return to the room with Maria, she took her hawk from the back of the chair upon her hand, and so drew near to Adolf's bed.

"My good brother!" cried Maria, kissing his pale cheek, "you are better! Now I shall be rid of those frightful dreams! O, how glad I am! How often have I wept by your bedside with bitter pain of heart! How often have I thought that death could surely not be far from you! But now my heart is lighter. Will you drink, my brother?"

"No, my good Maria," answered Adolf, "I have never had to suffer thirst, so anxiously has my generous Lady Matilda cared for me. As soon as I am strong enough to make a pilgrimage to St. Cross, I will go and pray to God for blessings upon her head, and that sorrow may ever be far from her."

Matilda meanwhile was busily employed in whispering the good news to her bird, which now, seeing its mistress in recovered spirits, was dressing and pluming itself, and seemed to be making ready for the chase.

"Look, my faithful friend," she said, turning the creature's head toward Adolf; "look, now is Sir Adolf in the way of recovery, after we have so long seen him lying helpless there. Now we may speak together again, and not be sitting always in the dark. Our fear for him is all gone; and so methinks shall our other griefs pass away too, now that God has shown us His mercy and favor. Yes, my beautiful bird, so also shall have an end the sad captivity of—"

But here Matilda felt that she was about to say what the sick knight had better not be made aware of; but as she broke off, the word "captivity" had sounded strangely in Adolf's ear. The tears, too, which on awakening he had perceived on the maiden's cheek, filled him now with anxious foreboding.

"What say you, Matilda?" he exclaimed. "You weep! Heavens! What, then, has happened? of whose imprisonment did you speak?"

Matilda dared not answer; but Maria, more self-possessed, stooped down and whispered in his ear:

"Of her poor aunt Philippa's. But let us drop the subject; for she is always weeping about it. Now you are better, I shall, as soon as Master Roger allows it, have to talk to you of things of weight, but which are not for Matilda's ear; besides, I am at this moment expecting Master Roger. Be still awhile, and I will take her away into another chamber."

The knight laid his head upon the pillow, and

feigned to sleep; upon which Maria turned upon Matilda, and said:

"I think, Lady Matilda, we had better now leave my brother alone, that he may sleep, and not be tempted to speak too much; which the desire of expressing his gratitude to you might, I fear, lead him to do."

The two damsels left the room together; and presently afterward the surgeon presented himself at the door, and was conducted by Maria to her brother.

"Well, Sir Adolf!" said Roger cheerfully, "how goes it with you? Better, I see. Now all the danger is over, and you are safe for this time. There is no need of my dressing your wound again at present: only drink copiously of this beverage, keep as quiet as you can, and in less than a month you and I will take a walk together. That is my prognostic, if no unforeseen accident retard your recovery. Meanwhile, as your mind is in better case than your body, I have no objection to Lady Maria informing you of the sad events that have happened while you have been confined to your bed; but I pray you, do not lose your self-command, and keep yourself calm."

Maria now drew forward two chairs, upon which she and Master Roger took their places at the head of the bed; while Adolf regarded them with the greatest curiosity, and with an evident expression of anxiety upon his countenance.

The Lion of Flanders

"Let me finish what I have to say," began Maria, "without interrupting me, and bear yourself like a man, my brother. In that evening which was so unlucky for you, our Count called his faithful vassals together, and declared to them that he had resolved to set out for France, and cast himself at King Philip's feet. So it was determined, and Guy of Flanders journeyed with his nobles to Compiègne; but no sooner had they arrived than they were all arrested and cast into prison, and now our land is under French rule. Raoul de Nesle governs Flanders."

The effect which this short narration produced upon the knight was not so violent as might have been expected. He made no answer, and seemed deeply sunk in thought.

"What a calamity! is it not?" added Maria at last.

"O God!" exclaimed Adolf, "what felicity hast thou then in store for Guy of Flanders, that he must reach it through such miseries and humiliations? But tell me, Maria, is our Lion also a prisoner?"

"Yes, my brother, Lord Robert de Bethune is in prison at Bourges, and Lord William at Rouen. Of all the nobles that were with the Count, one alone has escaped this unhappy lot—the cunning Diederik."

"Now I understand the unfinished sentence

and the constant tears of the unhappy Matilda. Without father, without family, the daughter of the Count of Flanders has to seek shelter with strangers."

And as he spoke, his eyes lighted up, and a glow of indignation passed over his countenance. After a short pause, he went on:

"The precious child of my prince and master has watched over me as a guardian-angel! She is deserted—unhappy—and exposed to persecution; but I will remember what I owe to the Lion, and watch over her as the apple of mine eye. Oh, what a great and glorious mission is it which has fallen to my lot! How precious to me now is the life which I can devote to her service!"

Then, after a short moment of deep meditation, a cloud suddenly passed over his countenance; he cast a look of supplication on his physician, and said:

"O heavens, how grievous are my wounds to me now! how intolerable this confinement! My worthy friend, Master Roger, do, for the love of God, hasten my recovery all you can, that I may be able to do something for her who has so lovingly tended me on my bed of pain. Spare no expense—whatever drugs are costliest, procure them, if only I may the sooner rise from my bed; for now I feel as if I could rest no longer."

"But, Sir Adolf," answered Roger, "there is no

possibility of hastening your recovery from such a wound; nature must have time to unite the severed parts. Patience and rest will do more for you than all the drugs in the world. But this is not all that we had to say to you. You must know that the French are masters throughout the land, and are strengthening themselves in it every day. Hitherto we have succeeded in concealing our young Lady Matilda from them; but we dread every day lest she should be discovered; and then she too might fall into the hands of the wicked Queen of France."

"Truly you are right, Master Roger," exclaimed Adolf; "they would have no pity upon her. But what shall we do? Oh, what a misery, to lie stretched out here, when all the strength I have, all the help I can give, is so much wanted!"

"I know a place," observed Roger, "where Matilda would be safe enough."

"Your words relieve me. But where, then, is this place? quick, tell me!"

"Think you not, Sir Adolf, that she would be safe and in peace with her cousin William, in the country of Juliers?"

The knight was evidently not a little dismayed at this question. Must he let Matilda depart for a foreign land? Shall he render it impossible for himself to aid and defend her? To that he could by no means bring his mind; for he had already in his heart charged himself with the task of restoring Matilda to her father, and preserving her from every wrong and insult.

He strained, therefore, all his powers of invention to devise some other plan which would not remove her so far from him; and thinking he had hit upon such a one, he answered, with an expression of joy lighting up his countenance:

"Certainly, Master Roger, there could not be a safer retreat for her; but, according to what I hear from you, there are bodies of French troops dispersed in different garrisons throughout the whole of Flanders, which seems to me to render the journey a dangerous one for her. It would be impossible to furnish her with a proper escort, for that would only make the matter worse; and I can not possibly allow Robert de Bethune's daughter to set out alone, accompanied only by a few servants. No! I must watch over her as over my soul's salvation, that I may not be ashamed to appear before my Lord Count Robert when he demands his daughter at my hands."

"But, Sir Adolf, bethink you! you expose her to still greater danger by keeping her in Flanders. Who is there to protect her here? Not you, for you have not the power. The city magistrates will not; they are all body and soul given up to France. The French may easily get scent of her; and what would become of the poor girl then?"

The Lion of Flanders

"I have bethought me of a protector for her," answered Adolf. "Maria, send a servant to the Dean of the Clothworkers, and pray of him to come and see me here. Master Roger, what think you if we place our young lady under the protection of the commons? Is not that a happy thought?"

"Well enough, indeed, if only it were practicable; but the people are to the last degree embittered against all that calls itself noble, and will have nothing to do with any such. And in good truth, Sir Adolf, one can not blame them for it; for most part of the nobles hold with the enemy, and think of nothing but how most effectually to destroy the rights and liberties of the commons."

"I shall not allow such considerations to turn me from my purpose; of that assure yourself, Master Roger. My father was ever the good friend to the city of Bruges; it is to his intervention that they owe many of their privileges, and I do not think that the Dean of the Clothworkers and his company have forgotten it. And, after all, if I fail here, we can but look about for an opportunity of sending away our young lady quietly to Juliers."

After a space of some half an hour, which they spent in discussing their projects, Master Peter Deconinck, Dean or chief of the Guild of Clothworkers at Bruges, arrived, and was immediately introduced into Adolf's chamber.

The Lion of Flanders

A long gown or overcoat of brown woolen stuff covered him from neck to feet; and being totally without any kind of trimming or ornament, strikingly contrasted with the gay dresses of the nobles. It was easy to see that the Dean of the Clothworkers, in affecting this plainness of apparel, wished to make ostentatious display of his estate in life, and so to oppose pride to pride; for, in truth, this coarse woolen gown covered the most powerful man in Flanders. On his head he wore a flat cap, from under which his hair hung down half a foot long over his ears. A leathern belt drew in the wide folds of the gown about his body, and the hilt of a cross-handled knife glittered at his side. An excessive paleness, high cheek-bones, and a wrinkled forehead, threw an air of deep thought over his countenance; while the loss of an eye gave a somewhat unpleasing expression to his features. On common occasions there was nothing to distinguish him from ordinary men; but no sooner was he moved or interested than his glance became lively and penetrating; beams of intelligence and manly spirit shot from his remaining eye, and his bearing was proud and even imperious. On first entering the room, he cast a mistrustful glance on all present, especially Master Roger, in whom he at once perceived more of worldly craft than in the other two.

"Master Deconinck," commenced Adolf, "be

pleased to draw near to me. I have something to ask of you that you must not refuse me, for I have no other hope but in you; only you must first give me your solemn assurance that you will never divulge to any human being that which I am about to communicate."

"The just dealings and good offices of the lords of Nieuwland are not yet forgotten by the Clothworkers," answered Deconinck; "and you, noble sir, may ever count upon me as your faithful servant. Nevertheless, sir, allow me first to warn you, that if what you have in hand is in any way contrary to the rights of the commons, you will do well to keep it to yourself, and tell me nothing of it."

"Since when, then," cried Adolf, somewhat sternly, "have the Nieuwlands touched you in your rights? Such language is injurious to my honor!"

"Forgive me, sir, if my words have offended you," replied the Dean; "it is so hard to distinguish the evil from the good that one is obliged to mistrust all. Allow me to ask you only one question, the answer to which will remove all doubt from my mind at once; are you a Lilyard, noble sir?"

"A Lilyard!" cried Adolf, indignantly: "no, Master Deconinck! in my breast beats a heart that has nothing but abhorrence for our enemies; and the very scheme about which I wished to consult you is directed against them."

The Lion of Flanders

"Speak freely then, noble sir; I am at your service."

"Well, then; you know that our Count Guy is in prison, with all his faithful nobles; but there is still in Flanders one to whom all true Flemings owe their best and readiest aid—one who now needs it greatly because of her utter helplessness, and to whom it is due both on account of what she is, and of the sore trouble which oppresses her."

"You speak of the Lady Matilda, daughter of the Lord Robert de Bethune," observed Deconinck.

"How know you that?" inquired Adolf, surprised.

"I know yet more, sir. The Lady Matilda was not brought to your house so privily, but that Deconinck knew it, nor could she have left it again unknown to me. But be not alarmed, for I can assure you that but few besides myself at Bruges are in the secret."

"You are a wonderful man, Master Deconinck. But now to the point. I feel that I may trust in your magnanimity to defend this young daughter of our Lion, if need be, against any violence from the French."

Sprung from among the people, Deconinck was one of those rare geniuses who come before the world from time to time as the leaders of their age and country. No sooner had years ripened his capacity than he called forth his brethren out of the bondage in which they slumbered, taught them to understand the power which lies in union, and rose up at their head against their tyrants. The latter now found it impossible to resist the awakened energies of their former slaves, whose hearts Deconinck had so roused and kindled by his eloquence that their necks would no longer bear the yoke. Yet sometimes the fortune of war would favor the nobles, and the people for a time submitted, while Deconinck seemed to have lost at once his eloquence and his sagacity. Nevertheless he slumbered not, but still worked upon the spirits of his comrades with secret exhortations, till a favorable moment came; then the commons rose again against their tyrants, and again broke their bonds. All the political machinations of the nobles vanished into smoke before the keen intellect of Deconinck, and they found themselves thus deprived of all their power over the people, without any possibility of permanently holding their ground. With truth it might be said that a chief share in the reform of the political relations between the nobles and the commons belonged to Deconinck, whose waking thoughts and sleeping dreams were devoted solely to the aggrandizement of the people, who had so long groaned, so to say, in the dark dungeon and heavy chains of feudal bondage.

It was with a smile of satisfaction, then that he

listened to Adolf of Nieuwland's appeal in behalf of the young Matilda; for it was a great triumph for the people whose representative he was. In an instant he counted over the advantages which might be derived from the presence of the illustrious maiden for the execution of his great project of deliverance.

"Sir Adolf of Nieuwland," he answered, "I am greatly honored by this application. I will spare no effort which may contribute to the safety of the illustrious daughter of the Flemish prince."

Desirous of bringing the matter more entirely into the hands of the commons, he added, with cautious hesitation, "But might she not easily be carried off from hence before I could come to her aid?"

This remark was somewhat displeasing to Adolf; for he thought he saw in it a disinclination on the Dean's part to take up Matilda's cause with heart and soul. He therefore replied: "If you can not yourself give us efficient aid, I pray you, master, to advise us as to what is the best that can be done for the safety of our noble Count's daughter."

"The Clothworkers' Company is strong enough to stand between the lady and all fear of insolence," rejoined Deconinck; "I can assure you that she may live as peacefully and safely at Bruges as in Germany, if you will take counsel of me."

The Lion of Flanders

"What is your difficulty, then?" asked Adolf.

"Noble sir, it is not for such as me to make arrangements for the daughter of my prince; nevertheless, should she be pleased to do as I shall recommend her, I will undertake to be answerable for her safety."

"I hardly understand you, master. What have you to ask of the Lady Matilda? you would not carry her to another place?"

"Oh, no; all I desire is, that she should on no account leave the house without my knowledge, and should, on the other hand, at all times be ready to accompany me, should I judge it necessary. Moreover, I leave it to you to withdraw this trust from me the moment you feel any doubt of the loyalty of my intentions."

As Deconinck was universally held in Flanders as one of their ablest heads, Adolf doubted not that his demand was founded on good reasons, and therefore made no difficulty in granting all he asked, provided he would undertake to be himself answerable for the Lady Matilda's safety; and, as he was not yet personally acquainted with her, Maria went to request her presence.

On her entering the room, Deconinck made a low and humble obeisance before her, while the princess looked at him with considerable astonishment, not in the least knowing who he could be. But while he thus stood before her, and she awaited

The Lion of Flanders

an explanation of the scene, suddenly a noise of loud disputing was heard in the passage.

"Wait then!" cried one of the voices, "that I may inquire whether you can be admitted."

"What!" cried another voice of much greater power, "shall the Butchers be shut out while the Clothworkers are let in? Quick, out of the way, or you shall rue it!"

The door opened, and a young man of powerful limbs and handsome features entered the chamber. His dress was made like that of Deconinck, but with more of taste and ornament; the great cross-handled knife hung at his girdle. As he passed the threshold he was in the act of throwing back his long fair hair from his face; but the sight that met his eyes checked him suddenly in the doorway. He had thought to find there the Dean of the Clothworkers and some of his fellows; but now seeing this beautiful and richly-dressed lady, and Deconinck bowing thus low before her, he knew not what to think. However, he did not allow himself to be disconcerted, either by the unexpected presence in which he found himself, or by the inquiring look of Master Roger. He uncovered his head, bowed hastily all around, and went straight up to Deconinck; then seizing him familiarly by the arm, he exclaimed:

"Ha, Master Peter! I have been looking for you these two hours; I have been running all over the town after you, and nowhere were you to be found. Know you what is happening, and what news I bring?"

"Well, what is it then, Master Breydel?" inquired Deconinck impatiently.

"Come, don't stare at me so with your cat's eye, Master Dean of the Clothworkers," cried Breydel; "you know well enough that I am not afraid of it. But that is all one! Well, then, King Philip the Fair and the accursed Joanna of Navarre are coming to Bruges to-morrow; and our fine fellows of city magistrates have ordered out a hundred clothworkers, forty butchers, and I know not how many more of the rest, to make triumphal arches, cars for a pageant, and scaffolding."

"And what is there so wonderful in that, that you should waste your breath about it?"

"What, Master Dean! what is there in that? more than you think; for certainly not a single butcher will put his hand to the work, and there are three hundred clothworkers standing in front of your hall waiting for you. As far as I am concerned, it will be long enough before I wag a finger for them. The halberds stand ready, the knives are sharp; everything is in order. You know, Master Dean, what that means when I say it."

All present listened with curiosity to the bold words of the Dean of the Butchers. His voice was clear, and even musical, though with nothing of womanish softness in it. Deconinck's cooler judgment, meanwhile, soon perceived that Breydel's designs would, if executed, only be injurious to the cause, and he answered:

"I will go with you, Master Jan; we will talk over the necessary measures together; but first, you must know that this noble lady is the Lady Matilda, the daughter of Lord Robert de Bethune."

Breydel, in much surprise, threw himself on one knee before Matilda, lifted his eyes to her, and exclaimed:

"Most illustrious lady, forgive me the random speech I have heedlessly used in your presence. Let not the noble daughter of our lord the Lion remember it against me."

"Rise, master!" answered Matilda graciously; "you have said nothing I could take amiss. Your words were inspired by love for our country, and hatred against its enemies. I thank you for your faithful allegiance."

"Gracious Countess," pursued Breydel, rising, "your ladyship can not imagine how bitter are my feelings against the Lilyards and French tax-gatherers. Oh, that I could avenge the wrongs of the House of Flanders!—Oh, that I could! But the Dean of the Clothworkers here is always against me; perhaps he is right, for late is not never; but it is difficult for me to keep back. To-morrow the false Queen Joanna comes to Bruges; but unless

The Lion of Flanders

God gives me other thoughts than I have now she shall never see France again."

"Master," said Matilda, "will you promise me what I am going to ask of you?"

"Promise you, lady? say rather that you command me, and I will obey. Every word of yours shall be sacred to me, illustrious princess."

"Then I desire of you that you shall do nothing to break the peace while the new princes are in the city."

"So be it," answered Breydel, sorrowfully. "I had rather your ladyship had called upon me to use my arm or my knife; however, it's a long lane that has no turning, and if to-day is for them, to-morrow may be for us."

Then, once more bowing his knee before the princess, he added:

"I beg and pray of you, noble daughter of our Lion, not to forget your servant Breydel, whenever you have need of strong arms and stout hearts. The Butchers' Company will keep their 'good-days' and knives ready ground for your service."

The maiden started somewhat at an offer which savored so much of blood; but nevertheless she replied in a tone of satisfaction.

"Master," she answered, "I will not forget to make your fidelity known to my lord and father, when God shall restore him to me; for myself, I can not sufficiently express my thanks to you."

The Lion of Flanders

The Dean of the Butchers rose, and taking Deconinck by the arm, they went out together. Long after they had left the house this unexpected visit formed a topic of conversation for its inmates.

As soon as the two Deans were in the street Deconinck began:

"Master Jan, you know that the Lion of Flanders has always been the friend of the people; it is therefore our bounden duty to watch over his daughter as a sacred deposit."

"What need of so many words about it?" answered Breydel; "the first Frenchman that dare but look askance at her shall make acquaintance with my cross-knife. But, Master Peter, would it not be the best plan to close the gates, and not let Joanna into the town? All my butchers are ready, the 'good-days' stand behind the doors, and at the first word every Lilyard will be packed to—"

"Beware of any violence!" interrupted Deconinck. "To receive one's prince magnificently is the custom everywhere; that can do no dishonor to the commons. It is better to reserve our strength for occasions of more importance. Our country is at present swarming with foreign troops, and we might very easily get the worst of it."

"But, master, this is terribly slow work! Let us just cut the knot with a good knife, instead of taking all this time to untie it; you understand me."

"I understand you well enough; but that will not

do. Caution, Breydel, is the best knife; it cuts slowly, but it never blunts and never breaks. Suppose you do shut the gates, what have you gained then? Listen, and take my word for it. Let the storm go by a little, and things get quiet; let us wait till a part of the foreign troops are gone back to France; let the French and the Lilyards have their own way a little, and then they will be less on their guard."

"No!" cried Breydel, "that must not be! They are already beginning to be insolent and despotic more than enough. They plunder all the country round about, and treat us burghers as though we were their slaves."

"So much the better, Master Jan! so much the better."

"So much the better! what do you mean by that? Say, master, have you turned your coat? and do you mean to use your fox's wit to betray us? I know not, but it seems to me that you begin to smell very strong of lilies!"

"No, no, friend Jan! but just bethink you, that the more there is to irritate, the nearer is the day of deliverance. If they cloaked their doings a little, and ruled with any show of justice, the mass of the people would sit down quietly under the yoke till they grew accustomed to it; and then, adieu, once for all, to our hard-won liberties! Know that despotism is freedom's nursing-mother.

The Lion of Flanders

If, indeed, they ventured to make any attempt upon the privileges of our town, then I should be the first to exhort you to resistance; but even then not by means of open force—there are other means surer and better than that."

"Master," said Jan Breydel, "I understand you; you are always right, as though your words stood written upon parchment. But it is a bitter pill to me to have to put up so long with those insolent foreigners. Better the Saracen than the Frenchman! But you are right enough; the more a frog blows himself out, the sooner he bursts! After all, I must confess that understanding is with the Clothworkers."

"Well, Master Breydel, I, for my part, acknowledge that it is the Butchers that are the men of action. Let us ever put these two good gifts, caution and courage, together, and the French will never find time to make fast the irons about our feet."

A bright smile on the face of the Butcher acknowledged his satisfaction at this compliment.

"Yes," he replied, "there are fine fellows in our company, Master Peter; and that the foreign rascals shall know when the bitter fruit is ripe. But now I think of it, how shall we keep our Lion's daughter from Queen Joanna's knowledge."

"We will show her here openly in the light of day."

The Lion of Flanders

"How so, master? let Joanna of Navarre see the Lady Matilda? You can never mean that in your sound senses! I think you must have something wrong in your upper works."

"No; not yet, at any rate. To-morrow, at the entry of the foreign masters, all the Clothworkers will be under arms; so will you, with your Butchers. What can the Frenchmen do then? Nothing, as you know. Well, then, to-morrow I will put the Lady Matilda in a conspicuous place, where Joanna of Navarre can not but notice her. Then I shall be able to judge from the queen's countenance what her thoughts are, and how far we have to fear for our precious charge."

"The very thing, Master Peter! You are in very truth too wise for mortal man! I will keep watch over our princely lady; and I should only like to see the French offer to harm or affront her; for my hands itch to be at them, and that's the truth of it. But to-day I have to go to Sysseele to buy some oxen, so it will be your turn to keep guard over the young countess."

"Now, then, only be a little calm, friend Jan, and do not let your blood boil over: here we are at Clothworkers' Hall."

As Breydel had said, a considerable group of Clothworkers stood about the door. All had gowns and caps of the same form as their Dean, though here and there might be perceived a young journeyman, with longer hair, and something more of ornament about his apparel. This, however, was but an exception; for the company kept strict discipline, and did not permit in its members much of idle display.

Jan Breydel spoke a few words more with Deconinck in an undertone, and then left him in high satisfaction.

Meanwhile the Clothworkers had opened a passage for their Dean as he approached; and all respectfully uncovering their heads, followed him into the hall.

The Lion of Flanders

CHAPTER VII

The Lilyards had made unusual preparations for giving a magnificent reception to their new prince, whose favor they hoped by this means to earn. No cost had been spared; the fronts of the houses were hung with the richest stuffs the shops could furnish; the streets were turned into green avenues by means of trees brought in from the neighboring woods and fields, and all the journeymen of the different companies had been employed in erecting triumphal arches. On the following day, by ten o'clock in the morning, all was in readiness.

In the middle of the great square stood a lofty throne, erected by the Carpenters' Company, and covered with blue velvet, its double seat adorned with gold fringe, and furnished with richly worked cushions; two figures, Peace and Power, stood by, which with united hands were to place crowns of olive and laurel on the heads of Philip the Fair and Joanna of Navarre. Hangings of heavy stuffs descended from the canopy, and the very ground of the square was covered with costly carpets for some distance round.

The Lion of Flanders

At the entrance of the Stone street stood four columns painted in imitation of marble, and on each of them a trumpeter, dressed as a figure of Fame, with long wings and flowing purple robes.

Over against the great shambles, at the beginning of the Lady street, was erected a magnificent triumphal arch with Gothic pillars. Above, at the apex of the arch, hung the shield of the arms of France; lower, one on each pillar, those of Flanders and the city of Bruges. The rest of the available space was occupied with allegorical devices, such as might best flatter the foreign lord. Here might be seen the black lion of Flanders humbly cringing under a lily; there were the heavens with lilies substituted for stars; and many other like images, such as a spirit of base truckling had suggested to these bastard Flemings.

If Jan Breydel had not been kept in restraint by the Dean of the Clothworkers, the people would certainly not have been long scandalized by these symbols of abasement. As it was, however, he swallowed his indignation, and looked on in dark and desperate endurance. Deconinck had convinced him that the hour was not yet come.

The Cathelyne street was hung throughout its whole length with snow-white linen and long festoons of foliage, and every house of a Lilyard bore an inscription of welcome. On little four-cornered stands burned all kinds of perfumes in beautifully chased vases, and young girls strewed the streets with flowers. The Cathelyne gate, by which the king and queen were to enter the town, was decked on the outside with magnificent scarlet hangings; there, too, were placed allegorical pictures intended to glorify the stranger, and to throw scorn upon the lion, the ancestral emblem of victory. Eight angels had been secretly planted on the gatehouse to sound a welcome to the prince and announce his arrival.

In the great square stood the companies, armed with their "good-days," and drawn up in deep file along the houses. Deconinck, at the head of the Clothworkers, had his right flank covered with the egg-market; Breydel, with his Butchers, occupied the side toward the Stone street; the other companies were distributed in lesser bodies along the third side of the square. The Lilyards and principal nobles were assembled on a richly decorated scaffolding immediately in front of the town-hall.

At eleven o'clock, the angels who were stationed upon the gatehouse gave the signal of the king and queen's approach, and the royal cavalcade at last passed through the Cathelyne gate into the town.

First rode four heralds on magnificent white horses, from whose trumpets hung the banners of their master, Philip the Fair, with golden lilies on a blue field. They sounded a melodious march as they went, and charmed all hearers with the perfection of their playing.

Some twenty yards after the heralds came the king, Philip the Fair, on a horse of majestic figure and paces. Among all the knights about him there was not one that approached him in beauty of features. His black hair flowed in long waving locks upon his shoulders; his complexion vied with that of any lady for softness and clearness; while its light-brown hue imparted to his countenance an expression of manly vigor. His smile was sweet, and his manner remarkably captivating. Added to this, a lofty stature, well-formed limbs, and easy carriage made him in all externals the most perfect knight of his day; and thence his surname, by which he was known throughout Europe, of *Le Bel*, or, as we translate it, the Fair. His dress was richly embroidered with gold and silver, yet not overloaded with ornament; it was clear that good taste, and not love of display, had guided the selection. The silvered helmet which glittered on his head bore a large plume, which fell down behind him to his horse's croup.

Beside him rode his consort, the imperious Joanna of Navarre, upon a dun-colored palfrey, her apparel all one blaze of gold, silver, and jewels. A long riding-dress of gold-stuff, secured in front with a lace of silver cord, fell in heavy folds to the ground, and glistened as she went with its thousand ornaments. Both she and her palfrey were so beset with studs, buttons, and tassels of the most costly materials that scarcely a single vacant spot could be perceived upon them.

Arrogance and vanity filled the whole soul of this princess, and it might be seen in her countenance that the pomp of her entry had filled her heart with pride. Full-blown in insolence, she cast her haughty looks over the conquered people, who filled the windows, and had even climbed upon the roofs of the houses in order to look on at the magnificent show.

On the other side of the king rode his son, Louis Hutin, a young prince of good disposition, and who carried his greatness unassumingly. He regarded these new subjects of his house with a compassionate air; and the eyes of the citizens ever found a gracious smile upon his countenance. Louis possessed all the good qualities of his father, unalloyed by any of the vices that might have been looked for in the son of Joanna of Navarre.

Immediately after the king and queen came their personal attendants—gentlemen of the chamber and ladies of honor; then a numerous cavalcade of nobles, all magnificently arrayed. Among them might be distinguished Enguerrand de Marigny, De Chatillon, St. Pol, De Nesle, De Nogaret, and many others. The royal standard and

The Lion of Flanders

numerous other banners waved merrily over this princely company.

Last of all came a body of men-at-arms, or heavy cavalry, some three hundred strong, all of them armed from head to foot in steel, and with long lances projecting above their heads. Their heavy chargers, too, were steel-barbed from counter to crupper.

The citizens, every here and there gathered into groups, looked on in solemn silence; not a single cry of welcome ascended from all that multitude, no single sign of joy could anywhere be seen. Stung to the soul at the coldness of this reception, Joanna of Navarre was still more irritated at the looks of scorn and hate which she could perceive from time to time were turned upon her.

As soon as the procession reached the marketplace, the two figures of Fame, planted on the pedestals, put their trumpets to their mouths and blew a blast of welcome that resounded throughout the square; upon which the magistrates and other Lilyards (of whom, however, there were but few) raised the cry, "France! France! Long live the king! long live the queen!"

Still more intense was the inward rage of the proud queen, when not a single voice from the people or the companies joined in this cry and all the citizens stood motionless, without giving the slightest sign of respect or pleasure! Still, for the moment she swallowed her wrath, and contrived so to command her features that nothing of what she felt was perceptible on her countenance.

A little on one side of the throne was stationed a group of noble ladies, mounted on the most beautiful palfreys; and all, in honor of the occasion, so bedecked with jewelry that the eye could hardly bear to rest upon them.

Matilda, the fair young daughter of the Lion of Flanders, had her place in the front row, and was the very first that fell under the queen's eye. She was most magnificently attired. A high pointed hat of yellow silk, copiously trimmed with ribbons of red velvet, sat lightly and gracefully upon her head; from under it fell a flowing mantilla of the finest lawn, which, shading her cheeks, covered neck and shoulders, and reached down behind below her waist; while, suspended from its point, and fastened there by a golden button, fluttered a transparent veil bespangled with thousands of gold and silver points, which hung down upon her palfrey's back, and waved to and fro, following her movements as she turned her head. She wore an upper garment of cloth-of-gold, reaching only to the knee, and open at the breast, where it showed a corset of blue velvet laced with silver. From beneath this vestment descended a robe of green satin, of such length that it not only covered her feet, but reached down over the flank of her pal-

The Lion of Flanders

frey so as at times even to sweep the ground. An almost magical effect was produced by this stuff, which changed its color with every movement of the wearer: at one moment it would seem, as the sun shone upon it, all yellow, as if it were woven of gold, then it would turn to blue, and then, again, it would shade off into green. On her bosom, where the two ends of a string of the finest pearls met, shone a plate of beaten gold, with the Black Lion of Flanders artistically carved upon it in jet. A girdle, also bespangled with gold, and with silk and silver tassels, was fastened round her waist by a clasp, in which flashed two rubies of great value.

The harness of the palfrey, profusely enriched as it was with studs, drops, and tassels of gold and silver, corresponded in magnificence with the dress of the rider; and with like splendor were the other ladies attired in changing stuffs of every varied hue under heaven.

The queen, with her retinue, rode slowly up, and turned her eyes with spiteful curiosity upon these Flemish dames, who glittered so brilliantly in the sun's rays. As soon as she had arrived within a certain distance, the ladies rode up to her at a stately pace, and greeted her with many courtly speeches; Matilda alone was silent, and regarded Joanna with a stern unbending countenance. It was impossible for her to show honor to a queen who had thrown her father into prison. Her feelings were plainly traceable on her features, and did not escape Joanna's notice. She looked Matilda imperiously in the face, thinking to make the Flemish maiden quail beneath her frown; but in this she found herself mistaken; for the young girl proudly threw back glance for glance, without lowering her eyelids, even for an instant, before the angry queen, whose displeasure at the sight of so much magnificence had now become too great to be concealed. With evident annoyance she turned her horse's head, and exclaimed, while casting a look of scorn upon the band of ladies:

"Look you, gentlemen, I thought that I alone was queen in France; but methinks our Flemish traitors whom we hold in prison are princes one and all; for here I see their wives and daughters dressed out like queens and princesses."

These words she spoke aloud, so as to be heard by the nobles about her, and even by some of the citizens; then, with ill-concealed vexation, she inquired of the knight who rode next her:

"But, Messire de Chatillon, who is this insolent girl before me, with the Lion of Flanders upon her breast; what doth that betoken?"

De Chatillon, drawing nearer to her, replied: "It is Matilda, the daughter of Robert de Bethune."

And with these words he put his finger to his

The Lion of Flanders

lips, as a sign to the queen to dissemble and keep silence—a sign which she well understood, and accepted with a smile, a smile full of treachery, hatred, and revenge.

Any one who might have been observing the Dean of the Clothworkers at this moment could not have failed to perceive the steadfastness with which his eye was fixed upon the queen: not the slightest shade had come or gone upon her brow, but Deconinck had noted it down upon the tablet of his memory. In her features, he had plainly divined her anger, her wishes, and her plans; he knew, moreover, that De Chatillon was chosen to be the instrument of her designs; and he immediately occupied himself in devising the readiest means for defeating their attempts, whether made by stratagem or by force.

The king and queen now dismounted from their horses, and ascended the throne which had been erected for them in the middle of the great square. Their esquires and ladies of honor arranged themselves in two rows upon the steps; the knights remained on horseback, and drew up round about the scaffolding. When every one was in his place, the magistrates came forward with the maidens who were to represent the city of Bruges, and offered the foreign rulers the keys of the gates upon a costly velvet cushion. At the same moment the two figures of Fame blew a fresh blast upon their trumpets, and the Lilyards again cried, "Long live the king! long live the queen!"

All this time a dead silence reigned among the citizens; it seemed as though they affected indifference, that their dissatisfaction might be only the more thoroughly apparent; and in this they fully attained their aim, for Joanna was already turning indignantly in her mind how she might most effectually punish these insolent and disloyal subjects.

King Philip, who was of a less irritable temper, received the magistrates most affably, and promised to bestow his best consideration on all that might tend to the prosperity of Flanders. And this promise was no mere feigning; he was a generous prince and true knight, and might, under other circumstances, have been the blessing of his people both in France and Flanders. But there were two causes which completely neutralized all his good qualities. The first and worst of these was the influence of his imperious wife, who, whenever his better nature was about to prevail, came in like an evil spirit to turn him from good to evil. The other cause was his prodigality, which drove him on to use all means, whether good or bad, in order to provide for its gratification. Even now, his plans and resolves were all for the good of Flanders; but what could that avail, when Joanna of Navarre had already otherwise determined?

The Lion of Flanders

After the delivery of the keys, the king and queen remained for some time listening to the addresses of the magistrates; after which they left the scaffolding. They immediately took to horse again; and the cavalcade rode slowly through other streets on their way to the building called the Prince's Court, where a banquet was prepared for them, to which the chief men of Bruges and the principal Lilyards had also been invited. Meanwhile, the members of the companies returned to their homes, and the public festival was at an end.

Night had now set in; the guests had long since departed, and Queen Joanna was alone with her waiting-woman in her chamber. Already she had laid aside a great part of her cumbrous magnificence, and was busied in disarraying herself of all her jewelry. The hasty movements of her hands, and the irritable expression of her countenance, evinced the most violent impatience. The attendant in waiting could do nothing aright; and got from her mistress only sharp and angry words; necklaces and earrings were thrown hither and thither, as things of naught; while expressions of annoyance flowed incessantly from her mouth.

In a loose white robe the enraged queen kept pacing her chamber to and fro in deep thought, while her flaming eyes wandered fiercely around. At last her attendant, quite disconcerted at her strange manner and violent gesticulations, approached her, and respectfully inquired:

"Will your majesty be pleased to remain up any longer? Shall I go for a fresh light?"

To which the queen answered impatiently:

"No, there is light enough! Cease to annoy me with your tiresome questions. Leave me alone; begone, I tell you! Go to the anteroom, and wait there for my uncle De Chatillon. Let him come to me forthwith—go!"

While the damsel proceeded to execute the orders thus rudely given, Joanna sat down by a table and rested her head upon her hand. In this position she remained for some minutes, thinking upon the insult she had received; then, rising, she paced the room with hasty steps, at the same time violently gesticulating with her hands. At last she spoke in a suppressed voice:

"What! this paltry, insignificant people to put scorn upon me, the Queen of France! an insolent girl to stare me out of countenance! And shall I quietly put up with such an affront?"

A tear of anger glistened upon her burning cheek. Suddenly again she raised her head, and laughed with the malicious joy of a fiend as she continued:

"Oh ye insolent Flemings! you do not yet know Joanna of Navarre! you know not how fearfully her vengeance can fall! Rest and sleep without dread in your rash security! I know of means that will give you a fearful awakening. What a cup of bitterness shall not my hand mix for you! What tears shall I not make you shed! Then at least you shall know my power! Crawl before me you will, and supplicate me, insolent slaves! but you shall not be heard! With joy shall I set my foot upon your stubborn necks. In vain shall you weep and cry; for Joanna of Navarre is inexorable. That you know not yet, but you shall know it."

Hearing her attendant's steps in the passage, she now hastened to compose herself; and standing before a mirror, she gave her countenance a calmer expression, while her whole bearing assumed a more tranquil air. In the art of dissimulation, that great accomplishment of bad princes, Joanna was a perfect adept.

Soon De Chatillon entered the room, and bent one knee to the ground before the queen.

"Messire de Chatillon," she said, giving him her hand to rise, "it seems that you do not pay much attention to my wishes. Did I not appoint you to come to me long ere this?"

"True, madame; but I was detained by the king my master. Believe, I pray you, my illustrious niece, that I have been upon burning coals, so earnest was my desire to fulfil your royal pleasure."

"I thank you for your good-will, Messire; and

The Lion of Flanders

I am desirous this very day of rewarding you for all your faithful services."

"Gracious princess, it is itself a great boon to me to be permitted to follow and serve your majesty. Only let me always and everywhere accompany you. Let others seek office and power; for me, your presence is my best joy; I ask for naught besides."

The queen looked with a contemptuous smile upon the flatterer; for she knew too well how much his heart belied his words. With a peculiar emphasis, therefore, she continued:

"But what if I were to set you over the land of Flanders?"

De Chatillon, who had not reckoned on so speedy an attainment of his great object, almost repented of his words; and for the first moment knew not what answer to make. He soon recovered himself, however, and said:

"If it should please your majesty to give me so great a proof of confidence, I should not for a moment venture to oppose myself to your royal will; but should thankfully, and as a good subject, accept the gift, and kiss your gracious hand with love and reverence."

"Listen, Messire de Chatillon," cried the queen, impatiently; "I did not send for you to hear fine speeches; you will therefore greatly oblige me if you will put all such aside, and tell me without circumlocution, or disguise, what you think of our entry to-day. Has not Bruges given the queen of France and of Navarre a reception beyond all she could have looked or hoped for?"

"I pray you, my illustrious niece, leave these bitter jests, for the scorn that has been done you has touched me to the very heart. A vile and contemptible people has defied you to your very face, and your dignity has met with a grievous affront. But be not troubled; all is in our power now, and we shall soon find means to tame these insolent subjects, and bring them to their senses."

"Do you know your niece, Messire de Chatillon? Do you know how jealous is Joanna of Navarre?"

"In truth, madame, with the noblest and most laudable jealousy; for to wear a crown, and not to maintain its dignity, is to deserve to forfeit it. Your princely spirit is the object of universal admiration."

"Do you know, too, that it is no paltry vengeance that satisfies me? The punishment of those that have affronted me must be commensurate with my dignity. Both as a queen and woman I must be revenged: that is enough for you, to whom I am about to commit the government of Flanders, and who will have to execute my will."

"It is needless, madame, for you to trouble yourself further about this matter; be assured that your vengeance shall be complete. Peradventure I shall even exceed your wishes; for I have to avenge not only the affront to you, but also those which are daily offered to the crown of France by this rebellious and headstrong people."

"But, Messire de Chatillon, do not, I pray you, lose sight of sound policy. Be not too hasty in drawing the noose fast about their necks; break their spirit rather by gradual humiliation. Above all, fleece them bit by bit of the wealth which supports their obstinacy; and then, when you have them fairly in the harness, press down the yoke so tight upon their necks, that I may be able to feast my eyes upon their slavery. Be in no hurry; I have patience enough, when the end can be more effectually reached thereby. And the better to succeed, it will be advisable to take the first opportunity of removing one Deconinck from his place of Dean of the Clothworkers in this city, and to take care that none but our friends are admitted to offices of power."

De Chatillon listened attentively to the queen's counsel, and secretly admired her skill in the crooked ways of policy; and as his private revenge was equally interested in the establishment of despotism, he was highly delighted at being able to gratify at once his own passions and those of his niece. With evident joy he replied:

"I receive with gratitude the honor which your majesty confers on me, and will spare nothing to carry out the counsels of my sovereign lady, as a true and faithful servant. Have you any further commands for me?"

In putting this question he had the young Matilda in view. De Chatillon well knew that she had drawn upon herself the queen's enmity, and was convinced she would not be long without feeling its effects. Joanna answered:

"I think it might be as well to have away that daughter of Messire de Bethune into France; she seems full of Flemish pride and obstinacy; and I shall be pleased to have her at my court. Enough said—you understand me. To-morrow I leave this accursed land; I have had more than enough of their insolence. Raoul de Nesle goes with us; you remain here as governor-general of Flanders, with full power to rule the land at your discretion, and accountable only to ourselves for your fidelity."

"Say rather at the discretion of my royal niece," interposed De Chatillon, in a tone of flattery.

"Be it so," said Joanna; "I am gratified by your devotedness. Twelve hundred men at arms shall remain with you to support your authority. And now it is time for us both to go to rest, my fair uncle; so I wish you good-night."

"May all good angels watch over your majesty!" said De Chatillon, with a profound bow; and with these words he left the chamber of the evil-minded queen.

CHAPTER VIII

THE city magistrates and their friends the Lilyards had gone to great expense about the ceremonial of the royal entry. The triumphal arches and scaffoldings, and the precious stuffs with which they were adorned, had cost large sums of money; besides which, a quantity of the best wine had been served out to each of the king's men-at-arms. As all this had been done by order of the magistrates, and consequently had to be paid for out of the common chest, it had been regarded by the citizens with the greatest dissatisfaction.

All the machinery of the pageant had long been removed; De Chatillon was at Courtrai, and the royal visit almost forgotten, when one morning, at ten o'clock in the forenoon, a crier appeared before the town hall, at the usual place of proclamation, and by sound of trumpet called the people together. As soon as he saw a sufficient number of hearers assembled, he produced a parchment from a case which hung at his side, and read aloud:

"It is hereby made known to each and every citizen, that the worshipful the magistrates have ordered as follows, that is to say:

The Lion of Flanders

"That an extraordinary contribution be levied for covering the expenses of the entry of our gracious prince, King Philip.

"That each and every inhabitant of the city pay thereto the sum of eight groats Flemish, to be paid head by head, without distinction of age.

"That the tax-gatherers collect the same on Saturday next, from door to door; and that such as by force or fraud refuse or evade payment of the same be compelled thereto in due course of law."

Those of the citizens who heard this proclamation looked at one another with astonishment, and secretly murmured at so arbitrary an exaction. Among these were several journeymen of the Clothworkers' Company, who, without delay, hastened to make the matter known to their Dean.

Deconinck received the intelligence with extreme displeasure. Such a violent blow struck at the rights and liberties of the commonalty filled him with mistrust as to what might follow, for he saw in it a first step toward the despotism under which, with the aid of France, the nobles were endeavoring again to bring the people; and he determined to defeat these first attempts either by force or policy. He well knew that any opposition might easily be fatal to him, for the foreign armies still occupied Flanders; but no consideration could check his patriotic zeal: he had devoted himself body and soul to the weal of his native city. Sending immediately for the company's beadle, he thus commissioned him:

"Go round instantly to all the masters, and summon them in my name to meet forthwith at the hall. Let them lay all else aside, and ,delay not a moment, for the matter is urgent."

The Clothworkers' Hall was a spacious building with a round gable. A single large window in front, over which stood the arms of the company, gave light to the great room on the first floor; over the wide doorway stood St. George and the dragon, artistically cut in stone. In all other respects, the front was without ornament or pretension; it would have been difficult in fact to guess from its appearance that it was here the wealthiest guild in Flanders held its meetings, for it was far excelled in magnificence by many of the houses around it.

Notwithstanding the considerable number of large and small chambers which the building contained, not one of them was empty or unemployed. In a spacious room on the second story were to be seen the masterpieces, or specimens of work which every one had to show before he could be admitted to the mastership; and also patterns of the most costly stuffs that the looms of Bruges could produce. In an adjoining chamber were exhibited models of all the implements made use of by weavers, fullers, and dyers. In a third apartment were

The Lion of Flanders

laid away the dresses and arms which were used by the guild on occasions of ceremony.

The principal room, in which the masters held their meetings, lay toward the street. All the operations which the wool had to undergo, from those of the shepherd and shearer to those of the weaver and dyer, and even to the foreign merchant who came from distant lands to exchange his gold for the stuffs of Flanders, were exhibited upon the walls in well-executed paintings. Several oaken tables and a number of massive seats stood upon the stone floor. Six velvet-covered armchairs at the further end indicated the place of the Dean and Ancients.

The beadle once despatched, it was not long before a considerable number of master clothworkers were assembled at the hall, energetically discussing the matter which for the time most occupied them, and overspread every countenance with the deepest gloom. Most of them were violent in their expressions of indignation against the magistrates; nevertheless, there were some who seemed disinclined to take any extreme steps. While the assembly was thus each moment increasing, Deconinck entered the room, and passed slowly through the crowd of his fellows up to the great chair, where his place was. The Ancients took their seats beside him; the rest mostly remained standing by their seats, the better to catch sight of their Dean's countenance, and read off from his furrowed brow the full sense of his weighty and eloquent speech. The whole number present was sixty persons.

As soon as Deconinck saw the attention of his fellows directed upon himself, with an emphatic gesture of his hand he thus spoke:

"My brethren! give heed to my words, for the enemies of our freedom, the enemies of our prosperity, are forging fetters for our feet! The magistrates and Lilyards have flattered the foreigner who is become our master by receiving him with extraordinary pomp; they have pressed us into their service for the erection of their scaffoldings and arches, and now they require that we should make good the cost of their scandalous prodigality from the fruits of our honest labor; a demand which is an infringement alike on the liberties of our city and on the rights of our company. Understand me well, my brethren, and endeavor with me to penetrate the future; if for this once we submit to an arbitrary imposition, our liberty will soon be trampled under foot. This is the first experiment, the first pressure of the yoke that is hereafter to sit heavy upon our necks. The unfaithful Lilyards, who leave their Count, our lawful lord, in a foreign prison, that they may the better be able to gain the mastery over us, have long fattened upon the sweat of our brows. Long did the people serve

The Lion of Flanders

them—serve them as beasts of burden, and with sighs and groans. To you, men of Bruges, my fellow-citizens, was it first given to receive the heavenly beam, the light of freedom; you were the first to break the chains of slavery; you rose up against your tyrants like men, and never again shall you bow your necks under the yoke of despotism. At present our prosperity is the envy, our greatness the admiration, of all the people of the earth; is it not then our bounden duty to preserve for ourselves—to hand down to our children—those liberties which our fathers won for us, and which have made us what we are? Yes, it is our duty, and a sacred one! and whoso forgets it is a caitiff undeserving the name of man, a slave worthy only of contempt!"

But here one of the masters present, by name Brakels, who had already twice filled the office of Dean, rose from his seat, and interrupted Deconinck's speech with these words:

"You are always talking of slavery and of our rights; but who tells us that the worshipful magistrates intend to infringe upon them? Is it not better to pay eight groats than to break the peace of the city. For it is easy to see that if we resist, we shall not get off without bloodshed. Many of us will have to bury a child or a brother, and all for eight groats! If we were to take your word for everything, the Clothworkers would have their 'good-days' in hand oftener than their shuttles; but I hope that our masters will be too wise to follow your advice on this occasion."

This speech caused the greatest excitement among all present. Some, though but a few, made it apparent by their gestures that they thought with Brakels; but by far the greater number disapproved of the sentiments he had expressed.

Deconinck had narrowly watched the countenances of his brethren, and had told over the number of those upon whose support he could reckon. Having speedily convinced himself that the party of his adversary was but small, he replied:

"It stands written expressly in our laws that no new burden can be laid upon the people without their own consent. This freedom has been purchased at a very costly price; and no person, be he who he may, has the power to violate it. True it is that to one who does not look far forward, eight groats, paid once for all, are no great matter; and certainly it is not for eight groats' sake that I would urge you to resistance; but the liberties, which are our bulwark against the despotism of the Lilyards—shall we allow them to be broken down? No; that were at once most base and most improvident. Know, brethren, that liberty is a tender plant, which, if you break but a single branch from off it, soon fades and dies; if we allow the Lilyards to clip our tree, we shall soon have no longer power to defend its withered trunk. Once for all, whoever has a man's heart in his bosom does not pay the eight groats! Whoever feels true Claward blood in his veins, let him lift his 'good-day,' and strike for the people's rights! But let the vote determine; what I have said is my opinion, not my command."

To these words the master who had already spoken on the opposite side rejoined:

"Your advice is evil. You take pleasure in tumult and bloodshed, in order that in the midst of the confusion your name may pass from mouth to mouth as our leader. Were it not much wiser, as true subjects, to submit to the French Government, and so to extend our commerce over the whole of the great land of France? Yes, I say, the government of Philip the Fair will forward our prosperity; and every right-minded citizen therefore must regard the French rule as a benefit. Our magistrates are wise men and honorable gentlemen."

The greatest astonishment showed itself throughout the assembly, and not a few angry and contemptuous looks were cast upon him who held this unseemly language. As for Deconinck, he could no longer contain his wrath; his love for the people was unbounded, and moreover he felt it a dishonor to the whole guild that one of his own Clothworkers should thus express himself.

The Lion of Flanders

"What!" he exclaimed, "is all love for freedom and fatherland dead in our bosoms? Will you, out of thirst for gold, kiss the very hands that are riveting the chains about your feet? And shall posterity have it to say that it was the men of Bruges that first bowed their heads before the foreigner and his slaves? No, my brethren, you will not endure it; you will not let this blot come upon your name. Let the cowardly Lilyards barter away their freedom to the stranger for miserable gold, and peace such as dastards love; but let us remain free from reproach and shame. Let free Bruges once again pour out the blood of her free children for the right! So much the fairer floats the blood-red standard; so much the faster stands the people's power!"

Here Deconinck made a short pause; and before he could resume, Master Brakels again broke in:

"I repeat it, say what you will. What disgrace is it to us that our prince is a stranger? On the contrary, we ought to feel proud that we are now a part of mighty France. What matters it to a nation that lives and thrives by commerce to whose sway it bows? Is not Mahomet's gold as good as ours?"

The indignation against Brakels was now at the highest—so high, in truth, that no one deigned to answer him; only Deconinck sighed deeply, and at last exclaimed:

The Lion of Flanders

"Oh, shame! a Lilyard, a bastard, has spoken in our hall! We are disgraced forever!"

A tumultuous movement passed through the assembly, and many an eye flashed wrath upon Master Brakels.

Suddenly a voice was heard from the midst of the assembly, "Turn the Lilyard out! no French hearts among us!" and the cry was repeated again and again from one to another.

It now required all Deconinck's influence to keep the peace; not a few seemed inclined to violence; and the question was put, whether Brakels should be expelled the company, or fined in forty pounds' weight of wax.

While the clerk was busy taking the votes, Brakels stood with an unconcerned air before the Dean. He relied upon those who had received with favor his first speech; but in this he greatly deceived himself, for the name of Lilyard, a sore reproach in the eyes of all, had not left him a single friend. The sentence that he should be expelled the company was given without a dissentient voice, and received with general acclamation.

Upon this all the fury of the Lilyard burst forth, and a torrent of threats and abuse flowed from his mouth. The Dean sat on in his place with the greatest composure, without deigning a reply to his adversary's insults. Presently there came up two stout journeymen, who officiated as doorkeepers, and required Brakels to leave the hall forthwith, as no longer a member of their body. Full of spite and bitterness, he obeyed, and now thirsting for revenge, presented himself without loss of time before John van Gistel, the principal tax-gatherer, whom he informed of the opposition organized by the Dean of the Clothworkers.

Peter Deconinck continued at considerable length to address his fellows, the better to encourage them to the defense of their rights. It was far from being his desire, however, that they should do anything tumultuously; and he strictly enjoined them to confine themselves to refusing payment of the eight groats, until he should call them to arms.

All the members now left the hall, and made the best of their way homeward. Deconinck proceeded alone and in deep thought along the old Sack street, intending to have a conference with his friend Breydel. He foresaw how great would be the efforts of the nobles to reestablish their power over the people, and he was meditating on the means of preserving his brethren from falling again under the yoke. The moment he was on the point of turning into the Butcher street he found himself surrounded by some ten armed soldiers, while the high-constable of the town coming up to him required him, in the name of the magistracy, to surrender without resistance. His hands were bound behind his back, as if he had been a common criminal; to which, however, he submitted without complaint, well knowing that resistance was in vain. In this way he walked quietly on through four or five streets between the halberds of the sergeants, without seeming to pay any attention to the exclamations of wonder which everywhere greeted the procession; and was at last conducted into an upper chamber of the Prince's Court, in which the city magistrates were already assembled, and along with them the other chiefs of the Lilyards—John van Gistel, chief receiver of the taxes, and the warmest friend of France in all Flanders, being at their head. The latter no sooner saw Deconinck before him than with an angry voice he exclaimed:

"So, insolent citizen, you defy the authority of the magistrates! We have heard of your rebellious doings, and it shall not be long before you pay for your disobedience on the gallows."

To this insulting speech Deconinck calmly answered:

"The liberty of my people is dearer to me than my life. In such a death there is no shame, and for me there is no fear, for the people die not. There will still be men enough whose necks will never bend under the yoke."

"A dream, a vain dream," replied Van Gistel; "the people's reign is over. Under the rule of our gracious sovereign King Philip a subject must obey his lord. Your privileges, extorted by you from weak princes, must needs be reviewed and curtailed; for you have grown into insolence upon the favor shown you, and now rise up against us, as disobedient subjects, worthy not only of punishment, but of contempt."

Deconinck's eye flashed with indignation:

"God knows," he exclaimed, "whether it is the people who better deserve contempt, or the Lilyards, those bastard sons of Flanders, who forget alike their country and their honor, basely to fawn upon a foreign master! Submissively you kneel before this prince, who has sworn the downfall of your country; and to what end? that you may bring back into your hands your old despotic sway over the people; and that for greed of gold! But you shall not succeed; they who have once tasted of the fruits of the tree of freedom turn with disgust from the baits you offer. Are you not the slaves of the foreigner? And think you that the men of Bruges are sunk low enough to be the slaves of slaves? Sirs, you forget yourselves strangely! Our country has grown into greatness, the people have felt their own dignity, and your iron sceptre is gone from you forever."

"Be silent, rebel!" cried Van Gistel; "what have such as you to do with freedom? you were never made for it."

The Lion of Flanders

"Our freedom," answered Deconinck, "we have bought and paid for with the sweat of our brows and the blood of our veins; and shall we, then, permit such as you to wrest it from us?"

Van Gistel replied with a scornful smile:

"Idle words, Master Dean; your threats are mere smoke. We have now the French forces at our disposal, and shall soon show you that we can clip the wings of the many-headed monster. The insolence of the commons has long passed all bounds, and they must now be ruled by other laws. Our plans, be assured, are so well laid that Bruges shall humbly bow the neck; and as for yourself, you shall not behold to-morrow's dawn."

"Tyrant!" cried the Dean; "shame of Flanders! Are not the graves of your fathers dug in her soil? Do not their sacred ashes rest within the earth that you, unnatural that you are, would basely sell for the gold of the foreigner? Posterity shall judge you for your cowardice; and your own children, when they chronicle the deeds of these days, shall curse and renounce you!"

"It is time to make an end of these foolish and insolent declamations," exclaimed Van Gistel. "Here, sergeants, to the dungeon with him until the gallows is prepared!"

Upon this Deconinck was led away, down several flights of stairs, into an underground vault. He was heavily ironed; a chain round his waist made him fast to the wall, while by another his right hand was linked to his left foot. An allowance of bread and water was set before him, the massive door was closed and locked, and the captive was left alone in his solitary dungeon. He now saw clearly from the words of Van Gistel how seriously the freedom of his native town was threatened. In his absence, the Lilyards might overpower the citizens with the aid of the foreign mercenaries, and so annihilate the labors of his whole life. This was a frightful thought for him. Ever and anon as he moved under his chains, and their clanking struck his ear, he seemed to see his brethren lying thus bound before him, with shame and slavery for their portion; and a tear of regret would trickle down his cheeks.

The Lilyards, in truth, had long been busy with a plot of surprise and treachery. Hitherto they had never been able to lay any firm foundation for their ascendency in Bruges. The people were all armed, and could not be coerced. No sooner was any recourse to violence attempted than the terrible "good-days" appeared, and all their endeavors were in vain: the Guilds were too strong for them. At length, in order to remove, once for all, this hindrance out of their way, they had concerted a plan with De Chatillon, now governor-general of Flanders, for surprising and disarming the citizens on the morrow of this very day. An early

The Lion of Flanders

hour of the morning had been fixed upon for the execution of their design, when De Chatillon was to be ready to support them with five hundred French men-at-arms; but, however well their secret might be kept from ordinary observers, they greatly feared the activity and penetration of Deconinck, who, moreover, was evidently possessed of secret sources of information which they had in vain endeavored to trace out. The Dean of the Clothworkers was craftier than they all, as they well knew; they had therefore seized the first opportunity of arresting him in order to deprive the popular party of their ablest leader, and so fatally to weaken their ranks. Brakel's denunciation, and the intended resistance of the Clothworkers, had merely served them as a pretext.

Having thus begun, by the committal of Deconinck, the execution of their base plans for betraying their native city to the stranger, they were about to break up the assembly, when suddenly a tumult was heard without, the door was burst open, and a man forced his way through the doorkeepers, who, striding proudly up to the assembled magistrates, cried in a loud voice:

"The Trades of Bruges call upon you to say whether you will release Deconinck, the Dean of the Clothworkers—yes or no? I advise you not to be long in making up your mind."

"You have no concern, Master Breydel, in this

chamber," answered Van Gistel; "and I command you to quit it forthwith."

"I ask you once more," repeated Jan Breydel, "will you set at large the Dean of the Clothworkers, or will you not?"

Van Gistel, after whispering to one of the magistrates, cried in a loud voice:

"We reply to the threats of a rebellious subject with the punishment he deserves. Sergeant, seize him!"

"Ha! ha! Seize him!" repeated Breydel, with a laugh; "who will seize me, I should like to know? Take notice that the commons are at this moment about to make themselves masters of the building, and that each and every one of you shall answer with his life for the Dean of the Clothworkers. You shall soon see quite another dance, and to quite another tune too—that I promise you."

Meanwhile some of the sergeants in waiting had drawn near and seized the Dean of the Butchers by the collar, while one of them was already uncoiling a piece of cord with which to bind him. Breydel, intent upon what he was saying, had hitherto taken but little notice of these preparations; but now, as he turned away from the Lilyards, he perceived what the officers were about; and sending from his chest a deep sound, like the suppressed roaring of a bull, he cast his flashing eyes upon his assailants, and cried:

The Lion of Flanders

"Think you, then, that Jan Breydel, a free butcher of Bruges, will let himself be bound like a calf? Ha! you will wait long enough for that!"

And with these words, which he uttered in a voice of thunder, he struck one of the officers so violently with his heavy fist upon the head that the man speedily measured his length on the ground; then, while the rest stood stupefied with astonishment, he rapidly forced his way through them to the door, prostrating several of them right and left as he passed. In the doorway he turned round upon the Lilyards, and again exclaimed:

"You shall pay for it, insolent scoundrels! What! bind a butcher of Bruges! Woe to you, accursed tyrants! Hear me! hear me! the drum of the Butchers' Guild shall beat your death-march!"

More he would have said; but being no longer able to hold his ground against the multitude that was pressing upon him, he turned and descended the stairs, uttering threats of vengeance as he went.

An indistinct sound like the roar of distant thunder now fell upon the ear from the other side of the city. The Lilyards turned pale, and trembled at the coming storm; nevertheless, being determined not to release their prisoner, they strengthened the guard about the building, so as to secure it against assault, and retired to their homes, protected by an armed escort.

An hour afterward the whole city was in insurrection; the tocsin sounded, and the drums of all the Guilds beat to arms. The distant groan of the coming storm had given place to the formidable howl of a present tempest. Window-shutters were closed; doors were fastened, and only opened again for the grown men of the family to pass out in arms. The dogs barked fiercely, as though they had understood what was going on, and joined their hoarse voices to the angry shouts of their masters.

Here the people were grouped in masses; there they ran hither and thither with hasty steps; some armed with maces or clubs, others with "good-days" or halberds. Among the streaming multitude the butchers were easily to be recognized by their flashing pole-axes; the smiths, too, with their heavy sledge-hammers on their shoulders, were conspicuous among the rest at the place of meeting, which was near to the Clothworkers' Hall, and where already a formidable body of the Guilds stood drawn up in array. The multitude kept constantly increasing, as each newcomer ranged himself under his proper standard.

At last, the assembly being now sufficiently numerous, Jan Breydel mounted the top of a

The Lion of Flanders

wagon, which by chance was standing in the street, and, flourishing his heavy pole-ax about his head, in a stentorian voice thus addressed the throng:

"Men of Bruges! the day has arrived when you must strike for life and liberty! Now we must show the traitors what we really are, and whether there is a pound of slave's-flesh to be found among us, whatever they may think. They have Master Deconinck in their dungeon; let us release him, if it cost us our blood. This is work for all the Guilds, and a right good treat for the Butchers. Now, comrades, up with your sleeves!"

And while his fellows were obeying the word of command, he himself stripped his sinewy arms to the shoulder, and sprang down from the wagon, crying:

"Forward! Deconinck forever!"

"Deconinck forever!" was the universal cry. "Forward! Forward!"

And, like the surging waves of a stormy ocean, the angry multitude rolled onward toward the Prince's Court. The streets resounded with the cry of "Death to the tyrants!" while the terrible clash of arms might be heard, mingled with the baying of the dogs, the heavy toll of the bells, and the roll of the drums; the citizens seemed possessed one and all with sudden fury.

At the first approach of their frantic assailants

The Lion of Flanders

the guards of the Prince's Court fled in every direction, and left the building wholly undefended. But hurried as their flight was, it was not rapid enough to save them all; in an instant more than ten corpses lay on the ground in front of the palace.

Impatient of each moment's delay, and furious as an enraged lion, Breydel mounted the stairs by three steps at a time, and meeting a French servant in one of the passages, hurled him headlong among the people below, where the unhappy victim was received on the points of the "good-days," and instantly despatched with clubs and maces. Soon the whole building was filled with the people. Breydel had brought with him several of the smiths, and the doors of the dungeons were speedily broken open; but, to the dismay of the liberators, all were empty; Deconinck was nowhere to be found. Then they swore in their fury fearfully to avenge his death.

No sooner had the Clothworkers heard that their Dean had disappeared than their rage became perfectly ungovernable. Instead of making further search after him, they hurried off in detachments to the houses of the principal Lilyards, forced them open, and broke and destroyed everything in them; but of the Lilyards themselves not a single man was to be found; they had all foreseen the visit, and had been too prudent to await their coming.

Just as Breydel was about to leave the palace,

The Lion of Flanders

with thoughts full of despair and vengeance, an old gray-headed fuller came up to him, and said:

"Master Breydel, you know not how to search. There is another dungeon at the farther end of the building, as I have good reason to know; for at the time of the great disturbances, one mortal year of my life did I lie there. It is a deep underground hole; be pleased to follow me."

Accordingly, Breydel, with several others, followed the old man; and they passed on through many passages, till they reached a small iron door. Here their guide took a sledge-hammer from the hand of a smith who was with them, and with a stroke or two broke the lock; but the door still refused to open. Then, in a transport of impatience, Breydel snatched the hammer from the fuller, and struck the door such a blow that all the fastenings by which it was embedded in the wall became loose, the door fell from its place, and at once afforded them ready entrance into the dungeon.

In one corner stood Deconinck, fastened to the wall by a heavy chain. No sooner did Breydel perceive him, than in a transport of joy he sprang toward him, clasping him in his arms, as a brother that had been lost and was found again.

"Oh master!" he cried, "how happy is this hour to me! I knew not till now how much I loved you!"

The Lion of Flanders

"I thank you, my brave friend," was Deconinck's answer, while he cordially returned the Butcher's warm embrace; "I knew well that you would not leave me in the dungeon; I knew that Jan Breydel's was not the heart for that. No! he that would see a Fleming of the true metal, let him look at you!"

Then turning to the bystanders, he exclaimed, in a tone of feeling that touched the hearts of all who heard him:

"My brethren, this day you have delivered me from death! To you belongs my blood; to the cause of your freedom I devote every faculty of my being. Regard me no longer as one of your Deans of Guild, as a Clothworker living among you, but as a man that has sworn before God to make good your liberties against their foes. Here, in the dark vaults of these dungeons, let me record the irrevocable oath: My blood, my life, for my beloved country!"

A cry of "Long live Deconinck!" overpowered his voice, and long reechoed from the walls. From mouth to mouth the cry passed on, and soon resounded over the whole city. The very children lisped out:

"Long live Deconinck! long live Deconinck!"

A file soon relieved him of the chain with which he had been fastened to the wall, and the Dean of the Clothworkers proceeded along with Jan Brey-

The Lion of Flanders

del into the vestibule of the palace; but the irons on his hands and feet still remained, and were no sooner perceived by the people, than cries of fury again burst from every mouth. Every beholder's cheek was wet with tears at once of joy and rage, and again, with still greater energy, resounded the cry:

"Long live Deconinck! long live Deconinck!"

And now the Clothworkers pressed about their Dean, and, in their exultation, raised him aloft upon the blood-stained shield of one of the soldiers whom they had killed. In vain Deconinck resisted; he was obliged to allow himself to be carried in triumph through all the streets of the city.

Strange sight it was—that tumultuous procession. Thousands upon thousands, armed with such weapons as the moment had offered—axes, knives, spears, hammers, clubs—ran hither and thither, shouting as if possessed. Above their heads, upon the buckler, stood Deconinck, with the fetters on his hands and feet; beside him marched the Butchers, with bared arms and flashing axes. More than an hour was thus consumed; at last Deconinck called to him the Deans and other principal officers of the Guilds, and informed them that he must immediately confer with them upon a matter of the greatest importance to the common cause; he desired them, therefore, to assemble at his house that same evening, in order to concert together the necessary measures.

He then addressed the people, thanking them for their services and for the honor they had shown him; the irons were removed from his hands and feet, and amid enthusiastic acclamations, he was conducted by his fellow-citizens to the door of his house in the Wool street.

BOOK SECOND

CHAPTER I

JOHN VAN GISTEL and his Lilyards stood in the vegetable-market, fully armed. With them were some three hundred of their retainers, every man ready for battle. The strictest silence was maintained, for the alarm once given, their plot would fail. They awaited patiently the first beams of the morning sun, to fall upon the people and disarm them; then, without more ado, to hang Deconinck and Breydel as rebels, and, finally, to coerce the Guilds into complete subjection. The selfsame day De Chatillon was to make his entry into the disarmed city, and to establish, once for all, a new form of government in Bruges. Unfortunately for them, however, Deconinck's sagacity had penetrated their secret, and had already provided the means for frustrating their designs.

At the same moment, and in equal silence, the Clothworkers and Butchers, with detachments from some of the other trades, stood drawn up in arms in the Flemish street. Deconinck and Breydel were conferring together at a little distance from their corps, and laying out the plan for their morning's work. It was finally settled that the

The Lion of Flanders

Clothworkers and Butchers were to fall upon the Lilyards, while the men of the other Guilds should make themselves masters of the city gates, which they were forthwith to close, in order to cut off from the enemy all succor from without.

Hardly was the plan of operations agreed upon, when the morning bell began to sound from the church of St. Donatus, and the tramp of John van Gistel's horses was heard in the distance; upon which the men of the Guilds at once set themselves in motion, and marched upon the Lilyards, all in the deepest silence. It was upon the great marketplace that the two hostile bodies first caught sight of each other; the Lilyards, just turning the corner of the Bridle street, while the Guildsmen were still in the Flemish street. Great was the astonishment of the French party at finding their secret discovered; nevertheless, as good knights and men of valor, they determined to persevere, and were still confident of success.

The trumpets soon gave forth their inspiring tones, and horse and rider dashed in headlong charge upon the citizens, who had not yet extricated themselves from the defile of the Flemish street. The leveled spears of the Lilyards were met by the "good-days" of the Clothworkers, who in serried phalanx awaited the shock. But how great soever the courage and address of the Guildsmen, their unfavorable position made it impossi-

The Lion of Flanders

ble for them to hold their ground before the terrible onslaught. Five of their front rank fell dead or wounded to the ground, and so gave the enemy's horsemen the opportunity of breaking their array; three of their divisions were already driven back; the bodies of the Clothworkers strewed the pavement; and the Lilyards, now deeming themselves masters of the field, triumphantly raised their warcry: "Montjoie St. Denis! France! France!" Deconinck in the front held his ground valiantly, "good-day" in hand, and for some time succeeded in rallying the foremost ranks, who had alone to support the whole shock of the enemy, the narrowness of the street preventing the main body from taking their share in the fight. But the Dean's exhortations and example could not long uphold the fortune of the day; the French party pressed forward with redoubled efforts upon his van, and drove it back in confusion upon the rear.

All this had passed so rapidly that already many had fallen, before Master Breydel, who, with the men of his Guild, stood at the farther end of the street, was aware of what was going on; at last a movement ordered by Deconinck opened the ranks, and showed him at once the whole position of things, and the danger of the Clothworkers. Muttering some unintelligible words, he turned to his men, and cried in a loud voice:

"Forward, Butchers! forward!"

The Lion of Flanders

As if beside himself, he dashed onward through the opening made by the Clothworkers—he and his men after him, against the enemy. At the first blow his ax hit through headplate and skull of a horse; the second laid the rider at his feet. The next instant he strode over four corpses; and so he fought onward, until he himself received a wound on his left arm. At the sight of his own blood, he became as one possessed; with a hasty glance at the knight who had wounded him, he cast aside his ax, and stooping beneath the lance of his adversary, with headlong fury sprang upon the horse, and grappled body to body with the rider, who, firmly as he sat, could not resist the maddened force of Breydel, and, falling from the saddle, rolled with his assailant upon the ground. While the Dean of the Butchers was thus occupied in satiating his vengeance, his comrades and the other Guildsmen had fallen in a mass upon the main body of the Lilyards, and had already cast many of them under their feet. Obstinately was each inch of ground contested; men and horses, dead and dying, lay piled in heaps, and the pavement was red with blood.

Soon all effectual resistance on the part of the Lilyards was at an end; they were driven back into the market-place; and the Guildsmen being now at liberty to deploy, and avail themselves of their superior numbers, it became evident that their object was to surround their enemies, and that for this purpose they were extending their right wing toward the egg-market. Upon this the knights, seeing themselves defeated, turned their horses, and fled from the destruction that awaited them—the Butchers and Clothworkers following them with shouts of triumph, but without much effect; for, well mounted as they all were, they were soon beyond the reach of pursuit.

By this time the sound of the trumpets and the tumult of the battle had given the alarm throughout the city; all its inhabitants were in motion, and thousands of armed burghers filled the streets, hurrying to the aid of their brethren. The victory, however, was already won; the Lilyards had retreated to the castle, and were blockaded on every side by the Guildsmen.

While these things were proceeding in the market-place, the governor-general, De Chatillon, presented himself before the town with five hundred French men-at-arms. He had foreseen that he should find the gates closed, according to the old custom of the men of Bruges in such cases, and was therefore well provided for that event. His brother, Guy de St. Pol, was ordered to follow close upon him, with a numerous body of infantry, and all the engines necessary for storming the place. While waiting for this reenforcement, he was already planning his assault, and looking out

The Lion of Flanders

for the weak points of the fortifications. Although he saw but few people upon the ramparts, he did not deem it expedient to make his attack with his men-at-arms alone, knowing as he did the indomitable spirit of the men of Bruges. Half an hour after his arrival, St. Pol with his division appeared in the distance, the points of their spears and the blades of their halberds glancing from afar in the sun's early rays, while an impenetrable cloud of dust indicated the progress of the machines, with the horses that drew them.

The small number of the citizens who were in charge of the walls watched the approach of their numerous assailants with fear and trembling. As they saw the heavy battering machines brought up, the hearts of all were filled with the saddest forebodings, and the unwelcome tidings speedily circulated throughout the whole city. The armed Guildsmen were still posted about the castle, where the intelligence of this new force disturbed them in their operations. Leaving, therefore, a sufficient detachment to continue the blockade of the Lilyards, the main body hastened to the walls to meet the danger that now threatened them in that quarter. It was not without deep anxiety for the fate of their beloved Bruges that they perceived the French soldiers already busily engaged in setting up their battering engines.

The besiegers carried on their operations for

The Lion of Flanders

the present at a considerable distance from the walls, quite out of bow-shot, while De Chatillon with his men-at-arms covered the workmen against a sally from the town. Soon lofty movable towers, with drawbridges, by which to reach the walls, were seen rising within the French lines; battering-rams and catapults were also in readiness; and everything portended sad woes to Bruges.

But, great as the danger was, no coward fear was visible on the countenances of the Guildsmen. Anxiously and closely they watched the foe; their hearts beat hard and fast, and their breath shortened, as first the hostile squadrons met their sight; but that was soon over. Their eyes still bent upon their enemies, they felt the blood flow more freely in their veins; a manly glow overspread their cheeks, and the heart of every citizen burned within him with the noble fire of heroic wrath.

One man there was that stood joyous even to mirth upon the rampart; his restless movements, and the smile which flitted over his countenance, spoke of impatient anticipation, and of a moment long looked for and at last found. Ever and anon his eye, for a moment, quitted the enemy to rest upon the pole-ax in his stalwart grasp, and then he would tenderly and fondly caress the deadly weapon with his hand—Jan Breydel knew not what fear was.

And now the Deans of all the different companies surrounded Deconinck, and awaited in silence for his counsel—it might almost be said, his orders. He, after his manner, was in no haste to give his opinion, and gazed long in deep thought upon the French position, till the restless Breydel impatiently exclaimed:

"How now, Master Deconinck, what say you? Shall we make a sally and have at these French fellows where they are, or shall we let them come on, and pitch them into the ditch?"

Still the Dean of the Clothworkers made no answer; still he stood plunged in thought, his eye fixed upon the enemy's works, and scanning curiously the great engines of assault with which they were so abundantly provided. The bystanders strained their eyes and wits to anticipate from his countenance what his speech would be; naught, however, was discernible but calm and cool reflection. Deconinck's heart, meanwhile, with all its self-possession and courage, was not one of those that were elate with hope and confidence. He saw plainly that it would be impossible finally to resist the force of the besiegers; the gigantic catapults and lofty movable towers gave the French considerable advantage over the citizens, who were totally unprovided with any equivalent apparatus. He had soon convinced himself that the town must in the end be stormed, and so given up to fire and sword. He resolved therefore to recommend, sad

The Lion of Flanders

as it was, the one only possible means of safety; and, turning to his fellow-deans, thus slowly spoke:

"Comrades, our need is urgent! Our city, the flower of Flanders, has been traitorously sold over our heads, or rather behind our backs; and now our only safety is in prudence. However great the violence you must do to your noblest feelings, I pray you well to weigh that fact. As there is glory for the hero who pours out his blood for the rights of his fellows, even so there is bitter blame for the rash and reckless citizen who brings danger upon his country without need or without hope. Here, now, no resistance can avail us aught—"

"What? what?" interrupted impetuously Jan Breydel; "no resistance can avail us? What words are those? and what spirit are they of?"

"Even of the spirit of prudence and true patriotism," answered Deconinck. "We, as beseems good Flemings, can well die sword in hand upon the smoking ruins of our city—can fall with a shout of joy amid the bleeding corpses of our friends and fellows. We are men; but our wives, our children! —can we expose them, helpless and deserted, to the excited passions of our enemies?—to their vengeance, and worse still? No! courage has been given to man, that he may protect the defenseless ones of his kind. We must surrender!"

At this word the bystanders started, as though a thunderbolt had fallen amid them; and from every side looks of anger and suspicion were directed against the Dean. To some, his advice sounded even like treason; all regarded it as an insult. One universal cry of astonishment burst from their lips:

"Surrender? We?"

Deconinck met with unaltered mien their indignant looks, and calmly replied:

"Yes, fellow-citizens; however much it may afflict your free hearts, it is the only way that remains to save our city from destruction."

Jan Breydel, meanwhile, had listened to the words of the Dean in a very fever of impatience; and now, seeing that many of their fellows were wavering, and half-inclined to consent to a surrender, his indignation burst all bounds.

"The first of you," he passionately exclaimed, "that breathes a word of surrender, I will lay a corpse at my feet. Welcome a glorious death upon the body of a foe rather than life with dishonor! Think you that I and my Butchers are afraid? Look at them yonder, with their arms bared for the fight! How bravely their hearts beat, and how they long to be at their day's work! And shall I talk to them of surrender? They would not understand the word. I tell you, we will hold our own; and he whose heart fails him may keep house with the women and children. The hand that would open yon gates shall never be lifted again; this arm shall do justice on the coward!"

The Lion of Flanders

Fuming with rage, he hastened off to his Guildsmen; and pacing up and down in front of their ranks:

"Surrender! We surrender!" he exclaimed again and again, in a tone of mingled anger and contempt; and at last, in reply to the anxious questions of his comrades, he thus broke forth:

"Heaven have mercy on us, my men! My blood is ready to boil over at the thought; it is an insult —an intolerable insult! Yes; the Clothworkers would have us surrender our good town to the French villains yonder; but be true to me, my brothers, and we will die like Flemings! Let us say to ourselves, 'The ground we are treading upon has often been red with the blood of our fathers, and it shall be red with our own—with our own heart's blood—and that of the accursed foreigner!' Let the coward that hath no stomach for the fight depart; but he that will cast in his lot with us, let him cry, 'Liberty or death!'"

As he ceased to speak, one universal shout arose from the band of the Butchers, and the terrible word "death!" three times repeated, reverberated through their ranks like a hollow echo from the abyss. "Liberty or death!" was the cry which issued from seven hundred throats; and the oath by which they bound themselves to live or die together was mingled with the grinding sound of their axes as they whetted them upon their steels.

The Lion of Flanders

Meanwhile, the assembly of the Deans, or at least the greater part of them, convinced by the reasoning of Deconinck, and terrified at the sight of the engines of assault which now stood ready within the hostile lines, were disposed to submit to necessity, and to open negotiations with the enemy with a view to the surrender of the town; but Breydel, restless and suspicious, soon perceived their intentions. Raging like a wounded lion, and with words half-choked with fury, he rushed up to Deconinck; while his Butchers, easily comprehending the cause of his sudden movement, broke their ranks, and followed him in wild disorder.

"Slay! slay!" was the savage outcry; "death to the traitor! death to Deconinck!"

Not small was the peril in which the Dean of the Clothworkers now stood. Nevertheless, he saw the furious crowd approach without the slightest mark of terror upon his countenance; its expression, indeed, was rather that of deep compassion. With folded arms he coolly awaited the onset of the Butchers, while ever from out that raging throng arose the terrible cry, "Death to the traitor!"— already was the ax close to the great leader's head, and still he kept his ground unmoved, like some giant oak which defies the utmost violence of the storm. From the bastion on which he was standing he tranquilly looked down upon the frantic multi-

The Lion of Flanders

tude, as a ruler might look from his judgment-seat upon his people.

Suddenly a remarkable change came over the countenance of Breydel; he seemed as though paralyzed, and his ax fell powerless at his side. Seized with an irresistible admiration of the courage of the man whose counsels he abhorred, he thrust aside the foremost of the Guildsmen, whose ax was already raised over the head of the Dean, and that so roughly that the stalwart butcher measured his length along the ramparts.

"Hold, my men! hold!" he exclaimed in a voice of thunder, while at the same time he placed himself in front of the Dean; and swinging his heavy ax around him, he warded off the attacks of his comrades. The latter, perceiving the intentions of their chief, immediately lowered their arms, and with threatening murmurs awaited the event.

Meanwhile a fresh incident occurred, which greatly assisted Breydel in quelling the tumult which he had raised, by drawing off the attention of the excited crowd to another quarter. A herald from the French lines made his appearance at the foot of the rampart on which the occurrences just narrated were taking place, and with the usual forms made proclamation as follows:

"In the name of our mighty prince, Philip of France, you, rebellious subjects, are summoned by my general, De Chatillon, to surrender this city to

The Lion of Flanders

his mercy; and you are warned that, if within the space of one-quarter of an hour you have not answered to this summons, the force of the storming-engines shall overthrow your walls, and everything shall be destroyed with fire and sword."

As soon as this summons was heard, the eyes of all were turned with one accord on Deconinck, as if seeking counsel of him on whom they had so lately glared in murderous rage. Breydel himself looked at his friend with an inquiring gaze; but all in vain. Neither to him nor to the rest did the Dean give utterance to a single word; he stood looking on in silence, and with an air of unconcern, as though in no wise personally interested in what was passing around him.

"Well, Deconinck, what is your advice?" asked Breydel, at length.

"That we surrender," calmly replied the Clothworker.

At this the Butchers began to give signs of another outburst; but a commanding gesture from their Dean speedily restored them to order and Breydel resumed:

"What, then, do you really feel so sure that, with all our efforts, we can not hold out against the foe—that no courage, no resolution can save us? Oh, that I should see this day!"

And as he thus spoke, the deep grief of his heart plainly displayed itself upon his features. Even

The Lion of Flanders

as his eyes had lighted up with ardor for the fight, so now was their fury quenched and his countenance darkened.

At last Deconinck, raising his voice so as to be heard by all around him, addressed them thus:

"Bear witness, all of you, that in what I advise I have no other motive than true and honest love of my country. For the sake of my native city, I have exposed myself to your mad fury; for that same sake I am ready to die upon the scaffold that our enemies shall raise for me. I deem it my sacred duty to save this pearl of Flanders; cry me down as a traitor, and heap curses upon my name if you will—nothing shall turn me aside from my noble purpose. For the last time I repeat it, our duty now is to surrender."

During this address Breydel's countenance had exhibited, to an attentive observer, an incessant play of passion; wrath, indignation, sadness seemed in turns to move him. The convulsive twitching of his stalwart limbs told plainly of the storm which raged within, and the struggle which it cost him to restrain it; and now, with the word "surrender" sounding once again in his ear, as though struck by a sentence of death, he stood appalled, motionless, and silent.

The Butchers and the other Guildsmen turned their eyes upon one and the other of the two leaders, and stood waiting in solemn silence for what should happen.

"Master Breydel," cried Deconinck at length, "as you would not have the destruction of us all upon your soul, consent to my proposal. Yonder comes back the French herald; the time has already expired."

Suddenly, as if awakening from a stupor, the chief of the Butchers replied in a mournful and faltering voice:

"And must it be so, master? Well, let it be, then, as you say—let us surrender."

And as he spoke, he grasped the hand of his friend and pressed it with deep emotion, while tears of intense suffering filled his eyes, and a heavy groan burst from his bosom. The two Deans regarded each other with one of those looks in which the soul speaks from its inmost depths. At that moment they fully understood each other, and a close embrace testified to every beholder the sincerity of their reconciliation.

There stood the two greatest men of Bruges, the representatives respectively of her wisdom and her valor, clasped in each other's arms, heart against heart beating high with mutual admiration.

"Oh, my valiant brother!" cried Deconinck; "oh, great and generous soul! Hard, I see, indeed, has been the struggle; but the victory is yours; the greatest of victories, even that over yourself!"

The Lion of Flanders

At the sight of this moving spectacle, a cry of joy ran through the ranks, and the last spark of angry feeling was extinguished in the bosoms of the valiant Flemings. At Deconinck's command, the trumpeter of the Clothworkers called aloud to the French herald:

"Does your general grant to our spokesman his safe conduct to come and to return?"

"He gives full and free safe conduct, upon his faith and honor, according to the custom of war," was the reply.

Upon this assurance the portcullis was raised, the drawbridge lowered, and two of the citizens issued from the gate. One of them was Deconinck; the other the herald of the Guilds. On reaching the French lines, they were immediately introduced into the tent of De Chatillon, when the Dean of the Clothworkers advanced toward the general, and with a firm countenance thus addressed him:

"Messire de Chatillon, the citizens of Bruges give you to know, by me their delegate and spokesman, that, in order to avoid useless bloodshed, they have resolved to surrender to you the city. Nevertheless, since it is a noble and honorable feeling that leads them to proffer their submission, they can make it only on the following conditions: first, that the costs of his majesty's late entry be not levied by a new impost upon the commons; secondly, that the present magistrates be displaced from their offices; and, lastly, that no one be prosecuted or disturbed on account of any part he may have taken in these present troubles, by what name soever the same may be called. Be pleased to inform me whether you assent to these terms."

"What!" exclaimed the governor, his countenance overcast with displeasure; "what manner of talk is this? How dare you speak to me of conditions, when I have only to bring up my engines to your walls and batter them down, without hindrance or delay?"

"That is very possible," replied Deconinck firmly; "but I tell you, nevertheless—and do you give heed to my words—that our city ditch shall be filled with the dead bodies of your people, before a single Frenchman shall plant his foot upon our walls. We, too, are not unprovided with implements of war; and they that have read our chronicles have not now to learn that the men of Bruges know how to die for their country."

"Yes, yes, I know well that stiff-necked obstinacy which is the characteristic of all your race; but what care I for that? The courage of my men knows no obstacles; your city must surrender at discretion."

To say the truth, the sight of that warlike multitude in armed array upon the walls had filled De Chatillon with serious apprehensions as to the issue of the coming fight. Knowing as he did the indomitable spirit of the men of Bruges, and the probability of a desperate resistance, prudence strongly dictated to him the desirableness of gaining possession of the city, if possible, without a struggle. He was not a little rejoiced, therefore, when the arrival of Deconinck gave him hopes of the peaceful accomplishment of his wishes. On the other hand, the conditions proposed were by no means to his taste. He might, to be sure, at once accept them under a mental reservation, and afterward invent some pretext for evading them; but he had a supreme mistrust of the Dean of the Clothworkers, Deconinck, and greatly doubted whether he could safely rely upon what he had said. He resolved, therefore, to put his words to the test, and see whether it really was true, as he asserted, that the men of Bruges were determined to resist to the death rather than surrender at discretion; accordingly, in a loud voice he gave the signal for advancing the engines to the assault.

But Deconinck, like a skilful player, had closely watched the countenance of his adversary. It had not escaped his penetration that the resolute air of the French general was merely assumed, and that in reality he would gladly avoid the necessity of putting his threats into execution. Once convinced of this, he adhered firmly to the conditions he had proposed; while he regarded with apparent indifference the hostile preparations which were being made around him.

The cool self-possession of the Fleming was too much for De Chatillon. He was now convinced that the men of Bruges stood in no fear of him, and that they would defend their city to the very last extremity. Unwilling, therefore, to stake all upon this isolated point of the game, he at last condescended to enter into a negotiation; and, after some discussion, it was finally agreed that the magistrates should remain in office, while the other two points were conceded to the Flemings. The governor, on his part, expressly stipulated for the right of occupying the city with his troops, in whatever numbers he might think fit.

And now, the terms of capitulation having been regularly engrossed, and the instrument mutually executed with all formality, the envoys returned to the town. The conditions agreed upon were made known to the citizens by proclamations from street to street, and half an hour afterward the French force made their triumphant entry with banners and trumpets; while the Guildsmen, with their hearts full at once of sorrow and of wrath, departed each to his home, and the magistrates and Lilyards issued forth from the castle. A few hours more, and to a superficial observer peace reigned through the whole city.

The Lion of Flanders

CHAPTER II

BRUGES being now entirely at the mercy of the French party, De Chatillon began to think seriously of executing the several commissions with which he had been charged; and the first that occurred to him was the securing, according to the queen's desire, of the person of the young Matilda de Bethune. It might seem, indeed, as though nothing need stand in the way of his immediately carrying out this design, seeing that the city was occupied by his troops in overpowering force; nevertheless, a motive of policy restrained him for a time. He was anxious, in the first instance, to establish his dominion on a firm and permament basis; and this he conceived could be effected only by breaking once for all the power of the Guilds, and erecting a strong citadel in order to overawe the town; this accomplished, he was prepared without further delay to seize Matilda and send her off to France.

The arrival and entry of the French troops had filled Adolf of Nieuwland with the most serious apprehensions for his young charge, now in the midst of her enemies, and totally without defense; for though Deconinck, indeed, visited her daily, and watched over her without intermission, yet this was not enough to set at ease the mind of the young knight. After the lapse of some weeks, however, finding that in fact no molestation was offered to the fair girl, he began to think that the French had either forgotten her existence altogether, or else that they had ceased to have any hostile designs against her. Meanwhile his vigorous constitution, and the skilful care of his physician, had done their work; the color returned to his cheeks, and activity to his limbs; but not so peace and joy to his breast, in which was now opened, in truth, a fresh source of anxiety and sadness. Day by day it was his grief to behold the daughter of his prince and benefactor grow paler and paler; wasted and sickly, like a blighted flower, Matilda pined away in sorrow and anguish of heart. And he who owed his life to her tender and generous care could do nothing to help her, nothing to comfort her! Neither kind attention nor pleasant words would bring a smile upon the countenance of the sorrowing maiden; sighs and tears were the only utterance of her heart; sighs and tears for her father's unhappy lot, of whom no word of tidings reached her, and for the fate of the other dear prisoners, whom now she thought to see again no more. Adolf's endeavors to mitigate her grief were inces-

The Lion of Flanders

sant and fruitless; in vain he sought out for her the oldest legends and the newest toys; in vain he sang to his harp of the Lion's deeds of valor; nothing could rouse her from her depression, or dispel her dark forebodings. Gentle, indeed, she was, affectionate and grateful; but without life, without interest in aught around her. Even her favorite bird sat apart neglected, with dull, spiritless eye and drooping wing.

Some weeks had now passed since Adolf's complete recovery, when one day with sauntering steps he passed the city gates, and struck into a narrow pathway across the fields, which led him on in dreamy mood toward the little hamlet of Sevecote. The sun was fast sinking toward the horizon, and the western sky was already glowing with the tints of evening. With head bowed down, and full of bitter thought, Adolf walked on, following the path mechanically, and taking little heed whither he was going. A tear glistened from beneath his eyelids, and many a heavy sigh broke from his bosom. A thousand times had he strained his imagination to find some means of alleviating the young Matilda's lot, and as often had he fallen back into despair, so sad and hopeless did it appear. And, for himself, what wretchedness, what shame! each day, and all day long, to watch her pining away with sorrow, and sinking into an early grave, and thus to stand by the while with folded arms,

The Lion of Flanders

powerless alike to help, to counsel, or to console!
He was now at some distance from the city.
Wearied more with the burden of his sadness than
with the length of the way, he seated himself upon
a bank, and still allowed his thoughts to drift along
upon the drowsy current of his reverie. As he sat
there, with his eyes bent upon the ground, he suddenly
became aware that he was no longer alone—
a stranger stood before him.

The unknown was dressed in a friar's frock of
brown woolen, with a wide and deep hood; a long
gray beard hung down upon his breast, and his
bright black eyes were overhung by shaggy brows.
His complexion was deeply bronzed; his features
hard and strongly marked; his forehead scarred,
and deeply furrowed with wrinkles. Like some
wayworn traveler, he dragged his weary steps to
the spot where Adolf sat, and for an instant a
gleam of satisfaction seemed to light up his features,
as though he recognized one whom he was
glad to meet. This, however, was but for a moment;
the grave and cold expression, whether real
or worn as a mask, with which he had first regarded
the youth, instantaneously returned.

Adolf, aware of the friar's presence only when
the latter stood close before him, immediately rose
from his seat, and greeted the stranger in words of
courtesy. But the melancholy tenor of his thoughts
had communicated a tone of sadness to his voice;

and, to say the truth, he had to put some violence on himself to speak at all.

"Noble sir," responded the friar, "a long day's journey has wearied me, and the pleasantness of the spot which you have chosen tempts me to loiter a while to snatch a few moments' rest; but I pray you let me not disturb you."

So saying he threw himself upon the grass; and, motioning with his hand, invited Adolf to do the like: who thereupon, moved either by respect for the friar's sacred character, or by some secret wish to enter into conversation with him, resumed at once his former seat, and thus found himself side by side with the stranger.

Something there was in the strange priest's voice which had a familiar sound to Adolf's ear, and he endeavored to recollect when and where and under what circumstances he had heard it; but as all his efforts failed, he was at last obliged to dismiss the notion as a groundless fancy.

A short pause ensued, during which the friar regarded the young knight with many an anxious and inquiring glance; at length, however, he proceeded to open a conversation.

"Noble sir," he commenced, "it is now long since I left Flanders; and I should be greatly obliged by any information you could give me concerning the present state of things in our good city of Bruges. I pray you be not offended at my boldness."

The Lion of Flanders

"How could I be offended, father?" answered Adolf. "It will be a pleasure to me to serve you in any way I can. Things go ill enough, truly, in our good city of Bruges; the French are now our masters there!"

"That seems to please you but indifferently, noble sir. Nevertheless, I had understood that most of the nobles had renounced allegiance to their lawful Count, and done homage to the stranger."

"Alas! that is but too true, father. Our unfortunate Count Guy has been deserted by very many of his subjects; and still more of them there are who have tarnished the glory of their ancient name by base submission. Yet are there left some in whose veins the Flemish blood runs pure; still there are brave and loyal hearts, that have not given themselves up to the stranger."

At these words an expression of the liveliest satisfaction passed over the features of the friar. With more experience of life, Adolf might haply have perceived something both forced and feigned in the speech and countenance of his companion, betraying to a keen observer that he was playing a part which was not his own.

"Your sentiments, noble sir," he replied, "do you much honor. It is ever a true joy to me to meet with one of those generous souls who have not ceased lovingly to remember our old Count Guy in this his sad estate. God reward you for your loyalty!"

"Oh, father," cried Adolf, "would that you could look into the most secret depths of my heart, that so you might know the love I bear to our old lord—now, alas! so helpless—and to all his ancient house. I swear to you, father, that the happiest moment of my life would be that in which I might pour out for them the last drop of my blood."

The friar had good experience of men's hearts, and of their words and faces too; he could well see that there was no feigning in the young knight, and that Adolf was in very truth deeply attached to Count Guy, and devoted to his cause. After some reflection, he resumed:

"Then, if I should one day give you the opportunity of making good what you have just averred, you would not hold back; but would be ready, like a man and a true knight, to defy all danger."

"I pray you, father," cried Adolf, in a tone of supplication, "I pray you, doubt not either of my faith or of my courage. Speak now quickly; for your silence tortures me."

"Listen then—but calmly. To Guy of Flanders and to his illustrious house I am bound by the tie of countless benefits; and I have resolved, to the utmost of my power, to pay them in this their hour of need the debt of gratitude which I owe

The Lion of Flanders

them. With this resolve I have been traveling through France; and there, sometimes by money, sometimes under color of my priestly character, have found means to visit all the noble prisoners. I have carried to the father the greeting of the son, and brought back to the son the blessing of the father; yes, and I have even sighed and wept with poor Philippa in the dungeons of the Louvre. Thus have I mitigated their sufferings, and bridged over for a moment the gulf that separates them from each other. Many a time have I spent the night in long and toilsome journeys; many a time have I been repulsed with scorn: but little recked I of all this, if thereby I could serve my lawful princes in the time of their distress. A tear of joy which my arrival might evoke, a word of thanks which might greet me on my departure, was to me a reward against which all the gold in Flanders would have weighed as nothing."

"Blessings upon you, generous priest!" cried Adolf, "and a blessed reward shall one day be yours! But tell me, I pray you, how is it with Lord Robert?"

"Let me proceed, and you shall soon hear more of him. He lies in a darksome tower, at Bourges, in the land of Berri. Worse, however, his lot might be; for he is free from chains and fetters. The old castellan, under whose charge he is, long ago fought in the Sicilian wars under the banner of the Black Lion; and he is now a friend rather than a jailer to our prince."

Adolf listened with intense eagerness; and many a time were exclamations of heartfelt joy upon his lips. He restrained himself, however; and the friar meanwhile proceeded:

"His imprisonment would thus be tolerable enough, had he only himself to think of; but he is a father, and has a father's heart, and it is that which suffers most. His daughter is left behind in Flanders; and he fears lest the spiteful and cruel Queen Joanna should persecute his child, perhaps even to death. This dreadful thought will not suffer him to rest, and his prison is become to him a very pit of despair; his soul is filled with the bitterest anguish, and each day of his life is a day of torment."

Adolf was about to give vent to his compassion; and Matilda's name was already upon his lips, when a sign from the friar prevented him from speaking.

"Weigh well now," resumed the stranger in a solemn tone, "whether you in very truth are ready to risk your life for the Lion, your liege lord. The castellan of Bourges is ready to set him free for a season, upon his knightly word to render himself on the appointed day; but he must find some faithful and loving subject to take his place the while."

The Lion of Flanders

The young knight seized the priest's hands, and kissed them with tears in his eyes.

"Oh, happy hour!" he cried; "and shall it be mine to procure this consolation for Matilda? Shall she once more behold her father, and that by my assistance? How does my heart beat with gladness! Father, you see before you the happiest man upon earth. You can not tell what delight, what unmixed happiness, your words have given me. I will fly to my prison on the wings of joy! More precious to me than gold shall be the iron bars of my dungeon. Oh, Matilda! would that the winds could speed to you this rapturous news!"

Without interrupting the knight's transport, the friar now rose from his seat; Adolf followed his example, and they walked on together slowly toward the city.

"Noble sir," said the priest again, "I can not but admire the generosity of your spirit; but though I doubt not of your courage, think you, have you well weighed the risk you are about to run? The deception once discovered, the reward of your devotedness is death."

"Is death, then, a word to frighten a Flemish knight?" answered Adolf; "no, nothing shall keep me back. Did you but know how, day and night, for these six months past, I have had no other thought but to devise means how I might serve the House of Flanders at the peril of my life, you would hardly speak to me of danger or of fear. Even now, when first you saw me sitting sorrowfully beside the path, was I earnestly praying God to show me how I might best accomplish the object nearest to my heart; and He has answered me by you His priest."

"We must depart this very night, lest our secret be discovered," rejoined the friar.

"The sooner the better; in thought I am already at Bourges with the Lion of Flanders, my lord and prince."

"But remember, sir knight, you are somewhat young for the part you have to play. It may be that in feature you are not unlike to Robert de Bethune; but the difference of age is much too great. That, however, shall be no hindrance to us; in a few moments my art shall make up the deficiency in years."

"What mean you, father? how can you make me older than I am?"

"That indeed I can not do; but I can change your face, so that the very mother who bore you should not recognize you. This I can do by means of herbs, of which I have learned to know the virtues; think not that any unlawful art hath aught to do therewith. But, noble sir, we are now hard upon the city; can you tell me whereabout resides one Adolf of Nieuwland?"

"Adolf of Nieuwland!" exclaimed the knight;

"it is with him you are now conversing. *I* am Adolf of Nieuwland."

Great seemed the friar's surprise; he stopped, turned full upon Adolf, and regarded him with well-feigned astonishment.

"What! you Adolf of Nieuwland! Then it is in your house that the lady Matilda de Bethune now is?"

"That honor has fallen to its lot," answered Adolf. "Your news, father, will bring it consolation; and not before it was wanted; for Matilda's life is fast wasting away with sorrow."

"Here, then, is a letter from her father, which I commit to your charge to place in her hands; for I can well perceive that it will be to you no trifling satisfaction to be the bearer of such happy tidings."

With these words he drew from underneath his frock a parchment secured with a seal and silken cord, and handed it to the knight, who received it in silence and with deep emotion. Already he seemed to be in Matilda's presence, and to have a foretaste of the joy which her delight would give him. The friar's pace was now too slow for him; so urgent was his impatience that he always found himself a step or two in advance of his companion.

Once within the city, they soon stood before Adolf's house; and here the priest took a general but attentive survey both of it and of all the neigh-

The Lion of Flanders

boring buildings, as though fixing them in his memory for future recognition. At last he said:

"Sir Adolf, I must now bid you farewell; ere the day close I will be here again; probably it may be somewhat late; meanwhile, make all the necessary preparations for your journey."

"Will you not, then, allow me to present you to the lady? Moreover, you are weary; I pray you do me the honor of taking refreshment and repose beneath my roof."

"I thank you, sir; my duty as a priest calls me elsewhere; at ten o'clock I will see you again. God have you in His holy keeping!"

And with this greeting he parted from the astonished knight, and turned into the Wool street, whence he speedily vanished into Deconinck's house.

Transported with joy at his unexpected good fortune, which had come upon him like a golden dream, Adolf knocked with the greatest impatience at his door. His dear master's letter seemed to glow between his fingers; and as soon as the door was opened, he rushed past the servant and along the corridor like one mad.

"Where is the Lady Matilda?" he inquired, in a tone which demanded speedy answer:

"In the front room," replied the servant.

He hurried upstairs, and hastily opened the door of the chamber.

The Lion of Flanders

"Dry your tears, Lady Matilda," he cried. "No more sadness and sorrow! Light is breaking in upon our darkness!"

As Adolf entered, the young Countess was sitting disconsolately in the window, and from time to time sighing heavily. She looked at the knight for some moments with a countenance on which was depicted wonder, mingled with doubt bordering on incredulity.

"What mean you?" she cried at last; "what light can visit such darkness as mine?"

"Nay, but so it is, noble lady; a better lot awaits you. See, here is a letter: does not the throbbing of your heart already tell you from whose hand it comes?"

More he would have said; but, even as he spoke, Matilda sprang from her seat, and snatched the letter from his hand. Her bosom heaving, her cheeks glowing with a color that had long been a stranger to them, and tears of joy streaming down her cheeks, she broke the seal and tore off the silken cord; and thrice had her eyes wandered over the writing on the parchment ere she seemed to catch its purport. Then, at last, she understood it too well; unhappy maiden! her tears ceased not to flow, but the cause of them was changed; they were no longer tears of joy, but of new and bitter sorrow.

"Sir Adolf," at last she said, in a tone of deepest

The Lion of Flanders

suffering, "your joy adds torture to my grief. What was it you said? light! Read, and weep with me for my unhappy father."

The knight took the letter from Matilda's hands, and, as he read it, his countenance fell. For a moment he feared that the priest had dealt treacherously by him, and had made him the bearer of evil tidings; no sooner, however, had he fully possessed himself of the contents of the letter than his suspicions vanished; but recollecting his incautious exclamations, he was seized with self-reproach, and remained silent and lost in thought. And now compassion filled Matilda's breast; seeing him musing so sadly, with his eyes fixed mournfully upon the letter, she repented of her hasty words, and approached him where he stood, while a smile gleamed through her tears.

"Forgive me, Sir Adolf," she said; "be not thus troubled. Think not that I am angry with you for having raised my hopes too high; full well I know the fervor of your zeal for all that touches me and mine. Believe me, Adolf, I am not ungrateful for your generous self-devotion."

"Princely lady," he exclaimed, "I have not raised your hopes too high. I repeat, there is light for you, and my joy is not in vain. All that the letter tells you was known to me already; but it was not for that I so rejoiced. Dry your tears, lady, again I say, and cease your mourning; for soon your father shall press you to his heart."

"What!" cried Matilda, "can it indeed be true? Shall I, then, see my father, and speak to him? But why torture me thus? why talk to me in riddles? Oh Adolf! speak, I pray you, and free my heart from doubt."

A slight shade of vexation passed across the young knight's countenance. Gladly would he have given her the explanation that she sought; but his generous spirit could not bear to publish his own deserts. He answered therefore, in an earnest tone:

"I pray you, illustrious lady, take not my silence amiss. Be assured that you shall in truth see my lord, your father; that you shall hear his beloved voice, receive his warm embrace; and that too, on the soil of our own dear Flanders. More to tell you is not in my power."

But the young maiden was not to be thus put off. A double feeling—her woman's curiosity and a lingering doubt—alike impelled her not to rest till she had discovered the solution of the enigma. Evidently not well pleased, she began again:

"But do, Sir Adolf—do tell me what this is which you would fain conceal from me. You surely do not rate my discretion so low as to suppose that I shall betray your secret—I that have so much at stake?'

The Lion of Flanders

"I pray you, spare me, lady?" he replied: "it is impossible. I must not, I can not tell you more."

With each refusal or evasion of the knight, Matilda's curiosity grew more and more. Again and again she pressed him to disclose his secret; but all in vain. To curiosity succeeded impatience, to impatience, irritation; till at last she lost all self-command, and burst into a flood of tears, like a child that can not have its way.

Adolf could now resist no longer; he resolved to tell her all, however much it might cost him to be the herald of his own self-sacrifice. Matilda soon read her victory in his countenance, and drawing more closely to him, regarded him with a smile of pleasure, while he thus addressed her:

"Listen, then, lady, since it must be so, and hear in how wonderful a manner this letter and these joyful tidings reached me. I had wandered out toward Sevecote, and was sitting upon a bank deep in thought, fervently beseeching Heaven to have mercy upon my lawful but unhappy lord. Suddenly, happening to raise my head, to my surprise I saw before me a stranger priest. In the instant it seemed to me that my prayer had been heard, and that some consolation was at hand, of which this stranger was to be the minister. And so it was, lady; for it was from his hand that I received the letter, and from his mouth the happy news. Your noble father has obtained from a generous keeper the boon of a few days' liberty; but on condition that another knight takes his place in prison."

"Oh, joy!" exclaimed Matilda; "I shall see him! I shall speak with him! Ah, my father! how has my heart longed for one kiss from your lips! O Adolf, I am beside myself with joy! How sweet are your words, my brother! But who will be willing to take my father's place?"

"The man is already found," was the brief reply.

"The blessings of our Lord be upon him! How noble a spirit must his be who can thus devote himself for my father's safety! But tell me, now, who is this generous knight? Let me know his name, that I may ever think of it with love and gratitude; that is the least return I can make to one who thus restores me to life at the instant peril of his own."

For a moment Adolf hesitated; the words would not pass his lips. At last, bending one knee to the ground, with a hasty effort he exclaimed:

"Who else, lady, could it be than your servant Adolf?"

Her eyes were now fastened upon him with an expression of deep emotion; then, raising him from the ground, she said:

"Adolf, my good brother, how shall we be ever able to repay your self-devotion? Well do I know all that you have done to soften my hard lot. Have I not seen that my well-being has been the

The Lion of Flanders

one constant subject of your thoughts? And now you are about to take my father's place within his dungeon-walls—to risk your very life for him and me! Ungracious that I have been—thankless as I must have seemed—how have I deserved so much?"

An unusual fire sparkled in the eyes of the young knight, and communicated itself to his speech. In the exultation of his feelings he exclaimed:

"Does not the ancient blood of the Counts of Flanders flow within your veins? Are you not the beloved daughter of the Lion—of him who is the glory of our common country, the benefactor to whom I can never sufficiently express my gratitude? My blood, my life, are devoted to your illustrious house; and all that the Lion of Flanders loves is sacred to me."

While Matilda was still regarding him with astonishment, a servant came to announce the arrival of the stranger priest. Immediately after, the father himself entered the apartment.

"Hail to thee, illustrious daughter of the Lion our lord!" he began, making a lowly reverence, and at the same time throwing back his cowl.

The sound of his voice instantly attracted Matilda's attention. She eyed him with a close scrutiny, and anxiously taxed her memory to recall the name of one whose accents sounded so familiar to her ear. Suddenly she seized him by the hand,

and with eyes flashing with delight passionately exclaimed:

"Heavens! I see before me my father's bosom friend! I thought that all besides Sir Adolf here had deserted us; but now, thanks be to God, He has sent me a second protector!"

Diederik die Vos stood aghast; his art had failed before a woman's eye. With an air of something like chagrin, he threw off his beard, and now stood in his own character before his youthful friends; then turning to Matilda:

"In truth, lady," he exclaimed, "I must allow that your sight is sharp and piercing; I may now as well resume my natural voice. I had rather, indeed, have remained unrecognized; for the disguise which you have penetrated is of the last necessity for my noble master's weal. I pray you, therefore, be careful how you breathe a hint of who I really am; it might cost me my life, and what is of greater moment, defeat the mission I have in hand. Your countenance, lady, witnesses to the sufferings of your heart; but if our hopes do not deceive us, your sorrow will soon be over. Nevertheless, should your father's captivity be even yet prolonged, we must not cease to put our trust in the justice of Heaven. Meanwhile, I have seen the Lord Robert, and conversed with him. His lot is much alleviated by the courtesy of the castellan in whose charge he is; for the present, therefore, your heart may be at ease regarding him."

"But tell me all he said, Sir Diederik; describe his prison to me, and how he occupies his time; that I may have the pleasure of picturing it all to myself, since as yet I can not see him."

Thereupon Diederik began a minute description of the castle of Bourges; and related circumstantially to the lady all that he thought could interest her; answering with ready sympathy her most trivial questions, and comforting her with the hope of a happier future. Adolf meanwhile had left the room, to inform his sister of the journey he was about to undertake, and to give directions for horse and armor to be in readiness. He had also charged a confidential servant to inform Deconinck and Breydel of his absence, that they might keep closer watch over their young princess; a precaution, however, which was not, in fact, necessary; since Diederik die Vos had already concerted measures with them to that end.

As soon as the young knight returned, Diederik rose from his seat; "Now, Sir Adolf," said he, "we have not much time to spare; allow me, therefore, before we set out, to throw a little more age into your countenance. Sit down, and let me have my own way, and fear not; I shall do nothing that will harm you."

The Lion of Flanders

Adolf accordingly took a seat in front of Diederik, and leaned his head backward. Matilda, quite at a loss to understand the scene before her, looked on in astonishment; with curious eye she followed Diederik's fingers, as he traced many a deep line on Adolf's youthful visage, and darkened its complexion. Her astonishment increased, as at every stroke of the pencil Adolf's countenance gradually changed its expression, and assumed something that reminded her of her father's features. At last the work was completed, and Diederik desired his patient to stand up and show himself.

"There, it is done," said he; "you are as like the Lord Robert now as if the same mother had borne you; and if I did not know the work of my own hands, I should make my obeisance to you as to the noble Lion in person."

As for Matilda, she could only look from one to the other in speechless wonder, hardly able to believe her eyes, so like her father did Adolf stand before her.

"Sir Adolf," now proceeded Diederik, "if you would secure success to your generous enterprise, we shall do well to start without delay, lest perchance, should an enemy or an unfaithful servant see you in your present guise, you not only risk your life, but risk it fruitlessly."

The reasonableness of this caution was obvious,

The Lion of Flanders

and the young knight immediately assented. "Farewell, noble lady!" he exclaimed, "farewell! Think sometimes of your servant Adolf."

But what words can describe the maiden's emotion as she heard these few and simple words? Hitherto she had looked only at the bright side of Adolf's chivalrous undertaking; she was once again to behold her beloved father! But now at once the thought flashed upon her, that this happiness was to be purchased by the absence, perhaps the loss of her good brother—for so she called the knight. A pang shot through her heart; but she was sufficiently mistress of herself to suppress her tears; and loosening the green veil, which formed a portion of her headdress:

"Take this," she said, "from the hands of your grateful sister; let it serve to remind you of her who will never forget your noble deed; it is my own favorite color."

The knight received the pledge on bended knee, and with a look which bespoke his thanks, he pressed it to his lips.

"Lady," he said, "so great a reward exceeds my poor deserts; but the day may come when it shall be given me to pour out my blood for the House of Flanders, and to show myself not unworthy of your gracious favor."

"Come, a truce to compliments," cried Diederik; "it is time we were gone."

The Lion of Flanders

With pain the youth and maiden heard the summons. Each spoke but one word more:

"Farewell, Matilda!"

"Farewell, Adolf!"

The two knights hurried away; and passing out into the courtyard, mounted with all despatch. A few moments later and the streets of Bruges resounded with the hasty tramp of two horses, the last echo of which was heard under the gate toward Ghent.

The Lion of Flanders

CHAPTER III

In the year 1280 a terrible conflagration had caused the ruin of the old town hall in the market-place of Bruges; the wooden tower with which it was surrounded had perished in the flames; and all the charters and muniments of the city together with it. But in the lower part of the building some massive walls had resisted the general destruction, and some few chambers were still left standing, which were now used as a guardhouse. At present these half-ruined apartments were the chosen rendezvous of the French garrison; and there they whiled away their time in play and revelry.

A few days after Adolf of Nieuwland's departure, eight of these foreign mercenaries found themselves together in one of the innermost recesses of the ruin. A large lamp of coarse earthenware shed its yellow rays upon their swarthy faces, while a thick smoke curled upward from its flame, and hung sullenly in the groinings of the vault. The walls still retained traces of decorative painting; an image of Our Lady, with the hands broken off, and the features defaced by time or violence, stood at one end of the chamber. At a heavy oaken table sat four soldiers, intent upon the dice with which they were playing; others stood by, looking on and following with interest the chances of the game. It was evident, however, that some other game was afoot than that in which these men were for the moment engaged; for, with helmets upon their heads and swords at their belts, they had all the appearance of being prepared for action.

Soon one of the players rose from the table, at the same time angrily dashing down the dice upon it. "That old Breton's hands are not clean!" he exclaimed; "else how should I lose fifty times running? A plague on the dice! I'll have done with them."

"He is afraid to go on," cried the winner, with a provoking air of triumph. "What the fiend, Jehan! surely you are never cleaned out yet, man! Is that the fashion in which you face the enemy?"

"Try once more, Jehan," said another; "the luck can't go one way forever."

The soldier addressed as Jehan stood for some moments as if in doubt whether to try his luck again or not. At last, passing his hand within his shirt of mail, he drew from under it his last reserve, a necklace of fine pearls with richly wrought clasps of gold.

"There," he exclaimed, holding it out so that

all might see, "I will stake these pearls against what you have won from me to-night. It is as fair a necklace as ever shone upon the neck of a Flemish lady! If I lose this, I have not a stiver left of the whole booty."

The Breton took the jewel into his hand, and scanned it curiously. "Well, here goes," he cried; "how many throws?"

"Two," replied Jehan; "you throw first."

The necklace lay upon the table, and over against it a heap of gold pieces. All eyes were fixed on the dice as they rolled, while the hearts of the players beat high with excitement. At the first throw, the fickle dame Fortune seemed to be taking Jehan into favor again, for he threw ten, and his adversary but five. But, while preparing to throw again, and full of hope that he might this time retrieve his losses, he suddenly observed that the Breton secretly put the dice to his mouth, and moistened one side of them. He was now immediately convinced that it was not ill luck, but foul play, that had hitherto made him the loser. He took no notice, however, merely calling to his adversary:

"Come, why don't you throw? you are afraid now, I suppose!"

"Not I," replied the Breton, as the dice rolled from his hand upon the table, "the game is not lost yet. See there, twelve!"

The Lion of Flanders

And now it was Jehan's turn; he threw only six —so with an air of joy and triumph the Breton tucked the necklace under his mail, and Jehan stood aside from the table, with bitterness and vengeance in his heart, but sufficiently master of himself to put a good face on the matter, and even, with feigned good humor, to wish the winner luck with his prize. But for all this he was not at all disposed to let his adversary off so easily. While the Breton was in conversation with another of his comrades, Jehan whispered something in the ear of those who stood next to him, and then called across the table:

"Now, comrade, as you have cleaned me out, you must give me another chance. I will set my share of this night's earnings against an equal sum; what say you?"

"Done; I'm always ready."

Jehan took the dice, and in two casts threw eighteen. The other now took them up, and seemed, talking all the while, to hold them carelessly in his hand; the soldier who stood beside Jehan narrowly watched him; and now they distinctly noticed how the Breton again brought the dice to his lips, and by this device threw first ten, and then twelve.

"You have lost again, friend Jehan," he exclaimed. A tremendous blow of Jehan's fist was the answer. Blood gushed from the Breton's nose and mouth, and for a moment he stood stunned and motionless, so violent was the shock.

"You're a cheat, a thief!" shouted Jehan, now giving full vent to his fury; "have I not seen how you wetted the dice, and so won my money of me by false play? You shall give back all I have lost to-night, or by Heaven—"

But the Breton, now recovered from his stupor, gave him no time to finish his speech, but rushed upon him, sword in hand, with a volley of oaths and curses. Jehan, too, was ready for the fight, and swore vehemently that he would have the Breton's blood. Already the blades flashed in the lamplight, and a bloody issue seemed inevitable, when suddenly an additional actor, also in military equipment, appeared upon the scene.

The look of mingled command and reproof which the newcomer cast upon the combatants sufficiently indicated him to be one of their officers; and no sooner were they aware of his presence, than with abashed looks they slunk aside, the curses died away upon their lips, and the swords were hastily returned to the scabbards. Jehan and the Breton eyed one another in a manner which showed that they did but postpone the termination of their contest to a more convenient season; meanwhile they followed the example of the rest, and drew near their commander, who now spoke:

"Are you ready, men?" he asked.

The Lion of Flanders

"Ready, Messire de Cressines," was the answer.

"Remember, not a word spoken," proceeded the officer. "And remember, too, that the house to which this citizen will conduct you is under the especial protection of the governor; the first that lays a finger upon anything therein will bitterly repent it. Now, follow me."

The citizen alluded to, and who was about to serve as conductor to the French soldiers, was no other than Master Brakels, the same whose unpatriotic behavior had caused him to be expelled from the Guild of the Clothworkers. The whole party once in the street, Brakels took the lead, and silently led them through the darkness to the Spanish street and the mansion of the Nieuwlands. Here the soldiers ranged themselves close to the walls, on either side of the door, drawing their very breath cautiously, so fearful were they of giving the alarm. Master Brakels tapped very gently, as though on an errand which required caution. In a few moments a woman's voice from within inquired who it was that knocked at so late an hour.

"Quick, open!" replied Brakels. "I come from Master Deconinck with an urgent message for the Lady Matilda. Be quick, for there is danger in every moment's delay."

At this reply, the servant, suspecting no treason, immediately drew the bolts, and opened the door

The Lion of Flanders

with all the speed she could command; but what was her alarm when, at the heels of the Fleming, she saw that eight French soldiers had forced their way into the hall. With a scream which resounded through the house, she endeavored to make her escape; but in this she was prevented by Messire de Cressines, who, seizing her by the arm, awed her into silence by his threatening gestures.

"Where is your mistress, the Lady Matilda?" he asked, in a tone of perfect coolness.

"My lady retired to her chamber two hours ago, and is now asleep," stammered out the waiting-maid in a frightened tone.

"Go to her," pursued De Cressines, "and bid her rise and dress herself; for that she must go with us on the instant. She will do well to attempt no resistance, for we are prepared to use force if necessary."

The girl hurried upstairs to the chamber of Maria, whom she forthwith awoke. "Lady," she exclaimed, "make haste and rise, the house is full of soldiers."

"What say you?" cried Maria, terrified, "soldiers in our house! What is it they want?"

"They come to carry off the Lady Matilda, at this very instant. Make haste, I pray you, for she is asleep, and I fear every moment lest they should enter her chamber.'

The Lion of Flanders

In too much haste and astonishment to answer, Maria threw a loose dressing-gown over her shoulders, and descended the stairs, where she found De Cressines still in the entrance-hall. Two male servants, who had been awakened by the girl's scream, had been arrested and detained by the soldiers.

"Sir," said Maria, addressing herself to the officer in command, "please to inform me why you thus enter my brother's house by night."

"Certainly, noble lady. It is by order of the governor-general. The Lady Matilda de Bethune must accompany us without delay. You need be under no apprehension, however, as to the treatment she will receive; for I pledge you my honor that not a word shall be addressed to her otherwise than as beseems her rank."

"Oh, sir," replied Maria, "I wonder to see you employed on such an errand; for I have always heard you spoken of as an honorable knight."

"I can assure you, lady, that the employment is not to my taste; but, as a soldier, I have no choice but punctually to obey the orders of my general. Be pleased, therefore, to bring down to us the Lady Matilda; we can delay no longer, and you must yourself see that escape is hopeless."

Maria did, in fact, see too plainly that the blow was neither to be evaded nor resisted, and had she yielded to her fears she would have wrung her

The Lion of Flanders

hands in despair; but she had sufficient self-command to suppress her feelings before the stranger, though as her eye lighted on the Fleming, who stood by in one corner of the hall, her whole countenance assumed an expression of ineffable contempt. Master Brakels's heart quailed beneath that look of scorn; he trembled too for the vengeance which he saw hanging over his head, and retreating a few steps, seemed as though about to make his escape by the doorway.

"Keep an eye on yonder Fleming, that he does not give us the slip," cried De Cressines to his men; "after betraying his own friends, he may likely enough play us false too."

In an instant Brakels was roughly seized by the arm, and dragged into the midst of the soldiers, who seemed to take delight in showing their contempt of the traitor, even while they were profiting by his treachery.

Meanwhile Maria had again ascended the stairs; and with heavy heart entered the chamber of her young friend. For a moment she stood in silence before the bed, and contemplated the unhappy Matilda as she slept—slept indeed profoundly, yet not peacefully. Her breath came heavily and hurriedly; ever and anon, with a convulsive motion of her hand, she seemed striving to repel some threatening vision; and amid many inarticulate sounds might be distinguished the oft-repeated

The Lion of Flanders

name of Adolf, which she uttered in the tone of one who calls for help in danger.

Tears flowed from Maria's eyes; for the spectacle moved her innermost heart, which was still more deeply touched by the thought of the sad awakening so soon to follow. But, painful as it was to be the bearer of evil tidings, there was no time to be lost; a few moments' delay might fill the chamber with rude soldiers. To spare her friend a worse shock, she must hasten to startle her from her slumber; taking, therefore, Matilda's hand, she roused her with the words:

"Awake! awake! dear friend; I have that to say to you which will not brook delay."

At Maria's first touch the maiden started from her sleep in alarm, opened wide her eyes, and regarded her friend with mingled doubt and terror.

"Is it you, Maria?" she exclaimed, hastily passing her hand over her eyelids; "what brings you to me at this strange hour?"

"My poor friend!" cried Maria, bursting into tears, "you must get up and let me dress you. Nerve yourself as best you can, and above all make haste. A great misfortune has befallen you."

In her bewilderment Matilda rose from her bed, fixing a look of anxious inquiry upon Maria, who immediately began dressing her, sobbing bitterly the while, and making no answer to the terrified girl's repeated questions, till, at the moment

The Lion of Flanders

of handing her a long riding-dress, with a painful effort she said:

"You are about to take a journey, dear Matilda! May St. George protect and keep you!"

"What means this, my Maria? Ah, now I see what lot awaits me! My sad dream, then, was a true one; for, even as you woke me, methought I was being carried off to France, to Joanna of Navarre. Now is all hope gone from me! never again shall I behold my beloved Flanders! And you, my father, never again, in this world, shall you embrace your child!"

Overcome with grief, Maria had sunk into a chair; her voice inarticulate with sobs, was unable to offer a word of comfort, when she felt her neck encircled by Matilda's arms, and heard her tender accents sounding in her ear:

"Weep not for me, sweet friend. Sorrow upon sorrow is nothing new to my sad heart; and for the house of Flanders there is left no joy, not even peace."

"Oh hapless, yet ever noble girl!" Maria at last found words to say; "you know not that the French soldiers who are to carry you hence already guard the house!"

At these words Matilda turned pale, and an evident shudder passed over her frame. "Soldiers!" she exclaimed, "am I then to be exposed to the insolence of ruffian hirelings? Save me, my Maria!

The Lion of Flanders

Oh God! that I might now die! My father! my father! you know not what insults are offered to your blood!"

"Be not thus terrified, my Matilda; their leader is a good knight and a noble gentleman."

"The fated hour, then, is come. I must leave you, Maria; and the wicked Joanna will cast me, too, into a dungeon. Be it so; there is a Judge in Heaven, and He will not forget me!"

"Quick, now, and put on the riding-dress; for I hear the soldiers approaching."

While Matilda was fastening her dress about her, the door opened, and the waiting-maid entered.

"Madam," she said, addressing herself to Maria, "the French knight desires to know whether the Lady Matilda is yet ready, and whether it is permitted him to present himself before her?"

"Let him come," was the unhesitating answer.

Messire de Cressines had followed closely upon his messenger, and now made his appearance. He bowed respectfully to the ladies; and his compassionate looks sufficiently testified his distaste for the commission with which he was charged.

"Noble countess," he commenced, "bear with me if I call upon you to accompany me without further delay. I assure you I have already allowed you all the time that it is possible for me to grant."

"I will follow you, Messire, on the instant," answered Matilda; "but I trust that I may rely on your knightly honor to secure me against any unworthy treatment."

"I swear to you, lady," replied De Cressines, deeply moved by her resignation, "that so long as you are in my charge, you shall meet with nothing but respect."

"But your soldiers, Messire."

"As for my soldiers, lady, not a man among them, I assure you, shall address one word to you. Let us now be going."

Anxiously and tenderly the two friends embraced one another, while tears trickled down their cheeks. Often was the bitter word "farewell" repeated, and the last embrace given, only to be commenced anew. At length they left the room, and began to descend the stairs.

"Messire," said Maria, earnestly, "tell me, I entreat you, whither are you conducting my unhappy friend?"

"To France," he replied; and then turning to his soldiers:

"Mark my words well," he said, in a voice of stern command: "let no unseemly word pass the lips of any of you in this lady's presence. It is my will that she be treated in every respect as becomes her noble rank; bear this well in mind, or—you know me. Now let the horses be brought round."

The Lion of Flanders

The horses came; the last word, the last embrace were exchanged amid sobs and tears; Matilda was lifted upon her palfrey; Master Brakels and the two servants were released; the party hastened away through the streets of Bruges, and were soon far beyond its walls.

The night was dark, and all nature seemed to slumber in solemn stillness. Messire de Cressines rode at Matilda's side, scrupulously refraining, however, from intruding upon her grief by any attempt at conversation; so that probably the entire journey would have passed without the interchange of a word, had she not herself broken silence by asking:

"Is it in your power, Messire, to give me any information as to the fate which awaits me? And may I inquire by whose command I am thus forcibly removed from the residence I had chosen?"

"The order was given to me by Messire de Chatillon; but it is by no means impossible that it may have, in the first instance, proceeded from a still higher authority; for Compiègne is the place of your destination."

"Ah, so I might have imagined! It is Joanna of Navarre from whom this blow comes. It was not enough that she should imprison in her dungeons my father and all my kindred; her vengeance was not complete while I remained. Oh,

The Lion of Flanders

Messire, you have an evil woman for your queen."

"A *man* should not dare say that in my presence with impunity, lady; nevertheless, it is true that our queen deals hardly with the Flemings, and especially with the House of Dampierre. From my heart I grieve for Messire Robert; still I may not hear my princess blamed."

"Forgive me, Messire; you speak like a true knight, and your fidelity demands my esteem. I will vent no more reproaches against your queen, and will even deem myself fortunate that in my calamity I have fallen into the hands of one who has the heart of a true and honorable knight."

"I should have rejoiced, noble lady, could I have been your conductor throughout the entire journey; but that is a pleasure which is denied me. It is but for some short quarter of an hour more that I shall have you under my charge; you will then proceed under other escort. That circumstance, however, can make no change for the worse in your condition; no French knight will fail to remember what is due to your sex, your rank, and your misfortunes."

"True, Messire, the nobles of France have ever borne themselves courteously and honorably toward us; but what assurance have I that I shall always be escorted in such wise as beseems one of my noble father's race?"

The Lion of Flanders

"You need be under no apprehension on that score, lady. I am now conducting you to the Castle of Male, where I am to deliver you over to the custody of the castellan, Messire de St. Pol. So far only does my mission extend."

The conversation continued till they found themselves in front of the castle, which for the present was their journey's end. The warder announced their arrival from his station above; the gates opened, and prisoner and escort passed on into the interior of the fortress.

The Lion of Flanders

CHAPTER IV

MONTHS had now gone by since the surrender of Bruges. De Chatillon had appointed Messire de Mortenay governor of the city, and had himself returned to Courtrai; for he knew enough of the true feelings of the men of Bruges to feel himself ill at ease within their walls. Meanwhile the garrison which he had left behind to ensure submission indulged themselves in deeds of violence of every description—plundering, insulting, and wantonly annoying the citizens in a thousand ways. The foreign merchants, disgusted at this state of things, had mostly betaken themselves elsewhere; the commerce of the city fell off from day to day, and with it the prosperity of the manufacturing and working classes, whose sullen dislike of their new rulers had thus gradually ripened into active hatred, which waited only an opportunity to exhibit itself in open rebellion. The time to attempt this, however, with any hope of success was not yet come. The French garrison was too numerous, and every possible means had been adopted by them in order to secure what they had already won. The city had been dismantled, in a great measure, of its defensive works, and a strong citadel was in progress of erection, by which they hoped more effectually to overawe the inhabitants.

To the great surprise of his fellow-citizens, Deconinck allowed all this to proceed without opposition, and, as far as the public could discern, went quietly on his way, as though now only intent upon his own affairs. In the private assemblies of his guild, however, he was all the while encouraging, by his fervent exhortations, the hearts of his fellows, and cherishing in their hearts the warmest and noblest aspirations for the deliverance of their country.

As for Breydel, there seemed to be nothing of his former self remaining. Ever darkly musing, with knitted brows and downcast eyes, the gallant Butcher went about as if bowed under the weight of years. It was seldom, indeed, that he left his house. Bruges, enthralled and oppressed, was to him but a wider prison, whither the light and air of freedom could no more enter; upon the forehead of each brother-citizen he read only the brand of shame; in the eye of each stranger glanced the insulting taunt, "Slave! slave!" For him there was neither joy nor comfort more. In this mood he was one day pacing his shop in the early morning, and fitfully continuing the dreams of the past night—now plunged in gloomy thoughts, now fuming with rage; at one moment grimly smiling upon his

The Lion of Flanders

ax as he poised it in his hand, and at another wrathfully casting it from him as the useless plaything of a slave—when suddenly the door opened, and to his surprise the Dean of the Clothworkers stood before him.

"A good-morning to you, master," said the Butcher; "what evil tidings is it that brings you to me thus early?"

"My friend Jan," answered Deconinck, "I ask not why you are sad; the thought of slavery—"

"Silence, Deconinck! I pray you, speak not that word; the very walls of my house seem to reecho it around me in a thousand tones of insult. Oh, my friend, would that I had died that day upon the ramparts of our city! I should not then have fallen unrevenged; and, oh, what bitterness of spirit should I have been spared! But I lost that chance, and—"

Calmly, but not unmoved, Deconinck interrupted him:

"Be of good cheer, my noble-hearted friend," said he; "our day shall yet come. The embers still glow under the ashes; and the time will surely arrive, though it is not yet. Let the chains press more sorely still upon our necks, until they become too galling even for cowards to bear; and our Black Lion shall yet again float aloft, with Bruges in the van."

A smile full of confidence flitted over the countenance of Breydel; and as he seized the Dean's hand he joyfully exclaimed, "You alone, my friend, you alone know how to comfort me; you alone understand my heart."

"But now, Master Jan," proceeded the Clothworker, "to the object of my visit. You have not forgotten our promise to keep guard over the Lady Matilda?"

"What now!" cried Breydel, hastily, his cheeks flushing at once with anxiety and anticipated indignation.

"She was seized and carried off by the French last night."

The Butcher took a step forward, caught up his ax, and furiously swung it round his head. For a moment he was unable to speak; then a torrent of incoherent curses burst from his lips; at last he exclaimed:

"Deconinck, this is too much—not a word more! I listen to no put off now; to-day I must see blood if I die for it."

"Softly, my friend, softly; be reasonable. Your life belongs to your country, and you must by no means risk it uselessly."

"Not a syllable will I hear! I thank you for your good advice; but I neither can nor will follow it. Spare your words, therefore, for they are all in vain."

"But be reasonable, Master Jan," rejoined the

Clothworker; "you can not drive the French out all by yourself."

"What care I for that? My thoughts carry me not so far. Vengeance and death!—"

The violence of his emotion prevented further speech. After a few instants' pause, however, he continued more calmly:

"Well, Master Deconinck, after all, I will be cool, as you tell me. What more, then, do you know about this matter?"

"Not much. This morning, before daylight, I was disturbed by an urgent message from Sir Adolf of Nieuwland's house, to the effect that the Lady Matilda had been carried off in the night by the French, and that it was the traitor Brakels who had acted as their guide."

"Brakels! There is another for my ax! He shall not play the spy for the French much longer."

"Whither they have taken her I know not," continued Deconinck; "but I suspect it may be to the Castle of Male; for the servant who brought me the message had heard this name mentioned more than once among the soldiers. You see well, Breydel, that it will be better to wait for some further information than to take any step hastily, especially as there is every probability that the countess is by this time already in France. It seems that the only course is to stay at home and bide our time."

The Lion of Flanders

"You preach to the deaf, my friend," replied the Butcher; "at all events, I must and will go out. Forgive me if I now leave you."

And with these words, concealing his ax under his garment, he moved toward the door. By a sudden side movement, however, Deconinck so placed himself as to intercept his passage.

"Have done with this childish impatience," said the Clothworker, while Breydel looked round as though seeking some other exit, and in default of that seemed ready to spring through the window; "forth with that ax you shall not go. You are by far too dear a friend to me, and too valuable to our cause, that I should let you thus rush upon destruction."

"Let me pass, Master Peter. I pray you, let me go out; you keep me on the rack."

"Not so, Master Jan. Think you that you are your own property, and may risk your life at pleasure? No, no, master; God has given you your great gifts for nobler ends than that. Remember your high calling, master; think of your country, and of the service you may do her. How shall you aid and save her if now you fling away your life upon a useless vengeance?"

While Deconinck was speaking, Breydel had gradually cooled down, and now answered in a calmer tone:

"You are right, my friend," he said; "I am too

The Lion of Flanders

easily carried away. There, now, see my ax is hung up in its place again. You can let me out now; for to-day I must to Thourout to buy cattle."

"Well, I will keep you no longer; though I know well enough that it is not to Thourout you are going to-day."

"Indeed, what I tell you is true, master; I haven't a hoof left, and I must provide myself a fresh supply this very day."

"You can not pass that off upon me, Master Jan. I have known you too long, and I can see into your soul through your eyes: you are going to Male."

"You are certainly a conjurer, Master Peter; I believe you know my thoughts better than I do myself. Yes, I am going to Male; but I give you my word it is only to reconnoitre, and if possible to procure some intelligence of our unfortunate princess. I promise you to put off the reckoning till a more convenient season; but I warrant you they shall pay with interest when they do pay, or my name is not Jan Breydel."

The two deans now went out together, and parted, after exchanging a few more words, in the street. Breydel started off without delay, and a rapid walk of half an hour brought him to the village of Male, which at this time consisted of some thirty thatched cottages, scattered here and there in the immediate neighborhood of the castle. All around stretched away impenetrable forests, amid which the industry of the villagers had cleared an open space of cultivated fields. To judge by the fertility of the soil and abundance of the harvests, the peasantry should have been rich and prosperous—a supposition, however, which was strangely belied by their dress and general appearance, which in all respects bespoke the deepest poverty. Slavery and despotism had borne their fruits. The peasant did not labor for himself; all belonged to his feudal lord; and he thought himself fortunate if, after payment of all exactions, he could, by unremitting exertion, secure for himself even the barest maintenance.

At some little distance from the castle was an open space, round which stood a few houses of stone, built somewhat closer together than the rest; in the middle rose a tall stone pillar, to which was attached a chain with an iron collar, in fact, a kind of pillory, which betokened the criminal jurisdiction possessed by the lord. On one side was a small chapel, the wall of its churchyard encroaching a few paces upon the square. Adjoining the chapel stood a tolerably lofty house, the only place of public entertainment which the village boasted. A stone image of St. Martin above the door served for a sign; but so rudely chiseled that its representation of a human figure might be regarded as purely conventional. The whole ground-floor was occupied by a single apartment, one end of which

The Lion of Flanders

was almost entirely taken up by a projecting fireplace, so disproportionately wide that it left only a recess at either end used as a drying-place for herbs and roots. The other walls were whitewashed, and hung all over with various cooking utensils in wood and pewter: a halberd, and several large knives in leathern sheaths, occupied a place apart. The whole aspect of the place was gloomy in the extreme. The rafters overhead were black with smoke, and a perpetual twilight reigned even when, as now, the sun shone brightly without; for but few of his rays were admitted by the small panes of the windows, which, moreover, were raised full seven feet above the floor. Some heavy wooden seats and still heavier chairs completed the furnishing of the room.

The hostess ran hither and thither hastily waiting upon her guests, who, at the time, happened to be unusually numerous. Flagons and beakers went their round incessantly, and the merriment of the revelers blended into one confused hubbub of voices, in which not one intelligible word could be distinguished. It was easy enough, however, to perceive that the result was not perfectly homogeneous, and that two distinct and different tongues combined together to produce it. From about the fireplace might be heard the manly and vigorous tones of the Flemish, while in the more polished and softer accents which sounded from the body of the apartment might be recognized the language of France. Among those who spoke in the foreign tongue, and belonged to the garrison of the castle, the principal leader was one Leroux, at least such he seemed to be, by the authoritative tone in which he spoke, and the air of superiority which he assumed. He was, moreover, but a simple man-at-arms, like the rest; it was only his extraordinary strength and lofty stature, and his readiness to profit by those advantages, which had procured him this kind of preeminence among his fellows of the garrison.

While the Frenchmen were thus lustily addressing themselves to their flagons, and merry jests and jovial shouts went freely round, another soldier of the garrison entered the room.

"Good news, comrades!" said he; "we shall soon be out of this cursed Flanders. I trust before to-morrow is over we shall see our own pleasant land of France again!"

At this, every man was instantly on the alert, and looked the newcomer in the face with an expression of mingled doubt and inquiry.

"Yes," he went on; "to-morrow we set off for France, with the lady that paid us a visit at such an out-of-the-way time last night."

"Is that so, indeed?" asked Leroux.

"Nothing more certain; Messire de St. Pol has sent me to desire you to be in readiness."

The Lion of Flanders

"I do not doubt you, for you are always a bringer of bad news."

"Why, what now? are you not then glad of the news? and don't you want to get back to France again?"

"No, not a bit of it! Here we are enjoying the fruits of victory, and for my part I don't want to leave the feast so early."

"Well, you needn't be so put out about it; 'tis only for a few days; we shall soon be back."

Just as Leroux was about to reply the door opened, and a Fleming entered, who, with a bold and careless glance at the French soldiers, sat down at a table by himself, and called out:

"Now, host! a stoup of beer. Quick, I'm in haste!"

"Anon, anon! I'm coming, Master Breydel!"

"He's a fine fellow, that Fleming!" whispered to Leroux the soldier who was sitting next him. "He's not so tall as you; but what a build! and what a voice too! He's no peasant, that!"

"He is a fine fellow, indeed," answered Leroux; "he has eyes like a lion. I like him."

"Host!" cried Breydel again, rising, "what are you about all this while? my throat is as dry as a smoked herring!"

"Tell me, Fleming," asked Leroux, addressing him, "can you speak French?"

"I'm sorry to say I can," answered Breydel in that language.

"Well, then, as I see that you're impatient and thirsty, accept a drink from me, till your own comes. Here, and good luck to you!"

The Fleming took the proffered cup with a motion of thanks, saying, as he raised it to his mouth:

"Health and long life to you!"

But hardly had a few drops of its contents passed his lips, when he hastily set it down again upon the table with an ill-suppressed look of disgust.

"What's that? why, the noble liquor frightens you! Ah! you Flemings are not used to it," cried Leroux, laughing.

"It's French wine!" answered Breydel, with careless indifference, as though his aversion had been a mere natural distaste.

The soldiers looked at one another, and a movement of displeasure contracted Leroux's brow. Nevertheless, Breydel's manner and countenance gave so little appearance of intention to his words that nothing was said, and the Fleming returned quietly to his table, where the beer he had called for stood ready waiting for him, and resumed his seat, taking no further notice of the French party.

"Now, comrades," cried Leroux, raising his beaker, "one draft more, that we may not go away with dry throats; here's to the health of this Flemish fair one, and may the devil fly away with her!"

The Lion of Flanders

At this toast Jan had some trouble to contain himself, but succeeded, and Leroux went on:

"If only by good luck all keeps quiet while we're gone! These rascally citizens are getting more than half-disposed to rebel, and there may be an outbreak any day. A pretty take-in it would be for us, if the others are at the plundering of Bruges while we are out of the way! We should have to thank this jade for it!"

Again Breydel's blood began to boil; but he remembered his promise and held his peace, listening, however, the more attentively as the Frenchman resumed:

"I should like to know who she is. I suppose she's the wife of one of the rebel nobles, and going to make one with the others they've got safe hold of there. Yes, yes! she'll not spend her time very pleasantly in France, depend upon it!"

Jan, meanwhile, felt that if he was to hold his peace he must find some vent for his feelings; accordingly he rose from his seat, and paced up and down at the farther end of the apartment, humming over in a low voice a Flemish popular song of the day:

> "The sable Lion! Mark him ramping
> So proudly on his golden field!
> Mark well his claws, his giant weapons,
> That tear the foe spite mail and shield!

The Lion of Flanders

Behold his eyes, for battle flashing!
 Behold his mane, how wild it flies!
That Lion is our Flemish Lion,
 That crouching still the foe defies."

The French soldiers looked at one another in astonishment. "Hark!" said one of them; "that is one of the Claward songs; and the insolent Fleming dares to sing it in our presence!"

These words Jan Breydel heard plainly enough; but he took no notice of them, and went on with his tune. He even raised his voice somewhat, as though in defiance of the Frenchmen:

"He showed his claws in Eastern regions,
 And trembling fled the Eastern host!
Before his keen eye paled the Crescent,
 The Saracen forgot his boast!
Returning to the West, his children
 He guerdoned for their deeds of fame;
He gave to Godfrey, gave to Baldwin,
 A royal and imperial name"

"Tell me, what is the meaning of that song they always have in their mouths?" inquired Leroux of a Fleming belonging to the castle, who was sitting by him.

"Well, the meaning of it is, that the Black Lion clawed the Saracens and their Crescent right hand-

The Lion of Flanders

somely, and made Count Baldwin Emperor of Constantinople."

"But I say, Fleming," cried Leroux to Breydel, "you must acknowledge that your terrible black lion has had to turn tail before King Philip's lilies; and now, I suspect, he's dead, for good and all."

Master Jan smiled contemptuously. "There's another verse to the song," he said; "listen:

" 'He slumbers now; the Gallic Philip
    Can his free limbs with chains oppress,
While robber-bands of foreign hirelings
    The Lion's fatherland possess.
But when he wakes—O, then, ye robbers,
    Then shall ye feel the Lion's claw!
Then shall in mud and blood your Lily
    Lie low beneath his mighty paw!'

There! now ask what that means!"

The sense of the verse was explained to Leroux, who immediately rose, thrust his seat hastily back, filled his drinking-cup to the brim, and exclaimed:

"Call me a coward my life long, if I don't break your neck, if you speak another word!"

"What, you think I am to be silenced by you?" answered Breydel, with a scornful laugh. "Not by all the like of you unhung; and to show you— here's to the Black Lion! and a fig for the French!"

"Comrades!" cried Leroux, trembling with rage,

The Lion of Flanders

"leave this Flemish dog to me! he shall die by my hand!"

And advancing toward Breydel, he shouted at him: "You lie! the Lily forever!"

"Liar yourself! and the Black Lion forever!" retorted Breydel.

"Come on!" pursued the Frenchman. "You are strong enough: but I will show you that it is another Lion than yours that must tread down the Lily! Come on, and to the death!"

"With all my heart, and the sooner the better. It's a real pleasure to me to have to do with a brave enemy; it's worth all the trouble!"

No sooner were the words uttered than they left the house, and straightway proceeded to seek out a convenient place for the encounter. This was soon found, and stepping a few paces apart, the two adversaries made their preparations for the fight. Breydel first took his knife from his girdle and threw it from him, then stripped up his sleeves to the shoulders, laying bare his sinewy arms, the sight of which struck with amazement the soldiers who were standing by. Leroux, too, threw from him his sword and dagger, and so remained totally unarmed; then turning to his comrades, he said:

"Mind, come what will, let there be fair play! He's a brave fellow, this Fleming!"

"Are you ready?" cried Breydel.

"Ready!" was the answer.

The Lion of Flanders

The word was given, and the combatants advanced upon each other, their heads thrown back, their eyes flashing, their brows knit, their lips and teeth forcibly pressed together; like two furious bulls they rushed upon each other.

A heavy blow resounded upon either breast, as of hammer upon anvil, and both reeled backward from the shock, which, however, did but inflame their rage the more. A short deep growl mingled with their heavy breathing, and with their arms they seized each other round the body as in a vise of steel. Every limb was strained to the uttermost, every nerve quivered, every muscle was in play; their veins swelled, their eyes became bloodshot, their brows from red grew purple, and from purple livid; but neither could win upon the other by an inch of ground; one would have said their feet were rooted where they stood.

After some time spent in this desperate struggle, the Frenchman suddenly made a step backward, twined his arms round Breydel's neck, and taking a firm purchase forced the Fleming's head forward and downward so as in some degree to disturb his balance; then, following up his advantage without the loss of a moment, Leroux made yet another effort with increased energy, and Breydel sank on one knee beneath the overpowering attack.

"The Lion is on his knees already!" cried the

The Lion of Flanders

French champion, triumphantly, dealing at the same time a blow on the head of the butcher that might have felled an ox, and wellnigh laid him prostrate on the ground. But to do this with effect, he had been obliged to release Breydel with one hand, and, at the very moment that he was raising his fist to repeat the blow, the latter extricated himself from the single grasp which held him, rose from the ground, and retreated some few paces; then rushing upon his adversary with the speed of lightning, he seized him round the body with a hug like that of a forest bear, so that every rib cracked again. The Frenchman, in his turn, wound his limbs about his foe with a terrible vigor, strengthened by practise and directed by skill, so that the Fleming felt his knees bend beneath him, and again they nearly touched the ground.

An unwonted sensation stole into Breydel's heart, as though for the first time in his life it had begun to fail him. The thought was madness; but even like madness, it gave him strength; suddenly loosening his hold, and again retreating, at the same time lowering his head, like a furious bull he rushed upon Leroux, and butted him in the chest, before the Frenchman could foresee, much less provide against this new attack. Reeling under the shock, blood burst from his nose, mouth, and ears; while at the same moment, like a stone

The Lion of Flanders

from a catapult, the Fleming's fist descended upon his skull; with a long cry he fell heavily to the earth, and all was over.

"Now you feel the Lion's claws!" cried the Fleming.

The soldiers who had been witnesses of the conflict had indeed encouraged the French champion by their shouts; but had rigorously abstained from any further interference. They now crowded about their dying comrade, and raised him in their arms; while Breydel, with slow and deliberate steps, retired from the ground, and made his way back to the room where the quarrel had begun. Here he called for another stoup of beer, from which he hastily and repeatedly drank to quench his burning thirst.

He had now been sitting there some time, and was beginning to recover himself from the fatigue of the combat, when the door opened behind him; and before he could turn his head, he was seized by four pair of powerful hands, and roughly thrown upon the ground, while in a moment after the room was filled by armed soldiers. For some time he maintained a fruitless struggle against numbers; but at last, exhausted with this new conflict, he ceased to resist, and lay still, regarding the Frenchmen with one of those terrible looks that precede a death-blow given or received. Not a few of the soldiers looked on the Fleming, as he lay, with hearts ill at ease, so fiercely and threateningly did his flaming eyes glare upon them.

A knight, whose dress sufficiently betokened his rank, now approached; and after ordering his men to keep a secure hold upon the prisoner:

"So, scoundrel!" said he, "we know one another of old: you are the ruffian that, in the forest near Wynandael, killed one of Messire de Chatillon's men-at-arms, and even went so far in your insolence as to threaten us knights with your knife; and now I find you murdering one of my best soldiers on my own ground. But you shall have your reward; this very day shall you be gibbeted upon the castle wall, that your friends in Bruges may see you dangling, and know what comes of rebellion."

"You belie me foully," exclaimed Breydel; "I have killed my opponent in fair fight and in self-defense; and only give me fair play, and I will show you the same over again."

"You dared to insult the royal banner of France—"

"I spoke up for our own Black Lion, and so I will do while breath is left me. But come, either lift me up or finish me at once; don't let me lie here like a slaughtered ox."

At a word from St. Pol, the soldiers raised their prisoner from the ground, but without, for a moment, loosening their hold, and cautiously led him to the door. Breydel walked slowly and quietly

The Lion of Flanders

along, two of the strongest of his captors holding him by the arms, and as many closely preceding and following him, so as to render resistance useless and escape impossible; and many a taunt had he to listen to the while from the soldiers who guarded him.

"Be easy, my fine fellow!" cried one; "show us a brisk dance upon nothing to-morrow, and we will keep the ravens from you afterward."

Breydel answered only by a look of withering scorn.

"If you dare to look at me so, you accursed Claward," cried the soldier, "I will give it you across the face."

"Coward Frenchmen!" retorted Breydel; "that is ever your way—to insult your enemy when he is in your power, base hirelings of a despicable master!"

A blow on the cheek from the soldier next him was the reply. Breydel ceased to speak, and bowed his head upon his chest, as though utterly cast down; but in truth his spirit burned within him all the while, like the fire which smolders deep in the bosom of a slumbering volcano. The soldiers, however, misinterpreted his silence, and jeered him all the more bitterly now that he answered them not a word.

Just at the moment, however, that they were about to step upon the drawbridge, their laughter suddenly ceased, and their faces became pale with terror. Breydel had suddenly collected all his strength, and extricated his arms from their grasp. Like a panther, he sprang upon the two soldiers who had been the most forward in jeering him, and like the wild beast's jaws his iron fingers clutched their throats.

"For you, Lion of Flanders, will I die!" he cried; "but not on a gallows, and not unrevenged."

And as he spoke, so fiercely did he grasp the throats of his two foes, that in a moment they hung senseless in his hands; then dashing their heads together with such violence that the blow reechoed from the castle walls, with one tremendous throw he cast them from him helpless upon the earth.

This feat of strength and energy was the work of less time than it has taken to describe it; and for a moment the surprise so paralyzed the whole party that Breydel gained time for flight, and was already at some distance from his enemies before they had fully recovered their senses. The soldiers were soon in pursuit of him, however, with shouts and curses; and the chase was vigorously kept up, till at last he succeeded, by a tremendous leap, in putting a wide ditch between himself and his pursuers, of whom only two were bold enough to follow him. On reaching the ditch, and attempting to cross, both fell into the water, and the pursuit was thereupon at an end. Without further molestation, the courageous Butcher returned to the city, and arrived safely at his own home.

On entering the house, Breydel found, to his astonishment, that no one was within except a young journeyman, who was himself just in the act of going forth.

"What is this? Where are my men?" he cried impatiently.

"Well, master," answered the youth, "they are all gone to our hall; a hasty message came to tell us that we were all to meet there."

"What is going on, then?"

"I don't rightly know, master; but this morning the city crier read a proclamation of the magistrates, enjoining all citizens who live by work or trade to pay every Saturday so much of their week's earnings to the tax-gatherers; and we suppose that this is the reason why the Dean of the Clothworkers has ordered all the trades to assemble at their halls."

"Stay you and shut up the shop," said Breydel, "and tell my mother not to be alarmed if I should not come home to-night; most probably I shall not."

He took his ax from where it hung, hid it under his gown, and was soon at the hall of his Guild, where his entrance was immediately greeted by a general murmur of satisfaction.

"Here is Breydel! here is the Dean!" was echoed

by all present, while the provisional president immediately made place for him in the chair of honor. Breydel, however, instead of occupying it as usual, seated himself upon a stool, and looking round with a grim smile upon his comrades, he exclaimed:

"Brothers, lend me your ears; for I have need of you. To-day a dishonor has been put upon me, and, in me, upon our whole Guild, such as we have never before had to endure."

Masters and journeymen alike pressed eagerly around their Dean. Never before had they seen him so violently excited; all eyes were accordingly fixed upon him as he continued:

"You, like myself, are true-born citizens of Bruges; you, like myself, have too long been suffering under the disgrace and burden of bondage; but all that is nothing to what I have had to endure to-day. By Heaven! I hardly know how to tell you of it for very shame."

The bronzed cheeks of the Butchers already glowed with wrath, though as yet they knew not the cause of offense; every fist was clenched, and muttered curses rose to the lips of all.

"Listen, my brothers," pursued Breydel, "and bear the shame as you best can; listen attentively, for you will scarcely believe your ears: a French dog has smitten your Dean upon the face—yes, on this very cheek!"

The Lion of Flanders

If the Butchers had been wroth before, they were furious beyond all measure on hearing these words. Cries of rage reechoed from the vaulted roof, and fearful oaths of vengeance burst out on every side.

"How," continued Breydel, "can such a blot be washed away?"

"With blood!" was the unanimous response.

"I see you understand me, brothers," said the Dean; "yes, that is the only way. Now, you must know that it is by the soldiers of the garrison at Male that I have thus been handled. Will you not say, with me, that when to-morrow's sun rises upon Male, he shall find no castle there?"

A unanimous cry of assent followed this appeal.

"Come, then," pursued Breydel, "let us go! Every one to his home. Let each take his keenest ax, and any other arms he can provide; we shall want, too, what may serve for scaling-ladders. At eleven o'clock to-night we assemble in the alder thicket behind St. Cross."

After a few special instructions to the Ancients, the assembly broke up.

That night, a little before the appointed hour, might be seen in the moonlight, upon the divers paths in the neighborhood of St. Cross, a multitude of figures, all wending their way in one direction, and finally disappearing in the alder thicket. Some of them carried crossbows, others clubs; the most of them, however, were without

The Lion of Flanders

any visible weapons. Already in the thickest of the little wood stood Jan Breydel, taking counsel with his fellow-leaders as to the side on which they should attack the castle.

At last it was unanimously determined to make the attempt from the side of the drawbridge, first filling in a portion of the ditch, and then endeavoring to scale the walls. A number of the young journeymen had been busily at work cutting brushwood and small trees, and binding fascines; and everything needful for the escalade being in readiness, the Dean gave the order to set forward.

The chronicles tell us that the men forming this expedition were seven hundred in number; nevertheless, so intent were they on effecting their purpose that the most perfect silence prevailed among them; not a sound was heard but the wary tread of their footsteps, the dragging of the branches along the earth, and the baying of the dogs, disturbed by the unwonted noise. At a bowshot from the castle they made halt, and Breydel, with a small party, advanced to reconnoitre. The sentinel, meanwhile, from his station above the gate, had caught the sound of their approach, though yet uncertain of its import, and now came forward upon the wall the better to pursue his observations.

"Wait a moment," cried one of the Butchers; "I will quickly rid you of this listening dog."

And as he spoke a bolt from his crossbow rapidly winged its way toward the sentinel. The aim, indeed, was good, but the missile shivered itself upon the tempered steel of the sentinel's breastplate, and at the same instant the alarm was given.

"France! France! an attack! to arms! to arms!"

"Forward, comrades!" shouted Breydel. "Forward! Here with the fascines!"

No sooner was it said than done. The ditch was bridged, the ladders planted, and a scaling-party stood upon the walls before any effectual resistance could be opposed to them. Within, meanwhile, the garrison was hurrying to arms, and in a few moments more than fifty of them were in readiness to oppose the assailants. For an instant Jan Breydel and his followers had the worst of the fray; there were hardly more than thirty men yet within the castle, and without helm or mail as they were, the French arrows rained fearfully upon them. But this did not last long; in a short time all the Flemings had made good their entrance.

"Now, comrades, to work!" cried Breydel. "Follow me!"

And, like a plowshare through the earth, he opened a way through the enemy's ranks. Every stroke of his ax cost a foeman's life, and his garments were speedily drenched with the blood of the slain. His comrades advanced with no less fury, and drowned the death-cries of their victims with their shouts of triumph.

The Lion of Flanders

While the conflict was thus raging upon the ramparts and in the courtyard, the castellan, Messire de St. Pol, seeing that there was no longer any hope of defending the fortress, ordered some of his men-at-arms to get to horse with all possible speed. A few moments after, a female figure was led, weeping and trembling, from an inner chamber, and placed before one of the mounted soldiers. The sallyport was then opened, the little body of horsemen issued from the walls, and, swimming the ditch, soon disappeared amid the surrounding wood.

Surprised and outnumbered as they were, the garrison defended themselves with courage and obstinacy. All resistance, however, was vain, and an hour later not a Frenchman remained alive within the castle. All that had not fallen under the terrible axes of the Butchers had made their escape by the postern.

Breydel's wounded honor was now avenged; but his end was only half-attained, for the Lady Matilda had not yet been found. After a long and fruitless search in every corner and crevice of the castle, from its loftiest turrets to its deepest dungeons, under the guidance of one who knew it well, he was obliged to conclude that she had been carried off. And now, to make his vengeance complete, he set fire to the four corners of the building. Soon the flames mounted high into the heavens.

The Lion of Flanders

The walls cracked and fell, the infuriated assailants hewed down the gates, the bridge, the posts, and hurled them into the burning pile. Long before morning nothing was left of the magnificent castle of Male that the fury of the Butchers and the devouring fire could lay waste.

Round about the fire-bell resounded from village to village, and the peasants, as in duty bound, hurried up to help at the call; but they arrived only to be spectators of the scene of destruction, which, to say the truth, did not greatly displease them.

"There!" shouted Breydel, with a voice at once deep and clear, as the last turret fell in; "now let to-morrow's sun look down upon the place where the castle of Male once was!"

And the Butchers marched off in a body to Bruges, singing in chorus as they went the song of the Lion.

The Lion of Flanders

CHAPTER V

At the time of the conquest of West Flanders by the French, in the year 1296, the castle of Nieuwenhove had offered them an especially obstinate resistance. A great number of Flemish knights had shut themselves up within it under Robert de Bethune, fully resolved to listen to no proposals of surrender so long as a single man remained in a condition to defend himself. But their valor was in vain against the overpowering force of their assailants; most of them perished, fighting desperately on the ramparts. The French, on entering through the breach effected by their engines, found not a living soul within the walls; and for want of living beings upon whom to wreak their vengeance, they fired the castle, and afterward deliberately battered down what the flames had spared, and filled up the moat with the rubbish.

The ruins of the castle of Nieuwenhove lay some few miles from Bruges, in the direction of Courtrai, surrounded by a thick wood. At a considerable distance from any human habitation, it was

The Lion of Flanders

but seldom that the place resounded with the foot of man; the more so, as the incessant screeching of the night-birds, which harbored there in great numbers, had possessed the country people with the idea that the spot was haunted by the unquiet spirits of the Flemings who had fallen in the combat, and who now wandered upon earth crying for vengeance, or wailing after repose. But, though ruined for all purposes of defense or habitation, the castle was yet not so utterly destroyed but that its ground-plan could be distinctly traced. Even considerable remnants of the walls were still standing, though cracked in every direction; large pieces of the roofing lay on the ground beside the stonework which had formerly supported them; and windows might here and there be seen, of which the stone mullions were yet undestroyed. Everything betokened a devastation effected in haste; for while some portions of the building had been deliberately and effectually demolished, others again had been left comparatively uninjured. The castle yard still formed an enclosure, though but a broken one, and encumbered in every direction with heaps of rubbish and scattered stones. During six years, moreover, which had now elapsed since the assault and conflagration, time and nature had done their work to increase the wildness of the scene; a vegetation, rank and luxuriant, in part concealed, in part set off with its rich green the cold gray of the shattered walls, and was itself relieved in turn by the varied tints of the flowers which grew profusely among it.

It was four in the morning; a faint glimmering, forerunner of the rising sun, was just appearing upon the eastern verge of the horizon, the ruins of Nieuwenhove lay reposing in their dim shadow, and the face of the still slumbering earth showed itself only under uncertain tints—they could not yet be called colors—while the heavens had already begun to don their mantle of blue. Here and there a night-bird was still on the wing, screeching as it sought its hiding-place before the coming light.

The figure of a man was seated amid the ruins, upon one of the heaps of rubbish. A plumeless helmet covered his head, and the rest of his person was clothed in complete armor. His steel gauntlet rested upon a shield, of which the cognizance would have been sought in vain, so completely was it obliterated by a broad transverse stripe of some non-heraldic color. All his armor was black; even the shaft of the long spear which lay on the ground beside him was stained of the same funereal hue, as if to betoken the deep and hopeless sadness of the wearer's heart. At a little distance stood a horse as black as his rider, so completely barded with steel plates that it was only with difficulty the animal could bow its head so as to crop the tops

The Lion of Flanders

of the tall herbage. The sword that hung at the saddle-bow was of extraordinary size, and seemed as if suited only for the hand of a giant.

The silence which reigned in the ruins was broken by the knight's deep-drawn sighs; and ever and anon he motioned with his hands, as though engaged in an animated discourse. At last, after many anxious and suspicious glances around him in every direction, he ventured to raise the visor of his helmet, so far as to make his features visible. They were those of a man far advanced in years, deeply wrinkled, and with gray hair. Although his countenance bore all the signs of long and severe suffering, yet the extraordinary vivacity of his eyes testified of the fire which still glowed within his breast. For some moments he remained lost in thought, gazing fixedly upon the ruins; then a bitter smile passed over his lips, his head sank upon his breast, and he seemed intent upon something at his feet; at last a tear fell from either eye, as he thus spoke:

"Oh, my brave brothers in arms! these stones have been wetted with your noble blood, and here beneath my feet you sleep the long sleep of death! But happy you who have left this troublous life in your country's cause, and without having seen our beloved Flanders in bondage. The blood of him to whom you gave the proud name of the Lion bedewed this ground along with yours; but, less fortunate than you, he still survives—an outcast, left to sigh over your silent graves, like a helpless woman, impotent for aught but tears."

Suddenly the knight rose from his seat, and hastily closing his visor, turned toward the road, as if anxiously giving his ear to some distant sound. A noise as of a tramp of horses was now audible in the distance. As soon as he had convinced himself that his first impression had not deceived him, the knight seized his spear, and hastily mounting his charger, took up his station behind a portion of the wall, so as effectually to conceal himself from view. He had not long occupied this post, however, when other sounds fell upon his ear along with those which it had already caught; through the clank of armor and the rapid tramp of the horses, he could now distinctly hear the lamentations of a female voice. At this his cheeks grew pale under his helmet, not with fear—for that was a thing his heart knew not—but his honor as a knight, his feeling as a man, urged him to succor the helpless, and above all to protect a woman, while at the same time a high mission and a solemn vow forbade him to expose himself to recognition. The mental struggle which he had thus to undergo showed itself plainly in his countenance.

But soon the party drew nearer, and he could distinctly hear the maiden's words, as with an agonizing voice she cried: "Father! oh, my father!" a

The Lion of Flanders

voice, too, which, though he recognized it not, had yet something in its sound that spoke irresistibly to his heart. In an instant all hesitation was at an end; giving the spur to his horse, he hastily made his way over the heaps of rubbish, and came forth upon the open road a little in advance of a body of six horsemen, who were proceeding along it at a rapid pace, and who, by their accoutrements, appeared to be French. They were without lances, though otherwise armed at all points, and one carried before him upon the saddle a female, whose wild and terrified air, irrespective of the exclamations of distress which occasionally burst from her lips, sufficiently indicated that she was an unwilling captive in their hands. With leveled spear the black knight awaited them. The Frenchmen no sooner beheld this unlooked-for opponent than they reined in their horses, and regarded the stranger with looks of wonder not unmixed with fear; while he that seemed to have the command of the escort advanced to the front, and called out in a loud voice:

"Out of our way, sir knight, or we ride over you!"

"Stand, false and dishonorable knight!" was the answer, "stand and let go this lady, or you will have me to deal with!"

"Forward! down with him!" cried the leader to his men.

The Lion of Flanders

But the black knight gave them no time to make their onset; stooping upon his charger's neck, he dashed in full career upon the astonished Frenchmen, and in an instant one of them fell mortally wounded from his saddle. The rest meanwhile had fallen upon him from all sides with their drawn swords, and St. Pol, the leader of the band, had already with a tremendous blow cut away one of the sable champion's shoulder-plates. Seeing himself thus beset, the knight dropped his spear and drew his giant sword, and, wielding it with both hands, speedily cleared a space around him; for, after a short experience of his prowess, no one of his opponents dared to venture within its sweep. St. Pol, whose horse, irritated by a wound, was no longer fully at his command, perceiving now that the issue of the conflict was less certain, at all events less immediate, than he had anticipated, made a sign to the soldier on whose horse the prisoner rode to make his escape with his charge. But the black knight was as vigilant as he was valiant. By a sudden movement he barred the way, and, dexterously parrying the blows which rained upon him, "For your life, set her down!" he cried in a voice of thunder; and, as the soldier turned off on the road, and sought to slip by him on one side, the mighty sword descended quickly upon his head, and cleft him to the teeth. In two red streams the blood gushed from the unhappy man, encrimson-

The Lion of Flanders

ing the white drapery of the young girl, and bedabbling her fair locks. For a moment the arms of the dying man convulsively retained their hold, and then both sank together to the ground. The consciousness of the young maiden had failed her under the alternate agitations of hope and terror, and she lay beside the corpse of the soldier motionless and senseless.

Meanwhile the black knight had already laid prostrate another of his foes, of whom now only three remained. But these seemed rather exasperated than intimidated by the fall of their companions, and the fight continued with increased fury. The horses tore up the ground, and seemed themselves to take part in the conflict; wonder it was that the unconscious maiden was not crushed and trampled upon as she lay beneath their iron-shod hoofs. The combatants, though panting with fatigue, weak with loss of blood or severe contusions, seemed to have no idea of anything but fighting to the death. And now the black knight suddenly reined his horse back a few paces, while the Frenchmen's hearts leaped with exultation as they thought that he was at last about to retreat. But they did not long enjoy this pleasing illusion, for an instant after he rode at them at full speed; and so well had he calculated his blow, that, even as he reached the nearest of them, helmet and head went flying across the road. This dexterous feat completed the discomfiture of the foreigners; for, astonished and terrified, St. Pol and his one remaining companion instantly turned rein and fled, in the full conviction that it was no mortal adversary they had encountered.

These events, which have taken so many words to describe, were crowded into a few rapid moments. The sun had not yet risen above the horizon, the fields still lay in dim twilight; but the veil of mist was already lifting itself from off the woods, and the tops of the trees were beginning to show a brighter green.

The black knight, now finding himself master of the field, with no more enemies in view, made haste to dismount, bound his horse to a tree, and proceeded to bestow his care upon the lady he had rescued, and who still lay senseless, under the corpse of the soldier which had fallen upon her, and to which, probably, she in a great measure owed her escape from the hoofs of the horses. Her face covered with mire and blood, her long hair trampled in the mud, her features were totally indistinguishable; nor, indeed, did her deliverer for the present seek to examine them more closely, his first care being to convey her to some place of greater security. With this object he raised her carefully from the ground, and carried her in his arms within the ruins of Nieuwenhove. Having laid her gently down upon the herbage in the courtyard, he proceeded to investigate the yet remaining portions of the building, if perchance some place of shelter should be found. At last he discovered one chamber of which the vaulting had not fallen in, and which might, in default of better, serve for a place of temporary refuge. The window-panes were gone, but otherwise the shelter was complete; there were even some tattered remnants of tapestry hanging from the walls, and pieces of broken furniture scattered about the floor, from portions of which he succeeded in putting together a kind of couch, which, rude as it was, was at least better than the cold and damp ground.

Well pleased at the result of his search, he returned to his insensible charge, and carried her to the temporary bed he had prepared for her. Here, with anxious care he laid her down, pillowing her head with a bundle of the tapestry rolled together. This done, he first cautiously satisfied himself that she was still alive and uninjured, and that the blood with which she was covered was not her own; then, returning to the scene of combat, he filled one of the helmets with water at a neighboring spring, and led his horse back within the ruins. His next care was to cleanse the lady's hair, face, and hands, from mud and gore, as completely as the means at his disposal and the gloom of the vaulted chamber would allow—a gloom, in-

The Lion of Flanders

deed (notwithstanding that the sun was by this time peeping above the horizon), which still rendered her features wholly indistinct, even though the hideous mask which had concealed them was removed. Having now done all for her that the circumstances in which they were placed rendered possible, he left her for a while, in the hopes that rest and nature might gradually restore her.

The knight's attention was next bestowed on his horse and armor; a considerable time was spent in collecting a heap of forage for the one, and in cleaning the other from the marks of the combat. When this occupation was completed, and the sun stood high in the heavens, and the face of nature showed in all its varied colors, the sunbeams fell upon the window which lighted the chamber where the maiden lay; and thither the knight now returned, to avail himself of the increased light for making further acquaintance with his charge. He entered; she was sitting up upon her couch, surveying with an astonished air the bare and blackened walls of her apartment; but there was a wildness and fixedness in her gaze which spoke of deeper disturbance than mere astonishment. No sooner had the knight looked upon her than suddenly he turned ashy pale, a cold shudder ran over all his limbs, his blood seemed to turn to ice in his veins, and when he essayed to speak, he could only utter incoherent ejaculations; then, as suddenly,

The Lion of Flanders

he rushed forward, and clasped the maiden in his arms, exclaiming in tones of mingled love and anguish:

"My own child! my poor Matilda! Have I then left my prison only to find you thus in the arms of death?"

But the maiden pushed him back from her with a look and gesture of passionate aversion.

"Traitor!" she exclaimed, "how dare you deal thus insolently with a daughter of the House of Flanders? Ah, you think that I am helpless now! Neither fear nor shame restrain you. But I have still a protector—God, who watches over me. There is lightning yet in store for you—yes, your punishment is at hand! Hark, wretch! hear you how the thunder growls?"

In an agony of grief and terror, Robert de Bethune tore the helmet from his brow. "Oh, my own Matilda!" he cried, "you do not know me: I am your father whom you love so much, and for whose sorrows you have wept so many bitter tears. Heavens! she thrusts me from her!"

A smile of triumph curled Matilda's lip as she exclaimed:

"Now you tremble, vile ravisher! now fear seizes upon your base and coward heart! But there is no mercy for you. The Lion, my father, will avenge me; and not with impunity shall you have put affront upon the blood of the Counts of

The Lion of Flanders

Flanders. Hark! I hear the Lion's roar; I hear his tread; my father comes! To me he brings his dear embrace, and death to you."

Not one of these words but pierced the father's heart like a venomed arrow, and filled it with untold anguish. Burning tears ran down his furrowed cheeks; in despair he smote his breast.

"But, my poor child," he cried, "do you not know me? Laugh not so bitterly; you strike my soul with death. I am your father—I am the Lion, whom you love, whom you call to help you."

"You the Lion!" she replied in accents of contempt; "you the Lion! say rather, liar! Is it not the tongue of the Queen Joanna that I hear you speak with—the tongue that flatters to betray? The Lion, too, went with them. They said, 'Come'; and what found he? A dungeon! and soon, perhaps, poison and a grave!"

In a transport of grief the knight pressed her in his arms. "But do you not hear, my child," he cried, "that it is the speech of our fathers that is upon my lips? What unheard of sufferings have thus unhinged your mind? Do you not remember that our friend Sir Adolf of Nieuwland has procured my liberty? Oh, talk not thus; your words wring my very heart!"

At the name of Adolf, the convulsive strain of the features somewhat relaxed, and a soft smile replaced their painful expression, while she

The Lion of Flanders

answered more gently, and this time without repulsing her deliverer:

"Adolf, say you? Adolf is gone to fetch the Lion. Have you seen him? He told you of the poor Matilda, did he not? Oh, yes! he is my brother! He has composed a new song for me. Listen! I hear the tones of his harp. How sweet are those sounds! But what is that? Ah, my father comes! I see a ray of light—a blessed beam of hope! Begone, caitiff!"

Her words died away into inarticulate sounds, while her countenance was overshadowed with an expression of the deepest melancholy.

Half-distracted now with alarm and grief, the knight felt his heart sink within him, and he knew not what to do. Silently he took the maiden's hand within his own, and bathed it with his tears; but almost instantly she snatched it back, exclaiming:

"No; this hand is not for a Frenchman! A false knight may not touch it. Go, your tears defile it; but the Lion will wash out the stain with blood. Look! there is blood upon my garment too—French blood! See how black it is!"

Again the knight endeavored to make his wandering child comprehend who he was; again he took her in his arms, and would have pressed her to his bosom; but she violently pushed him from her, while in piercing tones she exclaimed:

"Begone! away with those arms! They coil

around me like envenomed serpents; their very touch is dishonor. Release me, villain! Help help!"

With a sudden and desperate effort she disengaged herself from her deliverer, and sprang shrieking from the couch, the knight hastily pursuing her to prevent her egress from the chamber. A heartrending scene here ensued. Beside himself with grief and alarm, he caught the unhappy maiden in his arms, and strove to carry her back to the couch; while she, nerved by all the energy of delirium and despair, resisted his utmost endeavors. Great as was the strength of the knight, she seemed for a while almost a match for him; but at last, making a gigantic effort, he succeeded in bearing her back to the couch. She now ceased from all further resistance; her mood appeared suddenly to change. She sat still, and, looking reproachfully on the knight, said with bitter tears:

"It well beseems you to set your strength against that of a maiden, false knight. And why do you delay to complete your crime? No one sees—only God! But God has placed death between us; a yawning grave divides us. Therefore do you weep, because—"

The unhappy father was too much overcome by his grief to catch the last words of the maiden. Full of despair, he had seated himself upon a stone, and was gazing upon her with eyes moist with

The Lion of Flanders

tears, unconscious of aught but a sensation of unutterable anguish.

Presently Matilda's eyes closed, and she appeared to sleep. As he perceived this, a beam of hope lighted up the heart of the afflicted father. Sleep might restore her; and finding in this thought support and consolation, he sat noiselessly by her side, watching with tenderness and anxiety every breath she drew.

The Lion of Flanders

CHAPTER VI

After the destruction of the Castle of Male, a short march brought the Dean of the Butchers and his comrades back to St. Cross. Already, on their way thither, they had received intelligence from Bruges that the French garrison was under arms, and prepared to fall upon them as they entered the city; but elated by their recent victory, and deeming themselves sufficiently strong to oppose any force the enemy could bring against them, they nevertheless continued their march. Scarcely however, had they passed St. Cross, when an unexpected obstacle presented itself, and brought them suddenly to a stand. From the village to the city gate, the whole road was covered with a multitude of people pressing forward in the opposite direction and so dense was the throng that all further progress on the part of the Butchers became impossible.

Notwithstanding the obscurity of the night, the latter at once perceived, by the confused hubbub of voices and the dark masses moving before them, that a large portion of the population was leaving the city. Surging onward came the multitude;

The Lion of Flanders

and Breydel and his men, full of wonder at the sight, ranged themselves on one side, so as to allow them to pass. The retreat of the fugitives, however, had none of the appearance of a disorderly flight; each family walked on by itself, forming a separate group, and keeping itself distinct from all the rest, without any appearance of mingling or confusion. In the centre of one of these groups might be seen a mother, weeping as she went, the gray-headed grandfather leaning upon her for support, an infant at her breast, and the younger children, crying and wearied, clinging about her knees, while the elder ones followed behind, toiling under the weight of furniture or other property which they carried upon their backs. Group after group followed each other, in what seemed an interminable succession. Some few among them had carts or other vehicles loaded with goods; others, though these were but rare exceptions, were themselves mounted.

It may easily be imagined that Breydel was not long in seeking to ascertain the cause of this strange procession; but the lamentations with which he was everywhere greeted in answer to his inquiries were far from affording him any satisfactory explanation.

"Master," cried one, "the French would have burned us alive; we are flying from a miserable death."

The Lion of Flanders

"Oh Master Breydel!" exclaimed another, in a still more piteous tone, "for your life go not back to Bruges; there is a gallows waiting for you at the Smiths' Gate."

As the Dean was about to pursue his inquiries, in the hope of obtaining some clearer information, a wild cry was heard in the rear, and a voice, strong and powerful, but hoarse with terror, shouted aloud:

"Forward! forward! the French men-at-arms are upon us!"

Then there was a general rush onward, and the living tide rolled by with incredible rapidity. Suddenly, from a multitude of voices, there arose the cry:

"Woe! woe! they are burning our city! See, our houses are in flames! Oh, woe to us! woe! woe!"

Breydel, who up to this time had remained motionless and silent from sheer astonishment, now directed his eyes toward the city; and there, indeed, ever and anon, might be seen red jets of flame shooting up amid volumes of lurid smoke, which curled high above the walls. Rage and anguish now combined to rouse him from his stupor, and pointing to the city, he exclaimed:

"What! men of Bruges! is there one among you coward enough thus to abandon your city to destruction? No! never shall our foes make merry round that bonfire! Room here! room! Let us pass through, and then—"

Thus saying, and followed by his comrades, he dashed with resistless impetuosity through the crowd, throwing it aside right and left, while a burst of shrieks arose from the affrighted multitudes, who in their terror imagined that now indeed the French troops were upon them. Regardless of the alarm he had excited, Breydel rapidly pursued his way, wondering all the while that no men of warlike age were to be seen among the throng, when all at once his progress was arrested by a body of Guildsmen who were advancing toward him in regular order. It was a band of Clothworkers, all armed, but not all armed alike; some had crossbows, others halberds, others axes —such arms, in fact, as each man had been able to lay hands upon at the moment; many had only their knives. Onward they came with measured tread, their leader at their head, stopping the way as completely as a fixed barrier; while beyond them again, and following close upon their steps, other similar bodies might be seen issuing successively from the gate. They amounted in all to five thousand men. Breydel was on the point of addressing himself to the leader of the troop for an explanation, when far in the rear, above the din of arms and the heavy tramp of the Guildsmen, resounded the well-known voice of Deconinck.

The Lion of Flanders

"Steady, my men," he cried; "courage. Keep well together. Forward, third division! Close up, rear ranks! Fall in there on the left!"

Instantly Breydel pushed forward till he came within call of his friend. "What means all this?" he exclaimed. "A pretty time you have chosen for your drill! Is this what you are about while the city is burning! running away like a set of cowards after the women and children?"

"Ever the same! ever hot and impatient!" was the answer. "What is it you say about the city? Take my word for it, the French dogs shall burn nothing there."

"But, Master Deconinck, are you blind? Do you not see the flames blazing up above the walls?"

"Oh, that is what you mean, is it? That is only the straw we set fire to, that we might not be hindered in getting our wagons through the gates. The city is safe enough, my friend; set your mind at ease, and come back with me. I have important tidings to communicate to you. You know that I look at things coolly, and so it often happens that I am right. Take my advice now, and order your men to face about, and proceed along with us to St. Cross. Will you?"

"In truth, Master Peter, it is the only thing I can do, as I do not yet know what is on foot. But your people must halt for a moment."

Deconinck gave the necessary order to the subordinate officers; and immediately afterward was heard in loud, clear tones, the voice of Breydel:

"Butchers, face about, and then forward! keep your ranks, and be quick!"

Then, after personally superintending the execution of the maneuvre, he added:

"Now, Master Deconinck, I am at your orders."

"No, Master Breydel," replied the Dean of the Clothworkers, "now that you are here, you must take the command; you will make a better general than I shall."

Not a little pleased at this flattering recognition of his abilities, the Dean of the Butchers lost no time in taking possession of his office. "Butchers and Clothworkers, forward!" he thundered out; "steady, and not too fast!"

Upon this the Guildsmen set themselves in motion, the little army advanced steadily along the road, and in a short time reached St. Cross, where they found the women and children, with the baggage, awaiting their arrival. Singular, indeed, was the appearance presented by this confused encampment. A wide range of plain was thickly dotted with groups, each consisting of a single family. The night was so dark that it would have been impossible to distinguish objects beyond the distance of a few yards; but the numerous fires which already lighted up the scene showed the unfortunate wanderers crouching round them; or, in more extended circles, illuminated the remote background with their flickering glare. Sad and strange as was the sight presented to the eye, the sounds that struck upon the ear were not less wild and mournful. The cries of the children, the low wailings of the mothers, weighed upon the heart like the last sigh of a dying friend. But above the universal din might be heard the shouts of those who had strayed from their companions, or were calling to the missing ones; and louder and sharper still was the fierce barking of the dogs, faithfully keeping watch over their masters' households, or searching for them amid the confusion of the night.

On their arrival at St. Cross, Deconinck took Breydel apart into a house by the roadside, the owners of which received them with the greatest respect, and readily granted them a chamber for more private conference. Here, by the light of a small lamp, and with every precaution taken against their being overheard or interrupted, the Dean of the Clothworkers proceeded to inform his colleague as to what had taken place in the city during his absence.

"First," he began, "as to the cause of our flying from the city in the manner you see, and at this hour of the night: it is entirely owing to your breach of promise, and your imprudent proceedings at Male. No sooner were the flames of the

The Lion of Flanders

burning castle seen from the city walls than the tocsin sounded in the streets, and immediately all the inhabitants flocked together in the utmost terror: for in these troublous times they ever have the fear of death before their eyes. Messire de Mortenay had his men under arms in the market-place; but only as a measure of precaution, for no one knew what was going on. At last, some of the French who had escaped from the burning castle came flying into the town, calling aloud for vengeance; then there was no possibility of keeping the troops in the city quiet, nothing would satisfy them but fire and sword, and Messire de Mortenay had to threaten them pretty sharply with the gallows in order to keep them within bounds. You may imagine that, in such a state of things, I had lost not a moment in summoning my Clothworkers together, that at least we might not fall without making a determined fight for it. Perhaps we might even have succeeded in driving the French out; but such a victory could only have damaged the cause, as I shall presently show you. Then I had an interview with Messire de Mortenay, under safe conduct, and obtained from him a pledge that the city should be respected on condition of our forthwith evacuating it. Any Clawards found in Bruges after sunrise will be hanged."

"What!" cried Breydel, not a little indignant at the cool tone in which his brother Dean recounted a capitulation which appeared to him so scandalous; "what! is it possible? let yourselves be turned out like a herd of sheep! Oh, if I had but been there! our Bruges should not have been—"

"Yes, indeed, if you had been there; know you what would have happened then? Bruges would have seen a night of fire and sword, and the morning sun would have risen upon a scene of carnage and desolation! Hear me out, my hasty friend, and, I know, in the end, you will say I was right. One thing is certain, that we men of Bruges can not accomplish our freedom alone; and do you not see that, as long as the other cities of the land lie bound hand and foot, the enemy has his strong places at our very gates? Besides, how can we think only of our city, and forget our country? No, all the Flemish towns must stand or fall together! I doubt not that you have often pondered over all this; only in the moment of action your spirit runs away with you, and you forget all difficulties. There is, however, another important point to be considered: pray answer me this question—who gave you and me the right to kill, burn, and destroy? Who has given us authority to do these things, which we shall one day have to answer for at the judgment-seat of God?"

"But, master," replied Breydel, with a somewhat displeased look, "I suspect you are trying to throw dust in my eyes with all these fine speeches of yours.

The Lion of Flanders

Who gave us a right to kill and burn, say you? And pray, who gave it to the Frenchmen?"

"Who? Why, their king, Philip. The head that wears a crown takes all responsibility upon itself; a subject does not sin by fidelity and obedience. The blood that is shed cries out against the master who commanded the blow, not against the servant who struck it. But if we go to work on our own account, we are answerable before God and the world, and the blood that is shed lies at our door!"

"But, Master Deconinck, what have we done? What else than defend our life and property, and uphold the right of our lawful prince? For myself, I feel that I have nothing either to be sorry for or ashamed of; and I hope my ax hasn't yet struck its last blow. But, after all, Master Peter, I will not find fault with anything you say or do, though I confess I do not understand you; your thoughts are beyond the ken of mortal man, and that is the truth of it."

"Well, in part you are right; there is something behind more than you know of yet, and that is the knot I am just going to unravel. I know, Master Jan, that you have always thought me too patient and slow of action; but listen now to what I have been doing while you were risking all on a piece of useless vengeance. I have found means to acquaint our rightful lord, Count Guy, with our plans for the liberation of our country, and he has been pleased to confirm them with his princely approbation. So now, my friend, we are no longer rebels, but the generals of our lawful sovereign."

"Oh, master!" interrupted Breydel, in a tone of enthusiasm; "now I understand you; now indeed I thank you! How proudly does my heart beat at that honorable title! Yes, now I feel myself a true and worthy soldier; ay, and the French dogs shall feel it too!"

"Of this authority," continued Deconinck, "I have secretly availed myself for the purpose of inviting all the friends of the country to a general rising. This effort has been attended with the fullest success; and at the earliest call every city of Flanders will pour forth its levy of brave Clawards, as if they sprang forth out of the ground."

Here, in a transport of feeling, he pressed Breydel's hand, while for a moment his voice faltered with emotion: "And then, my noble friend, shall the sun of freedom rise again for Flanders, and not one living Frenchman shall be left for him to shine upon. Then, too, for very terror of our further vengeance, they will give us back our Lion. And we—we, the men of Bruges, shall have done this—shall have delivered our country! Does not your spirit swell within you at so proud a thought?"

In a transport of delight Breydel threw his arms around Deconinck's neck. "My friend! my friend!" he exclaimed. "How sweetly do your words fall upon my ear; a joy possesses me such as I never felt before. See, Master Peter, at this moment I would not change my name of Fleming even for the crown of Philip the Fair himself!"

"But, Master Breydel, you do not yet know the whole. The young Guy of Flanders and Count John of Namur are to be with us; Sir John Borluut is to bring up the men of Ghent; at Oudenarde there is the noble Arnold; at Alost Baldwin of Paperode. Sir John of Renesse has promised to come and aid us with all his vassals from Zeeland, and several other distinguished nobles will do the like. What say you now to my patience?"

"I can only marvel at you, my friend, and thank God from my heart that He has given you such wisdom. Now it is all over with the Frenchmen; I would not give six groats for the life of the longest liver among them!"

"To-day, at nine o'clock in the morning," continued Deconinck, "the Flemish chiefs meet to appoint the day for action. The young Lord Guy remains with us, and takes the command; the rest return to their domains in order to have their vassals in readiness. It would be well that you too should be at the meeting, that you may not through ignorance disconcert the measures that may be adopted. Will you, then, accompany me to the White Thicket in the Valley?"

The Lion of Flanders

"As you will, master; but what will our comrades say to our leaving them?"

"That I have provided for. They are prepared for my temporary absence, and Dean Lindens will for the present take the command. He is to proceed with our people to Damme, and there to wait for us. Come, let us start without further delay; for the day is beginning to break."

The Dean of the Clothworkers had taken care to have horses in readiness. Breydel in haste gave the necessary orders to his men, and the two friends set off together. There was but little opportunity for conversation during their hasty journey; nevertheless, Deconinck found time, in reply to Breydel's questions, to explain to him in brief terms the proposed scheme of general liberation. After an hour's sharp riding, they at last perceived the shattered towers of a ruined castle peeping out from among the trees.

"That is Nieuwenhove, is it not?" inquired Breydel, "where the Lion made such havoc of the French?"

"Yes; a little farther, and we are at the White Thicket."

"It must be acknowledged that our noble lord has not got his name for nothing; for a true lion he is when once the sword is in his hand."

These words were hardly out of Breydel's mouth, when they arrived at the spot on which the battle had been fought for the rescue of Matilda; there lay the corpses of the slain still weltering in their blood.

"Frenchmen!" muttered Deconinck as he rode by; "come on, master, we have no time to lose."

Breydel looked with fierce delight upon the bloody spectacle; and regardless of his companion's remonstrance, drew in his horse the better to contemplate it at his ease; and not only so, but he even urged his unwilling beast to trample the bodies under his hoofs until the Dean of the Clothworkers looking round, also reined in his steed, and turned back to the spot.

"Master Breydel!" he exclaimed; "what is this you are doing? For God's sake, hold! Surely you are taking a dishonorable revenge!"

"Let me alone," answered Breydel; "you do not know that these are some of the very rascals who struck me on the cheek! But listen! what is that? Don't you hear yonder among the ruins the sound as of a woman's cries? The thought is distraction; but it was by this very road that the villains carried off the Lady Matilda!"

With these words he leaped from his horse; and, without even stopping to secure it, started off at full speed toward the ruins. His friend proceeded to follow him without delay; but so much more deliberately that Breydel was already within the castle yard before Deconinck had dismounted and fastened the horses to the roadside. The nearer Breydel drew to the ruins, the more distinctly he heard the lamentations of a female voice; but finding, as he advanced, all further access barred, and unable at the instant to discern any entrance, he hastily mounted upon a heap of rubbish, and so obtained a view into the interior of the chamber from which, as he imagined, the sounds proceeded. At the first glance he recognized Matilda; but the black knight who forcibly held her in his arms, and whom with such desperate energy she sought to repulse (for she was again endeavoring to leave the couch, upon which exhaustion rather than slumber had for a while retained her), was altogether unknown to him, and could therefore appear to him only in the light of an assailant. Instantly he drew forth his ax from under his garment, climbed upon the window-sill, and dropped like a stone into the chamber.

"Villain!" he cried, advancing upon the knight, "base Frenchman! you have lived your time; you shall not have laid hands unpunished upon the daughter of the Lion, my lord and prince."

The knight stood amazed at the sudden apparition, not having in the instant perceived the manner of the Butcher's entrance, and for a moment he made no answer to his threats; quickly recovering himself, however, he replied:

"You are mistaken, Master Breydel; I am a true

The Lion of Flanders

son of Flanders. Be calm; the Lion's daughter is already avenged."

Breydel knew not what to think: his excited feelings had hardly yet subsided. Nevertheless, the knight's words, spoken in the Flemish tongue, and by one who seemed to know him well, were not without their effect. Matilda, meanwhile, still in her delirium, and accounting the black knight her enemy, welcomed the newcomer with joy as her deliverer.

"Kill him!" she cried, with a laugh of triumph; "kill him! He has shut up my father in prison, and now, false caitiff that he is, he is carrying me away to deliver me to the wicked Joanna of Navarre. Fleming, why do you not avenge the child of your ancient lords?"

The black knight looked upon the maiden with sorrowful compassion. "Unhappy girl!" he sighed, while tears filled his eyes.

"I see that you love and pity the Lion's daughter," said Breydel, pressing the knight's hand; "forgive me, sir; I did not know you for a friend."

At this moment Deconinck appeared at the entrance of the chamber; but no sooner had his eye fallen upon the scene which presented itself before him, than throwing up his hands above his head with astonishment, and then casting himself upon his knees at the feet of the black knight, he exclaimed:

The Lion of Flanders

"Oh heavens! our lord and prince, the Lion!"

"Our lord! our prince! the Lion!" repeated Breydel, hastily following Deconinck's example, and kneeling by his side; "my God, what have I done?"

"Rise, my faithful subjects," responded Robert; "I have heard of all your noble efforts in your Prince's service." Then raising them, he proceeded:

"Look here upon the daughter of your Count, and think how a father's heart must be torn at such a sight. And yet I have nothing wherewith to supply her needs—nothing save the shelter of these shattered walls, and the cold water of the brook. The Lord is indeed laying heavy trials upon me."

"Be pleased, noble Count," interposed Breydel, "to give me your commands; I will procure you all that you require. Accept, I pray, the humble services of your liege subject."

He was already on his way toward the door, when a gesture of command from the Count suddenly arrested him.

"Go," said Robert, "and seek a physician; but let it be no Lilyard, and exact from him an oath that he will reveal nothing of what he may see or hear."

"My lord," replied Breydel, with exultation, "I know precisely the man you want. There is a friend of mine, as warm a Claward as any in Flanders, who lives hard by, at Wardamme; I will bring him hither immediately."

"Go; but take heed not to utter my name to him; let my presence here remain a secret to all but yourselves."

Breydel hastened away on his errand, and the Count took the opportunity of questioning the Dean of the Clothworkers at some length concerning the state of affairs in Flanders. Then he said:

"Yes, Master Deconinck, I have heard in my prison, from Sir Diederik die Vos and Sir Adolf of Nieuwland, of your loyal though as yet fruitless endeavors. It is a great satisfaction to me to find that, although most of our nobles have forsaken us, we still have subjects such as you."

"It is true, illustrious sir," answered the Dean, "that only too many of the nobles have taken part against their country; nevertheless, they who remained true are more in number than the renegades. My endeavors, moreover, have not been altogether so fruitless as your highness may suppose; and even now the deliverance of Flanders is near at hand. At this very moment the Lord Guy and the Lord John of Namur, with many other nobles, are met together in the White Thicket in the valley to organize a powerful confederation for that purpose, and are now only waiting my arrival to proceed to the discussion of the necessary measures."

The Lion of Flanders

"What say you? So near to these ruins? my two brothers?"

"Yes, noble sir, your two illustrious brothers, and also your faithful friend, John of Renesse."

"O God! and I may not embrace them! Sir Diederik die Vos has doubtless told you upon what conditions I have obtained this temporary freedom; and I can not expose the lives of those to whom I owe it. Nevertheless, I must see my brothers; I will go with you, but with visor down. Should I judge it necessary to make myself known, I will give you a sign, and you shall then demand of all the knights present a solemn pledge of secrecy as to who I am. Till then I will abstain from uttering a word."

"Your will shall be executed, most noble sir," replied Deconinck; "be assured that you shall have reason to be satisfied with my discretion. But see, the Lady Matilda seems to sleep. May the rest benefit her!"

"She is not really asleep, poor child; she does but slumber heavily from exhaustion. But methinks I hear footsteps. Remember; my helmet once again upon my head, you know me no longer."

The next instant the physician entered, followed by Breydel. Offering a silent and respectful greeting to the knight, he at once proceeded to the patient's side. After a short examination of her state he declared that she must be bled; and this

The Lion of Flanders

having been done, and the arm bound up, she seemed again to slumber.

"Sir," said the physician, addressing himself to the black knight, who had turned away his face during the operation; "I assure you that the young lady is in no danger; with a moderate period of rest and quiet her senses will return."

Comforted by this assurance, the Count made a sign to the two Deans, who thereupon followed him out of the chamber.

"Master Breydel," he said, "to your care I commit my child; watch over the daughter of your Count until I return. And now, Master Peter, let us make haste to the White Thicket."

They quickly reached the appointed place, and here falling in with some dozen knights, who were already anxiously awaiting Deconinck's arrival, the whole party entered the wood together. In this secluded spot were assembled the chief men of the Flemish name and nation; among then John Count of Namur and the younger Guy, two brothers of Count Robert, William of Juliers, their cousin, a priest, and the provost of Aix-la-Chapelle; John of Renesse, the brave Zeelander; John Borluut, the hero of Woeringen; Arnold of Oudenarde, and Baldwin of Paperode. These, and others of scarcely less note and consequence, were here met together in their country's cause. The presence, however, of a stranger (for such the black knight appeared to be) occasioned them considerable uneasiness, and the looks which they directed toward Deconinck evidently demanded an immediate explanation; this, therefore, he proceeded at once to give.

"Illustrious sirs," he said, "I bring you here one of the noblest knights which our country can boast; one of the greatest enemies the Frenchman has to dread. Certain weighty reasons—reasons upon which the life and death of one of our best friends depend—forbid him for the present from making himself known to you; take it not amiss, therefore, that for the present he keeps his visor down, and maintains a strict silence; for to many of you his voice is no less familiar than his countenance. My long-tried fidelity to our common cause will vouch to you sufficiently that I am bringing no false brother among you."

The knights wondered greatly at this strange declaration, and racked their memories for a name which might belong to the unknown knight; but no one thought of the captive Lion—for how was it possible he should be here? Nevertheless, Deconinck's assurance was sufficient for them; and having taken all due precautions against surprise, they proceeded without further delay to the business of their meeting, which was thus opened by the Dean of the Clothworkers, who addressed himself especially to the two princes:

The Lion of Flanders

"I must first tell you, noble sirs," said he, "how painfully the men of Bruges have been afflicted at the captivity of your noble father, our lawful Count.

"True it is that we have often heretofore risen up against him in defense of our rights and liberties, and doubtless some of you may have imagined that we should therefore take part with his enemies; but of this be well assured—never will a free and generous people endure a foreign master. This, indeed, we have clearly shown; for since King Philip's traitorous plot against our rightful lord, ofttimes have we imperiled life and goods, and made many a Frenchman die the death in penalty for his king's unprincely deed, while the streets of Bruges have streamed with Flemish blood. This being so, I have ventured, noble sirs, to kindle in your hearts the hopes that animate my own of a speedy and general deliverance; for I am convinced that the yoke is now so loosened on our necks, that with one vigorous effort we might cast it from us forever. A fortunate accident has served us in a remarkable manner; the Dean of the Butchers, with his fellows, has destroyed the Castle of Male, whereupon Messire de Mortenay has driven all the Clawards out of Bruges, and now there are about five thousand Guildsmen in arms at Damme. Among them are seven hundred Butchers, who have joined us with their Dean, Jan

The Lion of Flanders

Breydel, at their head; nor do I hesitate to say that these bold men may safely be depended upon not to turn their backs before ten times their number; they are, indeed, a very band of Lions. Therefore, noble sirs, we have already in the field no despicable army, and may confidently hope to drive out the French, if only you, on your part, can bring to our assistance an adequate force from the remaining towns of Flanders. Such is my proposal; and may it please you, noble sirs, to approve the same, and to take speedy measures accordingly; for, believe me, the moment is most favorable. I place myself entirely in your hands, and am ready, to the best of my ability, to execute your commands as a true and faithful subject of your illustrious house."

"It seems to me," answered John Borluut, "that what we have most to deprecate is too great haste. The men of Bruges may be ready, and even now in arms; but in the other cities things are by no means so forward as yet. For my part, I should gladly see the day of vengeance postponed awhile, that we might collect larger reenforcements for ensuring it. Be assured that a vast number of Lilyards, those bastard sons of Flanders, will flock to the French standard. We must remember that it is the liberty of our country which is at stake, and that, too, on a single die; for if we throw away our present chance we shall hardly get another.

The Lion of Flanders

Once fail, and all we can do is to hang up our arms and quietly submit."

As the noble Borluut was universally famed for his skill and experience in war, his speech made a deep impression upon many of his hearers, John of Namur among the rest. Guy, on the other hand, was strongly opposed to the view he took of things.

"But bethink you, sirs," he passionately exclaimed, "that each hour of delay is an hour of suffering for my poor aged father, and for so many of our unhappy kindred; think what my glorious brother Robert is now enduring! he that could not brook even the suspicion of affront or wrong, and whom we are leaving to wear out his life in bondage, to our own eternal disgrace and shame! Do not our captive brothers call to us from their dungeons, asking us what we have done with our swords, and whether this be the way in which we acquit ourselves of our knightly duty? And what answer can we give them? None! none but the blush of shame! No! I will wait no longer! The sword is drawn! never shall it reenter the scabbard until it has drunk deep of the blood of our foes! I hope that our noble cousin of Juliers agrees with me in this resolution."

"The sooner the better, it seems to me," responded William of Juliers; "we have looked on long enough at the injuries done to our house;

longer than it were meet or manly to do without attempting either help or vengeance. I have put on my harness, and will not lay it off till the need for it is over. I go hand and heart with my cousin Guy; and no procrastination for me!"

"But, noble sirs," resumed John Borluut, "allow me to observe that we all need time to get our forces on foot, especially if we are to avoid giving the alarm to the enemy. If you hurry on your rising prematurely, you will lose the aid we might otherwise afford you. I only repeat to you what Sir John of Renesse has just been saying to me."

"It will be absolutely impossible for me," observed the knight thus appealed to, "to have my vassals under arms in less than a fortnight; and I can not but earnestly conjure the Lords Guy and William to acquiesce in the views which the noble Borluut has just expressed. Besides, we must remember that the German men-at-arms whom we expect can hardly be brought into the field without some delay. What say you, Master Deconinck?"

"So far as the words of so humble a subject as myself can be of any weight with the princes, I would endeavor to persuade them to act for the present with caution and prudence. The number of fugitives from Bruges will certainly increase, and will necessarily betake themselves to our camp; in the meanwhile, these noble gentlemen

The Lion of Flanders

will have time to assemble their vassals, and the Lord William of Juliers to return with his men-at-arms from Germany."

The black knight did not seem to share the opinions expressed by the last speakers, to judge at least by the significant movements of his head, which were plainly indicative of dissent; but though evidently laboring under a great desire to speak, he still preserved an unbroken silence. At last, the Lords Guy and William, finding the rest unanimous against them, gave way; and it was eventually decided that Deconinck, with the men of Bruges, should encamp at Damme and Ardenburg; while William of Juliers should bring up his forces from Germany, and Guy, the younger, his brother's troops from Namur. John of Renesse agreed to set out for Zeeland, and the others each to his own lordship, to make things ready for a general rising.

But at the moment that they were exchanging their parting greetings, the black knight made signs to detain them:

"Noble sirs!" he began.

At the first sound of his voice all present started, and each looked hastily round upon the next; as if to see whether he could read his own thought upon his neighbor's countenance. While the others were interrogating each other's looks, Guy rushed forward and exclaimed:

The Lion of Flanders

"Oh, blessed hour! my brother! my dearest brother! his voice penetrates my inmost heart!"

Thus saying, he quickly plucked the helmet from the head of the disguised knight, while he clasped him in his arms with impetuous delight.

"The Lion! our noble Count!" was the universal cry.

"My unhappy brother," continued Guy, "what sufferings have been yours! how deeply have I mourned for you! but now, oh, happy moment! now I can once more embrace you; you have broken your chains, and Flanders has regained her Count. Bear with my tears; it is for you they flow, as I think of all you have endured. The Lord be thanked for this unlooked-for happiness!"

Robert pressed the young knight affectionately to his heart; then, after turning and embracing his other brother, John of Namur, he thus spoke:

"There are good and weighty reasons, noble sirs, why I should preserve my incognito for the present; nevertheless, the decision to which you have just come has rendered it a still more imperative duty for me to declare myself, that I may, if possible, induce you to reconsider your measures. You must know, then, that Philip of France has summoned all the great feudatories of the crown, along with their vassals, to wage war against the Moors. But as the sole ostensible motive of this

The Lion of Flanders

expedition is to reinstate the King of Majorca in his dominions, it seems certain that the real object of the king in collecting so numerous an army is the maintenance of his dominion in Flanders. The time of assembling is appointed for the close of June; so that one month more, and our enemy will have seventy thousand men in the field. Consider, therefore, whether it is not advisable that the day of our liberation should anticipate his preparations, lest afterward we find it too late. Remember, however, that I am but giving you information and advice; I lay no commands upon you, for tomorrow I must return to my prison."

There could be no difference of opinion as to the importance of this intelligence; it was therefore unanimously agreed that the utmost expedition was necessary, and that the plan of operations must be modified accordingly. It was decided that all should proceed immediately to cooperate with Deconinck at Damme, taking with them such forces as they could get together on the spur of the occasion. The young Guy, as, in Robert's absence, the next representative of the House of Flanders, was to take the chief command of the army, William of Juliers declining the office, as incompatible with his ecclesiastical character, and John of Namur being unable personally to join the Flemings, as his presence at home at this juncture was indispensable for the defense of his own territories.

The Lion of Flanders

The latter, however, undertook to furnish a considerable contingent of men.

The nobles now separated, and Robert was left alone with his two brothers, his cousin William, and the Dean of the Clothworkers.

"Oh, Guy!" he began, in a tone of the deepest grief, "oh, John! I bring you tidings so terrible that my tongue can hardly find words to utter them, and the mere thought of them blinds my eyes with tears. You know how basely Queen Joanna threw our poor Philippa into prison; how for six long years the unhappy maiden sighed in the dungeons of the Louvre, far from all she loved. Doubtless you think that she still lives, and continue to pray to God for her release. Alas! your prayers are in vain; my poor sister has been poisoned, and her body cast into the Seine."

For a moment Guy and John of Namur lost all power of speech; they stood pale and confounded, their eyes fixed on the ground. Guy was the first to rouse himself from his stupor:

"It is true, then," he exclaimed, "Philippa is dead! Oh, soul of my sister, look down upon me, and read in my bosom how my heart mourns for you, how it burns to avenge your death! I—yes, and you too—shall be avenged; torrents of blood shall expiate your wrongs."

"Let not your grief thus carry you away, my fair cousin," interposed William; "mourn for your sister, pray for her soul's repose, but let your sword be drawn only for the freedom of our country. Blood can not bribe the jealous grave to restore its victim."

"My brothers," interrupted Robert, "and you, my cousin, be pleased to follow me; I will lead you to my poor child Matilda. She is not far from hence, and on the way I have other matters of serious import to communicate to you. Let your attendants wait for you here."

Robert now related to them the wonderful manner in which he had rescued his daughter from the French soldiers, and all the anxiety and anguish he had undergone within the ruins of Nieuwenhove.

On entering the chamber where Matilda was lying, they found her to all appearance in a profound and peaceful slumber, her cheeks white as alabaster, and her breathings so imperceptible that she might almost have been taken for a corpse. Great was the emotion of the knights at the sight of the maiden with her disordered and blood-stained dress. Filled with sorrowful compassion, they stood with hands clasped tightly together, but without uttering a word; for the physician's finger, anxiously pressed upon his lips, had warned them that the most perfect silence was necessary for the welfare of his patient.

Guy was not, however, able altogether to repress

his feelings. "Can that be the noble daughter of the Lion?" burst from his lips, as in an agony of grief he threw himself upon his brother's bosom. The physician now motioned to the knights to withdraw from the chamber, and then at last he unclosed his lips.

"The young lady," he said, "has recovered her senses; but she still suffers greatly from weakness and exhaustion. She woke up in your absence, and recognizing Master Breydel, who stood by, she asked him many questions, as though seeking to collect her ideas. He comforted her with the assurance that she should soon see her father; and as in her present state it is very inadvisable to disappoint her, I strongly recommend you not to leave her. Meanwhile, no time should be lost in procuring her a change of clothes and a more fitting resting-place."

Count Robert having thrown aside his incognito unwillingly, and solely under the pressure of necessity, was still anxious to restrict the knowledge of his presence within the narrowest possible circle; he therefore made no reply for the moment to the physician's recommendations, but, returning with his companions to Matilda's side, sat gazing in silent sorrow upon the pale and seemingly lifeless form of his child. Soon her lips began to move, and she uttered from time to time half-audible sounds. Presently she drew a deeper breath; and

The Lion of Flanders

twice the sweet word "father," distinctly articulated, struck the listening ear of the Count. A long kiss imprinted on the opening lips expressed the parent's delight, and hastened the maiden's awakening; her blood seemed again to flow, the color returned to her lips, and began even faintly to tinge her cheeks, while her eyes opened to the light with a soft and cheering smile.

It would be impossible to describe the expression of the maiden's countenance at the sight which met her returning consciousness; she did not speak, but raised her arms as though to throw them about her father's neck, who, in his turn, bent over her to meet her fond embrace. Yet her manner of greeting him was not such as he expected; with fondling tenderness she pressed both her hands over his face, and then gently stroked his cheeks; for the moment father and daughter seemed to be lost in one absorbing dream of happiness. Nor were the bystanders, in their measure, less affected by the moving spectacle; they looked on in profoundest silence, cautiously suppressing every sound or movement that might disturb a scene of almost solemn interest. It was curious, however, to observe how differently the several persons gave expression to their feelings. John of Namur, who had most command over himself, stood gazing fixedly before him; William of Juliers, the priest, with bended knees and folded hands, sought composure in prayer; while, to judge from their varying gestures, and the changeful working of their countenances, Sir Guy and Jan Breydel seemed to be swayed alternately by fierce desires of vengeance and the tenderest emotions of sympathy. Deconinck, usually so cold in appearance, was now the most deeply moved of all; a stream of tears flowed from under the hand with which his eyes were screened. No living heart in Flanders beat more warmly for his honored lord than that of the patriotic Clothworker of Bruges; all that belonged to the greatness of his fatherland was holy in the eyes of this noble citizen.

At last Matilda awoke from her trance-like contemplation, clasped her father in her arms, and with a faint voice gave utterance to her feelings in words; to which he, on his part, in tones of heartfelt joy, mingled, however, with sorrow, as ardently responded.

Sir Guy now approached to welcome his niece.

"Ha!" she exclaimed, but still without loosing her hold of her father, "what is it that I see! my dear uncle Guy here, weeping over me! and my cousin William there on his knees, praying! and my uncle John of Namur! Are we, then, at Wynandael?"

"My dear, unhappy niece," replied Guy, "my heart is ready to break to behold you thus; let me

The Lion of Flanders

too embrace you; it will be some alleviation of my grief;" and he tenderly drew her from her father's arms into his own.

Then, somewhat raising her voice, she said:

"Come, my good cousin of Juliers, do you too give me a kiss; and you too, my kind uncle John."

Thus, as if once more within the bosom of her family, she seemed to forget her sorrows for a moment, and to catch a passing gleam of her old childlike happiness. But when William of Juliers approached, she regarded him with astonishment from head to foot, and exclaimed:

"Why, how is this, cousin William? You, a servant of God, in harness, and with sword by your side!"

"The priest who is in arms for his country is in his holy calling!" was the reply.

Deconinck, meanwhile, and Breydel, standing with uncovered heads at a little distance from the couch, participated in the general joy. Deeply grateful for the faithful affection they had exhibited toward her, Matilda again drew her father's head to her bosom, and whispered in his ear:

"Will you promise me one thing, my dearest father?"

"What is it, my child? It will be a delight to me to fulfil any wish of yours."

"Well, then, forget not, I pray you, to reward

The Lion of Flanders

these two good and faithful subjects according to their deserts. Daily have they risked their lives in the cause of our country and our house."

"Your desire shall be accomplished, my child. But loose your arms for a moment from my neck," he added, "that I may speak with your uncle Guy."

The two left the chamber together; and when they had reached a convenient spot, the Count said: "My brother, it is fitting that fidelity and affection such as these two good citizens have shown should not be allowed to pass unrewarded; and I am about to charge you with the execution of my wishes in their regard. Remember, then, that it is my desire, that upon the first suitable occasion, with the standard of our house unfurled, and in presence of the Guilds drawn up under arms, and in battle-array, you confer the honor of knighthood upon Peter Deconinck and Jan Breydel, that all may know that it is love for our country which confers the best patent of nobility. Keep this command secret until the time arrives for performing it. And now let us rejoin the rest; for it is high time that I should be gone."

They now returned together to the chamber, and Robert, approaching his daughter, took her hand in his. "My child," he said, "you know by what means I have obtained this temporary freedom; a generous friend is risking his life by taking my

The Lion of Flanders

place the while. Yield not to sadness, my Matilda; strive, like me, to bear with patience and—"

"I know too well what you would say," she interrupted; "you are about to leave me!"

"You have said it, my noble child; I must return to my prison. I have pledged my faith and honor to remain only one day in Flanders. But weep not, these evil days will soon be over."

"I will not weep—that were a grievous sin. I give thanks to God for this consolation which He has sent me, and will endeavor to deserve a renewal of such happiness by prayer and patience. Go, my father; one kiss more, and may all the holy angels be with you on your way!"

"Deans," said Robert, turning to the two citizens, "to you I entrust the command of the men of Bruges, to Master Deconinck especially, as principal leaders of the forces. But first, I pray you to procure the services of some good and trusty tire-woman for my daughter, and provide her with other clothing. Take her with you hence, and defend her from all wrong; into your charge I commit her, to be cared for as becomes the blood from which she springs. Master Breydel, be pleased to bring my horse out into the yard."

The Count now took leave of his brothers and of his cousin, and again embraced his daughter, fixing a long and tender look upon her, as though seeking to imprint her image in his memory. She, too, kissed him again and again, clasping him in her arms, as if she could hardly make up her mind to let him go.

"Be comforted, my child," he continued; "I shall soon return, I trust, for good and all; and in a few days your good brother Adolf will be with you again."

"Oh, tell him to make haste!—then, I know, he will give wings to his horse! Go now, and God be with you, dear father!—I will not weep."

At last the parting was ended, and the tramp of the horses was soon heard in the distance. Her father was no sooner gone, however, than Matilda forgot her promise, and a flood of tears rolled down her cheeks. Yet they were not tears of anguish; for a gentle feeling of consolation remained behind in her heart. Deconinck and Breydel executed their lord's commands with carefulness and speed; a female attendant and fresh clothing were procured; and before evening they were all safe in the camp at Damme with the fugitives of Bruges.

The Lion of Flanders

CHAPTER VII

DURING the week which succeeded to the events last narrated, more than three thousand of the citizens left Bruges and betook themselves either to Deconinck's camp at Ardenburg, or to Damme, where the Dean of the Butchers was in command. The French garrison, meanwhile, increasing in confidence and security as the able-bodied men left the city, abandoned themselves to every species of license, and treated those of the inhabitants that remained as though they had been their very slaves. Nevertheless, there were only too many at Bruges, who, so far from taking umbrage at the presence of the foreigners, consorted with them in all cheerfulness, as if they had been their very brethren. But these were such as had denied their country, and sought by their cowardice to curry favor with the stranger; they were even proud of their by-name of Lilyards, as if it had been a title of honor. The rest were indeed Clawards, true sons of Flanders, who hated the yoke, and were longing for the time when they could cast it off; but the worldly goods which they had earned to themselves by the sweat of their brows were too

The Lion of Flanders

dear to their hearts to be abandoned to the discretion of foreign marauders.

It was these Clawards, and the wives and children of the fugitives, who were made to feel the heavy yoke and the cruel exactions of an insolent foe. Having nothing now to check them in the gratification of their cowardly revenge, the invaders tyrannized and plundered without mercy or moderation; they carried off by force the goods out of the shops, and paid for them with insults or blows. Irritated with this oppression, the citizens with one accord ceased to expose their goods for sale, and the French could no longer procure provisions even for ready money. Not a loaf of bread, not a piece of meat, was to be had; all were hidden away underground, out of the way of the enemy's search. Before four days were over, the garrison was in such distress for food that foraging parties were sent to scour the neighboring country in quest of supplies. Luckily for them, the deficiency was in part provided for by the care of their Lilyard friends; but notwithstanding their assistance, a grievous scarcity reigned within the gates. All the houses of the Clawards were shut up, all business of sale and purchase was at an end; the whole city seemed asleep, with the exception of the cowardly Lilyards and the violent and restless soldiers. The working-people, being deprived of all employment, could no longer pay their assessment, and were

The Lion of Flanders

obliged to lurk about in order to conceal themselves from Van Gistel's perquisitions. On Saturdays, when the tax-gatherers went round for the silver penny, they found no one at home; it was as if all the people of Bruges had abandoned their city. Many of the Guildsmen made representations to Van Gistel that, inasmuch as they were earning nothing, they were unable to pay the dues; but the unnatural Fleming turned a deaf ear to all remonstrance, and proceeded to levy the arrears by force. A great number of the citizens were then cast into prison; some—for resisting, or for making public complaint—were even put to death.

Messire de Mortenay, the French governor of the city and commander of the garrison, more merciful than the Flemish tax-gatherer, when he perceived the extremity to which the people were reduced, would gladly have diminished the burdens which pressed so heavily upon them; and with this view sent an account of the alarming and distressing state of things to his superior, De Chatillon, then at Courtrai, requesting his authority for the abolition of the obnoxious tax. Van Gistel, however, well aware that his countrymen cried shame upon him as an apostate, and, like every apostate, hating those whom he had betrayed, seized the opportunity to urge De Chatillon to increased severity. He painted the rebellious spirit of the men of Bruges in the blackest colors, and called loudly

The Lion of Flanders

for chastisement on their headstrong obstinacy; representing that their alleged inability to procure employment was a mere pretense, and that they wilfully abstained from work in order that they might have a plausible pretext for refusing payment of the tax.

De Chatillon's wrath at this intelligence exceeded all bounds. Everything he had done for carrying out the king's commands seemed to have been without result; the Flemish people were unsubdued, and to all appearance still indomitable. In all the towns of Flanders tumults were every day occurring; everywhere hatred of the French name began to display itself more publicly; and not at Bruges only, but in other places, the servants of King Philip frequently fell victims to the popular fury, either in open fray or by secret assassination. There, too, were the ruined towers of Male, the fire still smoldering among its walls, and its stones still reeking with the Frenchmen's blood.

The fountain-head of this stream of disaffection was evidently Bruges; there it was that the spirit of revolt had first displayed itself, and thence it had spread over the whole land of Flanders. Breydel and Deconinck were the two heads of the dragon which thus obstinately refused to crouch under the sceptre of King Philip. All this considered, De Chatillon resolved on a vigorous demonstration, which should stifle, once for all, the

The Lion of Flanders

liberties of Flanders in the blood of the refractory. Drawing together in all haste seventeen hundred men-at-arms out of Hainault, Picardy, and French Flanders, he joined to them a large body of infantry; and thus, in complete battle array, marched upon Bruges. Fully determined to take summary vengeance on the patriots, he carried with him several large casks, containing the ropes with which he designed to hang Deconinck, Breydel, and such as supported them, from the windows of their own houses. His expedition, meanwhile, was kept a profound secret from all in the city, with the sole exception of the governor, as a precaution against any defensive measures which the Clawards might adopt.

It was on the 13th of May, 1302, at nine o'clock in the morning, that the French force entered the city, with the governor-general at their head. Stern and threatening was the aspect of De Chatillon, as he rode along the streets, while the hearts of the citizens were oppressed with painful anxiety, foreseeing, as they could not but do, a part at least of the fate which was awaiting them. The Clawards might easily be recognized by their troubled countenances and downcast bearing; still they did not apprehend much beyond a rigorous enforcement of the capitation-tax, and a general increase of severity.

The Lilyards had joined the garrison, and together with the latter stood drawn up under arms upon the Friday's market-place. To them the governor-general's arrival was a matter of rejoicing, for from him they looked to obtain retaliation for the contempt and abhorrence with which they were regarded by the Clawards; and as he approached, loud and repeated cries of "France! France! long live King Philip and our noble governor!" resounded from their ranks.

Attracted by curiosity, the people had flocked together from every quarter of the city, and now occupied in crowds the whole neighborhood of the market-place. Every countenance bore an expression of the deepest fear and anxiety; mothers pressed their children closer to their breasts, and from many an eye trickled the unconscious tear. But while all were terrified at the vengeance which seemed ready to descend upon their heads, not a single voice of greeting was raised for France or her representative. Powerless, indeed, they were for the present; but hatred against their oppressors burned fiercely in their hearts, and ever and anon flashed out in threatening glances from their eyes: they thought of Breydel and Deconinck, and of a day of bloody retribution.

While the population were thus looking on in moody silence, De Chatillon had drawn up his forces in the market-place in such wise that either side of it was lined with men-at-arms, while one end was entirely occupied by a strong body of infantry—the troops thus forming three sides of a square, of which the fourth remained open; an arrangement which allowed the citizens a full view of all that was passing in the centre. He then despatched, as quietly as possible, a strong body of men to each of the city gates, with instructions to seize, secure, and defend them.

The governor-general, accompanied by some of his principal officers, now advanced into the centre of the square. Here the chancellor Peter Flotte, the governor of the city De Mortenay, and John van Gistel the Lilyard entered with him into what seemed an animated discussion upon some subject of pressing importance; at least if one might have judged from the passionate gesticulations of the speakers. Although they were careful not to raise their voices so as to be heard by the citizens, their words were nevertheless occasionally audible to the French officers; and more than one brave knight cast looks of compassion upon the anxious people, and of contempt upon the traitor Van Gistel, as he thus addressed the governor-general:

"Believe me, Messire, I know the headstrong nature of my countrymen; your lenity will serve only to increase their insolence. Warm the serpent in your bosom, and it will sting you! I judge from long experience; and I say, the men of Bruges will never bear the yoke quietly so long as these firebrands of sedition live among them; these must you quench, or you never will be master in this city."

"Methinks," said th echancellor with a malicious smile, "that Messire Van Gistel's countrymen are not much beholden to him for his good word. If we were to believe him, I trow there would not be many alive in this populous city to-morrow morning."

"On my honor, noble sirs," replied Van Gistel, "it is only out of faithful regard for the king's interests that I speak. I repeat it, nothing but the blood of the ringleaders can quench the mutinous spirit of our citizens. I can give you a list of all the thorough-paced Clawards here; and as long as they remain at large, I tell you there will never be any peace in Bruges."

"How many names might your list contain?" asked De Chatillon.

"Some forty," he coolly replied.

"How!" cried De Mortenay, in the highest indignation; "you would have forty of these citizens hung for your good pleasure! It is not those here, however, who deserve such punishment. The principal offenders have escaped to Damme. Hang Breydel, Deconinck, and their crew, with all my heart, when and where you can lay hands upon them; but not these poor defenseless creatures, on whom you are merely seeking to wreak your revenge."

"Messire de Mortenay," observed De Chatillon, "I think you wrote to inform me that the citizens refused to sell provisions to your men; what call you that but downright rebellion?"

"It is true, my lord governor, that in some respects they have passed all bounds, and have forgotten their duty as obedient subjects; but it is now six months since my people have received their pay, and the Flemings refuse any longer to sell except for ready money. I should, in truth, be deeply grieved were my letter to be the occasion of any extreme measures."

"This tenderness for the rebels can end only in the direst results to the interests of the crown of France," insisted Van Gistel; "and I wonder much to hear Messire de Mortenay thus pleading in their behalf."

There was a sneering tone in these words of the Fleming, which incensed De Mortenay even more than the speech itself. Casting a look of the deepest scorn upon the Lilyard, the noble-hearted soldier thus replied:

"If you felt for your country as an honest man should feel, it would not be necessary for me, a Frenchman, to defend your unhappy brethren against your bloodthirsty malice. And now, listen, I tell you to your face, before Messire de Chatillon here, the citizens never would have refused to sell us provisions, if you had not gone so nefariously to work in exacting the capitation tax. It is to you we owe these troubles; for all your thought is how to trample under foot your own people. No wonder they are full of the bitterest hatred against us and our government, when power is entrusted to such as you."

"I call every one of you to witness that I have only, with zeal and in all fidelity, executed the orders of Messire de Chatillon."

"Call you that zeal and fidelity?" exclaimed De Mortenay; "say rather your own malignant spite against your countrymen for the just contempt they bear you. It was a grievous oversight of the king our lord to set one whom all the world cries shame upon over his revenue in Flanders."

"Messire de Mortenay," cried Van Gistel, passionately, "you shall answer to me for this!"

"Sirs," interposed the governor-general, "let there be an end of this! I forbid you to exchange another word in my presence; let your swords decide your quarrel at a fitting opportunity. At the same time I tell you, Messire de Mortenay, that the fashion of your speech displeases me, and that in all things Messire van Gistel has demeaned himself according to my will. The honors of the French crown must be avenged; and were it not that the ringleaders have left the city, there should be more gibbets this day in Bruges than there are crossways to plant them in. Meanwhile, however, and until a convenient time arrives for putting the rebels to the rout at Damme, I am resolved to make a severe example now and on the spot. Messire van Gistel, give me the names of the eight most obstinate Clawards in the city, and to the gallows with them without more ado."

Determined not to miss this first instalment of his revenge, Van Gistel passed his eyes along the multitude before him; and picking out eight persons from among the crowd, marked them on the instant to the governor-general. A herald was then called, who speedily made his appearance in front of the citizens; and having first, by a blast of his trumpet, warned them to keep silence, he thus proceeded to make proclamation:

"In the name of the most high and noble prince, our most gracious sovereign lord, King Philip, the citizens whose names I shall now read forth are hereby summoned to appear without delay before Messire James de Chatillon, governor-general of this land of Flanders, and that on pain of death in case of disobedience." He then proceeded to read out the names.

The stratagem fully succeeded; for as each name was called, the person designated came forth out of the crowd, and advanced up the square into the

The Lion of Flanders

immediate presence of De Chatillon. Little did they suspect what awaited them; though indeed their hearts boded them no good, and they would probably have sought safety in flight had that been possible. Most of them were men of some thirty years of age; but among them approached one gray-headed old man, with slow-drawn steps, and back bowed down with the weight of years, his countenance expressive of placid resignation without the slightest shade of fear. He stood before the governor, looking up at him with an inquiring air. "What would you with us?" his bearing seemed to say.

As soon as the last had obeyed the summons, at a sign from the governor the eight Clawards were seized and bound in spite of all resistance. The murmurs of the spectators were soon repressed by the threatening aspect of a party of men-at-arms detached with that intention. In a few moments a lofty gallows was set up in the middle of the square, and a priest might be seen standing by the side of the victims. At the sight of the fell instrument of death, the wives, children, and friends of the unhappy men called aloud for mercy, and the masses of people swayed tumultuously to and fro. A mighty sigh, mingled with curses and cries for vengeance, burst from the crowd, and ran along its ranks like the growling of the thunder which precedes the storm.

The Lion of Flanders

Again a trumpeter came forward, sounded a blast, and made proclamation:

"Know ye all, that whosoever shall disturb the lawful execution of the justice of my lord the governor-general by seditious cries, or otherwise, shall be treated as an accomplice of these rebels, and an accessory to their crimes, and as such be hanged upon the same gallows."

Immediately the murmurs died away, and a death-like stillness fell upon the multitude. The weeping women lifted up their eyes to Heaven, and addressed their supplications to Him whose ear is ever open to His creatures' prayers, though a despot's threats may seal their lips; the men, inwardly burning with rage and indignation, cursed their own impotence to help. Seven of the Clawards were brought up, one after another, to the gallows, and turned off before the faces of their fellow-citizens. The dismay of the terrified crowd changed into horror, their horror into desperation; as each fresh victim was thrust from the ladder, they averted their eyes or bowed their heads toward the ground, to avoid the spectacle of his dying struggles. To escape from the scene by flight was not allowed them, and the slightest appearance of movement among the throng was instantly repressed by the threatening weapons of the soldiery who barred the way.

Only one Claward now remained by the side

The Lion of Flanders

of Messire de Chatillon: his turn was come, he had confessed himself, and was ready for the executioner; but still De Chatillon delayed to give the word. De Mortenay was earnestly soliciting the pardon of the aged man (for he it was), while Van Gistel, who bore him an especial hatred, was as earnestly representing that he was one of the very men who had been busiest in stirring up the population against the garrison. At last, by the governor's command, the apostate thus addressed his countryman:

"You have seen how your fellows have been punished for their rebellious conduct, and you are yourself condemned to share their fate; nevertheless, the lord governor, out of regard for your gray hairs, is willing to deal graciously with you. He grants you your life, on condition that henceforth you bear yourself as a true and faithful subject of the French crown. Cry, 'France forever!' and you are pardoned."

With a bitter smile of mingled scorn and indignation, the aged patriot replied:

"Yes! were I such as you, I should do your bidding like a coward, and sully my white hairs by that last act of baseness. But God, I know, will give me grace to defy your threats and resist you to the death. You, vile traitor that you are, are not ashamed, like the reptile that tears its mother's entrails, to deliver over to the stranger the land that gave you birth and nourished you. But tremble for yourself; I have sons that will avenge me. You shall not die peaceably in your bed! and you know that the words of an expiring man fall not to the ground."

Van Gistel turned pale at this solemn denunciation. A terrible foreboding passed over his heart, and he repented already of his gratified revenge; for the dread of death is ever the strongest feeling in a traitor's soul. De Chatillon, meanwhile, had sufficiently read the old Claward's determination in his countenance.

"Well, what says the rebel?" he asked.

"Messire," answered Van Gistel, "he scoffs at me, and despises the mercy you offer him."

"Hang him, then!" was the stern reply.

The soldier who did the office of executioner now took the old man by the arm, and led him unresisting to the gallows.

The priest had given his final blessing, the victim had set his foot upon the first round of the ladder, and the rope was already about his neck, when suddenly a violent commotion showed itself in the crowd, which all the efforts of the soldiers were unable to subdue. Some strong impulse from behind seemed to be communicating itself to the multitude, driving some forward, others sideways against the walls of the houses, and a young man, with naked arms, and a countenance intensely agitated with rage and terror, forced his way through into the open space in front. Once clear of the obstruction of the throng, he cast a wild look round the square, and sprang forward with the speed of an arrow, exclaiming, "My father! my father; you shall not die!"

Even as he spoke the words he had reached the foot of the gallows; his cross-knife flashed aloft, and the next instant was buried in the heart of the executioner. With a single cry he rolled expiring on the ground, while the young Fleming seized his father in his arms, threw him upon his shoulder, and hastened with his sacred burden toward the crowd. For a moment the soldiers stood motionless with astonishment, like so many passive spectators of the scene; but De Chatillon's voice speedily aroused them, and before the young man had time to take a dozen steps under his load, more than twenty of them were upon him. In an instant he placed his father behind him, and confronted his assailants with his knife still reeking in his hand. Some fifty other Flemings stood about him; for he had already reached the foremost ranks of the multitude when overtaken by his pursuers, so that they had been compelled to push in among the throng in order to follow him. With what rage were the hearts of the Frenchmen now filled, as, one by one, they beheld their twenty comrades bite the dust; for suddenly the bystanders

The Lion of Flanders

rushed upon the soldiers, and with their knives stabbed them down without mercy, while many a gallant Fleming too perished in the fray.

Upon this the whole body of the men-at-arms made a furious onset upon the citizens, the large two-handed swords mowing down the helpless multitude, and the steel-clad chargers trampling them under their hoofs as they attempted to escape. They fell not, however, unavenged; for many a Frenchman gave his heart's best blood to swell the crimson stream that flowed upon the pavement. The father and the son lay one upon the other, both pierced by the self-same thrust; their souls had not parted company upon that last journey. The streets were thronged with fugitives, and resounded everywhere with cries of terror; each one hastened to gain the shelter of his habitation, doors and windows were closed and fastened, and Bruges soon presented the aspect of a city of the dead.

But the stillness did not last long. Soon the infuriated soldiery, fierce as untamed beasts, and thirsting for revenge, spread themselves through the deserted streets, the Lilyards acting as their guides, and pointing out the houses of the Clawards. Doors or windows were instantly forced in; money and goods seized and carried off, and whatever was not worth the trouble of removal broken and destroyed. The terrified women, dragged from their hiding-places, were subjected to the grossest outrage, the men who raised a hand in defense of wife or sister murdered on the spot. Every here and there upon the streets, before the doors of the plundered houses, lay a mangled corpse amid fragments of shattered furniture. No sound was to be heard but the furious cries of the soldiers and the screams of the unhappy women. The plunderers came laughing out of the homes they had laid desolate, their hands filled with Flemish gold, and red with Flemish gore; and as each party, sated with blood and booty, drew off from the spot, another worse than it followed in its place; and so the horrid work proceeded, till the full cup of misery was drained to the dregs by the despairing citizens.

In Peter Deconinck's house there was not an article of furniture but was broken into fragments; nor would the very walls have been left standing, but that the plunderers grudged the time which they had destined for more ruthless deeds. Another party hastened straight to the dwelling of Jan Breydel. In a few moments the door was shivered to pieces; and breathing threats of vengeance, some twenty of the bloodthirsty crew rushed into the shop, where, however, they could discover no one, though each possible and impossible lurking-place was rigidly examined. Chests and closets were forced open, and rifled of their contents; and then everything the house contained was wantonly broken up and demolished. At last, tired with their work of destruction, they were contemplating its results with malignant satisfaction, when one of the band who had mounted the staircase returned, saying, "I have heard something moving in the loft; I'll be sworn there are some Flemings lurking under the roof; and if we make a sharper search, depend upon it we shall find something better worth looking for; most likely they have the best of their gear with them."

Upon this the whole party hurried toward the stairs, each eager to be the first at the spoil; their comrade, however, checked their haste.

"Stay, stay!" said he; "you can't get in yet. The trap-door is ten feet above the floor, and they have drawn up the ladder; but that makes no odds—I saw a ladder in the yard. Wait a moment, and I will fetch it."

This was speedily effected, and they all ascended the stairs together, and mounted to the trap-door; but there was still an impediment—the trap was firmly fastened down and could not be raised.

"Well, then," cried one of them, taking up a heavy piece of wood from the floor, "if the door is locked, we must find a key to it."

So saying, he struck violently against the trap, which, however, still held fast, without showing the slightest sign of giving way; but a cry of terror and

The Lion of Flanders

lamentation, as though the very soul itself was passing out with it, sounded from the loft.

"Ha! ha!" cried the soldiers, "they are lying on the trap."

"Wait!" exclaimed another voice: "I will soon show them the way off it. Lend a hand there."

With their united strength they now lifted a massive beam, and plied it so fiercely against the trap that the shattered board soon fell down among them. With a wild shout of triumph they rushed up the ladder, and in an instant were all within the loft. Here they suddenly stood still. It seemed as if some strange and solemn spectacle had touched their hearts; for the curses died away upon their lips, and they looked at one another with an air of hesitation.

At the farther end of the loft stood a boy—he could not be above fourteen—with a pole-ax in his hand. His face was pale; his limbs quivered with agitation; no word or sound issued from his compressed lips. He held up his weapon in a threatening attitude against the intruders, and his blue eyes flashed with the heroism of despair; while the muscles of his delicate cheeks were violently contracted to an expression at once terrible and ghastly. There he stood, like the miniature statue of some Grecian hero. Behind the youth were two women kneeling upon the floor—an old gray-headed mother, with folded hands and eyes raised to Heaven; and a tender maiden, whose hair hung disheveled about her shoulders. The trembling girl had hidden her face in her mother's clothes, and was clinging to her as in the last extremity of terror.

Recovered from their first surprise, the soldiers pushed rudely forward upon the affrighted women, overwhelmed them with insults, and were about to lay hands upon them; serious opposition on the part of the boy they never for a moment contemplated. What, then, was their astonishment when, with his left foot planted firmly behind him, he fiercely brandished his ax, and defied them to come on. For a moment the young champion checked their onset; then, as one of them thought with a single thrust of his sword to pierce him through, he parried the weapon, and struck with the force of despair at the shoulder of his assailant, who immediately staggered backward and fell into the arms of his comrades. At the same moment the youth himself, as though he had received his death-wound from some unseen hand, fell heavily to the ground, and there lay senseless and motionless by the side of the women he had endeavored to protect. The soldiers, pressing about their wounded comrade, proceeded to remove his accoutrements and clothes amid frightful imprecations and threats of vengeance; while the elder female, still on her

The Lion of Flanders

knees, with floods of tears, and in heartrending accents, sued for mercy.

"Oh, sirs!" she cried, addressing the soldiers in their own tongue, "have but pity on us, miserable creatures that we are! Do not murder us, for the love of our merciful Lord, and as you shall one day yourselves look for mercy from Him! God knows we have suffered more than enough already; and what can the death of two defenseless women profit you?"

"That is the mother of the Butcher that made such slaughter of our people at Male," cried one; "death to her!"

"Oh, no, no, Messire!" pursued the old woman, "dip not your hands in my blood! I beseech you, by the bitter passion of our Lord, let us live! Take all we have: but spare our lives!"

"Your money—your gold!" interrupted a rough voice.

She immediately seized a casket that stood behind her, and threw it to the soldiers. "There, sirs," she said, "that is all we have left to us in the world—take it; I give it to you with good will."

The lid of the casket flew open as it fell, and a quantity of gold pieces and various costly jewels rolled from it upon the floor. A general scramble for the booty ensued; but while the rest were thus occupied, one of them seized the maiden by the arm, and threw her violently on the ground.

The Lion of Flanders

"Mother! help me, mother!" gasped the poor girl with a fainting voice that in an instant roused the parent's heart into a frenzy of desperation. With flashing eyes and quivering lip, she sprang like a wild tigress on the soldier, twined her arms about him, and dug her nails, as if they had been claws, into his face, so that the blood streamed down his cheeks.

"My child!" she screamed, "my child! Villain!"

Maddened with the pain, and yet unwilling to loose his hold, the soldier brought the point of his sword against the mother's breast, and pitilessly thrust it deep into her body. Instantly her grasp relaxed, her eyes grew dim, her blood gushed upon the floor, and staggering against the side-beams of the loft, she clutched at them for support.

Regardless of the maiden's screams, the soldier proceeded to tear the golden drops from her ears, and to strip the pearls from her neck and the rings from her fingers; then with a malignant smile he stabbed her to the heart. "Now," said he to the dying mother, with a devilish sneer, "now you can take your long journey in company, you Flemish jades!" With a last expiring effort she sprang forward, and, uttering a single piercing cry, fell dead upon the lifeless body of her child.

All this scene of horror had occupied but a few short moments; and the mother and daughter had already exchanged this world for a better ere the

The Lion of Flanders

other soldiers had finished their scramble for the contents of the casket. When that was over, and everything that the loft contained of any value appropriated, the plunderers left the house to repeat the like elsewhere; while throughout the city the unhappy burghers, driven from their habitations by force or terror, wandered through the streets, exposed to the insults of their oppressors, and deeming themselves fortunate to escape so easily. At last, about midday, a strong party of men-at-arms traversed the city to call back the troops, Messire de Chatillon deeming that the honor of the French crown was now sufficiently avenged; and proclamation was at the same time made that all might freely bury their dead, and return without fear to their homes.

Some of Breydel's Claward friends now proceeded to his house, took up the bodies of his mother and sister, and conveyed them on a bier to the gate leading toward Damme. Here was to be seen a new spectacle of misery, enough to move with pity the hardest heart. Crowds of wailing mothers, weeping children, and men feeble with age were beseeching on their knees for permission to leave the city; while the soldiers, whose orders were to keep the gates closed, disregarded their entreaties, and only made a mock of their tears and lamentations. Thus they waited and supplicated for some time in vain, till one of the women conceived the happy thought of offering her ornaments as a bribe to the guard; and many others following her example, there speedily lay no inconsiderable pile of costly jewelry before the gate.

Greedily the venal mercenaries caught at the glittering ransom, and promised to open the gates if all the articles of price which the women bore about them were forthwith delivered up. The bargain was soon concluded. Each one hastened to throw down whatever of value she had upon her, and the gates were opened amid a shout of gladness from the liberated multitude. Mothers took their children in their arms, sons supported their aged parents; and thus they streamed forth from the town, the men who carried the corpses of Breydel's family following them through the gate, which was immediately after closed upon the fugitives.

The Lion of Flanders

CHAPTER VIII

Jan Breydel and his seven hundred butchers had pitched their camp near the small town of Damme, in the immediate neighborhood of Bruges. Three thousand Guildsmen from the other companies had also voluntarily placed themselves under his command; so that he now found himself at the head of a force, not numerous indeed, but formidable from its fearless and devoted courage; for there was not a man among them whose heart was not possessed with the single thought of liberty and vengeance. The wood which the Dean had selected as the place of encampment was thickly crowded for a considerable space with huts and tents; and on the morning of the 18th of May, a little before De Chatillon's entry into Bruges, numberless fires were smoking in front of the lines. Few, however, of the Guildsmen were visible about the tents. Of women and children there were indeed enough; but it was only here and there that a single man showed himself, and he was evidently a sentinel on duty. At some little distance from the actual camp, behind the trees which spread their branches over the tents, was an open space free from trees and entirely unoccupied. From this quarter might be heard incessantly a confused murmur of voices, the monotony of which was ever and anon relieved by the sharp or heavy resound of workmen's implements. The hammers rang upon the anvils, and in the wood the largest trees came thundering down under the axes of the butchers. Here long wooden shafts were being rounded and smoothed and pointed with iron; there stood piles of pikes and "good-days" ready for use. Elsewhere the basket-makers were busily engaged in manufacturing frameworks for bucklers, which were then handed over to the tanners to be covered with ox-hides. The carpenters were at work upon the heavy siege-artillery of the day, especially catapults and other engines of assault. Jan Breydel ran about hither and thither, animating his comrades with words of encouragement. Occasionally he would himself take the ax in hand from one of his butchers; and then, as he hewed away to the astonishment of all that saw him, one of the largest trees would speedily fall under his vigorous blows.

On the left of this open space stood a magnificent tent of sky-blue cloth, with silver fringe. At its summit hung a shield, showing a black lion on a golden field, and thus denoting the abode of a member of the princely house of Flanders. Here it was that the Lady Matilda was for the present lodged, under the special protection of the Guilds,

The Lion of Flanders

to which she had committed herself. Two ladies of the illustrious house of Renesse had left their home in Zeeland to attend upon her and bear her company; and in no respect did she want for anything. The most sumptuous appointments, the most costly apparel had been amply supplied for her use by the noble Zeelander. A party of butchers, axes in hand, stood on either side of the tent as bodyguard to the young countess. The Dean of the Clothworkers was pacing up and down before the entrance, apparently immersed in thought, with his eyes bent upon the earth. The guard looked on at him in silence; not a word was spoken among them, out of deep respect for the meditations of the man who was so great and noble in their eyes. The object of his thoughts was a plan for a general encampment. Hitherto, for the better convenience of provisioning, he had distributed the whole force into three divisions. The Butchers and the various Guilds were encamped at Damme, under the command of Breydel; Dean Lindens lay with two thousand Clothworkers at Sluys; and Deconinck himself, with two thousand men of the same Guild, at Ardenburg. But he was far from satisfied with this scattered disposition of the forces, and would gladly have seen the whole reunited into one corps before the arrival of Guy to take the supreme command. It was for this reason that he was now at Damme; and, his consulta-

The Lion of Flanders

tion with Breydel being concluded, he was waiting till he should be admitted to pay his respects to the daughter of his lord.

While he walked, thus meditating on his project, the portion of hanging that formed the door of the tent was drawn on one side, and Matilda stepped slowly forward over the carpet that was spread before it. Her countenance was pale, and expressive of much languor; her steps seemed to totter under her, and she leaned for support on the arm of the young Adelaide of Renesse, who accompanied her. Her dress was rich, but plain; for she had laid aside all ornament, and the only jewel she wore was the golden plate upon her breast, with the Black Lion of Flanders enameled on it.

Immediately on her appearance, Deconinck uncovered his head, and stood before her in an attitude of deep respect. A sweet smile lighted up the gloom with which the maiden's features were overcast; for it was with pleasure that she beheld the firm and faithful friend of her house and country, and with a faint voice she thus addressed him:

"Welcome, Master Deconinck, my good friend; how is it with you? With me, you see, it is ill enough. Every breath I draw is painful to me: but I can not always keep my tent: the narrow room oppresses me. I have come out to see my father's loyal subjects at their work—if, indeed, my feet will carry me so far; and you, Master Deconinck, shall accompany me. I have many things to ask you; and, I pray you, answer truly to my questions. I hope to find in your discourse some refreshment for my weary heart. There is no need for the guards to follow us. Ah! the bright morning sunshine does me good; it cheers me."

She moved forward with Deconinck by her side, who replied to her inquiries as they walked along. With that admirable tact and facility of expression by which he was distinguished, he continued to suggest matter for consolation and cheerful hope, and so for the while dispelled the heavy melancholy that weighed upon her spirits. Everywhere, as she passed, the Guildsmen greeted the young girl with loud expressions of homage and affection, and soon one universal shout of "Long live the Lady Matilda! long live our noble Lion's daughter!" resounded through the wood. Matilda felt a genuine thrill of joy as she received these testimonies of warm and loyal attachment to her father and her father's house; and approaching the Dean of the Butchers with a gracious smile:

"Master Breydel," she said, "I have been noticing you from afar. You really labor harder than the lowest of your Guildsmen; work seems to be a pleasure to you."

"Lady," answered the delighted Breydel, "we are making 'good-days' for the deliverance of our country and of our lord the Lion, and that is a work

The Lion of Flanders

I enjoy with my whole heart; for I feel as if each one we finish bore a Frenchman's death upon its point, and every blow I strike seems struck upon the body of an enemy."

Matilda could not look without admiration upon the young hero, in whose countenance, as in that of some Grecian deity, the fierce energy of passion was marvelously softened and tempered down by the noble refinement of the features. Its manly beauty seemed but the mirror of the generous soul within, and its whole aspect glowed with the fervor of self-devotion and patriotic zeal. Again graciously smiling on him, she replied:

"Come with us, I pray you, Master Breydel; it will give me pleasure to have your company in my walk."

Quickly Jan Breydel cast his ax aside, stroked back his long fair locks behind his ears, set his cap more jauntily on his head, and followed the princess, his heart bounding and his step elastic with honest pride.

"If my father," she whispered softly to Deconinck, "had but a thousand such, so fearless and so true, our enemies would not long keep foot in Flanders."

"Flanders has but one Breydel," replied the Clothworker. "It is but seldom that nature sets so fiery a soul in so mighty a body; and that is a wise providence of God, else should men, when they learnt to know their force, become too proud of heart, like the giants of old, who sought to climb up into Heaven—"

He would have proceeded; but at this moment he was interrupted by a sentinel running breathlessly up, and calling out aloud to Breydel:

"Master Dean, my fellows of the watch have sent me to let you know that a thick cloud of dust has been seen rising in the distance from just before our city gates, and that a noise as of an army in full march is clearly audible. Some considerable body is leaving the city, and advancing toward our camp."

"To arms! to arms!" cried Breydel in a voice that was heard far and near through the encampment; "each man to his place!—quick!"

The work-people hastily seized their arms, and ran confusedly hither and thither; but this was only for a moment. The companies were speedily formed, and soon the Guildsmen might be seen standing firm and motionless in their serried phalanx. Breydel's first care was to post five hundred chosen men about Matilda's tent, to which she had with all speed returned; a carriage, too, well horsed, was drawn up before it, and every preparation made for her escape in case of need; then with the whole remainder of his force he issued from the wood in full array, and ready at all points for battle.

The Lion of Flanders

It was not long ere they became aware that it was a false alarm. The body which raised the dust was evidently advancing in no kind of order; and it was soon perceptible that a large proportion of it consisted of women and children confusedly mingled together. A prominent object was a bier, or rather handbarrow, borne by men, round which the women crowded, filling the air with the most piteous lamentations. But although the cause of alarm no longer existed, the Guildsmen still kept their ranks, resting upon their arms, and awaiting with anxious curiosity the solution of the enigma. At last the approaching train drew near; and while wives and children pressed through the ranks to embrace a husband or a father, a frightful spectacle presented itself to the assembled multitude.

The four bearers of the bier carried it to within a short distance of the Dean of the Butchers, and there set it down upon the ground. Upon it lay two female corpses, their clothes dabbled with blood, their features indiscernible, being concealed from sight by a black veil thrown over the heads. The women meanwhile still kept up their cries; one continued heartrending "Woe! woe!" was all that could be heard, till at last a voice exclaimed:

"The French soldiers have murdered them!"

Hitherto the Guildsmen had looked on silently in mingled surprise and curiosity; but as these fearful words reached their ears, their hearts swelled with revengeful fury, and disorder would have ensued but for Breydel's loud command.

"The first man that leaves the ranks shall be severely punished!" he exclaimed.

He himself, tortured by a terrible presentiment, rushed impetuously to the bier, and tore away the veil that concealed the faces; but, oh God! how fearful the sight that met his eyes! He uttered not a sound, he moved not a limb; he stood there as struck with sudden and universal palsy. Paler he was than the corpses themselves, and his hair stood on end upon his head. His lips quivering, his eyes fixedly bent upon the eyes now glazed in death, one would have said that he felt his last hour upon him.

Thus he stood, but for a few moments only. Soon, with a mighty bound, he sprang forward in front of the ranks, threw both arms up into the air, and in a voice of agony exclaimed:

"Woe! woe is me! My aged mother! my poor sister!"

With these words he flung himself into Deconinck's arms, and lay powerless and almost senseless upon his friend's bosom. With vague and wandering eyes he stared around, while his comrades shuddered with horror and compassion. Anon he furiously raised his ax; but it was instantly caught away out of his hand. Deconinck now gave the word for all to return to their work until further orders. The men, indeed, thought of naught else but speedy vengeance; but no one ventured to dispute the command, for they knew that the Dean of the Clothworkers had been duly appointed their general-in-chief. Giving vent, therefore, to their feelings in murmurs, they returned into the wood, and resumed, though unwillingly, the labors which this incident had interrupted.

By Deconinck's care Breydel was speedily conveyed to his own tent, where, exhausted alike in mind and body, he threw himself upon a seat, and rested his head upon the table. He said nothing; but when his eyes met those of his friend, there was a singular expression in them. A bitter mocking smile distorted his features; it was as though he were scoffing at his own wretchedness.

At last Deconinck broke the silence. "My unhappy friend," he said, "be calm, for God's sake!"

"Calm! calm!" repeated Breydel; "am I not calm? Have you ever seen me so calm before?"

"Oh, my friend!" resumed the Clothworker, "full well can I conceive how intense must be the agony of your soul; I seem to see death upon your countenance. Comfort you I can not; your calamity is too great. I know of no balm for such a wound."

"Not so, say I," replied Breydel; "the balm for my wound I know well enough; it is the power to procure it that fails me. Oh, my poor mother! they have shed your blood because your son is a true Fleming; and that son—oh, misery!—can not avenge you!"

As he uttered these words, the expression of his countenance altered; he ground his teeth violently together; his hands grasped the legs of the table as though he would snap them asunder. Then, again, he became more quiet, and seemed to sink into a state of the deepest depression.

"Now, Master Breydel, bear up like a man," Deconinck began again, "and give not way to despair, that worst enemy of the soul. Strengthen your heart against the bitter calamity that has this day befallen you; your mother's blood shall not have cried in vain for vengeance."

Again the fearful smile curled Breydel's lip. "Vengeance!" he exclaimed; "how easily you promise what it is not in your power to accomplish—who can avenge me? Can you yourself? and could torrents of French blood refill my mother's veins? Can the tyrant's life redeem his victims from the grave? No; they are dead, gone from me forever, my friend. I will suffer in silence and without complaint. There is no comfort left for me; we are too weak, and our foes too mighty."

Deconinck made no reply to Breydel's lament, and seemed to be revolving something weighty in his mind. He appeared like one who was putting

The Lion of Flanders

violence on himself, and controlling some strong inward feeling. The Dean of the Butchers regarded him with an inquiring look, deeming that something unusual was at work within him. Soon the painful expression passed away from Deconinck's face; he rose slowly from his seat, and in a tone of deep earnestness thus addressed his friend:

"Our foes are too mighty, say you? To-morrow you shall say so no more. They have gained their ends by fraud and treachery, and have not feared to pour out innocent blood like water, as though the avenging angel no longer stood before the throne of the Most High. They know not that the life of every one of them is even now in my hands; that I can break them in pieces, as though God had put His power into my hands. They seek their advantage in deceit, and cruelty, and all evil arts. Well, then, their own sword shall pierce them, and they shall perish by it. I have said it!"

At this moment Deconinck looked like an inspired prophet pronouncing the malediction of the Lord upon the crimes and backslidings of Jerusalem. There was such an authority in his voice and bearing, as he declared God's judgments on the foe, that Breydel listened to him with awe-struck emotion.

"Wait a little," he proceeded; "I will send for one of these newcomers, that we may know how it has all happened; but, I entreat you, do not let your feelings carry you away whatever account he may give. I promise you vengeance even beyond what you would yourself demand; for matters are now arrived at a point at which endurance would be disgrace."

His cheeks glowed with the intensity of his indignation. He who was usually so calm, was now inflamed with fiercer passion than Breydel himself, though his exterior did not betray to their full extent the feelings which agitated him. He left the tent for a few moments, and returned with one of the lately-arrived craftsmen, from whom he demanded a full and particular recital of all that had passed in Bruges. From him they learned the amount of the reenforcements with which De Chatillon had arrived, the execution of the seven citizens, and the circumstances attending it, together with all the frightful story of the sacking of the town.

Breydel, for his part, listened to the horrible recital dispassionately enough, for all was as nothing to him after the murder of her who had given him birth; but Deconinck's emotion sensibly increased as each scene in the hideous tragedy was unrolled before him. It was not the details of the narrative, however, exciting as they were, that thus affected him: patriotism and love of liberty were the two mainsprings of his soul, and in these all his energies were concentrated. He felt that the latest moment had arrived for commencing in earnest the work of regeneration; that moment must not be lost, or the event of that day would spread terror through the Flemish people, and utterly subdue their spirit. The necessary information obtained, he dismissed the craftsman, and sat for some time silent, his head supported on his hand, while Breydel awaited impatiently the result of his cogitations.

Suddenly he started from his reverie. "Friend," he exclaimed, "sharpen your ax; chase sorrows from your heart! Up; we will break the chains from off our country's neck!"

"What is it you mean?" inquired Breydel.

"Listen: the husbandman waits till the cold of the morning has driven the caterpillars into their nest, then he plucks it from the tree, sets his foot upon it, and with one stamp of his heel crushes the whole brood. Do you understand me now?"

"Apply your parable," replied the Butcher. "Oh, my friend, a bright gleam of hope breaks in upon me through my dark despair. But go on, go on!"

"Well, then, the French tyrants have preyed upon our country like noisome insects; and like them they shall be crushed—ay, as though a mountain had fallen upon them. Cheer up, Master Jan; judgment is gone forth against them.

The Lion of Flanders

Your mother's death shall be requited with usury, and the blood we will shed shall wash the stain of slavery from the Flemish name."

Breydel's eyes wandered restlessly round the tent, seeking in vain for his ax; at last he remembered that it had been taken from him. Seizing Deconinck's hand:

"My friend!" he said with strong emotion, "more than once you have been my preserver; but hitherto it was life alone I owed you; henceforth I shall be your debtor for all its peace and joy. But now make haste, and tell me by what means you meditate accomplishing this vengeance, that my satisfaction may be unalloyed, and free from any lingering doubt."

"Have patience for a moment, you will soon hear all; for I must immediately lay my project before a general council of the Deans, which I am now about to call."

He hurried out, and despatched one of the sentinels through the encampment, to summon the superior officers to meet at Breydel's tent. Shortly afterward, they all stood before it in a circle, to the number of thirty, when Deconinck thus addressed them:

"Comrades! the solemn hour is come, which must bring us liberty or death. Long enough have we borne the brand of shame upon our foreheads; it is time that we demand from our tyrants an ac-

The Lion of Flanders

count of our brothers' blood; and if it shall so be that we lose our lives in our country's cause—remember, comrades, that the slave drops his fetters on the threshold of the tomb; we shall sleep with our fathers, free, and without reproach. But no; we shall conquer—I feel it, I know it: the Black Lion of Flanders shall not die! Right and justice, I need not tell you, are all on our side. The strangers have plundered our land; they have imprisoned our Count, with all the nobles that were true to their prince and their country; the Lady Philippa they have poisoned; our good city of Bruges they have laid waste with the sword; and on our own proper soil and territory they have hung up our brethren as infamous malefactors. The blood-stained corpses of those who were nearest and dearest to our friends lie even now unburied among us; unhappy victims of these foreign despots, they have voices which cry in your hearts for vengeance! Well then, now to the purpose for which I have called you together; but remember, what I say to you you must bury in your hearts, as in the depths of the grave. The French garrison have wearied themselves out with this day's wicked work; they will sleep soundly—most of them only to wake, I trust, on the day of judgment. Say nothing to your men; but to-morrow morning, two hours before sunrise, have them ready under arms in the wood behind St. Cross. I shall myself proceed instantly to Ardenburg, to make my arrangements there, and to send the necessary orders to Dean Lindens at Sluys; for I must be in Bruges before the day is over. I see you are surprised; well, one thing there is that we must not forget; there is a Frenchman in Bruges whom we may not harm, for his blood would assuredly be upon our heads."

"The Governor De Mortenay," here interrupted several voices.

"The same," pursued Deconinck; "he has ever treated us with consideration, and shown that he feels for the calamities of our country. Many a time he has restrained that execrable wretch, Van Gistel, in his persecutions, and obtained pardon or mitigation of sentence for such as were condemned to suffer. We must not sully our rightful arms with the blood of the just; and it is to provide for this that I am about to risk myself in the city, be the danger what it may."

"But," objected one of the Deans present, "how shall we obtain entrance into the city to-morrow morning (for that, I suppose, is our object), since the gates are not opened till sunrise?"

"The gates will be opened for us," replied Deconinck; "I shall not leave the city walls till our vengeance is secured. And now, for the present, I have said enough; to-morrow, at the rendezvous, I will give you further orders; meanwhile do you get your companies on foot. I will take immediate measures for removing the Lady Matilda from the neighborhood of a spectacle which befitteth not her presence."

All this Breydel had listened to without any expression of approbation, though his countenance sufficiently betokened the intensity of his satisfaction; but no sooner was the assembly broken up, and he found himself again alone with his friend, than, throwing himself upon Deconinck's neck, while tears trickled down his cheeks: "My best friend!" he exclaimed; "you have brought me back from the bottomless pit of despair. Now can I with an undisturbed heart weep over the remains of my poor mother and sister; and when I lay them in the earth, devoutly add my prayer to the last solemnities. But then—oh, then, when the grave has closed over them, what have I left upon earth to love or to live for?"

"Our country, and our country's greatness!"

"Yes, yes; country and liberty—and vengeance! But now, my friend, understand me well; when our land is fairly clear of the French, nothing will remain for me but to shed tears of rage. For then there will be no more heads for my ax to cleave, no corpses for me to trample on, as the hoofs of their horses have trampled down our brothers. What is liberty to me? only the sight of streaming blood can give me joy, now that they have poured out that of the heart from which my own veins were filled. But haste away, and God be with you! I am athirst after the promised vengeance."

"Secrecy and caution, my friend!" was the response; and Deconinck took his leave.

His first care was for the safe removal of the Lady Matilda, for which he speedily made all necessary arrangements; and then, after a short audience with her, he mounted his horse and disappeared in the direction of Ardenburg.

Meanwhile the bodies of Breydel's mother and sister had been duly washed and laid out by the women. A tent had been lined with black stuff, and the two corpses placed upon a bed in the centre of it—their faces exposed to view, the rest of them concealed under an ample pall. Round them burned eight large tapers of yellow wax; and a crucifix, with a silver vessel of holy water, and some palm branches—the emblem of martyrdom—stood at the bed's head. A crowd of women, weeping as they muttered their prayers, knelt by.

Immediately upon Deconinck's departure, Breydel proceeded to the wood, stopped the work, and dismissed his men to their tents, with orders to take all the rest they could without delay, and to be ready for marching the next morning before dawn. He also gave some further directions respecting the women and children, who were to remain at the camp, and then betook himself to the tent where the bodies were laid out. As soon as he had entered, he bade all present depart, and shut himself in alone with the dead.

More than one leader came up to ask for orders or instructions from his chief, but all in vain; to their loudest entreaties for admission no answer was returned. For some time they respected his sorrow, and waited patiently till he should appear; but when, after hours of expectation, still no sound was heard nor sign given from within the tent, then a terrible fear came over them. They dreaded— they dared not say what. Was Breydel dead? Had he perished of grief, or peradventure by his own hand?

While thus they anxiously speculated, suddenly the tent opened, and Breydel issued forth; but without seeming to take any note of their presence. No one spoke; for the Dean's countenance had that in it which chilled the heart and silenced the tongue. His cheeks were deadly pale, his eyes wandered vaguely around; and many remarked that two fingers of his right hand were red with blood. No one ventured to approach him; an inexpressible ferocity flashed forth in his glances, each one of which sank as an arrow into the soul of him on whom it fell. Above all, the blood which clung to his fingers caused a shudder of horror in the beholders; whence it came they could well divine. Ghastly thought! but doubtless he had laid his hand upon his mother's breast and that blood came from the heart which had so dearly loved him; that fearful touch it was which filled him with his frenzied thirst for vengeance, and lent him the superhuman strength to take it. Thus he wandered speechless through the wood, till the shades of evening falling upon the encampment concealed him from his comrades' eyes.

Arrived at Ardenburg, Deconinck placed his two thousand Clothworkers under the command of one of the chief men of the Guild, and despatched a messenger with instructions to Dean Lindens. The needful measures taken for concentrating the three divisions at St. Cross, he again mounted, and proceeded straightway to Bruges, stabling his horse at a roadside inn not far from the gate, and entering the city on foot. Impediment to his progress there was none; the gates were not yet closed; but the evening was far advanced, and no soldiers were to be seen save the sentinels upon the walls; a dead and awful stillness reigned in all the streets through which he had to pass. Soon he stopped before a house of mean appearance behind the church of St. Donatus, and would have knocked, but on approaching for that purpose, he perceived that the door was gone, and its place supplied by a piece of cloth hung over the entrance. He was evidently well acquainted with

The Lion of Flanders

the inmates, and familiar with its interior arrangements; for, lifting up the hanging, he stepped forward without the slightest hesitation through the shop into which the doorway opened, and passed on into a little chamber behind it. The shop was quite dark; the room which he now entered was doubtfully lighted by a small lamp, the flickering rays of which, however, enabled him to discern at a glance the state of things within. The floor was strewn with the fragments of shattered furniture—a woman sat weeping by a table, with two young children pressed against her bosom, amid alternate sighs and kisses, as thanking Heaven that they at least, her best and dearest portion of this world's goods, were spared to her. Further on, in a corner, but half-illuminated by the lamp's pale beams, sat a man, with his head resting on his hand, who seemed to be asleep.

Alarmed at Deconinck's unexpected apparition, the woman clasped her babes still closer to her breast, while a loud cry of terror escaped her lips. The man started up, and hastily grasped his cross-knife; but in a moment, recognizing his Dean, "Oh master!" he exclaimed; "what a heavy burden did you lay upon me when you ordered me not to leave the city! By God's grace we have escaped the massacre; but our house has been pillaged, we have seen our brothers murdered by the hangman or the soldiery; and what to-morrow may bring

The Lion of Flanders

Heaven alone knows. Oh, let me quit this place, I pray you, and come out to you at Ardenburg."

To this request Deconinck made no answer; but with his finger beckoned the Guildsman out into the shop. "Gerard," he then commenced in a low voice, "when I quitted the city, I left you and thirty of your comrades behind, that I might have means of intelligence as to the proceedings of our French masters. I chose you out for this service, from my knowledge of your unflinching courage and disinterested patriotism. Perhaps, however, the sight of your brethren upon the gallows has shaken your heart; if so, you have my leave to go this very day to Ardenburg."

"Master," replied Gerard, "your words grieve me deeply; for myself I fear not death, but my wife, my poor children, are here with me, and exposed to all the horrors of the times. They are pining away before my eyes with terror and anxiety; they do nothing but weep and mourn the whole day, and the night brings them no repose. Only look at them, how pale and worn they are! And can I see their suffering without sharing it? Am I not a husband and a father, and ought I not to be the guardian of those who have me alone to look to for protection? Yet what protection can I give them here? Oh, master, believe me, in such times as these a father has more upon his heart than those weaker ones themselves. Nevertheless, I am

The Lion of Flanders

willing to forget all for my country—yes, even the dearest ties of nature; and so, if you can make any use of me, you may safely count upon me. Now speak; for I feel that you have something weighty to communicate."

Deconinck seized the brave Guildsman's hand and pressed it with much emotion. "Yet one more soul like Breydel's!" he thought.

"Gerard," said he, "you are a worthy Fleming; I thank you for your fidelity and courage. Listen, then; for I have but little time to spare. Go round in haste to your comrades, and give them notice to meet you this night with all possible secrecy in Pepper Lane. Do you alone mount upon the city wall, between the Damme Gate and that of St. Cross; lie down flat upon the rampart, and look out in the direction of St. Cross. Presently you will see a fire lighted in the fields, at the foot of the wall; then do you with your comrades make haste to fall upon the guard and open the gate; you will find seven thousand Flemings before it."

"The gate shall be opened at the appointed hour; fear not," answered Gerard, coolly and resolutely.

"You give me your word on it?"

"My word on it."

"Good-evening, then, worthy friend. God be with you!"

"His angels attend your steps, master!"

The Lion of Flanders

The Guildsman returned to his wife, and Deconinck left the house. He proceeded to the neighborhood of the Town Hall, and knocked at the door of a magnificent mansion which was immediately opened to him.

"What will you, Fleming?" asked the servant.

"I wish to speak with Messire de Mortenay."

"Good; but have you arms? for you folks are not to be trusted."

"What's that to you?" replied the Dean. "Go, and tell your master that Deconinck would speak with him."

"What! you, Deconinck? then 'tis sure you have some mischief in hand."

With these words, the servant hastily departed; and in a few moments almost as hastily returning, invited Deconinck to follow him upstairs. The door of a small cabinet was opened and closed again, and the Dean of the Clothworkers stood before the French Governor of Bruges.

De Mortenay was sitting beside a table, on which lay his sword, helmet, and gauntlets; he regarded his visitor with no small astonishment, while Deconinck, with a low obeisance, opened his errand.

"Messire de Mortenay," he commenced, "I have put myself in your power, trusting in your honor, and feeling sure, therefore, that I shall not have to repent of my confidence."

The Lion of Flanders

"Certainly," answered De Mortenay; "you shall return as you have come."

"Your magnanimity, noble sir, is a proverb among us," resumed the Dean; "and it is on that account, and that you may see that we Flemings know how to respect a generous enemy, that I now stand before you. The governor De Chatillon has condemned eight innocent men of our citizens to the gallows, and has given up our town to the fury of his soldiery; you must acknowledge, Messire de Mortenay, that it is our bounden duty to avenge the death of those who have thus suffered; for what had the governor to lay to their charge, except that they refused obedience to his despotic will?"

"The subject must obey his lord; and, however severely that lord may punish disobedience, it is not for the subject to sit in judgment on his acts."

"You are right, Messire de Mortenay, so goes the word in France; and as you are a natural-born subject of King Philip the Fair, it is fitting that you should execute his commands. But we free Flemings—we can no longer bear the galling chain. The governor-general has carried his cruelty beyond all bounds of endurance; be sure that erelong blood shall flow in torrents, and that, if the fortune of war goes against us, and the victory is with you, at least it will be but a few wretched slaves that are left you; for we have re-

The Lion of Flanders

solved, once for all, to conquer or to die. However, be that as it may, happen what will—and it is to tell you this that I am come—not a hair of your head shall be injured by us; the house in which you abide shall be to us a sanctuary, and no Fleming shall set his foot across its threshold. For this Deconinck pledges you his faith and honor."

"I thank your countrymen for their regard," replied De Mortenay; "but I can not accept the protection which you offer me, and indeed shall never be in a situation to require it. Should aught occur such as you prophesy, it will be under the banner of France, and not in my house, that I shall be found; and if I fall, it will be sword in hand. But I do not believe that things will ever come to such a pass; as for the present insurrection, it will soon be at an end. But for you, Dean, do you make haste away to some other land; that is what I counsel you as your friend."

"No, Messire, I will never forsake my country, the land in which the bones of my fathers rest. I pray you, consider that all things are possible, and that it may yet be that French blood shall be poured out like water; when that day comes, then bethink you of my words. This is all that I would say to you, noble sir. So now, farewell; and may God have you in his keeping!"

As De Mortenay, when left to himself, pondered over Deconinck's words, he could not but feel an

The Lion of Flanders

anxious foreboding that some terrible secret lay hidden under them: he resolved therefore that he would the very next day warn De Chatillon to especial vigilance, and himself take extraordinary measures for the security of the city. Little deeming that what he feared, and thought to provide against, was so near at hand, he now retired to his bed, and soon fell asleep in all tranquillity.

The Lion of Flanders

CHAPTER IX

BEHIND the village of St. Cross, at some few bowshots from Bruges, rose a little wood, in summer a favorite Sunday's resort of the citizens. The trees were so planted as to afford ample space between them, and a soft turf covered the ground with its flowery carpet. This was the appointed place of rendezvous; and already, at two o'clock in the morning, Breydel was there. The night was impenetrably dark, the moon was hidden behind dense clouds, a gentle wind sighed among the foliage, and the monotonous rustling of the leaves added a mystic terror to the scene.

In the wood itself, at the first glance nothing was discernible; but upon more attentive observation numerous shadowy figures might be perceived, as of men extended side by side upon the ground, each with a strangely glimmering light close to it, making the turf look like a faint reflex of the starry heaven above, so thickly was it studded with luminous points; which, in truth, were naught else but the bright blades of the axes, reflecting from their polished steel the few wandering rays which they could gather amid the darkness. More than two

The Lion of Flanders

thousand Butchers lay thus in rank and file upon the earth; their hearts beat quick, their blood bounded in their veins; for the long yearned for hour, the hour of vengeance and liberation, was at hand. The deepest silence was maintained by this vast multitude; and all conspired to throw a veil of necromantic horror over the mysterious band.

Breydel himself had his place deep in the interior of the wood; beside him reclined one of his comrades, whom for his well-tried courage he especially affected; and thus in suppressed whispers the two discoursed together as they lay:

"The French dogs little expect the rousing up they will get this morning," began Breydel; "they sleep well; for they have seared consciences—the villains! I am curious to see the faces they'll make when they wake up and see my ax, and their death upon its edge."

"Oh! my ax cuts like a lancet; I whetted it till it took off a hair from my arm; and I mean to blunt it this night, or never to sharpen it again."

"Things have gone too far, Martin. They treat us like so many dumb beasts, and think that we shall crouch beneath their tyranny. They fancy we're all like those accursed Lilyards: but they little know us."

"Yes, the bastard villains cry, 'France forever!' and fawn upon the tyrants; but they shall have something for themselves to do; I didn't forget them when I took so much pains about sharpening my ax!"

"Oh, no, Martin, no; no Flemish blood must be shed. Deconinck has strictly forbidden it."

"And John van Gistel, the cowardly traitor! is he to come off scot-free?"

"John van Gistel is to hang; he must pay for the blood of Deconinck's old friend. But he must be the only one."

"What! and the other false Flemings are to escape scatheless? Master Breydel, Master Breydel, that's too much for me; I can not away with it."

"They'll have punishment enough; disgrace will be their portion; shame in their hearts, and contempt on the lips and countenances of all good men. Were it nothing, think you, that each comer should throw bastard, coward, and traitor in your face? That's what remains for them."

"Faith, master, you make my blood run cold; a thousand deaths were better than that. What a hell upon earth for them, if only they had one spark of the true Fleming in their souls!"

They were now silent for a few moments, listening attentively to a sound as of distant footsteps which caught their ears; but it soon died away, and then Breydel resumed:

"The French savages have murdered my poor aged mother. I saw with my own eyes how the sword had pierced her heart through and through—that heart so full of love for me. They had no pity on her, because she had given birth to a right unbending Fleming; and now I will have no pity on them; so shall I avenge my country and my own blood together."

"Shall we give quarter, master? Shall we make prisoners?"

"May I perish, if I make a single prisoner, or grant one single man his life! Do they give quarter? No, they murder for murder's sake, and trample the corpses of our brethren under their horses' hoofs. And think you, Martin, that I, who have the bloody shade of my dear mother ever before my eyes, can so much as look upon a Frenchman without breaking into a fit of downright madness? Oh, I should tear them with my teeth, were my ax to break with the multitude of its victims! But that can never be; my good ax is the long-tried friend and faithful partner of my life."

"Listen, master, again there's a noise in the direction of Damme. Wait a moment."

He put his ear to the ground, then raised his head again.

"Master, the Weavers are not far off," he said; "maybe some four bowshots."

"Come, then, let us up! Do you pass quietly along the ranks, and take care that the men lie still. I will go and meet Deconinck, that he may

The Lion of Flanders

know what part of the wood is left open for his people.

In a few moments four thousand Weavers advanced from different sides of the wood, and immediately lay down upon the ground in silence, according to the orders they had received. The stillness was but little broken by their arrival, and all was soon perfectly quiet again. A few men only might have been seen to pass from company to company, bearing the order to the captains to meet at the eastern end of the wood.

Thither, accordingly, they all repaired, and grouped themselves round Deconinck to receive his instructions, who proceeded thus to address them:

"My brothers, this day's sun must shine upon us as freemen or light us to our graves. Arm yourselves, therefore, with all the courage which the thought of country and liberty can kindle in your bosoms; bethink you that it is for the city in which the bones of our father's rest, for the city in which our own cradles stood, that we are this day in arms. And remember—no quarter! Kill is the word; death to every Frenchman who falls into your hands! that not a root of foreign tares may remain to choke our wheat. We or they must die! Is there one among you that can entertain a spark of compassion for those who have so cruelly murdered our brothers, on the gallows and under the

The Lion of Flanders

hoofs of their horses? for the traitorous foes who have imprisoned our lawful Count in foul breach of faith, and poisoned his innocent child?"

A low, sullen, terrible murmur followed, and seemed to hover for a moment under the overarching branches.

"They shall die!" was the universal response.

"Well, then," pursued Deconinck, "this day we shall once more be free. But that is not enough; we shall still need stout hearts to make good our freedom; for the French king will soon have a new army in the field against us; of that doubt not."

"So much the better," interrupted Breydel; "there will only be so many more children weeping for their fathers, as I do now for my poor murdered mother. God rest her soul!"

The interruption had broken the flow of Deconinck's harangue; lest, therefore, time might fail him, he proceeded at once to give the necessary instructions:

"Well, then," he said, "now hear what we have to do. As soon as the clock of St. Cross strikes three, you must get your men upon their feet, and bring them into the road in close order; I shall be on before you under the city walls, with a body of my own people. The gates will almost instantly be opened to us by the Clawards inside; do you then march in as quietly as possible, and each of you take the direction I shall now give you. Mas-

The Lion of Flanders

ter Breydel, with the Butchers, will occupy the Spey Gate, and then all the streets round about Snaggaert's Bridge. Master Lindens, do you take possession of the Catherine Gate, and advance your men into the adjacent streets up to Our Lady's Church. The Curriers and Shoemakers are to occupy the Ghent Gate, and from thence to the Castle. The other Guilds, under the Dean of the Masons, will hold the Damme Gate, and all the neighborhood of St. Donatus' Church. I, with my two thousand men, will proceed to the Bouverie Gate and cut off the whole quarter from thence to the Asses' Gate, including the Great Market-place. When once we have surprised all the gates, then each keep your station as quietly as possible; for we must not wake the French up before all is ready. But as soon as ever you hear our country's cry—'The Lion for Flanders!' let every man repeat it, that you may know one another in the darkness. And then, at them! Break open the doors of all the houses where the French are quartered, and make as short work as you can of them."

"But, master," remarked one of the captains, "we shall not know the French from our own townspeople, finding them, as we shall, almost all in bed and undressed."

"Oh, there is an easy way to avoid all mistakes on that score. Whenever you can't make out at the first glance whether it's a Frenchman or a Fleming, make him say, "*Schild en vriend!*" [shield and friend]. Whoever can not pronounce those words properly has a French tongue, and down with him!"

At this moment the clock of St. Cross resounded thrice over the wood.

"One word more," added Deconinck hastily. "Remember, all of you, that Messire de Mortenay's house is under my especial protection, and I charge you to see it most strictly respected; let no one set his foot over the threshold of our noble foe's dwelling. Now to your companies with all the speed you can; give your men the necessary orders, and in all things do exactly as I have told you. Quick! and as little noise as possible, I pray you."

Thereupon the captains returned to their companies, which they immediately led forward in order to the edge of the road, while Deconinck advanced a large body of Weavers to within a very moderate distance of the city walls. He himself approached still nearer, and endeavored with his eye to penetrate the darkness; a burning port-fire, the end of which he concealed in the hollow of his hand, shed its red glow from between his fingers. So he walked on, keeping a sharp lookout, till at last he espied a head peering over the wall; it was that of the Clothworker Gerard, whom he had visited the evening before. The Dean now produced

The Lion of Flanders

a bundle of flax from under his garment, laid it upon the ground, and blew vigorously upon the port-fire. Soon a clear flame shot up, and gleamed over the plain and the head of the Clothworker disappeared from the wall. A moment more, and the sentinel who was posted on the rampart fell heavily forward, with a single sharp cry, and lay dead at its foot. Then followed a confused noise behind the gate—the clash of arms mingled with cries of the dying; and then all was still—still as the grave.

The gate was opened: in deepest silence the Guildsmen defiled into the city; and each captain drew off his company to the station assigned him by Deconinck. A quarter of an hour later all the sentinels on duty at the gates had been surprised and cut off, each Guild had taken up its position, and at the door of every house occupied by a Frenchman stood eight Clawards, ready to force an entrance with hammers and axes. Not a single street was unoccupied; each division of the city swarmed with Clawards, eagerly awaiting the signal to attack.

Deconinck was standing in the middle of the Friday market-place: after a moment of deep thought, he pronounced the doom of the French with the words, "The Lion for Flanders! Whoso is French is false; strike home!"

This order, the doom of the alien, was echoed

The Lion of Flanders

by five thousand voices; and it is easy to imagine the fearful cries, the appalling tumult that followed. The Clawards, thirsting for revenge, rushed into the bedchambers of the French, and slaughtered all who could not pronounce the vital words, "*Schild en vriend.*" In many of the houses there were more Frenchmen than could be reached in so short a time, so that many had time to dress themselves hurriedly, and seize their weapons; and this was the case especially in the quarter occupied by De Chatillon and his numerous guards. In spite of the furious rapidity of Breydel and his comrades, about six hundred Frenchmen had collected in this manner. Many also, although wounded, contrived to escape from the fray; and the number of the fugitives was thus so much increased that they resolved to stand, and sell their lives as dearly as they could. They stood in a compact mass in front of the houses, and defended themselves against the Butchers with the energy of despair. Many of them had crossbows, with which they shot down some of the Clawards; but the sight of their fallen companions only increased the fury of the survivors. De Chatillon's voice was everywhere heard animating his men to resistance; and De Mortenay was especially conspicuous, his long sword gleaming like a lightning-flash in the darkness.

Breydel raged like a madman, and dealt his

The Lion of Flanders

blows right and left among the French. So many of the foe had fallen before him that he already stood raised some feet above the ground. Blood was flowing in streams between the dead bodies; and the cry, "The Lion for Flanders! strike home!" mixed its terrible sound with the groans of the dying. John van Gistel was, of course, among the French. As he knew that his death was inevitable if the Flemings gained the victory, he shouted incessantly, "France! France!" hoping thus to sustain the courage of his troops.

But Jan Breydel recognized his voice. "Comrades," said he, wild with rage, "I must have the soul of this traitor. Forward! he has lived long enough. Whoso loves me, let him follow me close."

With these words, he threw himself with his ax among the French, and soon struck down every foe within reach of his arm. So furious was their onslaught that they soon drove the enemy back against the walls of the houses; and five hundred of them fell beneath the axes of the Butchers. In this moment of extreme peril, of terrible agony, De Mortenay remembered the word and promise of Deconinck. Rejoicing that he yet had the power to save the governor-general, he cried:

"I am De Mortenay, let me pass." Immediately the Clawards made way for him with every token of respect, and opposed no obstacle to his passage.

The Lion of Flanders

"This way, this way; follow me, comrades!" cried he to the surviving Frenchmen, hoping thus to rescue them from their fate.

But the Flemings closed in again upon them, and dealt their blows pitilessly around. The number of the fugitives was so small that, besides De Chatillon, not more than thirty reached De Mortenay's house; the rest lay weltering in their blood. Breydel made his men halt at the door of the house, and forbade them to enter; he invested it on all sides, so that no man might escape, and himself kept guard at the entrance.

While this fray was going on, Deconinck was occupied in hunting out the few remaining Frenchmen in the Stone street, near Saint Salvator's; and the other Guilds were following his example in the quarters assigned to them. The dead were thrown from the houses; and the streets were soon so obstructed that it was scarcely possible to traverse them in the gloom. Many of the soldiers had disguised themselves, hoping thus to escape through one or other of the gates; but this was of no avail, for every one was required to pronounce the words, "*Schild en vriend.*" At the first sound of their foreign accent, the ax descended on their necks, and they fell groaning to the earth. From every quarter of the city resounded the shout, "The Lion for Flanders! Whoso is French is false; strike home!" Here and there a Frenchman fled before

The Lion of Flanders

a Fleming, but only to meet his death, a few steps farther on, from the weapon of another foe.

This scene of vengeance lasted until the sun stood high in the heavens: it shone on the dead bodies, and dried the flowing blood of five thousand of the French. Yes, in this night five thousand aliens were offered to the shades of the murdered Flemings; it is a bloody page in the chronicles of Flanders, that wherein this number is written.

Before the dwelling of De Mortenay was a strange and appalling sight. A thousand Butchers lay spread out on the ground, with their axes in their hands, their threatening revengeful eyes riveted on the door. Their naked arms and their jerkins were smeared with blood; around them were piled heaps of uncounted slain. But of all this they took no heed. Here and there among the Butchers passed Guildsmen, seeking among the slain for the dead bodies of the Flemings, that they might receive honorable burial.

Although their hearts were full of rage, yet no word of reviling escaped the lips of the Butchers. The dwelling of De Mortenay was to them sacred, in virtue of their plighted word. They respected Deconinck's pledge, and had, moreover, a great esteem for the governor of the city; so they contented themselves with investing the entire quarter and keeping careful watch.

The Lion of Flanders

Messire de Chatillon and John van Gistel, the Lilyard, had taken refuge in De Mortenay's house. They were overpowered by an extreme dread; for an inevitable death hovered before their eyes. De Chatillon was a man of courage, and awaited his fate with coolness; but the face of John van Gistel was bloodless, and his whole frame quaked with fear. Notwithstanding all his efforts, he was unable to conceal his terror, and excited the pity of the Frenchmen—even of De Chatillon, who was in equal peril. They occupied an upper room, overlooking the street; and from time to time they ventured to the window, and gazed with awe on the Butchers, who lay in wait about the door, like a pack of wolves lurking for their prey. Once, as John van Gistel showed himself a moment at the window, Jan Breydel caught sight of him, and threatened him with his ax. An angry, impetuous movement arose among the Butchers; all raised their axes toward the traitor, whose death they had sworn.

The heart of the Lilyard throbbed with anguish, as he saw in the gleam of these thousand axes his doom of death; and, turning to his companions, he said, in a tone of despair:

"We must die, Messires; there is no mercy for us, for they thirst for our blood like famished hounds. You will never leave this place. My God, what shall we do?"

The Lion of Flanders

"It is a disgrace," replied De Chatillon, "to meet one's death at the hands of this rabble; rather would I be slain sword in hand. But so it must be."

The coolness of De Chatillon disquieted Van Gistel still more.

"So it must be!" repeated he. "Oh my God, what a moment of agony! what torture they will inflict upon us! But, Messire de Mortenay, I pray you, for God's sake—you have much influence over them—ask them now if they will grant us our lives for a heavy ransom. Rather than die by their hands, I would give them whatever they might ask, no matter how much."

"I will ask them, indeed," answered De Mortenay; "but do not let yourself be seen, or they will drag you from the house by force."

He opened the window, and cried, "Master Breydel, Messire van Gistel wishes to ask you whether you will give him safe conduct for a heavy ransom. Ask whatever you please; name the required sum; and do not delay, I pray you."

"Comrades," shouted the Dean to his companions, with a bitter laugh, "they offer us gold! they think they can buy off the revenge of a people with gold; shall we accept it?"

"No; we will have the Lilyard!" cried the Butchers; "he must die: the traitor—the dastard, degenerate Fleming!"

This exclamation echoed hideously in Van Gistel's ears, and it seemed to him as though he already felt the sharp edge of the ax upon his neck. De Mortenay allowed the stormy cries for vengeance to pass away, and then again called out:

"You promised me that my house should be an asylum and sanctuary; why, then, do you violate the pledge you have given?"

"We will not violate your dwelling," answered Breydel; "but I swear to you that neither De Chatillon nor Van Gistel shall leave the city alive; their blood must atone for the blood of our brothers, and we will not leave this spot until our axes have given them the death blow."

"And may I leave the city without molestation?"

"You, Messire de Mortenay, are at liberty to go whithersoever you please, with your personal retinue; and no one shall touch a hair of your head. But do not attempt to deceive us; for we are too well acquainted with those of whom we are in quest."

"I give you notice, then, that in an hour from this time I shall take my departure for Courtrai."

"May God protect you!"

"And have you no compassion for unarmed knights?"

"They had no compassion on our brethren, and their blood must be shed. The gallows which they themselves erected still stands in the market-place."

The Lion of Flanders

De Mortenay closed the window, and said to the knights:

"I commiserate you, Messires; they insist on shedding your blood. You are in very great peril; but I hope that, by God's assistance, I shall yet be able to rescue you. There is an outlet behind the courtyard, through which you may be fortunate enough to escape from your bloodthirsty enemies. Disguise yourselves, and mount your horses; then I and my servants will leave the house by the principal entrance; and while I thus draw off the attention of the Butchers on myself, you may be able to make your escape along the walls. At the Smiths' Gate there is a breach through which it will not be difficult for you to gain the open country, and your horses will secure you from being overtaken."

De Chatillon and Van Gistel joyfully embraced this last hope. The governor-general put on the clothes of his castellan, and Van Gistel those of one of the meaner servants; the thirty remaining Frenchmen led their horses from the stables and made them ready, in order that they might fly with their commander.

When all were mounted, De Mortenay and his servants issued forth into the street, in which the Butchers lay, as it were, encamped. The latter, having no suspicion of deceit, stood up, and regarded with careful scrutiny all those who accom-

The Lion of Flanders

panied the governor-general. But soon the cry, "The Lion for Flanders! Whoso is French is false! strike home! to the death!" resounded in another street, and the clattering hoofs of horses at full gallop were heard round the corner. In the greatest haste the Flemings ran, bewildered and shouting, to the place whence the sound had come; but it was too late. De Chatillon and Van Gistel had escaped. Of the thirty men who accompanied them twenty were struck down, for they were assailed by the foe on every side; but fortune was propitious to the two knights. They fled to the city wall, and reached the Smiths' Gate; then they sprang into the moat, and swam across it at the peril of their lives. De Chatillon's groom sank with his horse, and was drowned.

The Butchers had pursued the flying Frenchmen as far as the gate; but when they saw the enemies they most detested disappear between the trees in the distance, they raged and yelled in baffled wrath; for now their revenge seemed to them unsated. After remaining some moments gazing on the spot where De Chatillon had disappeared from their view, they left the wall and returned to the Friday market-place. Soon another tumult arrested their attention. From the centre of the city arose a shout of mingled voices, filling the air with prolonged sounds of rejoicing as though a prince were making his festal entry. For some

The Lion of Flanders

time the Butchers could not distinguish the triumphant cries, for they came from too great a distance; but by degrees the exulting crowd drew nearer and nearer, and the shouts became intelligible:

"Long live the Blue Lion! long live our Dean! Flanders is free!"

An innumerable multitude, consisting of all the inhabitants of Bruges, poured itself through the streets in dense throngs. The acclamations of the liberated Flemings echoed back from the houses, and filled the city as with the booming of thunder. Women and children ran confusedly among the armed Guildsmen; and the joyous clapping of their hands mingled with and harmonized the uninterrupted shouting: "Hail! hail to the Blue Lion!"

From the midst of this crowd rose a white standard, on the waving folds of which was wrought, in blue silk, a lion rampant. It was the great banner of the city of Bruges, which had for so long a time disappeared before the lilies of France. Once more it came forth from its concealment into the light of day; now it waved over the prostrate bodies of its foes; and the resurrection of this holy standard was greeted with ten thousand shouts of rejoicing.

A man of small stature bore the banner, and with his arms crossed over his breast pressed it to his heart, as though it inspired him with the deepest

The Lion of Flanders

love. Abundant tears flowed down his cheeks—tears of love of fatherland mingled with tears of joy and sadness; and an unutterable expression of happiness beamed from his every feature. He who had shed no tear for his greatest personal misfortunes, now wept when he brought back the Lion to the city of his fathers—to the altar of freedom.

All eyes were turned toward this man; and the cries, "Long live Deconinck! Hail to the Blue Lion!" were echoed and reechoed ever louder and louder. As the Dean of the Clothworkers drew near to the Friday market-place holding aloft the standard, an inexpressible joy filled the hearts of the Butchers; they, too, swelled the exulting shout of victory, and clapped their hands with an impetuous outburst of love. Breydel rushed eagerly to meet the banner, and stretched his impatient hands toward the Lion. Deconinck resigned it to him, and said:

"There, my friend, this hast thou this day won—the palladium of our freedom." Breydel answered nothing—his heart was too full. Trembling with emotion, he embraced the drapery of the standard and the Blue Lion. He hid his face in the folds of the silk, and wept; for a few moments he remained motionless; then the banner fell from his grasp, and he sank exhausted by his transport on Deconinck's breast.

The Lion of Flanders

While the two Deans held each other in this warm embrace, the people ceased not their shouts; loud exulting cries poured from the lips of all, and their quick and impassioned gestures attested the rapturous gladness of their hearts. The Friday market-place was too small to contain the thronging citizens. In the Stone street, far away to Saint Salvator's, were clustering swarms of men; the Smiths' street and Bouverie street were crowded with women and with children.

The Dean of the Clothworkers turned himself toward the centre of the market-place, and advanced to the gallows. The bodies of the Flemings who had been hanged had been already taken down and buried; but the eight ropes had been purposely left dangling in the air as signs and memorials of the tyranny which had put them to death. The standard with the Lion of Bruges was planted close to the apparatus of murder, and, greeted afresh with cries of joy. After regarding for a few moments in silence the reconquered banner, Deconinck slowly bent his knee, bowed his head, and prayed with folded hands.

When one throws a stone into still water, the movement spreads in tremulous circles over the entire surface, and awakens the ripples of the whole lake; so the thought and the act of Deconinck communicated themselves to the crowd of citizens, although but few could positively see

The Lion of Flanders

him. First, those who were immediately near to him knelt silently down; then the movement extended itself further and further among the more distant, until every head was bowed in prayer; the voices of those in the centre of the vast circle were first hushed, and so further and further spread the silence, until it pervaded the whole multitude. Eight thousand knees touched the yet bloody earth; eight thousand heads humbled themselves before the God who had created men for freedom. What a harmony must have swelled up to the throne of the Most High in that moment! How grateful to Him must have been that solemn prayer, which, like a cloud of fragrance, was wafted upward to His footstool!

After a short time Deconinck arose, and availed himself of the unbroken stillness to address the following words to his assembled fellow citizens:

"Brothers! this day the sun shines on us with fairer splendor, the breeze of Heaven is purer and more exhilarating in our city; the breath of the foreigner pollutes it no more. The haughty Frenchmen deemed that we were their slaves forever; but they have learned, at the price of their lives, that our Lion may indeed slumber awhile—die, it never can. Again have we reconquered the heritage of our fathers, and washed out in blood the footprints of the aliens. But all our enemies are not yet overcome; France will send us yet more armed hirelings, for blood demands blood. That, indeed, is of small moment, for henceforth we are invincible; but, nevertheless, think not that you may sleep after the victory achieved. Keep your hearts firm, bold, quiet; never let the noble fire which at this moment glows in your breasts waver or wane. Let each betake himself now to his abode, and rejoice with his family in the victory of this day. Exult, and drink the wine of gladness; for this is the fairest day of our lives. Those citizens who have no wine may go to the hall; there a measure shall be dealt out to each."

The shouts, which gradually became louder, prevented Deconinck from saying more; he made a sign to the surrounding Deans, and went with them up to the Stone street. The crowds reverently made way for him, and on him above all, were bestowed the greetings and blessings of the joyous citizens.

END OF VOLUME ONE

THE BEACH AT SCHEVENINGEN

Lion of Flanders Vol. II

HENDRIK CONSCIENCE

The Lion of Flanders

Volume Two

TRANSLATED FROM THE FLEMISH

INTRODUCTORY ESSAY ON
FLEMISH AND DUTCH FICTION
BY A. SCHADE VAN WESTRUM

A FRONTISPIECE AND A
BIOGRAPHICAL SKETCH

Fredonia Books
Amsterdam, The Netherlands

THE LION OF FLANDERS

VOLUME TWO

CONTENTS

THE LION OF FLANDERS
(CONCLUDED)

BOOK THIRD

	PAGE
CHAPTER I	5
CHAPTER II	26
CHAPTER III	45
CHAPTER IV	64
CHAPTER V	83
CHAPTER VI	106
CHAPTER VII	136
CHAPTER VIII	152
CHAPTER IX	176

THE LION OF FLANDERS

BOOK THIRD

CHAPTER I

Two years had gone by since the foreigner had set foot in Flanders, and cried: "Bow your heads, ye Flemings! ye sons of the north, yield to the children of the south, or die!" Little thought they that there had been born in Bruges a man endowed with large sagacity, and inspired with heroic courage; a man who shone forth as a bright light among his contemporaries; and to whom, as to His servant Moses, God had said: "Go, and deliver thy brethren, the children of Israel, from the thraldom of Pharaoh."

When the desolating bands of the French first trod the soil of his fatherland, and darkened the horizon with the dust of their march, a secret voice spoke in Deconinck's soul, and said:

"Take heed, these are in quest of slaves!"

At its sound, the noble citizen quivered with anguish and wrath:

"Slaves! *we* slaves!" groaned he; "forbid it, oh Lord our God! The blood of our free-born fathers hath flowed in defense of Thine altars; they have died on the sands of Arabia with Thy holy name on their lips. Oh, suffer not their sons to bear the debasing fetters of the alien; suffer not the temple which they have raised unto Thee to have bondsmen for worshipers!"

Deconinck had breathed this prayer from his deepest soul, and all his heart lay open to his Creator. He found therein all the noble courage and energy wherewith He had endowed the Fleming; and He sent down an answering ray of trust and hope. Instantly filled with a secret strength, Deconinck felt as though all his capacities of thought and action were doubled in energy; and, impelled by a true inspiration, he cried:

"Yea, Lord, I have felt Thy strong and Thy strengthening hand; yes, I shall ward off this degradation from my fatherland; the graves of Thy servants, my fathers, shall never be trodden down by the foot of the alien. Blessed art Thou, oh my God, who hast called me to this!"

From that moment one only feeling, one only deep yearning lived in Deconinck's heart; his every thought, his every faculty, all were consecrated to the great word—my fatherland! Business, family, repose, all were banished from his ample heart, which held but one, one only affection —his love for the native soil of the Lion. And what man more truly noble than this Fleming, who

The Lion of Flanders

a hundred times risked life and liberty itself for the freedom of Flanders? what man was ever endowed with more ample sagacity? Alone and unaided, in spite of recreants and Lilyards, who would have sold their country's freedom, he it was who baffled the efforts of the King of France —he alone it was who preserved for his brethren a lion's heart even under the chains of slavery, and thus gradually achieved their deliverance.

The French knew this well—well they knew him who at every moment shattered the wheels of their triumphal chariot. Gladly would they have rid themselves of this troublesome guardian of his country's weal; but with the cunning he combined perfectly the prudence of the serpent. He had raised up for himself a secure rampart and defense in the love of his brethren; and the stranger well knew that a dire and bloody revenge would follow any attempt upon him. During the time that the French ruled all Flanders with the rod of tyranny, Deconinck lived in entire freedom among his townsmen; and he was indeed the master of his rulers, for they feared him much more than he feared them.

And now seven thousand Frenchmen had on one day atoned with their lives for the oppressions of two long years; not a single foreigner breathed within Bruges, the victorious and free; the city echoed the joyous lays wherewith wandering min-

The Lion of Flanders

strels celebrated this deliverance, and from the watch-tower the white flag displayed the Blue Lion on its waving folds. This ensign, which had once waved from the battlements of Jerusalem, and commemorated so many proud achievements, filled the hearts of the citizens with lofty courage. On that day it seemed impossible that Flanders should again sigh in the chains of captivity; for on that day the people remembered the blood their fathers had shed in behalf of liberty. Tears rolled down their cheeks—those tears which relieve the heart when it is overful, when it throbs with too strong and sublime an emotion.

One would have thought that, now his great work was done, the Dean of the Clothworkers would have occupied himself in the reconstruction of his plundered and desolated home. But no; he thought neither of the dwelling nor of the wealth of which he had been despoiled; the welfare and the peace of his brethren were his first care. He knew that disorganization might soon follow upon inaction, and therefore, on that very day, he placed at the head of each Guild, with the concurrence of the people, an old experienced master. He was not chosen to the presidency of this council, no one devolved any duty on him; but he undertook and accomplished all. No one ventured to do anything without him; his judgment was in everything an injunction; and without issuing a

The Lion of Flanders

single command, his thought was the absolute rule of right to the republic, so transcendent and all-subduing is the way of genius.

The French host was, indeed, destroyed; but it was certain that Philip the Fair would send fresh and more numerous troops to Flanders to avenge the insult put upon him. The greater part of the citizens thought little about this terrible certainty; it was enough for them to enjoy the freedom and the gladness of the moment. But Deconinck did not share the common joy; he had almost forgotten the present in his schemes for averting future disaster. He well knew that the exhilaration and courage of a people vanish at the approach of danger, and endeavored by every means in his power to keep alive a warlike spirit in the city. Every Guildsman was provided with a "good-day" or other weapon, the banners were put in order, and the command issued that all should be ready for battle at a moment's notice. The Guild of Masons began to repair and strengthen the fortifications, and the Smiths were forbidden to forge anything but weapons for the people. The tolls were again imposed, and the city dues collected. By these wise regulations, Deconinck made every thought, every effort of the citizens converge to one object and one aim; and so he warded off from his beloved city the manifold evils which a great insurrection, how noble soever its cause, is apt to inflict on a people. All was as orderly as if the new government had existed for years.

Immediately after the victory, and while the people were drinking in every street the wine of gladness, Deconinck had sent a messenger to the encampment at Damme, to recall the remaining Guildsmen, with the women and children, into the city. Matilda had come with them, and had been offered a magnificent dwelling in the Princes' Court; but she preferred the house of Nieuwland, in which she had passed so many hours of sorrow, and with which all her dreams were associated. She found in the excellent sister of Adolf a tender and affectionate friend, into whose heart she could pour all the love and all the grief which overflowed her own. It is, indeed, a consolation for us, when our hearts are pierced with mortal anguish, to find a soul which can understand our sufferings because itself has suffered: a soul that loves those whom we love, and whose wailings are the echo of our own. So two tender saplings interweave their tendrils, and, supported by this mutual embrace, defy the devastating hurricane which bows their frail heads. To us mourning and sorrow are a hurricane, whose icy breath chills the life and wastes the fire of our souls, and brings down our head untimely to the grave, as though each year of unhappiness were reckoned as two.

The sun was rising in glowing splendor for the

The Lion of Flanders

fourth time over the free city of Bruges. Matilda was sitting in the same room of Adolf von Nieuwland's house which she had formerly occupied. Her faithful bird, the beloved falcon, accompanied her no more—it was dead. Sickness and sorrow had spread their paleness over the soft features of the maiden; her eyes were dimmed, her cheek had lost its fulness, and her whole appearance showed that a deep grief lay, like a gnawing worm, in her heart.

Those who are visited with long and bitter suffering take pleasure in sad and gloomy dreams; and, as if the reality were not painful enough, fashion to themselves phantoms, which appal them yet more: and thus was it with the hapless maiden. She fancied that the secret of her father's liberation had been discovered; she saw in imagination the murderers, bribed by Queen Joanna, mingling poison with his scanty food; and then she would shudder convulsively, and tears of agony would stream down her cheeks. Adolf was dead to her: he had expiated, with his life, his love and his magnanimity. These heartrending fancies passed ever and anew before Matilda's soul, and ceaselessly tortured the poor maiden.

At this moment her friend Maria entered her room. The smile which passed over Matilda's features as she greeted her friend was like the smile which, after a death of anguish, lingers a while on the face of the departed; it expressed more of pain and profound sorrow than the bitterest wailing could have done. She looked at Adolf's sister, and said:

"Oh! give me some comfort, some alleviation of my suffering!"

Maria drew near to the unhappy girl, and pressed her hand in tender sympathy. Her voice took its softest tone, and sank like music into the soul of the sufferer, as she said:

"Your tears flow in stillness, your heart is breaking with anguish and despair; and there is nothing, nothing to lighten your heavy burden! Alas! you are indeed unhappy."

"Unhappy! say you, my friend? Oh, yes! There is a feeling in my heart which fills it to bursting. Can you imagine what hideous fancies are ever floating before my eyes? and can you understand why my tears unceasingly flow? I have seen my father die of poison; I have heard the voice as of one dying—a voice that said, 'Farewell, my child; thou whom I have loved.'"

"I pray you, maiden," interposed Maria, "banish these gloomy shadows of your fancy. You rend my heart with sorrow. Your father is yet alive. You sin grievously in abandoning yourself thus to despair. Forgive me these words of severity."

Matilda seized Maria's hand and pressed it gently, as though she would express to her what

The Lion of Flanders

comfort these words had given her. Nevertheless, she continued her desponding discourse, and seemed even to find a kind of comfort therein. For the wailings of an oppressed soul are, as it were, tears which lighten the burden of the heart. She continued:

"I have seen yet more than this, Maria: I saw the headsman of the inhuman Joanna of France—he swung his ax over the head of your brother, and I saw that head fall on the dungeon floor!"

"Oh God!" cried Maria, "what horrible fancies!" She trembled, and her eyes glistened with tears.

"And I heard his voice—a voice that said, 'Farewell! farewell!'"

Overpowered by these hideous thoughts, Maria threw herself into Matilda's arms; her tears fell fast on the heaving breast of her unhappy friend, and the deep sobbing of the two maidens filled the room. After they had held each other in a long and motionless embrace, Matilda asked:

"Do you understand my sufferings now, Maria? Do you understand now why I am slowly wasting away?"

"Oh, yes," answered Maria, in an accent of despair; "yes, I understand and feel your sufferings. Oh, my poor brother!"

The two maidens sat down exhausted, and without uttering a word. They looked at each other

The Lion of Flanders

a while with unutterable sorrow; but their tears gradually lightened their grief, and hope returned into the hearts of both, they knew not how. Maria, who was older than Matilda, and more self-possessed in suffering, first broke the deep silence, and said:

"Why should we allow our hearts to be thus crushed by false imaginations? There is nothing to confirm the painful apprehensions which torment us; I feel sure that no harm has befallen Lord Robert, your father, and that my brother has already set out on his return to his fatherland."

"Yet you have wept, Maria! Does one weep at the smiling expectation of a brother's return?"

"You are torturing yourself, noble damsel. Oh! anguish must have struck deep its roots in your heart ere you could cling with such passionate energy to the dark dreams which are overshadowing you. Believe me, your father yet lives; and who can say how near his liberation is? Think of the joy you will feel when his voice, the very voice that rings so frightfully in your disturbed fancy, shall say to you, 'My chains are broken!' when you shall feel his warm kiss on your brow, and his loving embrace shall call forth again the roses upon your blanched cheek. Once more shall the fair castle of Wynandael open its gates to welcome you; Messire de Bethune will ascend the throne of his fathers, and then shall you tend him again with loving care; then you will remember no more the sorrows of the present, or remember them only as sorrows which you endured for your father's sake. Tell me now, Matilda, will you not admit one solitary ray of hope into your heart? Can not these thoughts of joyful promise bring you any consolation?"

At these words a sensible change came over Matilda; a gentle gladness beamed again in her eyes, and a sweet smile played on her lips.

"Oh Maria!" she sighed, throwing her right arm around her friendly comforter, "you can not imagine what relief I feel, what happiness beyond hope you have poured, like a healing balm, into my heart! So may the angel of the Lord minister comfort to you in your last hour! With what soothing words has friendship endowed you, oh my sister!"

"Your sister!" repeated Maria. "This name beseems not your handmaiden, noble damsel; it is a sufficient reward to me that I have been enabled to dispel the gloom of death from your soul."

"Accept this title, my beloved Maria; I love you so tenderly. And has not your noble brother Adolf been brought up with me? Has not my father given him to me as a brother? Yes, we belong to one family. Alas! I pray the livelong night, that the holy angels may shield Adolf on his dangerous journey. He can yet comfort me, yet cheer me. But what do I hear? Can my prayer have been answered? Yes, yes, that is our beloved brother!"

She stretched forth her arm, and remained standing motionless, pointing toward the street. She stood like a marble statue, and seemed to listen eagerly to a distant sound. Maria was terrified; she thought the maiden had lost her senses. As she was about to reply, she heard the echo of a horse's hoofs in the street; and then the meaning of Matilda's words flashed upon her. The same hope filled her breast, and she felt her heart beat with redoubled energy.

After both had listened a while in silence, the noise suddenly ceased; and already was the glad hope deserting their hearts, when the door of the chamber was violently thrown open.

"There he is! there he is!" cried Matilda. "God be praised that mine eyes have seen him once more!"

She ran eagerly toward the knight, and Adolf as eagerly hastened to meet her, when a sudden emotion overcame him, and he well-nigh fell trembling to the ground.

Instead of the youthful blooming maiden whom he expected to see, he beheld before him a worn and wasted figure, with haggard cheeks and sunken eyes. While yet in doubt whether this shadow could be Matilda, a cold shudder ran through him; all his blood rushed to his oppressed heart, and he turned pale, pale as the white robe of his beloved one. His arms dropped, he fixed his eyes intently on Matilda's wasted cheeks, and remained as one struck by a thunderbolt. A moment he remained in this attitude; and then suddenly his eyes fell, and hot tears rolled down his cheeks. He spoke not a word—no lament, no sigh escaped his lips. He would probably have remained yet longer in this stupor of despair—for his heart was touched with too keen a pain to admit of his finding alleviation in words—but his sister Maria, who had hitherto remained in the background out of respect to Matilda, threw herself on his breast, and the warm kisses which she imprinted on the lips of her beloved brother, in the intervals of the most tender words, soon aroused him from his stupor.

The noble maiden beheld with emotion this outburst of sisterly love; she trembled, and a deep trouble filled her heart. The paleness of Adolf's features, the consternation which had so visibly seized him, said to her: "Thou art ill-favored, thy wasted cheeks and thy dimmed and lustreless eyes inspire fear and abhorrence; he whom thou callest thy brother has shuddered at thy look of death." A dark despair overcame her; she felt her strength desert her; only with great effort did she succeed in reaching a couch, and then sank down faint and

The Lion of Flanders

exhausted. She hid her face in her hands, as though to exclude from her view a spectre that appalled her; and thus remained, still and motionless. After a few moments, all was quiet in the room; she heard no more, and thought that she was left alone in that dreadful solitude.

But soon she felt a hand which pressed hers; she heard a gentle voice, which spoke to her in sorrow and in sympathy:

"Matilda! Matilda! Oh my hapless sister!"

She looked up, and saw Adolf standing before her, weeping. The tears fell thick and fast from his eyes, and his look expressed the warmest affection, the profoundest compassion.

"I am ugly; is it not so, Adolf?" she sighed forth. "You are shocked at me; you will no more love me as in days that are past?"

The knight trembled at these words; he looked at the maiden with a strange and significant expression, and replied:

"Matilda, can you entertain a doubt of my affection? Oh, then, you wrong me much. You are, indeed, changed. What illness, what sufferings have brought you so low, that the roses have thus withered on your cheek? I have wept, and have been alarmed indeed; but it is from sympathy and compassion, from the deep anguish which your hard lot has caused me. Ever, ever will I remain your brother. Matilda! I can comfort you now

The Lion of Flanders

with joyous tidings; I can heal your sorrows with a message of gladness."

Gradually a feeling of joy and consolation stole into the maiden's heart. Adolf's voice exercised a wondrous power over her, and she replied, with cheerful animation:

"Good tidings, do you say, Adolf? Good tidings of my father? Oh speak, speak then, my friend."

With these words, she drew two chairs near her couch, and motioned to Maria and her brother to sit down upon them.

Adolf reached forth one hand to Matilda, the other to his beloved sister; and so he sat between the two maidens, as an angel of consolation, on whose words one lingered as on those of some holy hymn.

"Rejoice, Matilda, and thank God for His goodness. Your father returned to Bourges; in sadness, indeed, but in safety and in health. No one but the old chatelain and Diederik die Vos know the secret of his temporary liberation. He is already free even in his captivity; for his jailers have become his warmest friends."

"But should the evil-minded Joanna desire to avenge on him the insult which has been offered to France, who will then shield him from the executioner? You are no longer with him, my noble friend."

The Lion of Flanders

"Listen, Matilda. The guardians of the castle of Bourges are all old warriors, who, by reason of their wounds, are no longer equal to active warfare. Most of them witnessed the heroic deeds of the Lion of Flanders at Beneventum. You can not imagine with what love, with what admiration, they regard him at whose name the armies of France have so often trembled. Were Robert to seek to escape without the permission of the castellan, their master, doubtless they would prevent him. But I assure you—and I know well the noble souls of those warriors, who have grown gray beneath their coats of mail—that they would shed their last drop of blood for him whom they revere, were but a hair of his head threatened. Fear not, then; the life of your father is assured; and, but for the sorrow he felt on account of your sad fate, he would have borne his captivity in patience."

"You bring me such good tidings, my friend—your words sink so consolingly into my relieved heart—that I seem to drink in fresh life from your smile. Speak on still, if it be only that I may hear the accents of your voice."

"And yet fairer hopes has the Lion given me for you, Matilda. It may be the deliverance of your father is very near at hand; it may be that you will very soon be with him, and all your dear relations, in the beautiful Wynandael."

The Lion of Flanders

"What are you saying, Adolf? It is your friendship that prompts these words; but do not mock me with hope of a bliss that is impossible."

"Be not thus unbelieving, Matilda. Listen to the grounds of this joyful hope. You know that Charles de Valois, that noblest of Frenchmen, has drawn the bravest of the knights after him into Italy. He has not forgotten at the court of Rome that he is the guiltless cause of the captivity of your relatives. It has been a bitter thought to him that he himself, like a traitor, had delivered his friend and companion in arms, the Lion of Flanders, into the hands of his enemies; and he has been striving, in every possible way, to effect his liberation. Ambassadors have been already sent from Pope Boniface to King Philip the Fair, and have demanded of him, with urgency, the release of your father, and of all your relatives. The Holy Father is sparing no effort to restore to Flanders its rightful princes; and the court of France seems already inclined to peace. Let us embrace this consoling hope, my dear friend."

"Yes, indeed, Adolf, gladly might we surrender ourselves to these consoling thoughts; but why should we flatter ourselves with hopes so deceitful? Will not the King of France avenge his fallen soldiers? Will not De Chatillon, our most rancorous enemy, goad on his terrible niece Joanna? Think, then, Adolf, what pangs can not this bloodthirsty woman imagine, to avenge on us the bravery of the Flemings?"

"Torment not yourself; for your fears are without foundation. Probably the horrible death of his soldiers has convinced Philip the Fair that the Flemings will never bow their free necks to the yoke of the alien. His own interest will constrain him to set at liberty our country's lords; otherwise he will lose the fairest fief of his crown. You see, noble damsel, that everything is propitious to us."

"Yes, yes, Adolf; in your presence all my sorrows melt away, and disappear utterly. Your speech is so full of comfort, you awaken such sweetly-echoing tones in my heart."

They conversed thus a long time peacefully together on their fears and their hopes. When Adolf had given Matilda all the information in his power, and had filled her heart with comfort, he turned with brotherly love to his sister, and held with her a soothing discourse, which attuned them all to gladness and serenity. Matilda forgot her bygone sufferings; she breathed freely and with courage, and the veins which were spread over her cheeks like delicate network were filled with warmer blood.

Suddenly they heard a loud tumult in the street; a thousand voices rang from the roofs of the houses, and the jubilant shouts of the crowd were mingled in indistinguishable confusion; only at intervals

The Lion of Flanders

was the cry intelligible amid the joyous clapping of hands: "Flanders, the Lion! hail, hail to our Count!" Adolf and the two maidens had drawn near to the window; they saw the countless heads of the crowds hastening to the market-place. Women and children swelled the procession, which passed before the curious maidens like a billowy sea. In another street resounded the tramp of a multitude of horses, so that they were confirmed in their conjecture that a troop of cavalry had entered Bruges. While they were discussing the probable reasons of this popular commotion, a servant announced the arrival of a messenger, who craved an audience, and who entered the room immediately on receiving permission.

It was a youthful page, a delicate boy, whose features bore a peculiar expression of innocence and truthfulness: he was clothed in black and blue silk, set off with manifold adornments. As he drew near to the ladies, he respectfully uncovered his head, and made lowly obeisance without speaking a word.

"What good tidings do you bring us, dear boy?" asked Matilda graciously. The page raised his head, and replied with his gentle voice:

"For the most illustrious daughter of the Lion, our Count, I bring a message from my lord and master Guy, who has just entered the city with five hundred horsemen. He sends his greeting to his

The Lion of Flanders

fair niece, Matilda de Bethune, and will in a few moments express his deep affection to her in person. This is the message, noble maiden, which I was charged to deliver to you."

And with these words he made a reverential bow, and disappeared at the door. In fulfilment of the promise which he had made to Deconinck in the wood, near the ruins of Nieuwenhove, the young Guy had arrived with the promised succors from Namur. He had taken Castle Wynandael on his way, and had put the French garrison to the sword. He had razed to the ground the Castle of Sysseele, because the castellan was a sworn Lilyard and had offered the French a refuge within its walls. The victorious entry of Guy filled the citizens of Bruges with exulting joy, and in every street resounded the cry, "Hail to our Count! Flanders! the Lion!"

When the young general with his suite had reached the Friday Market-place, the masters of the Guilds presented him with the keys of the city; and he was thus proclaimed Count of Flanders, until the liberation of Robert de Bethune, his brother. The citizens already deemed their liberty secure; for now they had a chief who could lead them forth to the fight. The horsemen were quartered among the most distinguished citizens; and so great was the zeal and the joy of the inhabitants that there was quite a struggle to seize the

The Lion of Flanders

reins of the horses; for every one wished to receive into his house one of the Count's followers; but it is easy to imagine with what kindness and courtesy these valuable auxiliaries were welcomed.

As soon as Guy had assumed the government which Deconinck had established and secured, he hastened to the house of Nieuwland, embraced his afflicted niece, and recounted to her with joy how he had driven the aliens from their beloved Wynandael. A costly banquet awaited them, prepared by Maria in honor of her brother's return. They drank the wine of joy for the liberation of the enslaved Flemings, and consecrated a tear to the mournful memory of the poisoned Philippa.

The Lion of Flanders

CHAPTER II

AFTER the fearful night in which the blood of the French had flowed in such abundant streams, De Chatillon, John van Gistel, and the few others who had escaped death, were received within the walls of Courtrai. In the city they found a numerous garrison, trusting in peaceful security to the strength of the castle; for on this place the French counted most confidently, as its fortifications were really unassailable. De Chatillon, a prey to hopeless despair on account of his defeat, was burning with the desire of vengeance. He hastily drew some small companies of mercenaries from the other cities to Courtrai, in order still further to protect it in the event of an attack, and he entrusted the command of these troops to the castellan Van Lens, a bastard Fleming. Using the utmost despatch, he visited the other frontier cities, placed within them the troops that yet remained to him in Picardy, gave the command of Lisle to the chancellor, Pierre Flotte, and hastened to France, to the court of Philip at Paris, where the tidings of the defeat of his army had already preceded him.

The Lion of Flanders

Philip the Fair received the governor-general of Flanders with marked displeasure, and reproached him angrily with the tyrannical conduct which had been the cause of the disaster. De Chatillon would have undoubtedly fallen into disgrace, had not Queen Joanna, who, as we know, hated the Flemings and exulted in their oppression, found means to exculpate her uncle so dexterously that Philip at length began to believe that he deserved thanks rather than reproofs. And thus the whole wrath of the king was again turned back on the Flemings, and he swore that he would exact from them a dire revenge.

An army of twenty thousand men had been already assembled at Paris, in order to deliver the kingdom of Majorca from the hand of the infidel; and these were the troops of whose gathering Robert de Bethune had spoken to the lords of Flanders. They might easily have marched this host upon Flanders; but Philip would run no risk of defeat, and resolved therefore to postpone his vengeance a short time in order to collect more soldiers.

A proclamation was borne throughout France by swift messengers; the great vassals of the kingdom were informed how the Flemings had put to death seven thousand Frenchmen; and that the king summoned them to Paris with all the troops at their command, and with the utmost speed, in order to avenge the insult. In those times warfare and feats of arms were the sole occupation of the nobles, and they exulted at the very mention of battle; so we need not wonder that this appeal met an immediate and hearty response. From every quarter, from every castle of mighty France, poured the great feudatories of the crown with their vassals; and in a very short time the French army counted more than fifty thousand men.

After the Lion of Flanders and Charles de Valois, Robert d'Artois was the ablest warrior that Europe boasted at that time; and indeed his great and varied experience, gained in numerous expeditions, gave him, in some respects, an advantage over these two commanders. For eight whole years he had never laid aside his armor; his hair had literally grown gray beneath the helmet. The unrelenting hatred with which he regarded the Flemings, who had slain his only son at Furnes, determined the queen to give him the chief command of the whole army; and in truth no one was better qualified for this honorable post than Robert d'Artois.

Want of money, and the daily arrival of the more distant vassals of the crown, retarded for some time the departure of the host. The excessive ardor and precipitation with which the French nobles usually entered on their expeditions had so often proved prejudicial to them, and they had learnt at such heavy cost that pru-

The Lion of Flanders

dence and foresight are important elements of strength, that they resolved on this occasion to take every precaution, and proceed with the greatest deliberation.

The fiery queen of Navarre sent for Robert d'Artois, and urged him to chastise the Flemings with the utmost cruelty. She enjoined on him, for instance, "to rip up all the Flemish swine, and to spit their whelps on the point of the sword, and to strike every Flemish dog dead." The swine and the whelps were the women and children of Flanders; and the dogs were those heroes who, sword in hand, were defending their fatherland. The faithful chronicles have preserved for us these shameless words of a queen and a woman, as a token of Joanna's ferocious spirit.

In the meantime, the Flemings had greatly increased their army. The illustrious Master John Borluut had excited the citizens of Ghent to rise and drive out of their city the French garrison; and seven hundred were slain in this insurrection. Oudenarde and several other cities effected their freedom in like manner; so that the enemy retained possession only of a few fortified places, in which the flying Frenchmen found refuge. William van Gulick, the priest, came from Germany to Bruges with a numerous troop of archers, and as soon as Master John van Renesse had assembled four hundred Zeelanders, they united their forces, and, ac-

The Lion of Flanders

companied by a crowd of volunteers, moved toward Cassel, in order to fall upon and expel the French garrison. This city was exceedingly well fortified, so that it could not be taken by surprise. William van Gulick had counted on the cooperation of the citizens; but the French kept so vigilant a guard that they could not make the slightest movement; so that Master William found himself compelled to begin a regular siege, and await the arrival of the necessary stores and battering machines.

The youthful Guy had been received with acclamations in all the most important cities of West Flanders; his presence everywhere infused courage, and inspired every man with a burning ardor to defend his fatherland. Adolf van Nieuwland had also visited the lesser towns, in order to summon together all who were capable of bearing arms.

In Courtrai there lay about three thousand French under the command of the castellan Van Lens. Instead of endeavoring to win the affections of the people by kindness, they exhausted their patience by continued acts of depredation and petty tyranny. Encouraged by the example of the other cities, the inhabitants rose suddenly against the French, and slew more than half of them; the remainder made their escape to the citadel, which they hastily fortified in the best way that they could. There they revenged themselves by shoot-

The Lion of Flanders

ing burning arrows into the city; so that many of its finest buildings, especially those surrounding the market-place and the Beguinage, became a prey to the flames. The citizens thereupon invested the citadel with their whole forces; but they did not number sufficiently strong to be able to expel the French. Filled with the mournful apprehension that their city would soon be entirely destroyed by fire, they sent messengers to Bruges with an earnest request to the young Count Guy for aid.

The messenger reached Guy in Bruges on the 5th of July, 1302, and made him acquainted with the melancholy condition of the city, and its urgent need of aid. The Count was deeply moved by the account they gave, and determined to hasten without delay to the hapless city. As William van Gulick had taken all the troops with him to Cassel, Guy had no other resource than to call together the Guildsmen. He caused all the Deans to be immediately summoned to the upper hall of the prince's castle, and betook himself thither with the few knights who were about him. An hour later, all the Deans, thirty in number, were assembled, and awaited, with uncovered heads and in silence, the subject to be proposed for their deliberation. Deconinck and Breydel, as leaders of the two most powerful Guilds, occupied the foremost place. Count Guy sat in a rich armchair at the upper end

The Lion of Flanders

of the hall; near him stood Messire John van Lichterwelde and Messire van Heyne, both peers of Flanders. There were four noble families in Flanders, of which the heads were called Beers, or peers; when the race of the Count became extinct, the new prince was to be chosen from among these Beers. The other gentlemen attending the Count were: Messire van Gavem, whose father had been slain by the French at Furnes; Messire van Bornhem, a knight templar; Robert van Leeuererghem; Baldwin van Raveschoot; Ivo van Belleghem; Henry, Lord of Lonchyn, in Luxemburg; Gorwyer van Goetzenhove and Jan van Cuyck of Brabant; Peter and Louis van Lichterwelde; Peter and Louis Goethals of Ghent; and Henry van Petershem. Adolf van Nieuwland was standing on the right hand of the Count, and engaged in confidential conversation with him.

In the centre of the vacant space, between the Deans and the knights, stood the herald of Courtrai. As soon as each had taken his place, Guy commanded him to repeat his tidings in presence of the Deans; and the herald obeyed, and began:

"The good citizens of Courtrai greet you by me, noble lords, and inform you that they have driven the French from their city, and that five hundred of them have bitten the dust. But now the city is in the greatest straits. The traitor Van Lens has fallen back on the citadel, and daily discharges

The Lion of Flanders

burning arrows upon the houses, so that the fairest portion of the city is already reduced to ashes. Messire Arnold van Oudenarde has brought them some succors, yet is the number of the enemy too great. In this their need and distress, they beseech the Count Guy in particular, and you, friendly citizens of Bruges, in general, to send them aid; and they hope that you will not delay a single day the rescue of your distressed brothers. Such is the message which the good citizens of Courtrai send to you by my mouth."

"You have heard, Deans," said Guy, "that one of our noblest cities is in peril of utter destruction; I do not think that the cry of distress from your brothers of Courtrai will fall in vain on your ears. The matter demands haste; your aid alone can deliver them from their danger; wherefore I pray you all instantly to summon your Guilds to arms. How long time do you require to prepare your comrades to set forth?"

The Dean of the Clothworkers replied: "This afternoon, most illustrious Count, four thousand Clothworkers will stand full armed on the Friday Market-place: I will lead them whithersoever you command."

"And you, Master Breydel, you will be there also?"

Breydel advanced proudly, and replied: "Your servant Breydel will place at your disposition, my

The Lion of Flanders

Lord Count, not less than eight thousand of his craftsmen."

A cry of astonishment ran along the circle of knights. "Eight thousand!" said they, all at once.

"Yes, truly, messires," continued the Dean of the Butchers; "eight thousand and more. All the Guilds of Bruges, except that of the Clothworkers, have elected me their captain; and God knows how I can repay this honor. This very afternoon, if you will it so, the Friday Market-place shall be filled with your trusty townsmen; and I can assure you that in my butchers you have a thousand lions in your host; the sooner the better, noble Count; our axes are beginning to rust."

"Master Breydel," said Guy, "you are a brave and a worthy vassal of my father. The land in which such men live can never long remain enslaved. I thank you for your hearty good-will."

A smile of satisfaction showed how much pleasure Breydel's words had given to the circle of knights; but the Dean turned back again, and whispered in Deconinck's ear: "I pray you, master, be not angry with me for speaking thus to the Count. You are and will ever be my superior; for without your counsel I should do but little good. My words have not caused you displeasure?"

The Dean of the Clothworkers pressed Breydel's hand in sign of friendship and perfect accord.

"Master Deconinck," inquired Guy, "have you

made known to the Guilds my former request? Will the requisite gold be provided for me?"

"The Guilds of Bruges place all their wealth at your disposal, noble Count," was the answer. "If you will but send some of your servants with a command in writing to the Guildhall, as many marks of silver will be delivered to them as you may require. The Guilds beseech you not to spare them; freedom can never cost them too dear."

Just as Guy was about to acknowledge the goodwill and confidence of the citizens with words of gratitude, the door of the hall was opened, and every eye was fixed with astonishment on a monk, who entered boldly and uninvited, and drew near to the Dean. A robe of thick brown cloth was confined by a girdle around his loins; a black hood overhung his face, and so concealed his features as to render it impossible to recognize him. He seemed very old; for his body was bent, and a long beard floated on his breast. With hasty and furtive glances, he regarded the knights who were present; and his keen eye seemed to pierce the lowest depth of their hearts. Adolf van Nieuwland recognized in him the same monk who had brought him the letter of Robert de Bethune, and was about to greet him with a loud voice; but the gestures of the monk were so extraordinary that the words died away on the lips of the young man. All who were present began to kindle with anger;

the daring looks which the unknown bent on them were such as they would not willingly endure; yet they gave no indication of their displeasure, for they saw that the riddle would soon be solved.

When the monk had well scrutinized each of those who were present, he loosed his girdle from his loins, threw his robe and his hood on the ground, and remained standing in the middle of the hall. He raised his head proudly; he was a man of about thirty years of age, tall and of noble frame; he looked round upon the knights as though he said, "Do you not recognize me?"

The answer did not come quickly enough, and he cried out: "You are astonished, messires, to find a fox under this coat; yet he has lain concealed in it for two years."

"Welcome, welcome, dear Diederik, good friend!" exclaimed the nobles all at once; "we thought you had been long since dead."

"Then you may thank God that I have risen again," continued Diederik. "No, I was not dead; our captive brother and Adolf van Nieuwland can bear testimony to that. I have been able to console all; for as an itinerant priest I had access to the prisons; and may God forgive me the vile Latin I have uttered. Yes, you may laugh, messires, but I have spoken Latin. I bring you, moreover, news from all our hapless countrymen for their relatives and friends."

The Lion of Flanders

Some of the knights wished to make more particular inquiry concerning the fate of the prisoners; but he put them aside, and continued: "For God's sake, cease these questions; I have far more important tidings to announce to you. Hear, and tremble not; for I bring you evil news. You have shaken off the yoke, and have fought and won the battle of your freedom; I grieve that I could not share this joy with you. Honor to you, brave knights and trusty citizens; honor to you that you have freed your fatherland. I assure you that if the Flemings do not wear new chains within fourteen days, not all the devils in hell will be able to rob them of their liberty; but the new chains that are preparing make me anxious and sad."

"Explain yourself more clearly, Messire Diederik," cried Guy; "explain your meaning, and do not torture us with enigmatical hints."

"Well, then, I tell you plainly that sixty-two thousand Frenchmen are encamped before Lille."

"Sixty-two thousand!" repeated the knights, gazing in alarm on one another.

"Sixty-two thousand!" echoed Breydel, rubbing his hands for joy; "what a fine flock!"

Deconinck's head sank on his breast, and he was lost in deep thought. Soon, however, he had estimated the greatness of the danger, and considered the means to avert it.

"I assure you, messires," continued Diederik

die Vos, "that they number more than thirty-two thousand horse, and at least as many foot. They plunder and burn as though they were thereby rendering an acceptable service to Heaven."

"Are these evil tidings well founded?" asked Guy anxiously; "has not he who told you this deceived you, Messire Diederik?"

"No, no, noble Count, I saw it with my own eyes; and last evening I ate my supper in the tent of the Seneschal Robert d'Artois. He swore on his honor, in my presence, that the last Fleming should die by his hand. Consider now what it behooves you to do. For myself, I shall buckle on my armor without delay; and if I stand alone against these two-and-sixty thousand accursed Frenchmen, I will not yield an inch of ground; I, at least, will no longer witness the slavery of Flanders!"

Jan Breydel could not keep himself still a moment; his feet were in perpetual motion, and he swung his arms in angry impatience. Could he but dare to speak; but reverence for the lords who stood around restrained him. Guy and the other nobles looked at one another in helpless dismay. Two-and-thirty thousand well-equipped and warlike horsemen! It was altogether impossible that they could hope to offer a successful resistance to a force like this. In the Flemish army there were only the five hundred horsemen of Namur, whom

The Lion of Flanders

Guy had brought with him; and what could this handful avail against the frightful number of the foe?

"What is to be done?" asked Guy. "Speak; how is our fatherland to be delivered?"

Some were of opinion that they should throw themselves into Bruges, and there await the dispersion of the French army from want of provisions. Others wished to be let loose upon the enemy, and to fall upon them that very night. Many projects were discussed, of which the greater part were rejected as dishonorable, and the remainder as impracticable.

Deconinck stood with his head still bowed in deep thought; he heard, indeed, every proposition that was made, but the attention he gave did not hinder the course of his own reflections. At last Guy addressed him, and asked what way of escape he saw from this critical position.

"Noble Count," replied Deconinck, raising his head, "were I commander-in-chief, I should begin operations thus: I should march with all speed with the Guildsmen of Bruges upon Courtrai, in order to expel thence the castellan Van Lens. That fortress would no longer be a stronghold and place of reserve for the French, and we should have a secure shelter for our women and children, as well as for ourselves; for the citadel of Courtrai is strong, while Bruges, in its present condition, could not stand a siege, but might easily be taken by storm. I would further despatch mounted messengers into all parts of Flanders to announce the nearness of the enemy, and to summon all the Clawards to Courtrai; Messires van Gulick and Renesse should also fall back on the place. In this way, I am sure, noble Count, that the Flemish army would within four days amount to thirty thousand picked men of war, and then we need have no great fear of the French."

The knights listened in eager silence; they could not help being astonished at the extraordinary man who had in a few minutes thought out so able a method of defense, and given them such appropriate counsel. Though they had long known Deconinck's high qualities, they could scarcely believe that they were the endowments of a Clothworker, a man from the class of the people.

"You have more wisdom than all of us together," cried Diederik die Vos. "Yes, yes, it is so indeed; we are far stronger than we thought. Now we turn over a new leaf; and I am inclined to think the French will have good reason to rue their journey hitherward."

"I thank God, who has inspired you with these counsels, Master Deconinck," said the youthful Count; "your good service shall not lack its fitting reward. I will act on the plan you have advised; it is most wise and most prudent. I hope, Master

The Lion of Flanders

Breydel, that you will not fail to supply us the men whom you have promised."

"Eight thousand, did I say, most noble Count?" replied Breydel. "Well, now I say ten thousand. No Guildsman nor apprentice shall remain in Bruges; young and old, all must forth to the fight. I will take care that the French shall not make their entry into Flanders except over our dead bodies, and their Deans, my friends, will do the same, I know right well."

"Certainly, noble lord," exclaimed the Deans with one voice; "no man will fail in his duty, for all are longing eagerly for the fight."

"Our time is too precious to be consumed in talking," said Guy. "Go now and gather the Guildsmen together with what speed you can; in two hours I shall be ready to depart, and will place myself at the head of the expedition in the Friday Market-place. Go now, I am right well pleased with your zeal and courage."

All then left the hall. Guy immediately despatched numerous messengers in all directions to the nobles who still remained loyal to their fatherland; and at the same time he sent directions to William van Gulick and John van Renesse to fall back on Courtrai.

The alarming tidings were spread in a few moments over the whole city. As the rumor diffused itself, the number of the enemy was exaggerated

The Lion of Flanders

in a wonderful manner, and now the French host was more than one hundred thousand strong. One may imagine with what terror and grief the sorrowful intelligence struck the women and children. In every street were weeping mothers embracing their terrified daughters with loving compassion. The children began to cry because they saw their mothers weep and tremble, and without any notion of the danger that threatened them. Their agonized sobs and the expression of mortal terror on their countenances contrasted singularly with the lofty and impatient bearing of the men.

From all sides hastened the Guildsmen to the place of rendezvous; the clatter of the iron plates, with which many were covered, mingled, like a jocund song, with the wailing cries of the women and children. Whenever a party of men met in the street, they halted a moment to exchange a few words, and kindle each other's courage to the fight for victory or for death. Here and there might be seen a father at the door of his house, embracing one by one his children and their mother; then dashing the tears from his eye, and disappearing like an arrow in the direction of the Friday Marketplace; and the mother would linger on the threshold of the house, gazing on the corner round which the father of her children had vanished. That farewell seemed to her a separation forever; tears

The Lion of Flanders

rolled down from beneath her eyelids—she pressed her children to her throbbing breast, and turned back despairingly into her home.

Already the Guildsmen stood in long files in the market-place; Breydel had kept his promise; he counted among his men twelve thousand Guildsmen of all crafts. The axes of the Butchers glittered like mirrors in the sunshine, and dazzled the beholder with their broad and fiery flashings. Over the heads of the Clothworkers arose two thousand "good-days," with keen iron heads, and one division of them carried crossbows. Guy was standing in the middle of the square, surrounded by a retinue of about twenty knights; he was awaiting the return of the remaining craftsmen, who had been despatched into the city to collect wagons and horses. A Clothworker whom Deconinck had sent to the great bell-tower advanced into the market-place at this moment with the great standard of Bruges. No sooner had the Guildsmen caught sight of the Blue Lion than they raised a deafening shout of joy, and ever anew was repeated the war-cry which had given the signal of vengeance on that night of blood:

"Flanders and the Lion! all that is French is false!"

And then they brandished their weapons, as though already in presence of the foe.

When all that was necessary had been disposed

The Lion of Flanders

in the wagons, the bugles gave forth their shrill tones, and the men of Bruges left their city, with waving banners, by the gate of Ghent. The women were now left without any protection; their distress was greater than ever; they saw nothing before them but misery and death. In the afternoon, Matilda left the city with all her maidens and attendants; this hasty departure led many to imagine that they would find a more secure retreat in Courtrai. They hastily gathered together a few necessaries, shut up their houses, and followed in the steps of their husbands through the gate of Ghent. Numberless families ran in this manner with bleeding feet the whole distance from Bruges to Courtrai, and watered with their bitter tears the grass which skirted the way; while in Bruges reigned a stillness—as of the grave.

The Lion of Flanders

CHAPTER III

It was already dark night when Guy reached Courtrai with about sixteen thousand men. The inhabitants, apprised of their approach by mounted messengers, stood in dense crowds on the walls of the city, and welcomed their rightful lords with glad and joyous acclamations, amidst the blaze of innumerable torches. As soon as the host had entered the city, and been distributed throughout its various quarters, the citizens of Courtrai brought forth every kind of food and refreshment; they placed before their weary brethren large flagons of wine to restore their exhausted strength, and kept watch over them the whole night. While they were embracing one another with transport, and expressing their affection in every possible manner, some hastened to meet the wearied women and children, and to relieve them of the burdens they carried. Not a few of these poor creatures, whose feet were torn and bleeding with their painful march, were borne to the city on the broad shoulders of the brave citizens of Courtrai; all were lodged and carefully tended, and comforted in every way. The gratitude of the men of Cour-

The Lion of Flanders

trai, and their extreme kindness, strengthened wonderfully the courage of the men of Bruges; for men's souls are ever enlarged and elevated by frank and noble treatment.

Matilda and Maria, the sister of Adolf van Nieuwland, with a considerable number of the noble ladies of Bruges, had been some hours in Courtrai before the army arrived. They had been already received by their friends, and had busied themselves in providing shelter and quarters for the knights and nobles, their relatives and friends; so that on their arrival, Guy and his companions found supper already prepared for them.

Early the next morning Guy and a few of the most distinguished inhabitants reconnoitred the fortifications of the citadel; and found, to their great dismay, that it was impossible to take it without a large siege-train. The walls were far too lofty, and the overhanging towers allowed too many arrows to be discharged on the advancing besiegers. He saw that a bold attack might easily cost him a thousand men; and, after mature deliberation, he determined not to storm the citadel at once. He gave orders for the construction of battering-rams and movable towers, and for the collection of every material in the city that could be available for the assault. It was clear that this could not take place for five days at least; but the delay was no disadvantage to the citizens of Courtrai, for since the

The Lion of Flanders

arrival of the Flemish troops, the French garrison had ceased to shoot burning arrows into the city; the soldiers were, indeed, seen standing with their bows at the loopholes of the battlements, but yet they did not discharge them. The Flemings could not conceive the reason of this cessation; they thought that some artifice lay concealed therein, and remained carefully on their guard. Guy had forbidden every aggression; he would attempt nothing until he had all his machines ready for storming the citadel, and could securely reckon on the victory.

The castellan Van Lens was at his wits' end; his archers had but a very slender supply of arrows left, and prudence compelled him to reserve them for the assault. His provisions, too, were so far exhausted that he could supply only half-rations to his soldiers. Still he hoped to elude the vigilance of the Flemings, and to find some opportunity to send a messenger to Lille, where the French army lay encamped.

Arnold of Oudenarde, who had a few days before brought the citizens of Courtrai a reenforcement of three hundred men, had bivouacked with his soldiers on the Gröningen Place, close to the abbey and the walls of the city. This place was especially fitted for a general encampment, and had been chosen for that purpose by Guy and his council of war. While the Carpenters' Guild was laboring at

The Lion of Flanders

the storming-engines, the other Flemings were set to work the next morning to dig trenches. The Clothworkers and the Butchers wielded each a pickax and a spade, and set to work with great ardor; the entrenchments and siege-works arose as by enchantment; the whole army toiled with emulous zeal, and each sought to surpass his neighbor in exertion. The spades and pickaxes rose and descended like gleams of lightning, so that the eye could not follow them; and the thick clods of earth fell on the entrenchments like showers of stones thrown down on the assailants from a besieged city.

As soon as a part of the earthworks was completed, the soldiers hastened to pitch the tents. Ever and anon the workmen would leave the poles sticking in the earth and scramble away to work at the entrenchments; and then would arise a loud shout of welcome greeting, and the cry, "Flanders and the Lion!" boomed in the distance as an answering echo. And this happened, too, whenever reenforcements arrived from the other cities. The Flemish people had unjustly accused their nobles of disloyalty and cowardice: true, a large number had declared for the alien, but the loyal were far more numerous than the traitors. Fifty-and-two of the noblest knights of Flanders pined in the prisons of France; and to these prisons their love for their fatherland and for their native princes had con-

The Lion of Flanders

signed them. The rest of the true-hearted nobles who remained in Flanders deemed it a degradation to take part with the insurgent townspeople; to them the tournament and the battle-field were the only places fit for deeds of arms. The manners of the time had given them this notion; for then the distance between a knight and a citizen was as great as that between a master and a servant now. So long as the struggle was carried on within the walls of the cities, and under the command of popular leaders, they remained shut up in their castles, sighing over their country's oppression; but now that Guy had placed himself at the head of his people, as the general-in-chief appointed by their Count, they poured in from all sides with their retainers.

On the first day, early in the morning, there entered Courtrai Messires Baldwin of Papenrode, Henry of Raveschoot, Ivo of Belleghem, Solomon of Sevecote, and the lord of Maldeghem. Toward midday a cloud of dust arose over the distant trees in the direction of Moorseele, and amid the loud shouts of the men of Bruges, fifteen hundred men of Furnes entered the city, with the renowned warrior Eustachius Sporkyn at their head. They were accompanied by a multitude of knights who had joined them on their march. Among these the most distinguished were Messires John van Ayshoven, William van Daekenem, and his brother

The Lion of Flanders

Peter; Messire van Landeghem, Hugo van der Moere, and Simon van Caestere. John Willebaert of Thorout had also placed himself, with a small contingent of troops, under the command of Van Sporkyn. Each moment, moreover, some stray knight would enter the camp: not a few of these were from surrounding countries, and gladly came to lend their aid to the Flemings in their struggle for liberty. In this way Henry van Lonchyn of Luxemburg, Goswyn van Goetzenhove and John van Cuyck, two nobles of Brabant, were already with Guy when the troops of Furnes marched into the city. As soon as each newcomer had recruited his strength, and refreshed himself with food, he was sent into the camp, and placed under the command of Messire van Renesse.

On the second day arrived in haste the men of Ypres. Although they had their own city to care for, they could not allow Flanders to be liberated without them. Their troops were the finest and richest in equipment of all the army. They were five hundred clubmen, all arrayed in scarlet, and with magnificent feathers in their glittering morions; they wore also breastplates and kneeplates, which gleamed wondrously in the sunshine. Seven hundred others carried enormous crossbows, with bolts of steel: and their uniform was green turned up with yellow. With them came Messires John of Ypres, armor-bearer of Count John of

The Lion of Flanders

Namur, Diederik van Vlamertinghe, Joseph van Hollebeke and Baldwin van Passchendale; their leaders were Philip Baelde and Peter Belle, the Deans of the two principal Guilds of Ypres. In the afternoon arrived two hundred well-appointed warriors from east and west Vrye, the villages around Bruges.

On the third day, early in the morning, Messires William van Gulick, the priest, and John van Renesse returned from Cassel. Five hundred knights, four hundred Zeelanders, and another detachment of the men of Bruges, marched with them into the camp.

And now from every part the knights and warriors who had been summoned had arrived. Men of all arms were ranged under the command of Guy. It is impossible to express the joy which filled the hearts of the Flemings during these days; for now they saw that their fellow-countrymen had not degenerated, and that their fatherland still counted loyal and valiant sons in every quarter. Already one-and-twenty thousand men lay encamped, fit and ready for battle, under the banner of the Black Lion; and their number was being hourly increased by small reenforcements.

Although the French had an army of sixty-two thousand men, of which the half was cavalry, yet not the slightest fear found entrance into the hearts of the Flemings. In their enthusiasm they would

The Lion of Flanders

cease their work, and embrace one another, exchanging words of confidence and triumph, as though there were nothing that could rob them of their victory.

Toward evening, as the laborers were returning to their tents, the cry, "Flanders and the Lion!" arose anew over the walls of Courtrai. All ran back to the entrenchments to see what the sound could mean. No sooner did their eyes range freely over the ramparts than they sent back a loud and joyous answering shout. Six hundred horsemen, all cased in steel, sprang into the trenches amid deafening acclamations. They came from Namur; and Count John, the brother of Robert de Bethune, had sent them into Flanders. The arrival of these horsemen greatly raised the spirits and increased the joy of the Flemings; for it was in cavalry that they were particularly deficient. Although they knew right well that the men of Namur could not understand one word they said, they overwhelmed them with words of greeting and welcome, and brought them wine in profusion: and when the foreign warriors saw this friendly reception, they felt themselves animated by a like spirit of affection; and they swore that they would sacrifice both blood and life for their good hosts.

Ghent alone had sent neither message nor contingent to Courtrai. It had been long known that the Lilyards were very numerous there, and that the

The Lion of Flanders

governor was a stanch ally of the French. Nevertheless, seven hundred French mercenaries had been slain by the townsmen, and John Borluut had promised his aid. The matter was doubtful, and so the Flemings did not venture openly to accuse their brethren of Ghent of disloyalty; nevertheless, they entertained great suspicion of them, and not seldom gave free expression to their displeasure. In the evening, when the sun had already disappeared more than an hour behind the village of Moorseele, the laborers had dispersed themselves among the tents. Here and there was still heard a song, interrupted at intervals by the clapping of hands and the chink of drinking-glasses, and the concluding verse of which was caught up and enthusiastically repeated by a multitude of voices. In other tents was heard a confused murmur, which, when one listened attentively, resolved itself into an interchange of encouragements and exhortations. In the midst of the camp, at a little distance from the tents, a large fire was blazing, which illuminated a portion of the entrenchments with its ruddy glare. About ten men were appointed to keep it burning, who, from time to time, threw large branches of trees upon it; and then would be heard the voice of the captain, saying, "Gently, my men, gently; lay the branches carefully, and do not drive the sparks toward the camp."

A few steps from this fire was the tent of the

The Lion of Flanders

camp sentinels. It was a covering of ox-hides, the framework of which rested on eight massive beams; the four sides were open, so that it commanded the camp in all directions.

It was Jan Breydel's duty to keep watch this night with fifty of his Butchers: they sat on little wooden stools round a table under the roof, which protected them from the dew and the rain; their axes shone in their hands like weapons of glowing flame. The sentinels they had sent out were seen in the gloom, striding slowly backward and forward. A large cask of wine and some tin cans stood on the table; and although drinking was not forbidden, one could see that they drank with unusual moderation, for they raised the cans but seldom to their lips. They laughed and chatted pleasantly together, to while away the time; each telling what splendid blows he meant to discharge on the Frenchmen in the coming battle.

"Well," said Breydel, "they may say, if they will, that the Flemings are not as good men as their fathers, now that such a camp as this has been got together by volunteers alone. Let the French come on, if they like, with their two-and-sixty thousand men. The more game, the finer hunt! They say we are nothing but a pack of ill-natured hounds. We will give them reason to pray that they mayn't get thoroughly well worried; for the hounds have right good teeth."

The Lion of Flanders

While the Butchers were roaring with laughter at the words of their Dean, a fine old Guildsman entered, whose gray beard attested his advanced age. One of them called out to him:

"And you, Jacob, do you think you can still manage to give a good bite?"

"My teeth may not be quite so good as yours," growled the old Butcher; "but for all that, the old dog has not forgotten how to use them. I am quite ready to stake twenty bottles of wine which of us two will give most Frenchmen a bloody grave."

"Bravo!" cried the others; "and we will join in drinking them out. Let us fetch them at once."

"Ho! ho!" interposed Breydel; "can't you keep yourselves quiet? Drink to-morrow, if you please; but whoever of you drinks to-night shall be shut up in Courtrai, and shall have no share in the fight."

This threat had a wonderful effect on the Butchers: their jests died away on their lips; they did not even dare to sing a song; the old Guildsman alone ventured to speak.

"By the beard of our Dean!" said he, "rather than suffer that, I would be roasted at this fire, like Messire St. Lawrence; for I can never expect to witness such another feast."

Breydel remarked that his threat had rather damped the spirits of his companions, for which he was sorry, as he was himself inclined to merriment. Anxious to restore their cheerfulness, he raised the cask, and, filling a bumper, he held up his can, and said:

"Well, my men, why are you so silent? There, take that, and drink that you may find your tongues. I am vexed to have spoken so to you. Do I not know you well? Do I not know that the true Butchers' blood flows in your veins? Well, then, here's to you, comrades!"

An expression of satisfaction burst from the company, and they broke out into a loud cheery laugh when they found that the threat of their Dean had no serious meaning.

"Drink again!" continued Breydel, filling his can afresh; "the cask is yours, and you may drink it to the dregs. Your comrades who are on guard shall have another supplied to them. Now we see that succors are arriving from every city, and that we are so strong, we may well be merry."

"I drink to the disgrace of the men of Ghent!" cried a Guildsman. "We have good reason to know that he who puts any trust in them leans on a broken staff. But it is no matter; they may stay at home now; and so our own good city of Bruges will have gained unshared the glory of the conflict and the liberation of our fatherland."

"Are they Flemings, those men of Ghent?" said another. "Does their heart beat for freedom? Are

The Lion of Flanders

there any butchers left in Ghent? Bruges forever! You have the true blood there."

"I do not know," added Breydel, "why Count Guy so earnestly desires their arrival. Our camp is not overstocked with provisions, and it is scarcely prudent to invite more guests to the meal. Does the Count imagine that we shall lose the game? One can easily see that he has been used to Namur; he knows not the men of Bruges, or he would not long so much for those of Ghent. I hope they will stay quietly at home; we shall do very well without them; and we want no cowards among us."

Like a genuine citizen of Bruges, Breydel bore no love to the men of Ghent. The two leading cities of Flanders kept up a hereditary rivalry, and almost enmity, with each other; not that the one boasted braver citizens than the other, but simply that each did his best to ruin or divert the trade and traffic of the other. And the same jealousy still continues.

So impossible is it to root out the feelings which are inborn in the mass of the people that, notwithstanding their many revolutions, and the changes of the times, this spirit has been perpetuated to our own day.

The Butchers continued their conversation in this strain for a long time, and many an execration was uttered against the men of Ghent, when suddenly a peculiar noise excited their attention: they heard

The Lion of Flanders

a sound of quarreling and wrestling at some little distance, as if two men were struggling together. All sprang up to see what it meant, but, before they could leave the tent, one of the Butchers, who had been on guard, entered it, dragging a man with him by main force.

"Masters," said he, pushing the stranger into the tent, "this roving minstrel I found behind the camp; he was listening at all the tents, and slinking about in the dark like a fox. I have been tracking him for some time; and I am convinced that there is some treason at the bottom of it, for look how the rascal is trembling."

The man thus dragged into the tent wore a blue cloak, and had on his head a small cap adorned with a plume; a long beard covered half of his face. In his left hand he held a small musical instrument, which had somewhat the appearance of a harp; and he made as if he would like to play some little piece to the assembled company. Yet he trembled with fright, and his face was pale as though his last hour were come. He evidently wished to avoid the eye of Jan Breydel; for he kept his head turned in the opposite direction, so that the Dean might not see his features.

"What are you doing in the camp?" exclaimed Breydel. "Why are you listening at the tents? Answer me instantly."

The minstrel answered in a language which bore

The Lion of Flanders

some resemblance to German; so that it was evident he came from another part of the country:

"Master, I come from Luxemburg, and have brought a message from Messire van Lonchyn. I had been told that some of my brothers were in the camp, and I came to find them out. I am overcome with shame and vexation that the sentinel should take me for a spy; but I hope that you will do me no injury."

Breydel felt his heart touched with compassion for the minstrel. Bidding the sentinel stand back, he offered a chair to the stranger, and said:

"You are surely weary with your long journey. There, my good minstrel, sit down and drink; the can is yours. Now sing us a few songs, and we will let you go in peace. Courage, man; you are among good friends."

"Excuse me, master," answered the minstrel; "I can not remain here, for Messire van Lonchyn awaits me. I am sure you would not wish to disappoint the noble knight by detaining me."

"We must have a song!" cried the Butchers. "You shall not go hence until you have sung us a song."

"Quick, then," said Breydel; "for I promise you that, if you do not sing us something, you will be kept here until the morning. If you would only have sung at once and with good-will, you would have finished ere this. Now sing, I bid and command you."

The terror of the stranger was sensibly increased by this peremptory speech. It was with difficulty that he could hold his harp; and he trembled so violently that the strings, touched by his clothes, gave forth some confused sounds. This yet further whetted the appetite of the Butchers for a lay.

"Are you going to play or sing to us at once?" exclaimed Breydel. "I assure you that if you don't make haste you will have cause to rue it."

The minstrel, in mortal fear, proceeded to touch the strings of the harp with his trembling fingers; but he drew forth only false and discordant tones. The Butchers saw at once that he could not play at all.

"He is a spy!" cried Breydel. "Strip him and search him, to see whether he has any treasonable papers about him."

In a moment the clothes of the stranger were torn from off him; and, in spite of his piteous cries for mercy, he was kicked about from one to another, and all that he carried about him thoroughly searched.

"Here it is! here it is!" exclaimed one of the Butchers, who had thrust his hand between the doublet and the breast of the stranger; "here is the treason."

He drew out his hand, and produced a piece of

The Lion of Flanders

parchment, folded three or four times over, and tied with a thread of flax, from which hung a seal. The minstrel stood aghast, as though he saw his end approaching: he looked at the Dean with anxiety and terror, and muttered a few indistinct words, to which the Butchers paid no attention whatever. Jan Breydel seized the parchment; but, eagerly as he gazed on it, its contents remained unknown to him, for he could not read.

"What is it, villain?" exclaimed the Dean.

"A letter for Messire van Lonchyn," stammered the confounded minstrel, with hesitating and interrupted words.

"We shall soon see that," continued Breydel; then taking his cross-handled knife, he cut the flax which was wound around the seal. As soon as he beheld on this seal the lilies, the escutcheon of France, he sprang wrathfully up, seized the unknown one by the beard, and roared out:

"Is that a letter for Messire van Lonchyn, traitor? No! it is one to the castellan Van Lens; and you are a spy. A bitter death shall you die!"

While speaking, he tugged so violently at the beard that the ribbons by which it was fastened gave way; in an instant Breydel recognized the miscreant, and thrust him away so violently that the spy fell against one of the poles of the tent.

"Oh, Brakels! Brakels! your last hour is come!" exclaimed the astounded Dean.

The Lion of Flanders

The cries of the Butchers had attracted a crowd from the surrounding tents; and all began to demand, with loud and angry clamor, that the traitor should be delivered up to their vengeance.

Brakels fell on his knees, and with clasped hands begged for mercy; he crawled to the feet of Breydel, and implored him:

"Oh, master! have compassion on me—I will serve our fatherland so loyally—spare me! do not put me to death!"

Breydel looked down on him with rage and contempt; and, in lieu of other answer, kicked him with his foot, so that he rolled to the other end of the tent. Meanwhile, the Butchers had the greatest difficulty in restraining the crowds, who were raging around the tent, and filling the air with cries of vengeance.

"Give us the scoundrel!" was their wild cry. "Into the fire with him! throw him into the fire!"

"I care not," said Breydel, with an authoritative look at his comrades, "that your axes should be stained with the blood of this viper. Give him up to the crowd!"

Scarcely were the words out of his mouth, when a man strode forth from the crowd, and threw a cord round the neck of Brakels; then, the other end being seized by a thousand hands, he was hurled to the ground and dragged out of the tent. His shrieks of agony mingled fearfully with the cries of the infuriated crowd. They dragged him round and round the camp, and then returning to the fire, still yelling and shouting, they drew him through it again and again, until the flames had obliterated every feature of his countenance. Then on they rushed in their mad race, and vanished in the darkness with the lifeless corpse trailing behind them. Long were their cries heard on the breeze; but at length wearied, and sated with revenge, they hung the mangled body of the traitor on a pole close to the fire; then every one betook himself to his tent; and an hour later a profound silence had succeeded to this hideous uproar.

The Lion of Flanders

CHAPTER IV

Guy had issued orders that the whole army, under its several captains, should muster on the Gröningen Place, in front of the camp, on the following morning; he wished to pass them all in review. In obedience to these orders, the Flemings were drawn up in a square on the appointed place. They stood like the four foundation walls of some mighty edifice, each troop being composed of eight closely compacted divisions. Deconinck's four thousand Clothworkers formed the front of the right wing. The first file of his troops consisted of archers, whose heavy crossbows hung diagonally over their shoulders; while a quiver, filled with steel-pointed shafts, was suspended at their side. They bore no other defensive armor than an iron plate, which was fastened over their breasts by four straps of leather. Over the six other divisions, thousands of spears arose ten feet high into the air. This weapon, the renowned "good-day," was with reason much dreaded by the French; for with it a horse might easily be pierced through and through. No armor could withstand its formidable stroke; the knight on whom it fell was inevitably unhorsed.

The Lion of Flanders

On the same side stood also the light troops of Ypres; their advanced division was composed of five hundred men, whose apparel was red as coral. From their graceful helmets downy plumes waved low as their shoulders; massive clubs, armed with points of steel, stood with the butt-end at the feet of each soldier; while the hilt, grasped by their strong fists, rested against their loins. Small plates of iron were buckled around their arms and thighs. The other divisions of this gallant host were all clothed in green, and their unstrung bows of steel reared themselves high above their heads.

The left wing was entirely composed of the ten thousand men furnished by Breydel. On one side of it the countless axes of the Butchers flashed before the eyes of their companions in arms, so that they were obliged to turn away their heads from time to time, so keen and dazzling were the rays of the sun reflected from these mirrors of steel. The Butchers were not heavily equipped; short brown trousers, and a jerkin of the same color, formed their only clothing. Their arms were bare to the elbows, according to their custom; for they took pride in displaying their compact and brawny muscles. Many were of fair complexion, but embrowned by exposure to the sun; huge scars, records of former combats, crossed their faces like deep furrows, and these they regarded as the laurel-wreaths which attested their bravery. The fea-

The Lion of Flanders

tures of Breydel formed a strong contrast to the sombre sharp-cut faces of his followers; for while the ferocious expression of most of these filled the beholder with terror, Breydel's appearance was pleasing and noble. Fine blue eyes glowed beneath his bushy eyebrows; his fair hair fell in long wavy curls over his shoulders; and a short and delicate beard lengthened still more the graceful oval of his countenance. The contour and expression of his features were most pleasing when, as at this moment, he was full of joy and content; but when excited by passion, no lion's face could surpass his countenance in hideous expressiveness: his cheeks would gather in folds and wrinkles, he would grind his teeth with fury, and his eyebrows would meet over his flashing eyes.

In the third wing were the men of Furnes, with the vassals of Arnold of Oudenarde, and Baldwin of Papenrode. The Guildsmen of Furnes had sent a thousand slingers and five hundred halberdiers; the former stood in the front rank, and were clothed entirely in leather, that they might wield their slings without impediment. About their loins was fastened a white leather girdle, which held the round pebbles with which they supplied their slings; and in their right hands they carried a leather thong, in the middle of which was a hollow depression. These were the slings—a fearful weapon—which they wielded with such fatal precision, that the heavy missiles which they discharged at the foe very seldom missed their aim. Behind these stood the halberdiers; they were sheathed in iron, and bore heavy helmets on their heads. Their weapon was a battle-ax, with a long handle; and above the steel of the ax was a thick, sharp-pointed piece of iron, with which they were accustomed to pierce both helmet and armor, so that they gained the name of helm-cleavers. The men of Oudenarde and of Papenrode, who were ranged on the same side, bore weapons of all kinds. The first two ranks, indeed, consisted entirely of archers; but the others carried spears, clubs, or broadswords. The last wing, which completed the square, comprised all the cavalry of the army (eleven hundred well-mounted men), whom Count John of Namur had sent to his brother Guy. These horsemen seemed as though they were made of steel and iron; nothing else was to be seen except the eyes of the rider flashing through the vizor, and the feet of his steed, which appeared beneath his trappings of mail. Their long broadswords rested on their mailed shoulders, and their graceful plumes fluttered behind them in the breeze.

The army was thus drawn up, in obedience to the command of their general. A deep silence reigned throughout the host; the few questions of curiosity asked by the men-at-arms were in so low

The Lion of Flanders

a tone, that they reached no further than the ears to which they were addressed. Guy and all the other knights who had contributed no troops were still in Courtrai; and although the whole army was drawn up in position, none of them had as yet made his appearance.

Suddenly the banner of Count Guy was descried beneath the gate of the city. Messire van Renesse, who commanded the troops in the absence of the general-in-chief, gave the word:

"To arms! Close up your ranks! Heads up! Silence!"

At the first word of the noble knight Van Renesse, every man brought his weapon into its proper position; then they closed their ranks, and stood in perfect order. Scarcely was this done, when the cavalry opened its ranks to allow the general and his numerous suite to pass into the centre of the square.

In advance rode the standard-bearer with the banner of Flanders. The Black Lion on his golden field floated gracefully over the head of his horse; and he seemed to the joyous Flemings as though he were stretching out his claws as omens of victory. Immediately behind the banner came Guy and his nephew William van Gulick. The youthful general wore a magnificent suit of armor, on which the escutcheon of Flanders was skilfully embossed; from his helmet a gorgeous plume fell

The Lion of Flanders

down over the back of his horse. The armor of William van Gulick bore only a broad red cross; from beneath his coat-of-mail his white priestly vestment fell down over the saddle. His helmet bore no plume, and his whole equipment was simple and unadorned. Immediately after these illustrious lords followed Adolf von Nieuwland. His armor was perfect in its grace and finish. Gilded studs concealed the joints of his coat-of-mail; he bore a plume of green, and his gloves were plated with silver. Over his shirt-of-mail might be discerned a green veil, the guerdon bestowed on him by the daughter of the Lion in token of her gratitude. Near him rode Matilda, on a palfrey white as driven snow. The noble maiden was still pale; but the arrival of her brother Adolf had put her sickness to flight. A sky-blue riding-habit of costly velvet, embroidered with silver lions, fell in long folds over her feet to the ground, and the silken veil which was fastened to the point of her peaked hat swept the mane of her palfrey.

Behind them followed a troop of about thirty knights and noble damsels, all adorned with costly magnificence, and with countenances as serene and joyous as though they were riding to a tournament. The procession was closed by four squires on foot; the first two bore each a rich suit of armor and a sword, while the others carried each a helmet and a shield. Amid the solemn silence of the whole army, this brilliant cavalcade reached the middle of the square, when all halted.

Guy beckoned to him his herald-at-arms, and gave him a parchment, the contents of which he was to publish to the assembled host.

"Only add to it," said he, "the warlike name of the Lion of Flanders; for that always gladdens our good folks of Bruges."

The curiosity of the soldiers was manifested by a slight movement, followed by a silence of deepest attention; they saw that some mystery lay hidden in all these forms of solemnity, for it was not for nothing that the daughters of their nobles wore their richest adornments. The herald advanced, sounded his trumpet thrice, and then proclaimed aloud:

"We, Guy of Namur, in the name of our Count and our brother, Robert de Bethune, the Lion of Flanders, to all who shall read or hear this our proclamation, greeting and peace!

"In consideration—"

He paused suddenly; a low murmur ran throughout the various divisions of the army; and while each was eagerly grasping his weapon, the archers strung their cross-bows, as though danger were at hand.

"The foe! the foe!" echoed on all sides. In the distance were seen numerous troops of men advancing; thousands of warriors were approaching

The Lion of Flanders

in dense masses; there seemed no end of their numbers. Still were all in doubt whether it could be the enemy, for no cavalry was visible among them. Suddenly a horseman was observed to leave the unknown host, and to ride at full gallop toward the encampment. He bent so low over the neck of his horse that his features could not be distinguished, though he was already at no great distance. When he had come quite close to the astonished troops, he raised his head and shouted:

"Flanders and the Lion! Flanders and the Lion! here come the men of Ghent!" The old warrior was at once recognized; joyous acclamations answered his shout, and his name passed quickly from mouth to mouth.

"Hail, Ghent! Hail, Messire John Borluut! welcome, good brother!"

When the Flemings saw their numbers increased by this unexpected reenforcement of troops so numerous, their impetuous joy could no longer be restrained: their commanders could scarcely keep them in their ranks. They moved about in violent commotion, and seemed beside themselves with pleasure; but Messire John Borluut cried:

"Be of good courage, my friends, Flanders shall be free! I bring you five thousand well-armed and intrepid warriors."

And then answered the whole host with irrepressible enthusiasm:

The Lion of Flanders

"Hail! hail to the hero of Woeringen! Borluut! Borluut!"

Messire Borluut then drew near to the young Count, and would have greeted him with courtly ceremony; but Guy hastily interrupted him:

"Spare these words of ceremony, Messire John; give me your friendly right hand. I am so glad that you are come; you who have passed your days in arms, and are so rich in experience. I was beginning to be troubled at your not arriving; you have delayed long."

"Oh, yes, noble Guy," was the answer, "longer than I wished; but those dastardly Lilyards have kept me back. Would you believe, noble lord, that they had actually formed a conspiracy in Ghent to bring back the French again? They would not let us leave the town to go to the aid of our brethren; but, God be thanked! their plot did not succeed; for the people's hatred and contempt of them exceed all bounds. The men of Ghent drove their magistrates into the citadel, and demolished the gates of the city. So here I am with five thousand intrepid men, longing for the fight more eagerly than for their dinners, though they have touched nothing this day as yet."

"I thought assuredly that some great obstacle must have detained you, Messire Borluut, and I even feared that you would not come at all."

"What, noble Guy! could I stay away from

The Lion of Flanders

Courtrai? I, who have shed my blood for strangers, was I not to stand by my fatherland in its hour of need? The French shall soon know this to their cost. I feel myself quite young again; and my men, noble lord, await only the day of battle to let you see how the French shall fall before the White Lion of Ghent."

"You gladden my heart, Messire Borluut; our men are full of fury and impetuous ardor; should we lose the fight, I can assure you very few Flemings will see their homes again."

"Lose the fight, say you? lose it, Count Guy? Never will I believe it; our men are all animated with too noble a courage; and Breydel—victory sits beaming already on his very countenance. Look you, my lord; I will wager my head, that if you would only allow Breydel to do what he likes, he and his Butchers would cut these two-and-sixty thousand to pieces just as easily as they would mow down a field of corn. Be of good courage; God and Messire St. George will be our aid. But, I pray you excuse me, Lord Guy; there are my men—I must leave you for a moment."

The men of Ghent had now reached the Gröningen Place; they were wearied and covered with dust, for they had made a forced march under the burning sun. Their weapons were of various kinds; and among them were all the classes of troops we have already described. About forty

The Lion of Flanders

nobles rode in advance, for the most part friends of the old warrior, John Borluut; and in the midst of the host floated the banner of Ghent with its white lion. Then the men of Bruges, who felt how unjustly they had reproached their brethren of Ghent, shouted again and again:

"Welcome, brothers, welcome! Hurrah for Ghent!"

In the meantime John Borluut drew up his men in front of the left wing of the square; he wished to make a good display of them, that the men of Bruges might see that they did not yield to them in love of their common fatherland. At Guy's command he then left the camp and entered Courtrai, that he might give his men the repose and refreshment which they so much needed. As soon as the men of Ghent had withdrawn, John van Renesse advanced into the square and cried:

"To arms! Silence!"

The group in the middle of the square returned to its former position; every one held his peace at the command of Messire van Renesse, and the attention of all was fixed on the herald, who again sounded his trumpet thrice, and then proceeded to read with a loud voice:

"We, Guy of Namur, in the name of our Count and our brother, Robert de Bethune, the Lion of Flanders, to all who shall read or hear this our proclamation, greeting and peace! In consideration of

The Lion of Flanders

the good and loyal service rendered to the whole country of Flanders and to ourselves, by Master Deconinck and Master Breydel of Bruges—we, willing to bestow on them, in presence of all our subjects, a token of our grace and favor—willing, moreover, especially to requite their noble-hearted love of our fatherland in such wise as is meet and fitting, that their loyal services may be held in everlasting remembrance; and whereas our Count and father, Guy of Flanders, hath thereto empowered us, we announce and declare that Peter Deconinck, Dean of the Clothworkers, and Jan Breydel, Dean of the Butchers, both of our good city of Bruges, and their descendants after them for all time, shall be, and shall be held to be, of noble blood, and enjoy all the rights and privileges appertaining to nobles, in our land of Flanders. And in order that they may be enabled to support this dignity honorably, we assign to each of them one-twentieth part of our good city of Bruges for the maintenance of his house."

Long ere the herald had made an end, his voice was drowned in the joyous acclamations of the Clothworkers and Butchers. The great favor conferred on their Deans was, as it were, the reward of their own bravery, an honor which was reflected upon their Guilds. Had not the loyalty and patriotism of the Deans been so well known, their elevation to the rank of nobles would undoubtedly have been received with suspicion and displeasure, as a stratagem of the nobility. They would have said:

"These feudal lords are depriving us of the asserters of our rights, and are seducing our leaders by these manifestations of favor." In any other case the suspicion would not have been unfounded; for men, for the most part, are easily perverted and seduced by the love of honor. Hence it is not to be wondered at that the people cherished a bitter hatred against such of their brethren as allowed themselves to be thus raised in dignity; for, instead of noble-minded friends of the people, they became, for the most part, fawning and craven flatterers, and upheld the power to which they owed their elevation. They knew that with it they must stand or fall; for they saw that the people whom they had forsaken regarded them with abhorrence and contempt as deserters and apostates.

But the Guilds of Bruges reposed too lofty a confidence in Deconinck and Breydel to admit of reflections such as these at that moment. Their Deans were now noble; they had now two men who were admitted to the councils of their Count, who dared look the enemies of their rights in the face, and oppose their lawless usurpations. They felt that their influence was thus greatly increased, and testified by repeated cries the rapturous joy they felt. At last the tumult subsided, and their

The Lion of Flanders

gestures and beaming countenances alone betrayed their gladness.

Adolf van Nieuwland advanced to the Deans, and summoned them to appear before the commander-in-chief; they obeyed, and joined the group of knights. The features of the Clothworker betokened no elation of spirit; he moved onward calmly and sedately, undisturbed by any exciting emotion; a peaceful serenity and a noble pride filled his soul. Not so the Dean of the Butchers; he had never learned to command himself—the most trivial incident, the lightest feeling which passed through his heart, expressed itself at once upon his countenance, and it was easy to see that sincerity was the chiefest of the many good qualities which he possessed. And now he tried in vain to restrain the tears which burst from his blue eyes; he stooped his head to conceal them, and thus, with beating heart, followed his friend Deconinck. All the knights and noble dames had dismounted, and given their horses into the care of their squires.

Guy then beckoned to the four esquires-at-arms to draw near, and presented to the Deans the costly suits of armor they carried; the several pieces were put on and adjusted, and the helmet, with its plume of blue, clasped on their heads. The men of Bruges regarded this ceremonial in breathless silence; their hearts were filled to overflowing with glad emotion, and each man felt that a measure of this honor was his own also. When the Deans were fully equipped, they were directed to kneel; and Guy, advancing, raised his sword over the head of Deconinck, and said:

"Be thou a true knight, Messire Deconinck; let thine honor know no stain, and grasp thy sword then only when God, thy fatherland, and thy prince shall summon thee thereto."

With these words he touched the shoulder of the Clothworker gently with his sword, according to the custom of knighthood; and then the same ceremony was gone through with Breydel.

Matilda now advanced from the group of ladies, and placed herself in front of the kneeling Deans. She took from the squires the two emblazoned shields, and attached them to the necks of the ennobled citizens. Many of the spectators remarked that she hung the shield round Breydel's neck first; and this she must have done advisedly, for in order to effect it she had to move some steps on one side.

"These coats-of-arms have been sent to you from my father," said she, turning herself rather toward Breydel. "I feel assured that you will preserve them in all honor; and I rejoice that I have been permitted to bear a part in this requital of your noble patriotism."

Breydel regarded the noble maiden with a look of profoundest gratitude—a look which was a pledge of the most ardent loyalty and devotion; he would certainly have thrown himself at her feet, had not the stately and ceremonious bearing of the surrounding knights checked his impetuosity. He remained as one petrified, without speech or motion; for he could scarcely comprehend what had happened to him.

"You are now at liberty to return to your troops, Messires," said Guy. "We hope that you will be present this evening at our council; we have need of long deliberation with you. Lead back now your troops to the camp."

Deconinck made a lowly reverence and retired, followed by Breydel; but the latter had gone but a few steps when he felt the movements of his body impeded and restrained by the weight of the armor. He turned quickly back to Guy, and said to him:

"Noble Count, I pray you grant me one favor."

"Speak, Messire Breydel, it shall surely be granted to you."

"Look you, most illustrious lord, you have this day conferred on me a signal honor; but yet you will not, of a surety, hinder me from fighting against our enemies."

The knights, astonished at these words, drew nearer to the Dean.

"What do you mean?" asked Guy.

"I mean that this armor constrains and oppresses me beyond endurance, noble Count. I can not

The Lion of Flanders

move in this coat-of-mail, and the helmet is so heavy that I can not bend my neck; in this prison of iron I shall be slain like a calf bound hand and foot."

"The armor will defend you from the swords of the French," remarked the knight.

"Yes," cried Breydel; "but that is quite needless in my case. So long as I am free, with my ax I fear nothing. I should cut a pretty figure standing in this stiff and ridiculous fashion. No, no, Messires, I will not have it on my body; wherefore, I pray you, noble Count, allow me to remain a simple citizen until after the battle, and then I will try to make acquaintance with this cumbrous armor."

"You may do even as you list, Messire Breydel," answered Guy; "but you are, and must remain, a knight for all that."

"Well, then," cried the Dean, eagerly, "I will be the knight of the ax! Thanks, thanks, most illustrious lord."

Thereupon he left the knightly group, and hastened toward his men. They received him with noisy congratulations, and expressed their joy in reiterated shouts. Before Breydel had reached his Butchers, the armor lay piecemeal on the ground, and he retained only the emblazoned coat-of-arms which Matilda had attached to his neck.

"Albert, my friend," he cried to one of his men, "gather this armor together, and lay it up in my

The Lion of Flanders

tent; I will not cover my body with iron while you expose your naked breasts to the foe; I will keep the Kermes Festival in my butcher's clothes. They have made me a noble, comrades; but I can not give in to this. My heart is, and will remain, a true butcher's heart, as I mean to let the French know. Come, we will return to the camp; and I will drink my wine with you as I have ever done, and I will give each of you a measure to drink to the success of the Black Lion."

The shouting recommenced on all sides; the ranks were thrown into confusion, and the soldiers were beginning to rush back to the encampment in disorder, so great was their joy at the promise of the Dean.

"Hold there, my men," interposed Breydel, "you must not march in that fashion. Let every one of you keep his rank, or we shall become very queer friends."

The other divisions were already in motion, and returned, with sounding trumpets and flying banners, to the entrenchment, while the party of knights entered the city gate and disappeared behind the walls.

In a very short time the Flemings were sitting in front of their tents discussing the elevation of their Deans. The Butchers sat on the ground in a large circle with their goblets in their hands; huge casks of wine were standing near them, and

The Lion of Flanders

they were singing, in exulting unison, the lay of the Black Lion. In their midst, upon an empty barrel, sat the ennobled Breydel, who began each stanza after the fashion of a precentor. He drank, in repeated drafts, to his country's liberation; and endeavored, by drawing more closely the bonds of their common hopes and sympathies, to obliterate the memory of his change of rank; for he feared that his comrades might no longer regard him as their friend and boon companion as in time past.

Deconinck had shut himself in his tent to avoid the congratulations of his Clothworkers; their expressions of affection moved him too deeply, and he could with difficulty conceal his emotion. He therefore passed the whole day in solitude, while the troops abandoned themselves to feasting and rejoicings.

The Lion of Flanders

CHAPTER V

The French general had pitched his camp in a broad plain at a short distance from the city of Lille, and the tents of his countless warriors covered a space of more than two miles in extent. The breastwork which surrounded the host might have led a distant spectator to imagine that he saw before him a fortified city, had not the neighing of horses, the cries of soldiers, the smoke ascending from their numerous fires, and the fluttering of a thousand flags betrayed the presence of a military camp. The part assigned to the nobles and knights was easily distinguished by the splendor and costliness of its standards and embroidered banners; and while their velvet pavilions glowed with every color of the rainbow, the rest of the camp showed only the ordinary tents of canvas, or huts of straw. It might have been matter of wonder that such an enormous host did not perish of hunger, for in those days armies seldom took stores with them; yet they were supplied in such overflowing abundance that corn was suffered to lie about in the mud, and the most valuable articles of food were everywhere trampled under foot. The French took the

The Lion of Flanders

best means at once to supply their own wants and to deepen the hatred with which the Flemings regarded them. They scoured the country day by day in large bands, plundering and laying waste on all sides; for the furious soldiers well understood the wishes of their general, Robert d'Artois, and their way was tracked by countless deeds of violence and devastation. As a symbol of the sweeping desolation with which they threatened Flanders, they had tied small brooms to the points of their spears; and their conduct amply redeemed their pledge, for in all the southern part of the country there remained not a house, not a church, not a castle, not a monastery, scarcely a tree standing—all were ruthlessly razed and destroyed. Neither sex nor age afforded any protection against the fury of the soldiers; women and children were pitilessly butchered, and their bodies thrown out to the birds of prey.

Thus the French commenced their expedition. In the midst of their ferocious course, no fear or apprehension of defeat occurred to them, so confidently did they rely on their overwhelming numbers. Flanders was doomed to a memorable destruction; they had sworn it. On the same morning on which Guy had bestowed on Deconinck and Breydel the meed of their loyal good service, the French general had invited his most illustrious knights to a sumptuous banquet. The tent of the

The Lion of Flanders

Count d'Artois was of unusual length and breadth, and divided into many compartments; there were rooms for the knights of his suite, rooms for the squires and standard-bearers, rooms for culinary purposes, rooms for all the various personages of his train. In the middle was a spacious saloon, capable of containing a large number of knights, and used alternately for revelry and for the deliberations of the council of war. The silk with which the tent was covered was powdered with *fleurs-de-lis;* at the entrance hung the shield of the house of Artois, and outside, on a small eminence, waved the royal standard of France. The saloon was hung with rich tapestry, and rivaled a palace in magnificence.

At the upper end of the table sat Count Robert d'Artois. He was still in the flower and full vigor of life, and a scar which traversed his right cheek at once gave evidence of his bravery and imparted to his countenance a more forbidding expression. Although his face was disfigured by deep wrinkles and stained with dark spots, yet his eyes gleamed like a fire from under his dark eyelashes with manly ardor and energy. His manner was harsh, and denoted the fierce and unrelenting man of war.

Close to him, on his right hand, sat Sigis, King of Melinde; age had silvered his hair and bowed his head, yet was he eager for the combat. In that company he felt his martial ardor return, and

The Lion of Flanders

boasted that he would yet perform glorious feats of arms. The countenance of the old man inspired respect; it bore the impress of goodness and gentleness. Certainly the good Sigis would never have taken arms against the Flemings had he known the real state of the case; but he had been persuaded, as many others had been, that they were bad Christians, and worse than Saracens, and that it was a good work in the sight of God to chastise and exterminate them.

On the left hand of the Count sat Balthasar, King of Majorca, an impetuous and daring warrior, the gaze of whose dark eyes it was scarcely possible to endure. A wild gladness lighted up his features; for he hoped now to reconquer his kingdom, which had been seized by the Moors. Near him sat De Chatillon, the late governor-general of Flanders, the man who, as the tool of Queen Joanna, was the cause of all this disturbance. His was the guilt that so many Frenchmen had been put to death in Bruges and in Ghent; and on his tyrant head lay the blood of all that were slain in this quarrel. He remembered how disgracefully he had been expelled from Bruges; he craved no petty revenge; and he sat with joy in his heart and smiles on his face, for he held it impossible that the Flemings could oppose the combined might of so many kings, princes, and counts. Next to him, and, like him, eagerly thirsting for revenge, was his brother, Guy.

The Lion of Flanders

de St. Pol. There might be distinguished also Thibaud, Duke of Lorraine, between Messires John de Barlas and Renauld de Trie; he had come to the aid of the French with six hundred horse and two thousand archers. On the left side of the table, next to Messire Henry de Ligny, sat Raoul de Nesle, a brave and noble-hearted knight; on his face were depicted displeasure and sorrow; it was evident that the ferocious threats which the knights were uttering against Flanders were not to his taste. About the middle of the right side, between Louis de Clermont and Count John d'Aumale, sat Godfrey of Brabant, who had brought the French five hundred horse. Near him sat one whose gigantic form might well strike the beholder with astonishment; it was the Zeelander, Hugo van Arckel; he raised his head proudly above the surrounding knights, and his powerful frame sufficiently indicated how terrible an adversary he must be on the battle-field. For many years he had had no other abode than the camp. Everywhere known and renowned for his feats of arms, he had gathered around him a troop of eight hundred intrepid men, well accustomed to war; and with them he roved from place to place wherever there was fighting to be done. Many a time had he decided a battle in favor of the prince whom he was aiding; and he and his men were liberally covered with wounds and scars. War was his element and his life; peace

The Lion of Flanders

and repose were unendurable to him. Now he had joined the French host, because many of his old companions in arms were there; impelled only by love of fighting, he recked little for whom or in what cause he did battle.

Besides these were present, among others, Simon de Piedmont, Louis de Beaujeu, Froald, governor of Douay, Alin de Bretagne. At the further end of the table, and apart from them, was a group of knights. It was the least honorable place; and as the French would not admit them to their company, they had found themselves obliged to occupy it. And truly the French were in the right; they were contemptible beneath contempt; for while their vassals, as genuine Flemings, were asserting their country's cause, these their feudal lords were banqueting with the foe! What blindness could lead these degenerate traitors to tear, like vipers, the bosom of their mother? They were marching under a hostile banner to shed the blood of their brethren and bosom friends on the soil of their common fatherland; and for what? that the country which gave them birth might be made a land of slaves, and humbled beneath the yoke of the alien. They had time to feel that shame and contempt were their portion, and to feel at their hearts the gnawing worm. The names of these recreants have been handed down to posterity: among many others, Henry van Bautershem, Geldof van Winghene,

The Lion of Flanders

Arnold van Eyckhove, and his eldest son, Henry van Wilre, William van Redinghe, Arnold van Hofstad, William van Cranendonck, and John van Raneel, were the most conspicuous.

The knights ate off silver dishes, and drank the choicest wines from cups of gold. The goblets which were placed before Robert d'Artois and the two kings were larger and more costly than the rest; their coats-of-arms were cunningly graven upon them, and their rims shone with rare and precious gems. During the meal, a lively conversation went on among the knights on the position and prospects of the expedition; and from its tone the fearful doom of Flanders might easily be gathered.

"Most undoubtedly," answered the general to a question of De Chatillon, "they must be all exterminated. Those cursed Flemings can be tamed only by fire and sword; and why should we let such wretched boors live? Let us make a thorough end of them, Messires, that we may not again have to stain our swords with their plebeian blood."

"Right!" said John van Raneel, the Lilyard; "you say right, Messire d'Artois. We must make no terms with the seditious rascals; they are too rich, and would soon give us trouble again. Already they refuse to recognize us, who are sprung from noble blood, as their rightful lords; they seem to think that the wealth which they gain by

The Lion of Flanders

their industry makes their blood nobler still. They have built houses in Bruges and in Ghent which surpass our castles in magnificence; and is not that an insult to us? Certainly, we will endure it no longer."

"Unless we wish to have a fresh outbreak every day," remarked William van Cranendonck, "all the craftsmen must be put to death; for the survivors will never be quiet; and therefore I am of opinion that Messire d'Artois ought not to spare one of them alive."

"And what are we to do when we have slain all our vassals?" asked the burly Hugo van Arckel with a laugh. "By my troth, we shall have to plow our land ourselves; a goodly prospect, truly!"

"Ha!" answered John van Raneel; "I have a good plan to remedy that. When Flanders shall be cleansed of this stiff-necked race, I mean to bring French peasants from Normandy, and establish them on my lands."

"And so we shall make Flanders a genuine province of France; that is a very good notion, and I will mention it to the King, that he may urge the other feudal lords to take the same course. I pledge myself that it will not be at all difficult."

"Surely not, Messire. Do you not think it a bright and excellent plan?"

"Yes, yes; and we will carry it out too; but let

us first begin by making a clean sweep of the ground."

The features of Raoul de Nesle were working with inward emotion. The conversation greatly displeased him, for his noble heart revolted against such ferocity; and he exclaimed with ardor:

"But, Messire d'Artois, I take leave to ask you—are we knights or not? and is it seemly that we should set to work after a worse fashion than Saracens? You are carrying your ferocity too far; and I assure you that we shall become a scorn and a by-word to the whole world. Let us attack and defeat the Flemings; that will be sufficient for us. Let us not call them a herd of boors; they will give us trouble enough; and then, are they not in arms under the son of their prince?"

"Constable de Nesle," cried D'Artois in anger, "I know that you are exceedingly fond of these Flemings. It is a love which does you honor, of a truth! It is your daughter, surely, who has inspired your breast with such amiable benevolence."

Adela, the daughter of Raoul de Nesle, was married to William van Dendermonde, one of the sons of the old Count of Flanders.

"Messire d'Artois," answered Raoul, "although my daughter dwells in Flanders, that does not hinder me from being as good and true a Frenchman as any one here present—my sword has given sufficient proof of that; and I shall have to demand a reckoning at your hand for the scornful words you have uttered before these knights. But what now lies nearest my heart is the honor of knighthood itself; and I tell you that you are imperiling it by your conduct."

"What mean you?" exclaimed the general; "is it not true that you wish to spare these seditious traitors? Have they not deserved to die, since they have put to death seven thousand Frenchmen without mercy?"

"Beyond a doubt they have deserved death; and therefore will I avenge on them the honor of the crown of my prince; but they shall find their death only on the battlefield, and with arms in their hands. I appeal to these knights whether they deem it fitting that we should stain our swords by doing the work of executioners on poor unarmed people while they are peacefully plowing their fields."

"He is right," exclaimed Hugo van Arckel, with loud and angry voice; "we are fighting like the very Moors. The very proposal is a disgrace to us; let us recollect, Messires, that we have to do with Christian men. Besides, Flemish blood flows in my veins, and I will not suffer my brethren to be dealt with like dogs; they offer us battle in open and fair field, and we must fight with them according to the laws of honorable warfare."

"Is it possible," replied d'Artois, "that you can

defend these base boors? Our good prince has made trial of all other means to reclaim them; but all have been in vain. Are we to allow our soldiers to be butchered, our king to be set at naught and put to shame, and then spare the lives of these dastard rebels? No, that shall never be! I know the commands which I have received, and I will both obey them and cause them to be obeyed."

"Messire d'Artois," interposed Raoul de Nesle with angry impetuosity, "I know not what commands you have received, but I declare to you that I will not obey them unless they accord with the honor of knighthood; the king himself has no right to stain my sword with dishonor. And hearken, Messires, whether I am right or not: this morning early I went out of the camp, and found everywhere the tokens of the most revolting rapine and devastation. The churches are burnt to the ground, and the altars desecrated; the dead bodies of young children and of women were lying exposed in the fields to be devoured by ravens. I ask you, is this the work of honorable warriors?"

Having uttered these words, he rose from the table, raised a portion of the hangings of the tent, and continued, pointing to the country: "Look you, Messires, turn your eyes in all directions; everywhere you behold the flames of this atrocious devastation; the sky is blackened with smoke; the

The Lion of Flanders

whole country is in a conflagration. What does such a war as this betoken? It is worse than if the ruthless Northmen had come again, and turned the world into a den of robbers."

Robert d'Artois became livid with anger; he moved himself impatiently in his chair, and cried:

"This has lasted too long; I can no longer permit any man to speak thus in my presence. I know well enough what I have to do; Flanders must be swept clean, and it is out of my power to prevent it. This strife of words discomposes me much, and I beseech Messire the Constable to speak no more in this tone. Let him keep his sword unstained; we will all do the same; for no disgrace can redound to us from the excesses of our soldiers. Let us now end this angry dispute; and each man see that he does his duty."

Then raising his golden goblet, he cried:

"To the honor of France and the extermination of the rebels!"

Raoul de Nesle repeated, "To the honor of France," and laid a significant emphasis on the words, so that every one might see that he would not drink to the extermination of the Flemings. Hugo van Arckel placed his hand on the goblet which stood before him; but he neither raised it from the table nor spoke a word. All the others repeated the words of the general exactly, and followed his example.

The Lion of Flanders

For some little time the countenance of Hugo van Arckel had assumed a peculiar expression; disapprobation and displeasure were depicted on it. At length he looked fixedly at the general, as though he had made up his mind to brave him, and exclaimed:

"I should do myself dishonor were I now to drink to the honor of France."

At these words the face of Robert d'Artois glowed with wrath; he struck the table so violently with his goblet, that he made all the drinking-vessels ring, and shouted:

"Messire van Arckel, you shall drink to the honor of France; it is my will."

"Messire," replied Hugo with imperturbable coolness, "I drink not to the devastation of a Christian land. Long have I warred, and in many lands; yet never have I found a knight who would defile his conscience with such base atrocities."

"You shall do my behest; I will it; I bid you."

"And I will not," answered Hugo. "Hearken, Messire d'Artois, you have already said that my soldiers demanded too high pay, and that they cost you too much; well then, you shall pay them no longer, for I will no longer serve in your camp, and so our contention is at an end."

These words caused an unpleasant sensation in all the knights, and even in the general himself; for the departure of Hugo would be no light loss.

The Lion of Flanders

The Zeelander meanwhile drew back his chair, threw one of his gloves on the table, and exclaimed with increasing anger:

"Messires, I aver that you are all liars! I scorn you all to your faces! There lies my glove; take it up who lists, I challenge him to mortal combat."

Almost all the knights, and among them even Raoul de Nesle, snatched eagerly at the glove; but Robert d'Artois threw himself so eagerly upon it, that he seized it before the others. "I accept your challenge," said he; "come, let us go."

But at this moment the old King Sigis von Melinde arose, and waved his hand in token that he wished to speak. The great veneration with which both the combatants regarded him restrained them, and they stood still in silence to hear him. The old man spoke thus:

"Messires, let your angry passions subside a while, and give heed to my counsel. You, Count Robert, are not at this moment master of your life. Were you to fall, the army of your prince would be deprived of its leader, and consequently exposed to disorder and disorganization; you can not resolve to risk this. And now, Messire van Arckel, I ask you, have you any doubt of the bravery of Messire d'Artois?"

"No, truly," replied Van Arckel; "I acknowledge Messire Robert to be a fearless and valiant knight."

The Lion of Flanders

"Well, then," continued the king, "you hear, general, that your personal honor is not called in question; there remains to you only the honor of France to avenge. I counsel you both to postpone the combat to the day after the battle. I pray you speak, Messires, is not my counsel wise and prudent?"

"Yes, yes," answered the knights; "unless the general will grant to one of us the favor of taking up the glove in his stead."

"Silence!" cried D'Artois; "I will not hear of it."

"Messire Van Arckel, do you agree to this?"

"That is no business of mine; I have thrown down my glove, and the general has taken it up; it behooves him to fix the time when he will give it back to me."

"Be it so," said Robert d'Artois; "and if the battle do not last until sunset, I shall come in quest of you that very evening."

"You may spare yourself the trouble," answered Hugo; "I shall be at your side before you are aware of it."

This was followed by threatenings on both sides; but they proceeded no further, for Sigis interposed with the words:

"Messires, it is not fitting that we should longer discuss this matter. Let us once more fill our goblets, and forget all bitter animosity. Be seated, Messire van Arckel."

The Lion of Flanders

"No, no," cried Hugo; "I sit here no longer. I leave the camp immediately. Farewell, Messires, we shall see one another again on the battlefield. Meanwhile, may God have you in His holy keeping."

With these words he left the tent, and called his eight hundred men together; and in a very short time one might have heard the sound of trumpets and the clanging armor of a departing band. The same evening he reached the camp of the Flemings, and we may imagine with what joy he was received by them; for he and his men had the reputation of being invincible, and, indeed, they had deserved it.

The French knights meanwhile had resumed the interrupted banquet, and continued to drink in peace. While they were discoursing of Hugo's temerity, a herald entered the tent, and inclined himself respectfully before the knights. His clothes were covered with dust, the sweat ran from his brow, and everything indicated that he had ridden in great haste. The knights looked at him with curiosity, while he drew a parchment from beneath his armor, and said, as he gave it to the general:

"Messire, this letter will inform you that I come from Messire van Lens at Courtrai, to report to you the extreme peril we are in."

"Speak, then," cried D'Artois impatiently; "can

The Lion of Flanders

not Messire van Lens hold out the citadel of Courtrai against a handful of foot-soldiers?"

"Permit me to say that you deceive yourself, noble lord," replied the messenger. "The Flemings have no contemptible army in the field; it has sprung up as if by magic; they are more than thirty thousand strong, and have cavalry and an abundant supply of provisions. They are constructing tremendous engines, in order to batter the citadel and take it by storm. Our provisions and our arrows are both exhausted, and we have already begun to devour some of our least valuable horses. If your highness shall delay but a day to bring aid to Messire van Lens, every Frenchman in Courtrai will perish; for there are no longer any means of escape. Messires van Lens, De Mortenay, and De Rayecourt beseech you urgently to extricate them from this peril."

"Messires," cried Robert d'Artois, "here is a glorious opportunity; we could have wished for nothing better. The Flemings are all gathered together at Courtrai; we will fall upon them where they are, and but few of them shall escape us; the hoofs of our horses shall avenge our wrongs on this vile and despicable people. You, herald, remain in the tent; to-morrow you shall return with us to Courtrai. Yet one toast more, Messires; then go and get your troops in readiness for departure; me must break up our encampment with all haste."

The Lion of Flanders

All now left the tent to obey the command of the general, and from every part of the camp resounded the flourish of trumpets summoning the dispersed troops, the tramp of horses, and the clash of armor; a few hours later the tents were struck, and the baggage-wagons packed—all was in readiness. Here and there a number of soldiers were occupied in plunder; but in so large a camp this excited no attention. The captains placed themselves at the head of their companies, arranged the cavalry two abreast; and in that order they marched out of the entrenchments.

The first band, which left the camp with banners flying, consisted of three thousand light cavalry, all picked men, armed with huge battle-axes, and carrying long swords hanging from the pommel of their saddles. These were followed by four thousand archers on foot. They marched onward in a dense mass, protecting their faces from the rays of the sun with their large square shields. Their quivers were full of arrows, and a short sword without a scabbard hung at their girdle. They were mostly from the south of France; but many were by nation Spaniards or Lombards. John de Barles, their captain, a brave warrior, rode here and there between the ranks to encourage them and keep them in order.

The second band was under the command of Reginald de Trie, and consisted of three thousand

The Lion of Flanders

two hundred heavy cavalry. They were mounted on horses of unusual height and strength, and carried each a broad and flashing sword on his right shoulder; armor of unpolished iron protected their bodies. Most of them were from Orleans.

Messire the Constable de Nesle led the third band. First came a troop of seven hundred noble knights, with glittering armor on their bodies, and graceful banderoles on their long spears; their plumes fell waving behind their backs as they rode, and their coats-of-arms were painted in various colors upon their armor. Their horses were covered from head to foot with iron, and more than two hundred embroidered banners fluttered over the troop. It was truly the most brilliant band of knights that could be seen, even in that age. After them came two thousand horsemen, with battle-axes on their shoulders, and long swords hanging at their saddle-bows.

At the head of the fourth band rode Messire Louis de Clermont, an experienced warrior. It was composed of three thousand six hundred horsemen, bearing spears, from the kingdom of Navarre; and it was easy to see that they were picked and choice warriors. In front of the first column rode the banner-bearer, with the great standard of Navarre.

Count Robert d'Artois, general-in-chief of the army, had taken the middle division under his es-

The Lion of Flanders

pecial command. All the knights who had brought with them no soldiers, or had enrolled them in other companies, were with him; and the Kings of Majorca and Melinde rode at his side. Among the others it was easy to distinguish Thibaut II, Duke of Lorraine, by the magnificence of his armor. And then there came the gorgeous banners of Messires John, Count of Tancarville, Angelin de Vimen, Ranold de Longueval, Farald de Reims, Arnold de Wexmael, Maréchal de Brabant, Robert de Montfort, and a countless number besides, who had formed themselves into a company. This band even surpassed the third in magnificence and splendor; the helms of the knights were covered either with silver or with gold, and their coats-of-mail were adorned with golden studs, by which their joints were secured. The burning rays of the sun fell on the glittering steel of their armor, and surrounded this peerless band as with a glowing fire. The swords which hung dangling at their saddle-bows fell with a sharp and iron clank on the trappings of their steeds, producing a peculiar sound, which seemed their fittest martial music. Next to these noble knights followed five thousand other horsemen, with battle-axes and swords; and this picked troop was accompanied by sixteen thousand infantry, drawn up in three divisions. The first consisted of a thousand crossbow men; their defensive armor was simply a

The Lion of Flanders

breastplate of steel and a flat square helmet; small quivers full of iron bolts were suspended at their girdles, and long swords hung at their side. The second was composed of six thousand men with clubs, studded at the end with horrible steel points. The third was made up of "helm-cleavers" with their long axes; and all these men were from Gascony, Languedoc, and Auvergne.

Messire James de Chatillon, the governor-general, commanded the sixth band. It consisted of three thousand two hundred horse. On the banderoles of their spears they had painted burning brooms, the emblems of the purification of Flanders; and their horses were the heaviest of the whole army. Then followed the seventh and eighth bands; the former under the command of John, Count d'Aumale, the latter under Messire Ferry of Lorraine. Each was composed of two thousand seven hundred horse, men of Lorraine, Normandy, and Picardy. These were followed by Godfrey of Brabant with his own vassals, seven hundred horsemen, who formed the ninth band. The tenth and last was entrusted to Guy de St. Pol; he was charged with the protection of the rear and of the baggage. Three thousand four hundred horsemen of all arms rode in advance; then followed a multitude of foot-soldiers with bows and swords, whose number might amount to seven thousand. On every side ran men with blazing torches, in order to set fire to everything within their reach. Behind came the endless succession of baggage-wagons, with the tents and camp-furniture and stores.

The French army, divided into ten bands, and exceeding sixty thousand strong, marched slowly through the country, and took the road to Courtrai. It is hard to conceive how far this numerous host reached; the van was already far out of sight ere the rear had left the entrenchments. Thousands of banners fluttered in the breeze above the marching host, and the sun was reflected with intolerable brightness from the armor of the valiant bands. The horses neighed and champed the bit beneath their heavy burdens; from the crash of arms arose a sound like the rolling of a stormy sea upon the strand; but it was too monotonous to break the stillness of the deserted fields. Wherever the troops had passed, the sky was ruddy with flame, and obscured by dense clouds of smoke. Not a habitation escaped destruction; neither man nor beast was spared; as the chronicles of the time bear record. The following day, when the flames were spent, and the smoke dispersed, there was neither man, nor work, nor trace of man, to be seen; from Lille to Douay and Courtrai, Flanders was so fearfully devastated that the French vandals might boast with reason that they had swept it as with a besom.

The Lion of Flanders

Deep in the night the army of Messire d'Artois arrived before Courtrai. De Chatillon knew the country very well, for he had long lived in the city; and he was accordingly summoned by the general to select a suitable spot for encamping. After a short deliberation, they turned a little to the right, and pitched their tents on the Pottelberg and in the adjacent fields. Messire d'Artois, with the two kings, and a few distinguished knights, took possession of a castle called Hoog-Mosscher, close to the Pottelberg. They placed numerous sentinels on guard, and then betook themselves in peace, and without suspicion, to rest; for they were too confident in their numbers to entertain any apprehension of an attack.

And thus the French army lay within a quarter of an hour's march of the camp of the Guildsmen of Flanders; the advanced pickets could see one another slowly pacing up and down in the gloom.

The Flemings, as soon as they had intelligence of the approach of the foe, had doubled their guard, and issued orders that no man should lie down to rest unarmed.

The Lion of Flanders

CHAPTER VI

THE Flemish knights who occupied Courtrai were fast asleep when the tidings of the arrival of the French, passing through the city, and diffusing terror on every side, roused them from their slumbers. Guy commanded the trumpets to sound and the drums to beat; and an hour later all the soldiers lodged within the city were assembled on the walls. As there was reason to fear that the Castellan van Lens would make a sortie into the city during the battle, the men of Ypres were summoned from the camp to watch the French garrison. At the Steenpoort a numerous guard was appointed to keep the women and children within the town; for they were so terrified, that they were bent on fleeing again during the night. Inevitable death seemed to threaten them: on the one side the Castellan van Lens, with his ruthless soldiers, might fall on them at any moment; on the other they saw the small number of their countrymen opposed to the countless hosts of France, and they dared not hope for victory. And truly, but that the heroism and intrepidity of the Flemings

The Lion of Flanders

blinded them to all thought of danger, they had done well to bethink them of a last parting prayer; for not only did the foot-soldiers in the French camp outnumber those in their own, but there were moreover the two-and-thirty thousand horsemen to be dealt with.

The Flemish commanders calculated with perfect coolness the chances of the coming battle; great as were their valor and eagerness, they could not conceal from themselves their critical position; heroism does not prevent a man from seeing the dark and threatening side of things, nor does it drive out the inborn dread of death; but it inspires a man with might to vanquish and to brave all depressing and disheartening forebodings—further than this the soul can not push its empire over the body. For themselves the Flemings had no fear; but their hearts were full of agonizing anxiety for the liberty of their fatherland—a liberty which was set upon this cast. Notwithstanding, however, the small hope which they dared to entertain, they resolved to accept battle, and rather to die as heroes on the bloody field than survive to endure a debasing slavery.

The youthful Matilda and the sister of Adolf, with many other noble ladies, were sent to the Abbey of Gröningen, where they would find a safe asylum, even in the event of the French becoming masters of Courtrai. When this and other pre-

The Lion of Flanders

liminary matters had been arranged, the knights returned to the camp.

The French general, Robert d'Artois, was a brave and experienced soldier; but, like many others of his fellow-countrymen, he was too rash and self-confident. He deemed it quite unnecessary to take ordinary precautions in his proceedings against the Flemings, so certain was he that his first attack would throw them into hopeless confusion. This rash confidence was shared by all his soldiers to such extent that, while the army of Guy was preparing for battle in the twilight, the French were sleeping on as unconcernedly as though they were quartered in a friendly city. Trusting to their numberless cavalry, they thought that nothing could resist them; whereas, had they been a little less thoughtless, they would have first inspected the field of battle, and disposed their van and rear accordingly. They would then have found that the ground between the two camps was not at all fitted for the action of cavalry—but why should they exercise a superfluous caution? Was the Flemish army worth it? Robert d'Artois thought not!

The Flemings were drawn up on the Gröningen Place. Behind them, to the north, ran the Lys, a broad river, which rendered any attack on that side impossible; in front flowed the Gröningen brook, which, though now but a narrow watercourse, was then a broad stream; and its shelving marshy banks opposed an insurmountable obstacle to the French cavalry. Their right wing rested on the portion of the walls of Courtrai near St. Martin's Church, and round the left ran a tributary of the Gröningen brook, so that the Flemings were posted, as it were, on an island; and any attempt to dislodge them must needs be difficult and perilous. The space which separated them from the French army was a succession of meadows, which lay very low, and were watered by the Mosscher brook, which converted them into a kind of marsh. Thus the French cavalry were obliged to cross two brooks before they could come into action; and this was a very difficult and tedious operation, because the horses' hoofs had no hold on the moist and slippery ground, and at every step the poor animals sank up to their knees in the morass.

The French general took no account of this; he made his plans as though the field of battle were firm and hard ground, and directed the attack in a manner quite at variance with the rules of strategy. So true is it that excessive confidence renders men blind.

Toward break of day, before the sun had shown his glowing disk above the horizon, the Flemings were drawn up in order of battle on the Gröningen brook. Guy commanded the left wing in person,

The Lion of Flanders

and he had about him all the lesser Guilds of Bruges. Eustachius Sporkyn, with the men of Furnes, occupied the centre; the second corps was commanded by John Borluut, and numbered five thousand men of Ghent; the third, composed of the Clothworkers and freemen of Bruges, was led by William van Gulick. The right wing, which extended as far as the city walls, consisted of the Butchers, with their Dean Jan Breydel, and the Zeeland men-at-arms; and it was commanded by Messire John van Renesse. The remaining Flemish knights had no definite post assigned them, but moved hither and thither, wherever they deemed their presence and aid necessary. The eleven hundred horsemen of Namur were stationed in the rear, behind the line of battle; they were not to be brought at once into action, lest they should throw the infantry into disorder.

At length the French army began to prepare for action. A thousand trumpets uttered their shrill voices, the horses neighed, and weapons rattled on all sides with a sound so ominous in the darkness that the Flemings felt a cold shiver thrill through them. What a cloud of foes was about to burst upon them! But to these valiant men this was nothing—they were going to die, that they knew: but their widowed wives and their children, what would become of them? At that solemn moment their thoughts reverted to those most dear to them.

The Lion of Flanders

Fathers thought bitterly of their sons, doomed to iron bondage; sons bewailed in agony their gray-headed fathers, left the helpless prey of tyranny. Within them were two contending emotions—inflexible resolution and crushing anguish; and when these meet in men's hearts in presence of a threatening danger, they combine and fuse into a transport of rage and fury. And this effect was now produced on the Flemings; their gaze was fixed and unpitying, their teeth were clenched in fierce resolve, a burning thirst made their mouths dry and parched, and their breath came thick and rapid from their panting breasts. An appalling silence reigned throughout the army; no one expressed his apprehensions or feelings to his comrade; all were plunged in thoughts of painful gloom. They were standing thus drawn up in a long line, when the sun rose above the horizon, and disclosed to them the camp of the French.

The horsemen were so numerous that their spears stood thick as ears of corn at harvest-time. The horses of the advanced columns pawed the ground impatiently, and besprinkled their glittering trappings of steel with flakes of snow-white foam. The trumpets sent their lively tones, like some festal rejoicing, to mingle with the sighing of the trees in the Neerlander wood; and the morning breeze played wantonly with the waving folds of the standards, and with the streamers attached to the

The Lion of Flanders

spears of the cavalry. At intervals, the voice of the general was heard above this tumult of war; and the war-cry, "Noël! Noël! France! France!" arose from one company; and as it was caught up by each in quick succession, a deafening echo ran through the whole host. The French horsemen were eager, and full of courage; they pricked the sides of their war-steeds with their spurs to goad them into fiercer fury, and then caressed them and talked to them, that they might the better know their master's voice in the thick of the fight. Who shall have the honor of the first blow? was the thought that filled every mind with eager excitement. This was a great point of honor in those days. Whenever this good fortune fell to the lot of a knight in an important battle, he boasted of it all his life long, as a proof and token of his superior valor; and hence each one held his horse in readiness, and his spear in rest, to rush forward at the first word of command, or at the slightest sign from the general.

In the meadows close about the army, the far-extended lines of the French infantry might be seen winding about the fields like the folds of some hideous serpent; the greatest stillness pervaded their ranks.

When Guy observed that the attack was about to commence, he sent a thousand slingers, under the command of Solomon van Sevecote, as far as the

The Lion of Flanders

second brook, to harass the French outposts and sentinels; then he disposed his various companies into a square, in such a manner that the eyes of all were directed toward its centre. At that point rose an altar constructed of turf, and over it waved the great banner of St. George, the patron of warriors; on its steps knelt a priest, arrayed in the vestments of his office, who proceeded to offer the Holy Sacrifice for the good success of the battle. When the Mass was ended, the priest, still standing at the altar, turned toward the army; and in a moment, inspired by one and the same sentiment, the troops sank to the ground, and received in solemn silence the benediction of the Most Holy Sacrament. The hearts of all were deeply stirred by this holy ceremony; a spirit of lofty self-devotion seemed to kindle within them, and they felt as if the voice of God called them to a martyr's death. Glowing with this holy flame, they remembered no more all that was dear to them on earth; they rose to the full stature of the heroism of their fathers; their breasts heaved more freely; the blood flowed more impetuously through their veins, and they longed for the battle, as for their deliverance from the oppressor.

And now, as all arose in deepest silence, the youthful Guy sprang from his horse, and standing in the middle of the square, addressed them thus: "Men of Flanders, remember the famous deeds of

The Lion of Flanders

your ancestors; never did they count their foes. Their invincible courage won for us that freedom of which an alien tyrant would now despoil us. You, too, will to-day pour out your hearts' blood in defense of this sacred heritage and deposit; and if we die, let us die a free and manly people, the never-tamed sons of the Lion. Think on God, whose temples they have burnt; on your children, whom they have sworn to slay; on your terror-stricken wives; on all that you love; on all that you hold sacred—and so, should we perish, the enemy shall not glory in his victory, for more Frenchmen than Flemings shall fall on the soil of our fatherland. Be wary of the horsemen; strike with your 'good-days' between the legs of the horses, and quit not your ranks. Whoso plunders a fallen enemy, whoso leaves his appointed post, strike him dead; this is my will and command. Is there a coward among you? let him die by your hands; his blood be upon my head alone!"

And then, as if impelled by a sudden and vehement inspiration, he stooped and took some mold from the ground; and placing it in his mouth, he raised his voice and cried:

"By this beloved earth, which I will bear within me to the fight, this day will I either conquer or die!"

And the whole host in like manner stooped, and swallowed each a little earth from the soil of their fatherland. This soil, so beloved, seemed to inspire their breasts with a calm concentrated rage, and a dark unrelenting yearning for revenge. A low and hollow murmur, like the rumbling of a tempest in the recesses of a cavern, was heard throughout the excited host; their cries, their oaths, became blended in one terrifice mass of sounds, among which were barely distinguishable the words, "We are ready and resolved to die!"

Again and in haste the order of battle was formed, and each returned to his position in front of the Gröningen brook.

Meanwhile Robert d'Artois, accompanied by some French generals, had approached close to the Flemish army to reconnoitre it. His archers were then brought forward and opposed to Guy's slingers, and the outposts exchanged a few arrows and stones while Robert was pushing forward his cavalry. Observing that Guy had disposed his troops in line, he arranged his own in three divisions; the first, under Raoul de Nesle, was ten thousand strong; the second, which he retained under his own command, was formed of the choicest companies, and numbered fifteen thousand picked horsemen; the third, destined for the defense of the rear and of the camp, he entrusted to Guy de St. Pol. While he was thus preparing for a tremendous attack on the Flemish position, Messire John de Barlas, captain of the foreign com-

The Lion of Flanders

panies, came to him, and addressed him in these words:

"For God's sake, Messire d'Artois, let me and my men be engaged in the battle; let not the flower of the French knighthood be exposed to die by the hands of this Flemish rabble, maddened as they are by rage and despair. I know their customs well; they have left their provisions and munitions in the city. Do you remain here in order of battle, and I, with my light horse, will cut them off from Courtrai, and keep them occupied with a feigned attack. The Flemings are great eaters; and if we can cut off their supplies, they will very soon be compelled by hunger to change their position, and we shall be able to attack them on more favorable ground than this; you will thus destroy all this rabble without shedding a drop of noble blood."

The Constable de Nesle, and many other knights, thought this counsel worthy of attention; but Robert, blinded by passion, would not even listen to them, and commanded John de Barlas to hold his peace.

During these preparations time had passed away; it was now seven o'clock in the morning; the French host were within two slings' cast of the Flemings. Between the French archers and the slingers lay the Mosscher brook, so that they could not come to close quarters; and very few fell on either side. Then Robert d'Artois gave Raoul de Nesle, general of the first division, the signal to begin the attack.

The horsemen sprang eagerly onward, and soon came to the Mosscher brook; but here they sank saddle-deep in the morass. One stumbled over another; the foremost were thrown from their horses, and either slain by the slingers or stifled in the swamp. The few who contrived to extricate themselves retreated at full speed, and dared not venture to expose themselves a second time so recklessly. The Flemings meanwhile stood motionless behind the second brook, looking on at the discomfiture of the enemy in silent composure.

When the Constable de Nesle saw that the passage was impracticable for cavalry, he came to Messire d'Artois, and said:

"Of a truth I tell you, Count, that we are exposing our men to great danger, by trying to force them over the brook; there is not a horse that either will or can ford it. Let us rather try to entice the enemy from their position. Believe me, you are staking all against fearful odds in this game."

But the general was too far carried away by vexation and anger to pay any attention to this wise counsel. "Constable," exclaimed he furiously, "that is advice befitting Lombards! Are you frightened at this pack of wolves, or are you of the same breed with them?"

Raoul, stung by this reproof, and by the insinuation it conveyed, burst forth in unrestrained wrath. He came up close to the general, and answered with an expression of bitter disdain:

"You throw doubt on my courage! you dare to taunt and insult me! But, I ask you, have you courage to go with me on foot and alone into the thick of the foe? I would lead you so far that you would return no more—"

Here some of the knights threw themselves between the angry generals, and endeavored by every argument to convince the seneschal that the brook was not fordable by cavalry; but he persisted in his refusal to listen to them, and ordered Raoul de Nesle to renew the charge.

The constable, beside himself with vexation, rode furiously with his troop toward the Flemish position. But at the brook all the horsemen of the front rank were thrown from their saddles; each thrust the other deeper into the morass, and more than five hundred perished in the confusion, either stifled in the mud, or slain by the stones of the Flemish slingers. Messire d'Artois now saw himself obliged to recall Raoul; but it was scarcely possible to restore order among the survivors, so utterly were they broken and dispirited.

Meanwhile Messire John de Barlas had found

The Lion of Flanders

a place at which the first brook could be forded, and had crossed it with two thousand cross-bow men. Having gained the open meadow, he drew up his men in a compact mass, and poured such a shower of arrows upon the Flemish slingers, that the sky was almost darkened by them, and a large number of Flemings fell dead or wounded to the ground, while the French archers continued to make a steady advance.

Messire Solomon van Sevecote himself had seized the sling of one of the fallen Guildsmen, in order to animate the survivors by his own example; but an iron bolt from a cross-bow pierced the vizor of his helmet, and flung him dead to the ground. Then the Flemings, seeing their general struck down, with so large a number of their comrades, and finding their supply of stones fall short, closed their ranks, and fell back on the camp in good order. Only one slinger from Furnes remained standing in the middle of the field, as though he scorned the arrows of the Frenchmen. He stood calm and unmoved, while the arrows flew hissing over him and around him. Slowly and with deliberation he placed a heavy stone in his sling, and measured carefully the distance of the spot at which he wished to take aim. After a few preparatory whirls, he let go the end of the sling, and the stone flew whistling through the air. A cry of anguish burst from the French captain, and in

The Lion of Flanders

a moment he lay lifeless on the ground—the stone had pierced his helmet and crushed his skull; and Messire John de Barlas lay weltering in his blood. Thus, in the first attack, perished the leaders of the first two divisions of the French army. The archers were so infuriated by this disastrous sight, that they threw away their cross-bows, grasped their swords, and impetuously pursued the slingers as far as the second brook, which ran in front of the Flemish encampment. At this moment Messire Valepaile, who was standing by the side of Robert d'Artois, seeing the advantage gained by the cross-bow men, exclaimed:

"Oh seneschal, the rascally foot-soldiers will, after all, gain the honor of the day. While they are counting the foe, what are we knights doing here? It is foul shame; we are standing still, as though we dared not fight."

"Mountjoy St. Denis!" shouted Robert. "Forward, constable! fall on them!"

At this command all the horsemen of the first division gave their horses the rein, and rushed on impetuously and in disorder; for each wished to be the first to strike the blow of honor. So eager was their onset, that they rode over the cross-bow men, and many hundreds of the hapless foot-soldiers were trampled to death beneath the hoofs of the horses, while the remainder fled in all directions over the meadow. Thus the cavalry robbed the

The Lion of Flanders

French of the advantage which the cross-bow men had gained, and gave the Flemish slingers time to fill up their ranks, and form again in order. Then arose from the prostrate horsemen a groan so fearful, a death-cry so general and so prolonged, that at a distance it might have been taken for the combined shoutings of a triumphant army; on they rushed, trampling down into the marsh those who had fallen, heedless of their deprecating cries. Scarcely had the shrieks of those who first sank died away on the air, when they who had trodden them under foot were in their turn overthrown and trampled down by others; and so the death-wail was continued unceasingly. The companies in the rear, thinking that the action was become general, spurred their horses on toward the brook, and thus increased the number of the victims of the seneschal's folly and imprudence.

As yet the Flemings had made no attack upon them; they stood motionless and silent, gazing with wonder and awe on the dismal tragedy enacted before them. Their generals proceeded with more skill and more prudence; other warriors would have thought this the fittest moment for a general attack, and so would perhaps have crossed the brook and fallen on the French; but Guy, and John Borluut, his chief adviser, would not relinquish the advantage which their position gave them.

The Lion of Flanders

At length both the brooks were filled with dead bodies of men and horses, and Raoul de Nesle had the good fortune to force a passage with about a thousand horsemen. He formed them in a close squadron, and shouted, "France! France! forward! forward!"

They charged with furious intrepidity into the centre of the Flemish troops; but the latter planted their "good-days" firmly on the ground, and received the horsemen on the points of these frightful weapons. A large number of the assailants were thrown from their horses by the shock, and quickly despatched. But Godfrey of Brabant, who had also crossed the brook with nine hundred horse, threw himself with such impetuosity on the squadron of William van Gulick, that he overthrew both this and the three first divisions, and so broke the line of the Flemings. And now began a terrible struggle; the French horsemen had thrown away their spears, and rushed on the Flemings with their long battle-swords. The latter defended themselves bravely with their clubs and halberds, and dismounted many a horseman; but still the advantage remained with Godfrey of Brabant; his men had made a clear space all around them, and there was thus a wide breach in the Flemish line. Through this opening poured all the French who had forded the brook, in order to fall on the rear of the Flemish divisions. This was

The Lion of Flanders

a critical and perilous maneuvre for the Flemings —were the foe once on their front and in their rear, they would have had no room to wield their "good-days," and would have been reduced to defend themselves with halberds, clubs, and swords alone; and this would have given the French an immense advantage: for, being mounted, their blows were better aimed, and more deadly in effect; it was easy for them to cleave the heads of those on foot, or to strike them from their bodies.

William van Gulick fought like a lion; he stood alone with his standard-bearer and Philip van Hofstade, surrounded by thirty of the enemy, who strove to capture his banner; but as yet every arm which had been put forth to seize it had been severed by his sword. At this moment, Arthur de Mertelet, a Norman knight, sprang over the brook, with a considerable number of horsemen, and dashed at full speed toward William van Gulick. Their arrival crushed the hopes of the Flemings; for the number of the foe was now too great, and their superiority too manifest; and when the Norman saw William's banner, he charged toward it with the speed of an arrow, and put his lance in rest to pierce the standard-bearer. Philip van Hofstade, perceiving his intention, dashed through the French foot-soldiers to stay the course of De Mertelet. The shock of the meeting of the two knights was so impetuous, that the lance of each pierced the heart of his antagonist; warrior and horse were in one moment bereft of motion; it seemed as though a preternatural influence had suddenly cooled their rage; one would have thought each was leaning on his spear with all his weight, in order to thrust it deeper into the body of his antagonist; but this was but for a moment; De Mertelet's horse made a slight convulsive movement, and the corpses of both fell to the ground.

Messire John van Renesse, who commanded the right wing, seeing the danger of William van Gulick, left his position, and, with Breydel and his Guildsmen, fell back behind the line of battle on the rear of the French. Nothing could resist men like the Butchers of Bruges; they exposed themselves to every weapon with naked breast, and before their death-scorning valor everything gave way. Their axes hewed the legs of the horses, or clave the skulls of their falling riders. A moment after their arrival, the ground was so cleared that scarcely twenty Frenchmen remained behind the line of battle. Among them was Godfrey of Brabant, who blushed not to fight against those who were his brethren both by birth and by language. When John van Renesse espied him, he shouted to him:

"Godfrey, Godfrey! your course is run—you shall die!"

The Lion of Flanders

"Apply your words to yourself," replied Godfrey, aiming at the head of Messire John a tremendous blow; but Van Renesse, with a dexterous and rapid movement of his sword from below, struck him so violently under the chin that he rolled out of his saddle to the ground. More than twenty Butchers fell immediately upon him, and he received innumerable wounds, the last of which was mortal. Meanwhile Jan Breydel and some of his men had penetrated further and further among the enemy, and had fought long enough to win the standard of Brabant; he regained his Butchers, defending his prize at every step with furious courage, and then, tearing the banner in pieces and throwing its pole scornfully from him, he exclaimed: "Shame and dishonor to the traitors!"

The men of Brabant burning to avenge this insult, rushed with redoubled rage upon the foe, and made the most extraordinary efforts to gain and to tear in pieces the banner of William van Gulick; but its bearer, John Ferrand, struggled with the strength of madness, with all who dared to approach him. Four times was he thrown to the ground, and four several times did he rise again, still grasping his banner, though covered with wounds. William van Gulick had already laid dead at his feet a large number of the French; and every fresh blow of his huge broadsword struck

The Lion of Flanders

down a foe. At length, wearied, covered with wounds, and exhausted by loss of blood, he grew pale, and felt his strength failing him. Filled with anger and vexation he retired to the rear to refresh himself and rest a while. John de Vlamynck, his squire, loosed the the plates of his armor and stripped him of his heavy mail, that he might breathe more freely. In the absence of William, the French had regained some of the ground they had lost, and the Flemings manifested a disposition to retreat. This threw Van Gulick into an agony of despair, and induced John de Vlamynck to adopt a singular device, which bore witness in its results to the fame of his master's bravery. He hastily put on the armor of Messire William, and threw himself into the thick of the enemy with the cry: "Give way,—back,—men of France! William van Gulick is here again!" He accompanied these words with a shower of well-directed blows, and stretched a considerable number of the bewildered foe on the ground; until at length the French gave way, and thus afforded the disordered troops time to close their ranks again.

Raoul de Nesle had thrown himself with the utmost impetuosity on the five thousand citizens of Ghent under John van Borluut; but all the efforts of the courageous Frenchmen to break their line were in vain. Thrice had the men of Ghent driven him back with prodigious slaughter, and

The Lion of Flanders

without his obtaining the slightest advantage. John Borluut thought it too rash to abandon his position in order to pursue the soldiers of Raoul, and so bethought himself of another plan. He hastily formed his three hindmost corps into two new battalions, and posted them behind the line of battle, one close in the rear, and the other further back in the meadow; he then ordered the central division to give way before the next attack of the French. When Raoul de Nesle had collected his scattered troops, and restored order among them, he made another vigorous attack upon the men of Ghent; the centre fell back immediately, and the French, thinking that they had at length broken their line, pushed on with shouts of joy: "Noël! Noël! Victory! Victory!"

They pressed forward into the opening made in the line and thought they had now turned the rear of the army; but everywhere they found walls of spears and halberds. John Borluut now quickly closed the wings of his division, and thus his five thousand men formed a compact circle, and the thousand Frenchmen were caught as in a net. Then began a fearful slaughter; for a quarter of an hour they were hacking, slashing, piercing, and trampling down one another; horses and men lay in helpless confusion on the ground, shrieking, howling, neighing—yet they heard nothing, spoke

The Lion of Flanders

nothing; but proceeded in silence with their work of death.

Raoul de Nesle continued a long time fighting over the dead bodies of his soldiers, though covered with wounds and besprinkled with the blood of his gallant followers; his death, he saw, was inevitable. John Borluut beheld the heroic knight with profound sympathy and compassion, and cried to him:

"Surrender, Messire Raoul; I would fain not see you die!"

But Raoul was beside himself with rage and despair; he heard, indeed, the words of Borluut clearly, and an emotion of thankfulness touched his heart; but the reproach of the seneschal had filled him with such bitter vexation that he no longer desired to live. He raised his hand and made a sign to John Borluut, as if to take a last farewell of him, and then, the same moment, struck dead two of the men of Ghent. At length, a blow from a club stretched him lifeless on the corpses of his brethren in arms. Many other knights, whose horses had been slain under them, would fain have surrendered; but no one listened to them—not a solitary Frenchman escaped alive from the net.

Meanwhile the battle raged with equal fury all along the line. Here was heard a shout: "Noël! Noël! Mountjoy St. Denis!" and this was an intimation that at that point the French had gained

The Lion of Flanders

some advantage; and there the cry: "Flanders! the Lion! all that is French is false! Strike home! to the death!" rose in mighty peals heavenward—a sign that there some body of French troops was broken and routed.

The Gröningen brook ran with blood, and was choked with the bodies of the slain. The mournful wail of the dying was scarcely drowned by the clash of arms; it was heard, low and continuous, like the roll of distant thunder, above the noise of the fight. Spears and clubs flew in pieces; in front of the line the dead lay in crowded heaps. The wounded had no chance of escape; no one thought of rendering them any assistance; and they were either stifled in the marsh, or trampled miserably to death beneath the hoofs of the horses. Hugo van Arckel meanwhile had penetrated with his eight hundred soldiers to the very centre of the French army, and was so surrounded by the enemy that the Flemings had lost sight of him altogether. They fought too valiantly and kept together too firmly to allow the enemy to break their small but compact mass; around them lay numbers of the French, and whoso dared to come near them expiated his temerity by death. At length he fought his way to the banner of Navarre, and wrenched it from the hands of the standard-bearer. The Navarrese, wild with rage, turned upon him, and laid many of his followers low; but Hugo defended the cap-

The Lion of Flanders

tured banner so well that the French could not retake it. He had already returned very near to the Flemish camp, when Louis de Forest struck him so tremendous a blow on the left shoulder that his arm was severed, and hung supported only by the shirt-of-mail. The blood gushed in streams from the wound, and the paleness of death overspread his features; but yet his grasp of the banner was unrelaxed. Louis de Forest was slain by some Flemings, and Hugo van Arckel reached the centre of the Flemish camp, gathered his ebbing strength to utter once more the cry, "Flanders! the Lion!" but his voice failed him, his life's blood was drained, and he sank, still grasping the conquered standard, to rise no more.

On the left wing, in front of Messire Guy's division, the conflict was yet more fierce and deadly. James de Chatillon charged the Guilds of Furnes with several thousand horse, and had cut down many hundreds of them. Eustachius Sporkyn lay grievously wounded behind the line, and employed his remaining strength in cheering on his men and urging them to hold their ground; but the impetuosity of the onset was too great—they were compelled to retreat. Followed by a large number of horsemen, De Chatillon broke the line; and the fight was continued over the prostrate Sporkyn, whose sufferings were soon ended beneath the tramp of the cavalry.

The Lion of Flanders

Adolf van Nieuwland alone remained with Guy and his standard-bearer; they were now cut off from the army, and their death seemed certain. De Chatillon made most strenuous efforts to get possession of the great standard of Flanders; but, although Segher Lonke, who bore it, had been many times thrown down, De Chatillon could not succeed in his attempt: he raged around it, and urged on his men, and dealt his blows in every direction upon the three invincible Flemings. Doubtless these could not long have continued to defend themselves against such a cloud of foes; but they had previously made such good use of their weapons that they stood surrounded and protected by a rampart of slain. Mad with rage and impatience, De Chatillon snatched a long spear from the hand of one of his horsemen, and dashed at full gallop toward Guy. He would infallibly have slain the Count; for, occupied with so many enemies, he did not notice De Chatillon's approach; the spear seemed to be already piercing his neck between the helmet and the gorget, when Adolf van Nieuwland swung his sword round with the rapidity of lightning, the spear flew in pieces, and the life of his general was saved.

The same moment, and before De Chatillon had time to seize his sword again, Adolf sprang over the heap of slain, and dealt the French knight so terrible a blow on the head that his cheek, and the

The Lion of Flanders

part of the helmet which covered it, were severed, and fell to the ground. The blood streamed from his wound; still he persisted in defending himself; but two mighty blows from Adolf's sword hurled him from his saddle under the hoofs of the horses. Some Flemings drew him out; and having carried him to the rear, hewed him in pieces, taunting him the while with his merciless ferocity.

While this conflict was pending, Arnold van Oudenarde had come to the succor of the left wing, and changed the fate of the battle. The men of Furnes, thus encouraged, returned with them; and soon the French were thrown into hopeless disorder. Men and horses fell in such numbers, and the confusion of the foe was so great, that the Flemings deemed the battle won, and from the whole line poured forth a loud and exulting shout:

"Victory! Victory! Flanders! the Lion! Whoso is French is false! strike all dead!" And over all the battle-field raged the Butchers, their arms, their bosoms, and their axes smeared with gore, their hair streaming wildly, their features rendered undiscernible by mire and blood and sweat, yet fixed in a grim expression of bitterest hatred of the French and intense enjoyment of the conflict.

While the first division of the French army was thus defeated and destroyed, the Seneschal d'Artois stood with the second division at a distance from the Flemish camp. As the front of the enemy was

The Lion of Flanders

not extensive enough to admit of a simultaneous attack with his whole army, he had not thought it necessary to advance. He knew nothing of the fortunes of the battle, but concluded that his troops were certainly victorious; for otherwise, he thought, some of them would have retreated. In the meantime he sent Messire Louis de Clermont with four thousand Norman cavalry through the Neerlander wood, to take the left wing of the Flemings in flank. De Clermont had the good fortune to find firm ground on this side; he crossed the brook without losing a man, and fell suddenly on the division of Guy. Attacked in the rear by fresh troops, while they were scarcely able to keep De Chatillon's men in check, they found it impossible to offer any resistance. The first ranks were broken, and cut to pieces; the others were thrown into confusion, and all this part of the Flemish army gave way and retreated. The voice of the youthful Guy, conjuring them by the memory of their fatherland to stand firm, inspired them with courage enough; but this was of no avail; the violence of the attack was too great; and all that they could do, in answer to their general's appeal, was to make their retreat as slow and orderly as possible.

At this moment Guy received so violent a blow on his helmet that he fell forward on the neck of his horse, and his sword dropped from his hand.

The Lion of Flanders

In this position, stunned and giddy, he could no longer defend himself; and would certainly have perished had not Adolf come to his rescue. The young knight sprang in front of Guy, and wielded his sword so skilfully and so valiantly that the Frenchmen were effectually prevented from striking at the Count. In a short time his arm waxed weak and weary in this desperate conflict; his blows became ever slower and weaker; the countless strokes that fell on his coat of mail made him feel his whole body bruised and swollen, and he was already on the point of taking a last farewell of the world; for he seemed to see death beckoning to him in the distance. In the meantime Guy had been carried behind the line of battle, and had recovered from his swoon. He now looked with anguish on the perilous position of his deliverer; and seizing another sword, he was in a moment at his side, and fighting with renewed vigor. Many of the most valiant of the Flemings had hastened after him; and the French would have been compelled to retreat, had they not received fresh reenforcements by way of the Neerlander wood. The intrepidity of the Flemings could not avail to check the advance of the enemy. The cry, "Flanders! the Lion!" was answered by, "Noël! Noël! the victory is ours! death to the rebels!"

The Flemings wavered, broke their ranks, and were thrown into inextricable disorder. The mar-

The Lion of Flanders

velous efforts of Guy failed to prevent their retreat; for there were at least ten horsemen to one Fleming, and the horses either trampled them down or drove them back with an irresistible impetus. Half of them fled before the advancing foe; great numbers were slain, and the remainder were so scattered that they could offer no resistance to the horsemen, and were pursued to the Leye, where many of them were miserably drowned. On the banks of this river Guy rallied a few of his men; they fought with desperation, but their heroic valor was of no avail. Though each of them had slain three or four of the horsemen, the French increased continually, while their own number diminished. Soon there remained but one hope, one thought—to die with honor avenged.

The Lion of Flanders

CHAPTER VII

Guy beheld the destruction of his troops, and deemed the battle lost. He could have wept aloud for anguish; but there was no room for grief in his manly heart—a moody rage had taken entire possession of it. In conformity with his oath, he desired to live no longer, and spurred his horse into the very thick of the exulting enemy. Adolf van Nieuwland and Arnold van Oudenarde kept close to his side; so desperate was their onset that the foe was appalled by their feats of valor, and the horsemen fell, on all sides, as if by magic, beneath their blows. Yet the Flemings were discomfited and almost all slain: the French continued their shouts of victory; for it seemed that nothing could extricate the remnant of Guy's division from their perilous position.

And now there appeared in the direction of Oudenarde, beyond the Gaver brook, an object that gleamed brightly between the trees; it drew rapidly near, and soon two horsemen might be distinguished in full career toward the field of battle. One was evidently a noble knight, as the magnificence of his armor attested. His coat-of-mail, and

The Lion of Flanders

all the steel that enveloped both himself and his horse, were covered with gold, and shone with wonderful brilliancy. An enormous blue plume streamed behind him in the wind, the reins of his horse were covered with silver plates, and on his breast was a red cross, surmounted by the word "Flanders" flashing in silver letters from a black ground.

No knight in the field was so gorgeously arrayed as this unknown; but what excited most attention was his unusual stature. He was at least a head above the tallest of the knights; and he was so powerfully built, in body and in limbs, that he might well have been taken for a son of the race of giants. The horse he rode was of a size and strength proportioned to those of its rider. Large flakes of foam flew from the mouth of the noble beast, and his breath rolled in two dense clouds from his expanded nostrils. The knight carried no other weapon than a huge ax of steel, which contrasted strangely with the golden splendor of his armor.

The other horseman was a monk, very meanly attired; his mail and helmet were so rusty that they seemed streaked with red; this was Brother William van Saeftinge. In his monastery at Doest he had heard that at Courtrai the Flemings were in conflict with the French; he went at once to the stable, took thence two horses, exchanged one for

The Lion of Flanders

the rust-eaten armor he wore, and spurred the other at his utmost speed toward the battle-field. He too was extraordinarily strong and brave; a long sword gleamed in his grasp, and the flash of his dark eye showed that he knew right well how to wield it. He had just fallen in with the wondrous unknown knight; and as both were bent on the same errand, they had continued their ride together.

The Flemings turned their eyes hopefully and joyfully toward the golden knight as he advanced in the distance. They could not distinguish the word "Flanders," and so knew not whether he was friend or foe; but in this their extremity they felt a hope that God had sent them one of His saints to deliver them. And everything combined to strengthen their hopes—the gorgeous armor—the extraordinary form and stature—the glowing red cross on the breast of the unknown. Guy and Adolf, who were fighting surrounded by foes, looked at each other with beaming joy—they had recognized the golden knight. It seemed to them as though they heard the death doom of the French, so absolute was their confidence in the prowess and skill of the new warrior. They exchanged a look which said:

"Oh, happy chance! there is the Lion of Flanders!"

At length the golden knight came near; and

The Lion of Flanders

before one could ask whom he came to aid, he fell with such impetuosity on the horsemen, and struck such fearful blows with his ax of steel, that the bewildered foe was smitten with a panic, and overthrew one another in their eagerness to escape from the dreaded strokes. Everything fell before his crushing ax—behind him he left a clear space, like the wake of a sailing ship on the waters; and thus, carrying death before him, he reached with marvelous rapidity the bands which were driven back upon the Leye, and cried:

"Flanders! the Lion! Follow me! Follow me!"

Repeating this cry, he hurled a number of Frenchmen into the marsh, and performed such prodigies of valor and strength that the Flemings looked on him with awe as a supernatural being.

And now the courage of the Flemings revived; with shouts of joy they rushed forward, and emulated the prowess of the golden knight. The French could no longer withstand the onset of the dauntless sons of the Lion: their front ranks gave way and fled; but they came in collision with those who were behind them, and the rout became general. A frightful slaughter began along the whole length of the line. The Flemings pushed on over heaps of slain. The cry, "Noël! Noël!" was no longer heard: "Flanders! the Lion!" alone resounded triumphantly from every part of the field.

The Lion of Flanders

Brother William, the monk, had dismounted, and was fighting on foot. He wielded his sword like a feather, and laughed to scorn every foe who dared to assail him. One would have thought he was playing at some amusing game, so joyous was he and so full of jests. At length he descried Messire Louis de Clermont with his banner at a little distance. "Flanders! the Lion!" shouted Brother William; "the banner is mine!" He fell on the ground like one dead, and crept on his hands and knees between the horses' legs, and suddenly stood by the side of Louis de Clermont, as though he had risen out of the earth. Blows rained on him on all sides; but he defended himself so well that he received only a few trifling scratches. At first the enemy did not observe that the standard was the object of his attack; but suddenly he turned with the speed of lightning, severed the arm of the standard-bearer at a stroke, and tore the fallen banner in a thousand pieces.

The monk would certainly have been slain, but at that moment began the general rout of the French, and in a short time he found himself surrounded by Flemings, with the golden knight at their head. Guy approached him, and hastily whispered to him:

"Oh, Robert! my brother! how I thank God for sending you to our aid! You have delivered the—"

The golden knight returned no answer, but in-

The Lion of Flanders

terrupted him by placing his finger on his mouth, as if to say, "Silence! it is a secret." Adolf, too, had observed the sign, and bore himself as though he did not recognize the Count of Flanders. Meanwhile the French were completing their own destruction. The Flemings pursued them closely, despatching every fallen horseman with their clubs and halberds. Horses and men were trampled down into the moist ground; the grass of the meadows was no longer visible, nor the Gröningen brook; everywhere were the ghastly corpses of the slain. The cries of the wounded and dying mingled with the exulting shouts of the Flemings, the flourish of trumpets, the clash of swords upon the coats-of-mail, and the dismal shrieks of the dying horses. The low rumbling of a volcano on the eve of an eruption may convey some faint notion of the terrors of that scene.

The town-clock of Courtrai struck nine ere the routed horsemen of De Nesle and De Chatillon reached the Seneschal d'Artois. Scarcely had the first fugitives brought him tidings of the defeat, than he resolved in his blind rage to attack the Flemings with his still numerous reserve. It was all in vain that some of the knights tried to dissuade him; followed by his men, he dashed wildly through and over the crowd of fugitives. The fury of their attack compelled Guy's army to fall back again behind the Gröningen brook; for there

The Lion of Flanders

the carcasses of horses formed a sort of breastwork, and impeded the action of cavalry.

The French knights could not keep their footing on the slippery soil: they fell over one another, and buried one another in the morass. Messire d'Artois lost all self-command: with some intrepid knights, he sprang across the brook and fell on the ranks of the Flemings. After a brief conflict, in which many Flemings were slain, he succeeded in seizing the great banner of Flanders, and tore a large piece of it away, with the front paw of the Lion on it. A cry of rage ran through the Flemish ranks—"Strike him dead! strike him dead!" The seneschal strove with all his strength to wrench the standard from Segher Lonke; but Brother William, throwing away his sword, sprang toward the horse of Messire d'Artois, threw his sinewy arms round the general's neck, hurled him from his saddle, and both rolled together to the ground. The Butchers had now come up; and Jan Breydel, burning to avenge the insults offered by Robert d'Artois to the standard of Flanders, struck off his right arm at a blow. The hapless seneschal saw that his end was near, and asked if there were no one of noble blood at hand to whom he might with honor surrender his sword? But his words were unintelligible to the Butchers, and were lost in their wild cry of vengeance: they hacked and hewed the luckless knight until death ended his sufferings.

The Lion of Flanders

While this was going on, Brother William had hurled the Chancellor Pierre Flotte to the ground, and had raised his sword to cleave his skull in twain. The Frenchman implored mercy; but Brother William, with a scornful laugh, struck him so violently on the back of the neck that he fell dead upon his face. De Tancarville and D'Aspremont perished in like manner beneath the arm of the golden knight; Guy clove the head of Renold de Longueval with a single blow; the kings of Majorca and Melinde, and more than a hundred nobles, fell beneath the blows of the men of Ghent.

The golden knight was now fighting, on the left wing, against a large body of horsemen; at his side were his brother Guy and Adolf van Nieuwland. The latter threw himself every moment upon the enemy; and was so often in imminent danger of death that it seemed as though he had resolved to die before the eyes of the Lion of Flanders. Matilda's father sees me! thought he; and his breath came more freely, his muscles acquired new strength, and his spirit rose with a loftier contempt of death. The golden knight warned him repeatedly not to expose himself so recklessly; but these warnings sounded in Adolf's ears like the sweetest praise, and made him only more rash and daring. It was fortunate for him that a stronger arm than his own shielded his life, and that one was by his

The Lion of Flanders

side who had vowed, in true paternal love, to protect him to the utmost of his power.

A single banner alone now remained standing in all the French host; the royal standard still waved its glittering folds, its silver lilies, and all the sparkling jewels with which the arms of France were embroidered. Guy pointed with his hand to the place where it stood, and cried to the golden knight, "Yonder stands our prize!"

They redoubled their efforts to break through the French host; but without avail, until Adolf van Nieuwland, finding a favorable spot, pierced alone the masses of the enemy, and fought his way to the great standard. What hostile hand, what envious spirit, impelled the youthful warrior thus to certain and untimely death? Had they known what hot and bitter tears were shed for him at that moment, how fervently and with how many repetitions his name came before God on the wings of a maiden's prayers, they could not have thus ruthlessly consigned him to destruction! For the royal banner was circled round by a band of noble and valiant knights, who had sworn by their troth and by their honor that they would die rather than suffer it to be taken from their keeping. And what could Adolf do against the flower of French chivalry? Words of scornful taunting greeted him, countless swords waved above his head; and, notwithstanding his marvelous intrepidity, he could no longer

The Lion of Flanders

defend himself. Already his blood streamed from beneath his helm, and his eyes were clouded by the mists of death. Feeling that his last moment was come, he cried, "Matilda! Matilda! farewell!" and gathering up his remaining strength, he threw himself, with the energy of despair, upon the swords of his foes, forced his way through them to the standard, and wrenched it from the standard-bearer; but it was torn from him in an instant by numberless hands, his strength forsook him, he fell forward on his horse, and the whelming sea of foes closed over him.

The golden knight saw in a moment the danger of Adolf; he thought of the hopeless anguish of the wretched Matilda were her beloved to die by the hand of the enemy; and turning to his men, he cried, with a voice which rose like a thunder-clap above the crash of battle:

"Forward, men of Flanders!"

Like the raging sea, which chafes against its embankment with fury irresistible—like that sea when, under some overmastering wave, the impediment to its mad career has been swept away, and it rolls its foaming billows over the plain, tearing up the trees by their roots, and dashing whole villages to the ground—so sprang forward the herd of Flemish lions at the cry of the unknown knight.

The French were burning with too fierce a courage for the Flemings to hope to overthrow them

The Lion of Flanders

by one impetuous onset; but the clubs and halberds fell thick and fast as hail upon them. Long and desperate was the struggle; men and horses were mingled together in indescribable confusion; but soon the French knights were so hemmed in that they could not move, and they were driven slowly from their position. The ax of the golden knight had cleared his way to the standard, and he was closely followed by Guy and Arnold van Oudenarde, with a few of the bravest Flemings. He looked anxiously in the direction of the banner for the green plume of Adolf van Nieuwland; but it was not to be seen, and he thought he perceived it further on among the Flemings. The forty chosen knights who stood ranged around the standard now rushed upon the golden knight; but he wielded his ax with such effect that not a sword touched him. His first blow crushed the head of Alin de Bretagne, his second broke the ribs of Richard de Falaise; and all around the Flemings emulated his valor. The bearer of the standard now retreated, in order to preserve it from capture; but Robert with one blow thrust aside three or four of his foes, and pursued him into the midst of a group of Frenchmen at some distance from the spot where the conflict was raging, and succeeded at length in grasping his prize. A whole troop of knights now assailed him to retake the banner; but the golden knight, placing it as a

The Lion of Flanders

spear in its rest, dashed impetuously among his pursuers. And thus he won his way back to the Flemish army, where he held aloft the captured standard, and cried, "Flanders! the Lion! the victory is ours!"

He was answered by a universal shout of joy; and the courage and strength of the Flemings seemed to increase every moment.

Guy de St. Pol was yet posted at the Pottelberg with about ten thousand foot-soldiers and a goodly troop of cavalry. He had already packed up all the valuables in the camp; and was about to save himself by flight, when Pierre Lebrun, one of those who had been fighting near the royal standard, dashed up to him, and cried:

"What, St. Pol! can you act thus? Can you fly like a dastard, and leave unavenged the deaths of Robert d'Artois and our brethren in arms? Stay, I implore you, for the sake of the honor of France! Let us rather die than endure this shame; advance your troops, and victory may yet be ours."

But Guy de St. Pol would hear nothing of fighting; fear had taken complete possession of him, and he replied:

"Messire Lebrun, I know my duty. I will not allow the baggage to be captured; it is better I should lead back the survivors to France than that I should hurry them to certain destruction."

"And will you, then, abandon to the enemy all

The Lion of Flanders

who are still fighting bravely sword in hand? Surely this is a traitor's deed; and if I survive this day, I will impeach you before the king for disloyalty and cowardice."

"Prudence compels my retreat, Messire Lebrun. I shall go, whatever you may think fit to say of me hereafter; for you are now too much excited to be capable of reflecting on all the circumstances of our position. Rage has bereft you of your reason."

"And you are benumbed and paralyzed by cowardice!" retorted Pierre Lebrun. "Do as you will; to show you that I am as prudent as yourself, I shall march with my division to cover and assist the retreat."

He then took a troop of two thousand foot-soldiers, and hastened with them to the field of battle. The number of the French was now so much reduced, and there were so many gaps in their line, that the Flemings were enabled to assail them at the same time in front and in rear. The golden knight observed at once Lebrun's movement and its intention; he saw clearly that St. Pol was about to make his escape with the baggage, and he sprang to the side of Guy to inform him of this plan of the enemy. A few moments after, several Flemish bands dispersed themselves over the plain. Messire John Borluut, with the men of Ghent, hurried along the wall of the city and fell on Lebrun's flank; while the Butchers, with their Dean,

The Lion of Flanders

Jan Breydel, made a detour round the castle of Nedermosschere, and fell on the rear of the French camp.

St. Pol's soldiers had not reckoned on fighting; they were busied in packing together a crowd of precious things, when the axes of the Butchers, and death in their train, took them by surprise. St. Pol, being well mounted, made good his escape, without bestowing further thought on the fate of his troops. Soon the camp was won, and in a few moments not a Frenchman remained alive within it; while the Flemings took possession of all the gold and silver goblets, and of the countless treasures which the French had brought with them.

On the field of battle the conflict had not yet ceased; about a thousand horsemen still persisted in their defense; they had resolved to sell their lives as dear as possible. Among them were more than a hundred noble knights, who had vowed not to survive this defeat, and so fought on with a calm and despairing courage. But at length they were driven on toward the walls of the city into the bitter marsh, and their steeds sank into the treacherous banks of the Ronduite brook. The knights could no longer manage or assist their horses; so they sprang upon the ground, ranged themselves in a circle, and continued the fight with desperate energy. Many of them were, however, stifled in the bitter marsh, which soon became a lake of blood, wherein were seen heads, and arms, and legs of slain warriors mingled with helmets and broken swords, and which has preserved a memorial of this dismal tragedy in its present name, "The Bloody Marsh."

When some Lilyards, among whom were John van Gistel, and a number of the men of Brabant, saw that escape was impossible, they mingled with the Flemings and shouted:

"Flanders! the Lion! Hail, hail Flanders!"

They thought thus to elude the notice of their countrymen; but a Clothworker rushed from the throng toward John van Gistel, and struck him a blow on the head which crushed his skull to fragments, muttering the while:

"Did not my father tell you, traitor, that you would not die in your bed?"

The others were soon recognized by the make of their weapons, and hewn down or pierced without pity, as traitors and recreants.

The young Guy felt a profound pity for the remaining knights who maintained so brave and obstinate a defense, and called to them to surrender, assuring them that their lives should be spared. Convinced that neither courage nor intrepidity could avail them, they yielded and were disarmed, and given into the custody of John Borluut. The most illustrious of these noble captives was Thibaud II, subsequently Duke of Lorraine; the re-

The Lion of Flanders

mainder were all of noble race, and famed as valiant knights; their number was about sixty.

And now there remained on the field not a single enemy to be vanquished; only here and there in the distance were seen a few fugitives hastening to secure a safe retreat. The Flemings, amazed that their fighting was over, and maddened with rage and excitement, rushed in crowds in pursuit of these hapless Frenchmen; near the Plague hospital at St. Mary Magdalen, they overtook a company of St. Pol's troops, and put every man to death; a little further on they found Messire William van Mosschere, the Lilyard, who had fled from the field with a few followers. Seeing himself surrounded, he fell on his knees and begged for mercy, pledging himself to serve Robert de Bethune as a loyal vassal. But no one listened to him; the axes of the Butchers ended his pleadings and his life. And thus passed the rest of the day; until within reach of the Flemings no Frenchman, nor ally or friend of Frenchmen, was any longer to be found.

The Lion of Flanders

CHAPTER VIII

ALTHOUGH a great part of the Flemish troops was engaged in pursuit of the flying enemy, there still remained some companies drawn up in order on the battlefield.

John Borluut gave orders to his men to keep a strict watch on the field until the following day, according to the custom of war. The division led by Borluut consisted now of three thousand men of Ghent; and in addition to these, many others had remained on the ground, either wounded or exhausted by fatigue. And now that the victory was won, and the chains of their fatherland broken, the Flemings testified their joy by repeated cries of, "Flanders and the Lion! Victory! Victory!" Their shouts were echoed back from the walls of the city by the men of Ypres and Courtrai with even greater energy. They, too, might well shout victory; for while the battle was raging on the Gröningen Place, the castellan, Van Lens, had made a sortie from the citadel, and would have reduced the city to ashes, had not the men of Ypres made so vigorous a resistance, that they drove him back into the citadel after a long conflict. The castellan found that scarcely a tenth part of his soldiers had escaped the rage of the citizens.

The captains and knights now returned to the camp, and thronged round the golden knight, to express to him their fervent gratitude; but, fearful of betraying himself, he answered not a word. Guy, who was standing at his side, turned to the knights, and said:

"Messires, the knight who has so wondrously delivered us and all the land of Flanders, is a crusader, and wishes to remain unknown. The noblest son of Flanders bears his name."

The knights were silent immediately; and every one was endeavoring to guess who this could be, who was at once so brave, so noble, and so lofty of stature. Those of them who remembered the meeting at the wood in the valley were not long in recognizing him; but remembering their pledge, they kept profound silence. Others there were who had no doubt that the unknown was the Count of Flanders himself; but the wish of the golden knight to remain unknown imposed on them also the obligation of secrecy.

After Robert had conversed a while with Guy in a low voice, he cast his eye over the surrounding group of knights; and then turning to Guy, with trouble depicted on his features, he said: "I do not see Adolf van Nieuwland; an agonizing doubt troubles me. Can it be that my young friend has fallen beneath the sword of the foe? **That** would indeed be to me an intolerable and an enduring grief: and my poor Matilda! how will she mourn her good brother!"

"He can not be dead, Robert; I am sure that I saw his green plume waving just now among the trees of the Neerlander wood. He must be in close pursuit of the foe; you saw with what irrepressible fury he threw himself upon the French in the battle. Fear nothing for him; God will not have allowed him to be slain."

"Oh Guy, are you speaking the truth? My heart is wrung that my hapless child can not taste the joy of this day without an alloy of bitterness. I pray you, my brother, let the men of Messire Borluut search the field, and see whether Adolf is among the slain. I will go to console my anxious Matilda; the presence of her father will be at least a momentary consolation."

He then greeted the knights courteously, and hastened to the Abbey of Gröningen. Guy gave orders to John Borluut to disperse his men over the field, and to bring the wounded and dead knights into the tents. As they began their search, they were seen suddenly to stand still, as though arrested by some sight of horror. Now that the heat and rage of the conflict had subsided, their eyes ranged over the broad plain, where lay in hideous confusion the mangled bodies of men and

The Lion of Flanders

horses, standards and broken armor. Here and there a wounded man stretched his hands toward them with a piteous cry, and a low wailing, more dismal than the dreariest solitude, filled the air: it was the voice of the wounded, crying, "Water! water! For God's sake, water!"

The sun poured its glowing rays upon the miserable men, and tortured them with unappeasable thirst. Flocks of ravens spread their dark wings over them; their hoarse cries were blended with the moans of the wounded; they fixed their talons in the yet quivering limbs of the dying; while troops of dogs, allured by the smell of blood, had poured forth from the city to deepen the horrors of the scene.

As the men of Ghent roamed over the field, they sought those in whose bosoms were yet some pulses of life, and brought them with care into the camp. One band was employed to fetch water from the Gaver brook; and it was a piteous sight to watch the eagerness with which the wounded seized it, and with what gratitude, with what glistening eyes, they welcomed the refreshing draft.

The soldiers had received orders to bring every knight they found killed or wounded, into the camp. They had already recovered more than half of the slain, and had traversed a considerable extent of the field of battle. As they drew near the place where the strife had been most deadly, they found the dead more numerous. They were busily removing the helmet of Messire van Machelen, when they heard close at hand a low moan, which seemed to issue from the ground. They listened, but all was still again; not one of the bodies around gave the faintest token of life. Suddenly the moan was repeated; it came from a little distance, from between two prostrate horses. After many efforts, they succeeded in drawing one of the horses aside, and found the knight from whom the sound proceded. He was lying stretched out across the bodies, and drenched in the blood of many of the foe. His armor was indented and broken by the tread of horses; his right hand still convulsively grasped his sword, while in his left was a green veil. His pallid features bore the impress of approaching death, and he gazed on his deliverers with restless wandering looks. John Borluut recognized in a moment the unfortunate Adolf van Nieuwland. They loosened in haste the joints of his mail, raised his head gently, and moistened his lips with water. His failing voice murmured some unintelligible words, and his eyes closed as if his soul had at length taken its flight from his tortured body. The cool breeze and the refreshing water had overpowered him; and he lost for some moments all consciousness. When he at length opened his eyes, like one whose life was ebbing fast, he pressed Borluut's hand,

The Lion of Flanders

and said—so slowly, that between each word there was a long pause:

"I am dying. You see it, Messire John; my soul can not linger much longer on earth. But bewail me not; I die contented, for our fatherland is delivered—is free—"

His voice here failed him. His breath grew shorter; his head drooped; he slowly brought the green veil to his lips, and imprinted on it a last kiss. This done, he lost all consciousness, and fell apparently lifeless in the arms of John Borluut. Yet his heart continued to beat, and the warmth of his body betokened remaining life; so that the captain of Ghent did not altogether abandon hope, but conveyed the wounded knight to the camp with the tenderest care.

Matilda had taken refuge in a cell of the Abbey of Gröningen during the battle, whither she was accompanied by Adolf's sister. Her terror and anxiety were extreme; her relatives, her beloved Adolf—all were in that fearful conflict. On the issue of this contest, waged by the Flemings against so overwhelming a foe, hung the freedom of her father; this field of battle would either win again for him the throne of Flanders, or forever crumble it to dust. Were the French victorious, she knew that the death of all she loved was inevitable, and that some horrible doom awaited herself. As the war-trumpets echoed over the field,

The Lion of Flanders

both maidens shuddered and grew pale, as if in that sound the stroke of death had descended on them. Their terror was too great to be expressed in words; they fell on their knees, buried their faces in their hands, and hot tears streamed down their cheeks. And thus they lay in fervent prayer, motionless, almost lifeless, as though sunk in heavy slumber, while from time to time a deep groan broke from their crushed hearts. As they caught the distant sounds of the fight, Maria sighed:

"O God Almighty, Lord God of Hosts, have mercy on us! Bring us help in this our hour of need, O Lord!"

And Matilda's gentle voice continued:

"O loving Jesus, Redeemer of men, shield him! Call him not to Thee, O Jesus most merciful! Holy Mother of God, pray for us! O Mother of Christ, consolation of the afflicted, pray for him!"

Then the roar of battle came nearer, and filled their hearts with fresh alarms; and their hands shook like the tender leaves of the aspen tree. Deeper sank their heads upon their breasts, their tears flowed more abundantly, and their prayers were murmured with fainter voice; for terror had paralyzed all their energies.

The strife lasted long; the appalling cry of the troops, as they fought hand to hand, resounded through the lonely cell. For long hours those low-

The Lion of Flanders

whispered prayers went forth; and still they prayed, when the golden knight knocked at the abbey-gate. The sound of heavy footsteps caused them to turn their eyes toward the door, and they were still and motionless with sweet anticipation.

"Adolf comes again!" sighed Maria. "Oh, our prayer is heard!"

Matilda listened with greater eagerness, and replied in tones of sadness:

"No, no, it is not Adolf; his step is not so heavy. Oh Maria, it may be a herald of evil tidings!"

The door of the cell turned on its hinges, a nun opened it; and the golden knight entered. Matilda's tender frame trembled with fear; she raised her eyes doubtfully and timidly to the stranger who stood before her and opened his arms to her. It seemed to her a delusive dream; but her agitation was fleeting as the lightning which flashes and is gone; she rushed eagerly forward, and was clasped in her father's arms.

"My father!" she exclaimed; "my beloved father! do I see you again free—your chains broken? Let me press you to my heart. O God, how good Thou art! Do not turn away your face, dearest father; let me taste all my bliss."

Robert de Bethune embraced his loving daughter with unutterable joy; and when their hearts at length beat more tranquilly, he laid his helmet and gloves of steel on the low stool on which Matilda had been kneeling. Wearied by his exertions, he sank into a couch. Matilda threw her arms around him, gazing with admiration and awe on him whose face had been ever to her so full of consolation and strength—on him whose noble blood flowed in her veins, and who loved her so deeply and tenderly; and she listened with beating heart to the words which that beloved voice murmured in her ear.

"Matilda," said he, "my noble child, God has long proved us with suffering: but now our sorrows are ended; Flanders is free—is avenged. The Black Lion has torn the Lilies to pieces, and the aliens are discomfited and driven back. Dismiss every fear; the vile mercenaries of Joanna of Navarre are no more."

The maiden listened with agonized attention to the words of her father. She looked at him with a peculiar expression; she could but faintly smile. Joy had come so suddenly upon her that she seemed deprived of all power and speech. After a few moments, she observed that her father had ceased speaking, and she said:

"O my God, our fatherland is free! The French are defeated and slain; and you, my father, I possess you once more. We shall go back again to our beautiful Wynandael. Sorrow shall no more cloud your days; and I shall pass my life joyfully and happily in your arms. This is beyond hope—be-

The Lion of Flanders

yond all that I have dared to ask of God in my prayers."

"Listen attentively, my child; and be calm, I beseech you; this day I must leave you again. The noble knight who released me from my bonds has my word of honor that I would return as soon as the battle was over."

The maiden's head sank again upon her breast, and she sighed, in bitter grief:

"They will put you to a cruel death, oh my poor father!"

"Do not be so fearful, Matilda," continued Robert; "my brother Guy has taken sixty French knights of noblest blood prisoners; Philip the Fair will be told that their lives are hostages for mine; and he can not allow the brave survivors of his army to be offered up as victims to his vengeance. Flanders is now more powerful than France. So I implore you dry your tears. Rejoice, for a blessed future awaits us; I will restore Castle Wynandael again, that we may live in it as in days gone by. Then we shall again enjoy the chase, with our falcons on our wrist. Can you not imagine how merry our first hunting party will be?"

An inexpressibly sweet smile and a fervent kiss were Matilda's answer. But on a sudden a thought of pain seemed to cross her mind; for her countenance was overspread with gloom, and she bent her eyes on the ground, like one who is overcome by shame.

Robert looked at her inquiringly, and asked:

"Matilda, my child, why is your countenance so suddenly overcast with sadness?"

The maiden only half raised her eyes, and answered with a low voice:

"But—my father—you say nothing of Adolf—why did he not come with you?"

There was a slight pause before Robert replied. He discerned that, unknown to herself, a profound feeling was slumbering in Matilda's heart; therefore it was not without design he answered her thus:

"Adolf is detained by his duty, my child; fugitives are scattered over the plain, and I believe he is pursuing them. I may say to you, Matilda, that our friend Adolf is the most valiant and the most noble knight I know. Never have I seen more manliness and intrepidity. Twice he saved the life of my brother Guy; beneath the banner-royal of France the enemy fell in numbers beneath his sword; all the knights are repeating his praises, and ascribe to him a large share in the deliverance of Flanders."

While Robert was uttering these words, he kept his eye fixed on his daughter, and scrutinized every emotion that flitted across her expressive features. He read therein a mingled pride and rapture, and had no further doubt that his conjecture was well founded. Maria, the while, stood with her eyes fixed on Robert, and drank in with eager joy the praises which he bestowed so lavishly on her brother.

While Matilda was gazing on her father in a transport of bliss, there was heard suddenly a confused noise of voices in the court of the monastery. After a few moments all was again still; then the door of the cell opened, and Guy entered slowly, and with a disturbed countenance; he came near to his brother, and said:

"A great disaster has befallen us, my brother, in the loss of one who is most dear to us all; the men of Ghent found him on the field of battle, lying under a heap of slain, and they have brought him here into the monastery. His life trembles on his lips, and I think the hour of his death can not be very distant. He anxiously begs to see you once more ere he quits this world; wherefore I pray you, my brother, grant him this last favor." Then, turning to Maria, he continued: "He desires to see you also, noble maiden."

One cry of bitter anguish broke from the hearts of both maidens. Matilda fell lifeless into her father's arms; and Maria flew to the door, and rushed from the chamber in an agony of despair. Their cries brought two nuns into the cell, who took charge of the unhappy Matilda; her father stooped and kissed her, and turned to visit the dying Adolf; when the maiden, perceiving his intention, tore herself from the arms of the nuns, and clinging to her father, cried:

"Let me go with you, my father; let me see him once more! Woe, woe is me! what a sharp sword pierces my heart! My father, I shall die with him; I feel already the approach of death. I must see him: come, come speedily; he is dying! Oh, Adolf! Adolf!"

Robert gazed on his daughter with tender compassion; he could not doubt now the existence of that secret feeling which had slowly and quietly taken root in his daughter's heart. The discovery gave him no pain, caused him no displeasure; unable to comfort her with words, he pressed her to his heart. But Matilda disengaged herself from these tender bonds, and drew Robert toward the door, crying:

"Oh, my father, have pity on me! Come, that I may once more hear the voice of my good brother, that his eyes may look on me once more before he dies."

She knelt down at his feet, and continued, amid burning tears:

"I implore you, do not reject my petition; hear me; grant it, my lord and my father."

Robert would have preferred leaving his daughter in the care of the nuns; for he feared, with reason, that the sight of the dying knight would completely overwhelm her; yet he could not deny her urgent prayers; he took her, therefore, by the hand, and said:

"Be it so, my daughter; go with me, and visit the unfortunate Adolf. But, I pray you, disturb him not by your grief; think that God has this day bestowed on us a great mercy, and that He may be justly provoked to anger by your despair."

Ere these words were ended they had left the cell. Adolf had been brought into the refectory of the monastery, and laid carefully on a feather-bed upon the floor. A priest, well skilled in the healing art, had examined him with care, and found no open wound; long blue stripes indicated the blows he had received, and in many places were large bruises and contusions. He was bled; and then his body was carefully washed, and a restorative balsam applied. Through the care of the skilful priest he had recovered a measure of strength: but yet he seemed at the point of death, although his eyes were no longer so dull and lustreless. Around his bed stood many knights in deep silence, mourning for their friend. John van Renesse, Arnold van Oudenarde, and Peter Deconinck assisted the priest in his operations; William van Gulick, John Borluut, and Baldwin van Papenrode stood at the left hand of the couch, while Guy, Jan Breydel, and the other more illustrious knights, gazed on

The Lion of Flanders

the wounded man with their heads bowed low in sorrow and in sympathy.

Maria was kneeling weeping near her brother; she had seized his hand, and was bedewing it with her tears, while Adolf bent on her an unsteady and almost vacant look. As Robert and his daughter entered the refectory, the knights were all struck with wonder and emotion. He who had come in their hour of need, their mysterious deliverer, was the Lion of Flanders, their Count! They all bowed before him with profound reverence, and said:

"Honor to the Lion, our Lord!"

Robert left his daughter's hand, raised Messires John Borluut and Van Renesse from the ground, and kissed both of them on the cheek; he then beckoned to the other knights to rise, and addressed them thus:

"My true and loyal vassals, my friends, you have shown me to-day how mighty is a nation of heroes! I wear my coronet now with a loftier pride than that with which Philip the Fair wears the crown of France; for of you I may well boast and glory."

He then approached Adolf, took his hand, and looked at him for some time in silence; a tear glistened awhile beneath each eyelid of the Lion, and at length dropped—a pearl of price—upon the ground. Matilda was kneeling at the head of Adolf's couch; she had taken her green veil from

The Lion of Flanders

his hand; and her tears fell hot and fast upon this token of her affection, and of his self-sacrifice and devotedness. She spoke not a word; she did not even steal a look at Adolf; but covered her face with her hands, and wept bitterly.

The priest, too, stood motionless, his eyes steadily fastened on the wounded knight. He marked some wonderful change passing over his features; something which, increasing every moment, spoke of returning life and vigor. And in truth his eyes had lost their fixed and glassy expression, and his countenance no longer bore the signs of approaching death. Soon he raised his eyes to Robert, with a look of intense love and devotion; and said slowly, and with a voice broken by suffering and weakness:

"Oh, my lord and Count! your presence is to me a sweet consolation. Now I can die in peace— Our fatherland is free! You will occupy the Lion's throne in peaceful and happy days— Gladly do I now quit this earth, now that the future promises so much happiness to you and to your noble daughter. Oh, believe me, in this my hour of death, your mischances were more grievous to me, your unworthy servant, than to yourself. Often have I, in the still night, moistened my bed with my tears, as I thought of the mournful lot of the noble Matilda, and of your captivity—" Then turning his head slightly toward Matilda, he made her tears flow yet more abundantly, as he said:

The Lion of Flanders

"Weep not, noble maiden; I merit not this tender compassion. There is another life than this! There it is my hope and trust I shall see my good sister again. Remain on earth, the stay and solace of your father's old age; and sometimes in your prayers think of your brother, who must quit you—"

Suddenly he stopped, and looked around him in astonishment.

"Merciful God!" cried he, turning an inquiring look on the priest, "what means this? I feel a renewed vigor; my blood flows more freely in my veins!"

Matilda arose at these words, and gazed at him in painful expectation. All looked anxiously and inquiringly at the priest, who had been attentively watching Adolf during this scene, and noting his most fleeting expression and emotion. He took Adolf's hand and felt his pulse, while all the bystanders followed his every movement with eager curiosity; and at length they read in the good priest's countenance that he had not abandoned all hope of restoring the wounded knight. The skilful leech opened the eyelids of his patient in silence, and attentively examined his eyes; he opened his mouth, and passed his hand over his uncovered breast; and then turning to the knights around the couch, he said, in a tone of decided conviction:

"I can now assure you, Messires, that the fever

The Lion of Flanders

which threatened the life of the youthful knight has subsided: he will not die."

A sensible tremor passed over all present, and one might have thought the priest had uttered a doom of death; but soon this convulsive thrill was succeeded by a bounding joy, which broke forth in words and gestures.

Maria had answered the assurance of the priest with a piercing cry, and clasped her brother to her breast; while Matilda fell on her knees, raised her hands toward Heaven, and cried with a loud voice:

"I thank Thee, O God all-merciful, full of compassion, that Thou hast heard the prayers of Thine unworthy handmaiden!"

And after this brief thanksgiving she sprang up, and threw herself, tremulous with joy, into her father's arms.

"He will live! he will not die!" she exclaimed, in a transport of gladness. "Oh, now I am happy!" and she rested a moment exhausted on Robert's breast. But soon she turned again eagerly back to Adolf, and exchanged words of joy and gratitude with him.

What appeared a miracle to all present was but a natural result of Adolf's condition. He had received no open nor deep wound, but many bruises; the pain which these occasioned him had induced a violent fever, which threatened his life; but the presence of Matilda seemed to have brought the

The Lion of Flanders

malady to a crisis, and, by imparting fresh energy to his soul, gave him strength to battle with it, and, as it were, to cast it off; and thus did she appear as an angel of life to rescue him from the grave, which already yawned to receive him.

Robert de Bethune allowed his daughter, who was beside herself with joy, to remain kneeling by Adolf's side; and, advancing toward the knights, he addressed them in these words:

"You, noble sons of Flanders, have this day won a victory, the memory whereof shall live among your children's children as a record of your lofty prowess; you have shown the whole world how dearly the alien has expiated his temerity in setting his foot on the soil of the Lion. The love of your fatherland has exalted you into heroes; and your arms, nerved by a most righteous vengeance, have laid the tyrant low. Freedom is a precious thing in the esteem of those who have sealed it with their heart's blood. Henceforth no prince of the South shall enslave us more; you would all rather die a thousand deaths than allow the alien to sing over you a song of triumph. Now this fear exists no longer. Flanders is this day exalted high above all other lands; and this glory she owes to you, most noble knights! And now our will is, that rest and peace should recompense the loyalty of our subjects; our highest joy will be that all should greet us by the name of father, so far as our loving care

The Lion of Flanders

and unsleeping vigilance can render us worthy of this title. Nevertheless, should the French dare to return, again would we be the Lion of Flanders, and again should our battle-ax lead you on to the conflict. And now let our victory be unstained by further violence; above all, pursue not the Lilyards; it behooveth us to protect even their rights. For the present I must leave you; until my return, I pray you obey my brother Guy as your liege lord and count."

"What! speak you of leaving?" cried the skeptical John Borluut; "you are surely not going back to France! They will avenge their defeat on you, noble count."

"Messires," said Robert, "let me ask you, who is there among you who would, from fear of death, break his word of honor and stain his knighthood's loyalty?"

All at once hung their heads, and uttered not a word. They saw with sorrow that they dared not oppose their count's return. He continued:

"Messire Deconinck, your lofty wisdom has been of essential service to us, and we hope to task it still further; you are now a member of our council, and I require you to live with us in our castle. Messire Breydel, your valor and fidelity merit a great reward; I appoint you commander-in-chief of all your fellow-citizens who may be able to assist us in time of war; I know how well this office be-

The Lion of Flanders

seems you. Moreover, you henceforth belong to our court, and will dwell there whenever it pleases you. And you, Adolf—you, my friend, deserve a yet richer recompense. We have all been witnesses of your prowess; you have approved yourself worthy of the noble name of your forefathers. I have not forgotten your self-devotion; I know with what care, with what love, you have protected and consoled my unhappy child; I know the pure, the profound feeling that has taken root and sprung up, unconsciously to yourselves, in the hearts of you both; and shall I allow you to outstrip me in noble generosity? Let the illustrious blood of the Counts of Flanders mingle its stream with that of the noble lords of Nieuwland, and let the Black Lion add its glories to your shield. I give you my beloved child, my Matilda, to wife."

From Matilda's heart burst one only word—the name of Adolf. Trembling violently, she seized his hand, and looked steadfastly in his eyes; then she wept precious tears, tears of joy, joy impetuous and overwhelming. The youthful knight uttered not a word; his bliss was too great, too profound, too sacred to be expressed in words. He raised his eyes, beaming with love, on Matilda; then turned them, full of gratitude, to Robert; and then upward in adoration to God.

For some little time a noise had been heard in the courtyard of the monastery; and it seemed as

The Lion of Flanders

though a large crowd of people were gathered there. The tumult waxed greater and greater, and at intervals was heard a mighty shout of joy. A nun brought the tidings that a great multitude stood at the abbey gate, and demanded, with repeated cries, to see the golden knight. As the door of the hall was opened, Robert caught distinctly the cry:

"Flanders! the Lion! hail to our deliverer! hail! hail!"

Robert turned to the nun, and said:

"Tell them that the golden knight, whom they demand to see, will appear among them in a few moments."

Then he approached the sick knight, seized his yet feeble hand, and said:

"Adolf van Nieuwland, my beloved Matilda will be your wife. May the blessing of the Almighty rest upon your heads, and give to your children the valor of their father and the virtues of their mother! You have merited yet more than this; but I have no more precious gift to bestow on you than the child who might have been the solace and the stay of my declining age."

While words of heartfelt gratitude flowed from Adolf's lips, Robert hastily approached Guy, and said:

"My dear brother, it is my wish that the marriage should take place as soon as possible, with all fitting magnificence, and with the customary religious ceremonies. Messires, I am about to leave you, with a hope that I shall soon return to you, free and unshackled, to labor for the happiness of my faithful subjects."

After these words, he again drew near to Adolf, and kissed him on the cheek:

"Farewell, my son," he said.

And pressing Matilda to his heart:

"Farewell, my darling Matilda. Weep no more for me; I am happy now that our fatherland is avenged; and I shall soon return again."

He then embraced his brother Guy, William van Gulick, and some other knights, his especial friends. He pressed with deep emotion the hands of all the others, and exclaimed as he took his departure:

"Farewell, farewell all, noble sons of Flanders, my true brothers-in-arms!"

In the courtyard he mounted his horse and resumed his armor; then he lowered his vizor, and rode through the gateway. A countless multitude was there assembled; and as soon as they caught sight of the golden knight, they drew back on both sides to make way for him, and greeted him with exulting acclamations.

"Hail to the golden knight! victory! victory! Hail to our deliverer!"

They clapped their hands, they gathered the

The Lion of Flanders

earth he trod, and kept it as a sacred relic; for in their simplicity they believed that St. George, who had been invoked during the battle in every church of Courtrai, had come to their aid in this majestic form. The slow measured tread of the knight, and his deep silence, confirmed them in their belief; and many fell on their knees as he passed by them. They followed him for more than a league into the country, and it seemed as if their gaze of veneration could never be satiated; for the longer they gazed, the more wonderful did the golden knight appear in their eyes. Their fancy lent him the form and features wherewith the saints are wont to be depicted; one sign from Robert would have laid them in the dust prostrate and adoring.

At length he gave his horse the spur, and vanished like an arrow into the wood. The people strove long to catch the gleam of his golden armor between the trees—but in vain; his charger had borne him far beyond the range of their vision; and then they looked sadly on each other and said with a sigh:

"He has gone back to heaven again!"

The Lion of Flanders

CHAPTER IX

OF the sixty thousand men whom Philip the Fair had sent to lay waste Flanders, only seven thousand succeeded in returning to France. Guy de St. Pol had gathered five thousand men at Lille, and hoped to march them safely to France: but a division of the Flemish army fell on them, and after an obstinate conflict nearly all who had fled from Courtrai were overcome and slain. The "excellente Chronike" tells us:

"And the number of those who fled and escaped may have been in all about three thousand men, sole remains of the enormous host which had gone forth to plunder and lay waste Flanders: and these had a tale to tell at home which was far from being edifying or joyous."

All the most illustrious nobles and bravest knights were slain at Courtrai. There was scarcely a castle of France where there was not wailing and lamentation for the death of a husband, a father, or a brother. The Flemish generals took care that the fallen kings and knights should receive honorable burial in the abbey of Gröningen, as appears

The Lion of Flanders

from an ancient painting still to be seen in St. Michael's Church at Courtrai. There is also in the Museum of Messire Goethals-Vercruyssen at Courtrai a stone which once lay on the grave of King Sigis; it bears his arms, and the following inscription:

"In the year of our Lord MCCCII, on St. Benedict's day, was fought the battle of Courtrai. Under this stone lies buried King Sigis. Pray God for his soul! Amen."

Besides the vessels of gold, costly stuffs, and rich armor, there were found on the battle-field more than *seven hundred golden spurs*, which knights alone had the privilege of wearing; these were suspended with the captured banners from the vault of our Lady's church at Courtrai, and thence this battle acquired the name of "*The Battle of the Golden Spurs.*" Several thousand horses also fell into the hands of the Flemings, who used them with great effect in subsequent battles. In front of the gate of Courtrai which opens toward Ghent, in the centre of the battle-field, there was in the year 1831 a chapel of our Lady of Gröningen; on its altar were to be deciphered the names of the French knights who had fallen in the fight, and one of the genuine old spurs of gold was still suspended from the vault. In Courtrai the anniversary of the battle was kept as a day of public rejoicing, and its memory still lingers in a Kermes, which is called

The Lion of Flanders

the Vergaderdagen, or day of gathering. Every year in the month of July, the poor of Courtrai go from house to house begging for old clothes, which they sell in commemoration of the sale of the rich booty of 1302. Then, accompanied by a player on the violin, they betake themselves to the Pottelberg, the old camp of the French, and drink and dance until evening.

When tidings of this terrible defeat reached France, the whole court was filled with consternation and grief. Philip burst into a furious passion with Joanna of Navarre, whose evil counsels were the cause of all these disasters, and of all their consequences; and his reproaches may be read in some quaint contemporary verses by Lodwyk van Vilthem. The historians of France, indeed, have described Joanna in much brighter colors; but it is an amiable peculiarity of their national character to handle very indulgently the vices of their monarchs, at least of their *dead* monarchs; and it is an undoubted truth that the Flemish chronicles give a far more trustworthy description of the odious disposition of Queen Joanna.

The magistrates of Ghent, who were all Lilyards, and thought that King Philip would send a fresh expedition into Flanders with all haste, closed their gates, intending to hold out their city as long as possible for France. But they met their punishment at the hands of the men of Ghent themselves. The people rushed to arms, the magistrates and every other Lilyard were put to death, and Guy received the keys of the city, and with them a pledge of everlasting fidelity, from the hands of the principal citizens.

Meanwhile Count John of Namur, brother of Robert de Bethune, returned to Flanders and assumed the government; he collected in haste a new and far larger army, to resist any further attempt on the part of the French, and restored order everywhere. Without allowing his troops any repose, he marched to Lille, where some disturbances had broken out; thence he proceeded to Douay, which he captured, taking the garrison prisoners; and Cassel yielded after a very brief resistance. After taking some other garrisons of lesser note he was obliged to return; for not an enemy remained on the soil of Flanders; and as he deemed a small band of picked soldiers sufficient for all purposes of defense, he disbanded his army.

The land was still and at rest; trade and commerce flourished with renewed vigor; the wasted fields were sown with better hope of a bounteous harvest, and it seemed as though Flanders had acquired new life and new strength. Men thought with reason that the lesson France had received was sufficient. Philip the Fair himself had, in fact, little desire to renew the strife; but the reproaches which burst from all France, the lamentations of

The Lion of Flanders

the knights whose brothers had fallen at Courtrai, and, above all, the instigations of Joanna, who thirsted for revenge, compelled him at length to declare war. He collected a force of eighty thousand men, among whom were twenty thousand cavalry; but it was far inferior to the former army, inasmuch as it consisted chiefly of mercenaries, or of recruits levied by force. The command was entrusted to Louis, King of Navarre; he was instructed, before venturing on a general action, to take Douay and other French frontier towns from the Flemings; and with this commission, he pitched his camp in a plain near Vitry, a few miles from Douay.

No sooner did the Flemings hear that a fresh army was being assembled in France than the cry "To arms!" resounded through the length and breadth of the land. Never was so universal and so intense an enthusiasm known; from every village the inhabitants poured forth with weapons of all kinds; on they came, singing and shouting in such numbers that John of Namur was obliged to send many of them back to their abodes, fearing that it would be impossible to provide for so enormous a host. Those who had formerly been Lilyards longed now to wipe out the stain, and implored, with tears in their eyes, to be allowed a part in the conflict; and this was readily granted them. Besides John of Namur, most of the knights

The Lion of Flanders

who had shared the glories of Courtrai repaired to the army. Guy, William van Gulick, John van Renesse, John Borluut, Peter Deconinck, Jan Breydel, and many others, were among them. Adolf van Nieuwland had not yet recovered from his wounds, and could not therefore accompany them.

The Flemings marched against the enemy in two divisions, and at first took up a position about three leagues from the French camp; but they soon advanced to the Scarpe, a small river near Flines. The Flemings daily challenged the French; but as the generals on both sides wished to avoid an action, day after day passed on without any result. The cause of this pacific attitude was, that John of Namur had sent ambassadors to France to treat with the king for the liberation of the old Count and of Robert, and to conclude, if possible, a treaty of peace. But the French court could not agree on the terms to be proposed or accepted, and the answer was unfavorable.

The Flemings meanwhile began to murmur, and longed to fall on the French, in spite of the prohibition of their general; and the discontent became at last so alarming, that John of Namur was compelled to cross the Scarpe and attack the enemy. A bridge of five boats was thrown across the stream, and the Flemish army passed over, singing and shouting with joy that they were at length going to fight; but an ambiguous message

The Lion of Flanders

from France kept them still for some days longer on the further side of the river. At length the army would be no longer restrained, and the murmurs threatened to become serious. Everything was ready for the attack, and the army was put in motion; when the French, not daring to meet it, hastily broke up their camp, and retreated in confusion. The Flemings put themselves in pursuit, and slew a great number of them; they possessed themselves beside of the castle of Harne, where the King of Navarre had taken up his quarters. Their stores, tents, and everything the French army had brought with them, fell into the hands of the Flemings; and after a few insignificant skirmishes, the French were driven back into France overwhelmed with disgrace.

When the Flemish generals saw that no enemy remained in the open field, they disbanded a part of their force, and retained only as many soldiers as were necessary to keep the French frontier garrisons in check, and to prevent their plundering expeditions.

For a long time there were occasional battles and enterprises of lesser importance and of various success. At length Philip collected a third army to avenge the defeat of Courtrai. The command was given to Walter de Chatillon, and he was instructed, on his arrival in Flanders, to take with him all the troops in garrison on the fron-

The Lion of Flanders

tier, which would make his army far more than one hundred thousand strong.

Philip, one of the sons of the old Count of Flanders, had inherited the territories of Tyetta and Loretto in Italy. As soon as he heard of the French levy, he hastened to Flanders with his troops, and was appointed by his brothers to the chief command of the army. He assembled about fifty thousand men, and marched on St. Omer to await the French assault.

The two armies soon met; for two days there were only some lesser actions, in one of which, however, Peter de Coutrenel, one of the French generals, fell, with his sons and many of his soldiers. Walter dared not stake all on a decisive battle; in the night he decamped, and marched on Utrecht; and this so quietly, that the Flemings knew nothing of his departure, until they opened their eyes with astonishment in the morning on a vacant encampment. Philip then took by storm several French towns, and the army returned laden with spoil.

The King of France saw at length that it was impossible to subjugate Flanders by force of arms, and sent Amadeus of Savoy to Philip with proposals of peace. The children of the captive Count were eager for the liberation of their father and brother, and inclined gladly to peace; they therefore smoothed all difficulties, and a truce was proclaimed, which was to last until a treaty of peace should be signed by both parties. This was framed at the French court, and contained many articles much to the disadvantage of the Flemings; but Philip the Fair hoped to obtain its acceptance by cunning. He liberated the old Count of Flanders, and allowed him to depart, on his word of honor that he would return to his prison in the following May, if he did not obtain the recognition of the treaty in all its articles.

Count Guy was received in Flanders with the utmost rejoicing, and returned to Wynandael. But when he read the treaty to the assembled states, it was rejected; and the old Count saw himself obliged to return, like another Regulus, to France in the following April. During the truce, Philip the Fair had made every exertion to collect a mighty army. Mercenaries were everywhere enlisted, and heavy taxes imposed to meet the expenses of the war. The king himself marched with the army to the Flemish frontier toward the end of June. Besides the land forces, a large fleet, commanded by Renier Grimaldi of Genoa, sailed along the coast of Flanders, to attack the young Guy and John van Renesse in Zeeland.

Philip of Flanders had meanwhile sent forth his proclamation through the land, and gathered a valiant army around his standard; and with these he marched to give battle to the enemy. On the first day there was a partial engagement, in which

The Lion of Flanders

one of the French generals was slain, with many of his men. The next day the Flemings stood drawn up eager for the fight, and prepared for an impetous attack; but the French were again panic-stricken, and fled to Utrecht, leaving their camp a prey to the Flemings. Then Philip a second time stormed Bassé, and burnt the suburbs of the city of Lens.

The king next resolved to attack Flanders on the side of Henegauw, and marched toward Doornyk; but the very first day the Flemings had overtaken him. He was the less willing to accept battle, that he had received no tidings of his fleet; and in order to avoid an engagement, he broke up his camp in the night, and fled from place to place, closely pursued by the Flemings.

The action between the two fleets was fought on the 10th of August, 1304; it lasted two whole days from morning to night. The first day the Flemings had the advantage, and would certainly have gained a total victory, had not some of their ships been driven on a sand-bank in the night. This gave the French a great superiority of force, so that they gained the battle with little difficulty, burnt all the ships, and even took the young Guy prisoner. John van Renesse, the valiant Zeelander, who was in garrison at Utrecht, wishing to leave the city, attempted to cross the river in a small barge. The barge was unhappily over-

The Lion of Flanders

laden; it sank in the middle of the stream, and the noble warrior was drowned.

When the news of the happy issue of the sea-fight reached the French camp, it was posted near Lille, on the Peuvelberg. Advantageous as the position was, Philip quitted it; and it was immediately taken possession of by the Flemings. The latter would no longer delay the action; the generals found it impossible to restrain their ardor, and so they drew them up in order for an attack. Philip the Fair no sooner saw this, than he sent a herald with conditions of peace; but the Flemings would not hear of peace, and struck the herald dead. They then fell with wild shouts, on the French army, which fled in astonishment and terror. The Flemings fought with even more intense bitterness of hatred than at Courtrai, and their commanding position helped them much. Philip of Flanders and William van Gulick pierced through the enemies' ranks, and reached the king himself, who was for a moment in extreme peril. His bodyguards were struck down at his side; and he would certainly have been taken, had not those who stood by removed his mantle and other insignia of royalty. He was thus enabled to escape unnoticed, with only a slight wound inflicted by an arrow.

The Flemings gained a complete victory; the oriflamme itself was seized and torn in

The Lion of Flanders

pieces. This battle was fought on the 15th of August, 1304.

William van Gulick the priest lost his life in this action. The Flemings were busy until evening pillaging the king's tent, and amassing incredible spoil. They then returned to the Peuvelberg to refresh themselves; and finding nothing there, marched on to Lille. The day after they resumed their march homeward.

Fourteen days after this, Philip the Fair came again with a large army, and laid siege to Lille. The citizens closed their shops, and seized their weapons; and Philip of Flanders collected the men of Courtrai, and marched them to Lille in a few days. When the king saw their numbers, he exclaimed:

"Methinks Flanders must spawn or rain soldiers."

He risked no further defeat; but, after some attempts at evasion, proposed a peace, and meanwhile proclaimed a truce. It was long before both sides could agree upon the terms of the treaty. While it was pending, the old Count died in prison at Compiègne, and was soon followed by Joanna of Navarre.

Not long after the peace was concluded, and the treaty signed by Philip the Fair and Philip of Flanders, Robert de Bethune, with his two brothers William and Guy, and all the captive knights, were set at liberty, and returned to Flanders. The people, however, were not content with the articles of the treaty, and called it the "Treaty of Unrighteousness"; but their dissatisfaction had no further consequence at the time.

Robert de Bethune was received on his return to Flanders with surpassing magnificence, and publicly recognized as Count. He lived seventeen years after his liberation, upheld the honor and the renown of Flanders, and fell asleep in the Lord on the 18th of September, 1322.

THE END

LaVergne, TN USA
29 January 2010
171503LV00001B/1/A